OTHER PEOPLE

THE HUSBAND

THE MAGICIAN

LIVING ROOM

THE CHILDKEEPER

A Novel

OTHER

by SOL STEIN

PEOPLE

HARCOURT BRACE JOVANOVICH

NEW YORK AND LONDON

Requests for permission to make copies of any part
of the work should be mailed to:
Permissions, Harcourt Brace Jovanovich, Inc.
757 Third Avenue, New York, N.Y. 10017

Printed in the United States of America

Library of Congress Cataloging in Publication Data

Stein, Sol.
Other people.

I. Title.
PZ4.S8195Ot [PS3569.T375] 813'.5'4 78-14082

ISBN 0-15-170447-3

First edition
B C D E

in memory of
TONY GODWIN
for whom this book was being written
and for
CHARLES L. BRIEANT, Jr.
friend and mentor in the law

ACKNOWLEDGMENTS

I am grateful for the counsel of three editors who saw me through the several drafts of this book, Patricia Day, Michaela Hamilton, and Marilee Talman, and to Judge Charles L. Brieant, Jr., whose voluminous notes on the law once again went beyond the demands of friendship. Tony Godwin, for whom this book was being written, died suddenly during the early stages of the work, but his severe requirements continued to instruct me. I want to thank also Dr. Alan Tulipan, who graciously gave his time, and Sheila Silver, a chance acquaintance who sent me a long letter that turned out to be more important to my purpose than she could know.

OTHER PEOPLE

Archibald Widmer

When I telephoned Thomassy that morning in March of 1974 and asked him to lunch, I counseled myself to muster a casual voice. As I waited for him to get on the line, I thought *the protections are gone.* I had reluctantly perceived that civil and well-educated people now accepted gratuitous violence against strangers as ordinary. Therefore I had to conclude that George Thomassy had chosen an appropriate profession in criminal law and I had not.

Thomassy misinterpreted my casualness. He was preparing for trial, he said, and wasn't taking time for restaurant lunches.

"I wouldn't mind joining you for a sandwich in your office," I said, hoping my insistence wouldn't seem pushy.

Thomassy said absolutely nothing. It wasn't ill breeding. I took it to be a technique for extracting the most information without the commitment of even an acknowledging word.

"George," I went on, "I wouldn't trouble you about something trivial. It's about a case."

"Yours?"

I realized he thought that I had run into a noncivil aspect of some client's case and was seeking his advice.

"The victim is mine, not the case," I said.

He waited for me to go on.

"It's my daughter, Francine."

Again, no sound from him.

"It's rather . . ."

He could have said *Go on.*

"George?"

He acknowledged his presence with a sound, but no more.

"Look George, hell, she's been raped."

At last he spoke. "Does she know the man?"

"Yes."

"Jesus, she's just a kid."

Any other lawyer of my acquaintance would have immediately said *I'm so sorry.*

"Francine is twenty-seven."

"When did this happen?"

"Tuesday," I said.

"Is she all right?"

It was ridiculous for me to expect from Thomassy the ritual responses I could hear from my friends. His questions were not etiquette. He was already at work.

"I said is she all right?"

"Yes," I said. Then, "No. She's frightened. The analyst she's been seeing suggested she consult a lawyer. I guess I'm the only lawyer she knows. She hadn't intended to tell me."

"Has she been to a hospital?"

"Yes. No serious damage. To her body, that is."

"Did they take the tests?"

"I didn't think to ask." The truth is I wouldn't have known to ask.

"Has she been to the police?"

"Yes. They took some notes. She's worried sick."

"Why?"

"The man lives in the apartment over her."

That was when Thomassy said, "All right, let's have lunch."

"When?" I asked.

"How about today?"

I didn't know whether we'd been disconnected or Thomassy'd simply hung up. I hated the idea of calling back, but I did.

"George, shall I bring Francine to lunch?"

"No."

"I thought I'd save you time."

"I want to hear what she told you without her around."

It's a different world, criminal law. "What time?" I asked.

"Twelve-thirty's okay."

"At your office?"

"Meet me at Dudley's," he said.

When I report to you that Thomassy is regarded by other lawyers like myself as the best criminal lawyer in Westchester County, what is it I mean by "the best"? When a man runs a mile faster than any living human has heretofore, he has achieved an absolute, but how few of life's activities—art, pleasure, the law—can be so precisely determined! I remember William York Tindall used to say that his idea of perfection was to be able to put his legs up after a fine meal and listen to Mozart while smoking a Romeo and Julieta cigar. I knew exactly what he meant, though Mozart was by no means my favorite composer, and since the cigar makers fled Havana, Romeo and Julietas are not the smoke we once prized. If I had to be restricted to seeing one painting for the rest of my life, even if it was a Rouault or a Rembrandt, I should soon weary of it, but I can think of a small collection, perhaps a dozen or so, that might keep my eyes content. However, if you have been involved in a crime, and you need to deal with the law, you'll find that very few private individuals can hire a battery of attorneys; you usually pick one, and if the matter is important, you narrow your choice to the best. Hence Thomassy.

At Yale, even before I entered the Law School, it was made clear to me that all of the lawyers who inhabited the social echelon I came from without exception practiced civil law. Criminal lawyers, even the best, had a touch of taint. Their affairs caused them to associate not with the kind of people they would invite to their homes, but with labor racketeers, embezzlers, Sicilians, and worse. Moreover, criminal law was comparatively unremunerative except for those few lawyers who were primarily actors or outlaws.

And so, since I knew what was expected of me, I prepared myself for a career of luncheons in executive dining rooms in which, even today, women are not permitted with grace, and for the gentle world in which adversaries were friends. When we met, we always talked of something else before we got down to business. The stakes in our kind of law are always measured, ultimately, in dollars. In criminal law, the stakes are usually a man's freedom, and under some conditions could mean a man's life.

Nevertheless, I was fascinated by criminal law, and read the cases as if they were a form of specialized pornography contrived for my pleasure. I kept in touch with a few criminal lawyers so that, on occasion, I could derive some vicarious satisfaction from the brinksmanship of their cases. Above all, I maintained my now decade-long acquaintanceship with Thomassy, who practiced in the county in which I had always made my home. I sometimes thought, if my ancestors had come from Armenia instead of England, and if I had the perfectionist zeal that animates a man moving up from the bottom of the ladder rather than the ennui that lazies one at the top, I might have been like Thomassy. In America we toy with the idea that because we are a highly mobile society, we are not greatly stratified; it is supreme nonsense. In a way we are more class conscious than the Europeans because you cannot always pigeonhole an American by his accent or dress, and with newcomers you are compelled to watch carefully for the telltale nuance. However, in all classes we share one addiction: we admire winners. We root for the underdog so long as he is pushing for the top. Pity never excites us as much as triumph. We think of ourselves as sportsmanlike, but what we do is savagely tear down goal posts when our team wins.

The very naive think winning unimportant. When trouble strikes, they are quick to change their minds. I was once involved in a matter that affected not only my client but also the national interest. The matter was out of my field because money was not the issue. Moreover, it was a matter in which the outcome could not be compromised; we either won or lost totally. I phoned Edward Bennett Williams in Washington, and though we had never spoken before, within two minutes of hearing the subject of my concern, he said, "Come on down." He took the case and, of course, won it. But most criminal matters—the felonies that attract our interest in newspapers and worry us when they invade our neighborhoods—are tried locally, and one wants as advocate a lawyer who knows the individuals and customs of the courts in the immediate area. Like the nearly million other inhabitants of Westchester, if I were accused of a crime, particularly if I were guilty, I would want only Thomassy to represent me. I dread the possibility that Thomassy might become a judge and hence unavailable to me except as a friend. Besides, the quality one pretends to look for in a judge is fairness. That is not Thomassy's virtue. The boxers and ball players whom we adulate are known for their victories and not for their sportsmanship.

Please don't misconstrue my intent; Thomassy has as many surface flaws as good leather. He doesn't pay attention to his clothes. A glen plaid suit for everyday wear, a dark blue suit for special occasions, a knit tie that shows up two or three times a week, cordovan wing-tip shoes that are rarely polished. I have observed him at dinner parties. He does not keep his left hand in his lap. He sometimes begins eating a moment before everyone else. If someone bores him, Thomassy does not dissemble. You'd think that the son of an immigrant would pay more attention to the tenuous signs of class, but Thomassy seems to lack interest in passing into the Wasp superstructure of lawyerdom. Yet there is about him none of that reserve from which some lawyers look down at humankind in trouble. He maintains the aspect of a calm observer, but one knows that sinew binds the bones of his lank frame, that he is a jungle fighter of Orde Wingate's class, a puma among the cats of criminal law.

Thomassy claims he was born on January 1, 1931, at 12:01 A.M. in Oswego, New York. The circumstances were suspicious. The *Oswego Herald* had offered, in that depression year, a $500 prize for the first child born in the new year, and it is said that the doctor attending Thomassy's mother took a potentially dangerous step in keeping the child's head from emerging for a full five minutes in order that his parents might win the award. Nineteen thirty-one was interesting for other reasons than Thomassy's slightly delayed birth. That year Elmer Rice's *Counsellor-at-Law* was a smash on Broadway. Across the ocean, Oswald Mosley formed a fascist party in Britain; Pierre Laval, of similar predilections, was elected Premier of France; German millionaires Hugenberg, Kirdorf, Thyssen, and Schroder undertook to support the Nazi Party; and Pius XI issued his encyclical on the new social order. In innocent America, Jane Addams and Nicholas Murray Butler shared the Nobel Peace Prize, and Jehovah's Witnesses greatly expanded their organization in anticipation of the apocalypse.

My name is Archibald Widmer, and I will always remember the lunch with Thomassy that changed the course of his life.

COMMENT BY HAIG THOMASSIAN

I talk to you the truth. I don't want to call the boy George. My wife Marya, may she rest in peace, herself named after the mother of Jesus, we are in this new country only four years, she gives birth to a son, and calls him George, an American name used by everybody, especially Greeks. He is son of successful horse dealer who owes money to nobody. He should have been christened Haig after me, or Armen after his grandfather. For me, George sounds like a foreigner.

Look you, my hands are rough from work but my head is full of Armenian truth from centuries. Greeks call themselves what, the cradle of civilization, assfuckers! Armenians took civilization out of the cradle! Smart Jews, America is full of them, they learn from suffering, eh? When George was a boy, millions of Jews killed in Europe, smart ones, dumb ones. When I meet a Jew I tell him before this century began, 200,000 Armenians in Turkey, massacred! In Constantinople, 7,000 killed like pigs. In 1909, in Cilicia and Syria, 20,000 more Armenians butchered. During the Great War, the Turks—may their women die in childbirth—tried to force our women and children to take Islam, to make Moslems out of the first nation to be Christian in the world!

In 1920, I have a good memory, this Woodrow Wilson, President of America, refuses to lift a finger to protect Armenia. My father says if America will not come to us, we go to America.

Armenians are the greatest horse breeders in the world. What is a man without a horse? As soon as we earn some extra dollars, I give to my son, who must carry on this holy tradition, a pony. I go out with him Saturday, Sunday, ride, ride, ride, and what Georgie says? He is bored by horses. Sick! I show him how I always sell right horse to right people, how, if hurt horse is brought to Haig Thomassian, I make horse well, not shoot. I never give up. I take Georgie to cowboy movies. I show him wagon trains. I tell George who do you think pulled them, Jews? Horses made America. America needs horsemen. I tell George a man on a horse is a man not to be conquered. The kid's face looks up at me with pretend respect but his eyes say bullshit. I shout at him a horse means freedom, he looks away. His eyes are already on college, the city, somewhere else.

I knew he would leave, but could I even in an old-country nightmare imagine he would change his name to Thomassy, an act of treason against his own father! He can blah-blah-blah in court, but what is he? An Armenian who cannot ride a horse is like a Jew. The cossacks slaughtered the Jews. Whoever saw a Jew master a horse?

In 1969 my wife dies. George Big Shot comes to Oswego, at the funeral tells the story of Marya, her whole life from a little girl, and I ask him where does he know so much, not from me. He shakes my hand as if I am the boy. I tell him now is the time to move back, we have plenty crime in Oswego, good business for lawyers. He refuses me. I tell you, in his soul my son is a Turk.

Sure, on my birthdays the telephone rings, his secretary says "George Thomassy calling," and I yell at her, "Thomassian, Thomassian!" Then I hear George's voice. I feel he wants to talk, ask questions about what I do, how I feel, but I give him the least words, "yes" or "no," until he gives up. Even if he becomes the biggest lawyer in the whole United States, to me, as an Armenian, he is nothing.

❖

Dudley's was a six-minute drive from Thomassy's office, an oddball restaurant on Rockledge Avenue in Ossining, wedged between houses that had seen better days. Around the corner from Dudley's was Liberty Street, which led to Sing Sing, and the caged vehicles carrying prisoners often passed Dudley's front door.

Inside, you stepped into another universe, thick purple carpeting, antique signs on the walls, and cascades of living plants under a bank of plant lights artfully concealed in the skylight. On Fridays, in the old days, you were likely to find John Cheever at a table with friends, the folk singer Tom Glazer, editors wooing authors, middle-class women with a fondness for Dudley's very large lunchtime cocktails, and the oversize carafes of wine. The menu was eccentric—wildflower omelets in season, superb soups, a cheesecake that rivaled that of Lindy's in its heyday. Dudley's had imperfections: the washrooms were sometimes cleaned so casually experienced customers would do their washing up elsewhere; the bench seats sometimes gathered enough breadcrumbs to satisfy a pigeon. The young waitresses, as lovely as the cascading plants, sometimes served the host before serving his guest, but one didn't mind. It was an ambience that made Thomassy comfortable.

Thomassy looked as if a make-up man had dusted shadows under his eyes. He had always seemed younger than his age, but now, despite his admirable energy, he looked forty-four. No longer the boy wonder.

"How've you been?" I asked him.

"I put on a blue sock and a black sock this morning. My secretary noticed."

"You ought to get yourself a wife."

"Thanks," he said and shut me off.

I hadn't meant it as an intrusion into his private life. I suppose we were all aware of the succession of attractive women he squired about on occasion. One couldn't help wondering why Thomassy avoided anything resembling a permanent relationship. It was as if his women were cases also, occupying his attention for a time, then put out of mind.

"Who's the analyst who suggested your daughter see a lawyer?"

"Remember you gave me a reprint of an article on the three types of human personality?"

"I gave a lot of those away. What was the name of the psychiatrist?"

"Gunther Koch," I said.

"That's right," said Thomassy. "Now I remember."

"You ever meet the man?"

"No. Damn, it's a small world. I give you something to read, and your daughter ends up on his couch. How long has she been seeing this Dr. Koch?"

"Maybe half a year or more. My wife and I encouraged her."

"Why is she seeing an analyst?"

"Insomnia."

"A lot of people have insomnia," he said impatiently.

"Not like hers. She'd go weeks without a good night's sleep. Deep circles under her eyes. On only two or three hours' sleep some nights, you get desperate. She did. I suspect she was taking at least three Seconals a night for a month when Priscilla and I found out."

"Who's her doctor?"

"She didn't get them on prescription. Someone at the U.N. was selling them to her. Anyway, it was a palliative, not a cure. We encouraged her to see Dr. Koch to get at the source of her restlessness."

"Was she that way as a child?"

"Not at all. It started right after college. George, you sound like an analyst."

"Any analyst who sounds like me ought to be fired. Did you ever witness a rape trial?"

"No."

"Read a transcript?"

"No."

"Everything gets dragged out."

I hated the seamy things adversaries seemed to have to pull out of witnesses in criminal trials. It violated my sense of privacy to open boxes that should have stayed shut.

"Ned, when it comes to cases of this sort, your daughter—and you, too—may bump into surprises. You don't like surprises."

"I'm glad you understand," I said.

"Sure you want to go further?"

"I'm merely the Miles Standish here," I said. "It's not my choice."

"You know Cunham?"

"Only by name."

"He's interested in cases that'll keep him in the newspapers."

"I don't want this in the newspapers."

Thomassy's forefinger circled the rim of his martini glass.

"Cunham's looking for corruption or multiple murder these days. He thinks rape is petty cash."

"Could you talk to one of the assistant D.A.s, perhaps one of the younger ones who might be sympathetic to a woman's point of view? I've really had no contact with those people."

Thomassy looked at me with what I thought was sadness. To him, I suppose, those of us who didn't know the D.A.s were businessmen, not lawyers. He had settled back in his seat, and so I leaned forward as if to bridge the chasm.

"Will you try to help her?"

"If I believe your daughter's story."

I could never say anything resembling that to a client to his face.

Thomassy went on, "Why doesn't she just move out of the building and be careful from now on."

"Not Francine."

"Tell me about her."

"She's part of the new generation, George."

"What does that mean?"

"She doesn't live by our rules. George, you know what Wasp families are like. We read people's expressions, but we don't comment on them. Francine does."

Thomassy smiled.

"Saying what you think all the time," I told him, "is very like high treason in our world. I've accommodated myself to her rebelliousness because it's temporary. Her children will revert to type."

"She might end up with a Sicilian."

It was my turn to be amused. "I can't believe she'd carry things that far," I said. "Although I must say she tried to quit Radcliffe in her last semester as a protest against the degree. I made her go back on grounds I was ashamed of. I told her how much I had already invested in that degree. She mocked me, but finished up. If she hadn't, she wouldn't have gotten her job."

"Where?"

"The U.N."

It made me nervous that Thomassy hadn't taken a single note. When a client first briefed me about a situation, I always had my long yellow pad in front of me, getting the details down. It gives them security, and me as well. Was Thomassy expecting to remember all this? Or did it not matter?

"Boy friend?" he asked.

"From time to time."

Thomassy laughed. "Surprised you haven't got her married off already."

"Young women don't get married off today, George. Judging by her friends, most of them don't get married even on their own initiative. No contracts."

"Tough for lawyers. Like you, I mean."

I wanted to respond to him, but I didn't want to get embroiled in a side issue. I had promised her a lawyer who could advise her how to go about getting the rapist convicted. But I abhorred the idea of being trapped in the middle. I wanted Thomassy to see Francine, not to question me.

The food came. Thomassy was tolerant. He let us eat. Then he said, "Tell me about the rape."

"George, I'd really prefer that you asked her."

"I'm asking you."

"She just said she was by the man who lived upstairs."

"No details?"

"I'm her father."

"If she doesn't have a current boy friend, who else would she tell the details to?"

"No one. Not even her sisters. She's like that."

"The details are important."

"Yes, I know."

"She'll have to tell me."

I nodded.

"Will she lie?"

"Francine tells the truth even when she should give other people the comfort of white lies. The original wild duck." It occurred to me that Thomassy might not know Ibsen.

"*The Wild Duck . . . ,*" I started to explain.

"I know," said Thomassy, cutting me off. "Who's going to pay?"

"I said she works at the U.N."

"This could cost a lot more than a young secretary can spare."

I was pleased to have caught him in a prejudice. "Francine," I said, "is the research assistant on the staff of the American Ambassador. Her compensation is quite adequate. She's very bright," I added. "I'll stand behind her bill, of course. Just in case."

Thomassy waved the offer away. Which meant he accepted it. It was a great relief to me to pass the ball to him. In over twenty years of practice, I've never had a client's wife or daughter involved in an incident of this sort. Statistically, it would seem that some must have been. Is it the subject that makes it impossible for them to broach? Or is it me?

COMMENT BY PRISCILLA GRAVES WIDMER, SMITH COLLEGE, '40

His full nomenclature was Archibald Edward Widmer III. No one was about to call him Archie or Eddie, and Edward sounded like the Duke of Windsor so everyone in our crowd called him Ned.

What was the chemistry? He looked good in white suits. He was clean. His forearms were muscular. He blew into my ear on our first date. From the start, I trusted him to look out for my interests. He made me feel safe. Men weren't adversaries in those days. We didn't put excessive weight on orgasmic response or subject our feelings to psychoanalysis. We aimed for wedlock.

My friends thought Ned prissy. Edith's Brock concealed something behind his facade of shyness I didn't want to get in bed with. And Alison's Peter—what ambisexual lusts were camouflaged by his toothsome flash of condescension at every man, woman, and pet that came into view. My Ned was not prissy once our bedroom door was shut.

Most men say they want sons. Ned wanted daughters and got them, Joan, then Margaret. He turned into a talented coddler of little girls, a fanny patter, body hugger, all in the guise of warm fatherhood. Then Ned went through that brief berserk period, announcing he was ready to resign his partnership and shoot off to Tahiti or somewhere with or without me. He'd make love everywhere except in bed. And during that wild time, Francine was conceived. What a beautiful thing she turned out to be. Blond hair that would never turn dark like her sisters' and mine, and two Indian touches, high burnished cheekbones, and eyes that were almost almonds in shape. Her pupils were a strange blue, as if Wedgwood could glisten. She never had to experiment with make-up, as her sisters had. She shot up there at a very young age, taller than any of us except Ned. Joan and Margaret went through the same gawky period I had, but Francine could have been a ballerina the way she moved. I found it difficult to connect her graces to our genes.

I remember when I first discovered Francine got the curse. It was time to tell her the facts of life just as I had Joan and Margaret, but when I did, Francine led me on a bit, pretending she didn't know what I was talking about, and then I learned she'd had it a year earlier without so much as a word to me. The older girls were so dependent on me for things like that. I told Francine she made me feel useless, and she said "No, no" and assured me she did want to hear about the private things from me, so I thought what the hell, and started bravely to explain about intercourse. Francine listened as if she were mesmerized. Or was she putting me on? "You know all about this," I said, and she said, "Please, Mom, tell me about fellatio and cunnilingus." Would you believe that in a thirteen-year-old? Where did she—from the others? Joan? Margaret? I was in a panic until Ned came home. When I told him, he just grinned, and I lost my temper at him.

"Priscilla," he said, "there is absolutely nothing we can do about something she already knows."

Children were discovering our secrets much too soon. I didn't want to give up at least trying to be a mother to Francine. Once, when she was fourteen, still growing taller too fast, I was overwhelmed by a feeling of desertion and panic and told her, "You are my last baby," and she said, "Mother, I am not a baby."

Bereft of my motherhood, I fled upstairs to my bedroom and smothered my face in the pillow to muffle my desperate sobbing at the prospect of being dutyless, jobless, useless, marking time till I would die. I wasn't ready yet for change of life or death, why did I feel pushed, what was the hurry?

I don't remember if I fell asleep for a moment or not. I do remember the stroking of my hair. I turned. Francine was bending over me. With her fingertips she touched the tears in the corners of my eyes, then took my hands in hers, squeezing them, saying, "Mama"—she hadn't called me that in the longest time— "Mama, you are not old."

In truth, I had been childishly tormenting myself and she, at fourteen, was comforting me with reality. Joan and Margaret had grown up without looking back, but Francine was constantly glancing over her shoulder, as it were, to see where I was, where Ned was. No wonder he loved her so. I truly don't think I was jealous of the way Ned treated her as a woman when she was still a girl. I never had doubts about Joan and Margaret finding their places, marriage, children, the right men. But would Francine find someone she could have regard for? At twenty she said she didn't have time to be serious about anyone. At twenty-five she said to me that men were boys. I worried about her. About something happening to her. I didn't think about rape. Though Ned must have, mustn't he?

COMMENT BY FRANCINE WIDMER

You've got to fix an image in your mind to visualize a person you haven't met. When I asked my father what Mr. Thomassy looked like, he said he was a very good lawyer! I pictured him dark-skinned and beak-nosed because of his name, not an American look, more like some of the not-quite-Caucasians I see at the U.N., flat cheeks, the kind that don't look slick shaven even in the morning. I imagined him leaning forward a bit, on the balls of his feet, ready to point. At me! Accusingly!

Driving to his office the first time, I got to the address without one wrong move. The place surprised me. It was a two-story professional building, new, in a good section of Ossining, near Briarcliff; from the way Dad had talked about Mr. Thomassy I had expected it to be a kind of nondescript store-front, walk-in sort of building. The directory in the lobby listed two doctors, a dentist, a real estate agent, and George Thomassy, attorney-at-law, by appointment only.

My appointment was for four o'clock and I turned the knob of the door to the outer office seconds before four. The reception room made you feel you were passing from a contemporary building into another world of paneled walls, subdued lighting, and heavy carpeting that had been put down a long time ago. At the left rear corner was the secretary's desk—I guessed she was his secretary—and she said, "Good afternoon, you must be Miss Widmer," and I thought *Do I look like my father?*

"I have an appointment," I said, which was a ridiculous thing to say since she knew who I was and there wasn't anybody else waiting.

"He'll be with you in a minute," said the secretary, glancing at her phone, "he's just finishing up a call."

I sat down on one of the brown leather chairs with brass upholstery nails. On the table in front of me lay an old *National Geographic,* a copy of *The New Yorker* that was falling apart, and some comic books. Who brought children along to waiting rooms like this?

When I looked up Thomassy was standing framed in the inner office door, watching me thumb through the comic books, Jesus! I felt like I'd been caught playing with myself. I stood up, put out a dumb hand to shake his outstretched hand, blushing. He didn't look at all like my conjuration of him; he was tall, lean, relaxed-limbed, loose, clean shaven, straight-nosed—no Arab, Greek, Turk, Armenian, whatever— firm, warm hand, and his grey eyes aimed straight at my eyes as he said, "Come in, Miss Widmer."

Those were the first words I ever heard from him and dozens of times since they have skimmed through my head, the mind-cutting bass rumbles of *Come in, Miss Widmer,* echoing again and again.

He stood aside to let me enter the inner office first. I was careful not to brush against him.

His desk near the window was cluttered with books, file folders, loose papers. In front of it was a brown leather armchair facing a matching couch. The rest was all bookshelves, closing the walls in around the cramped space.

He gestured me into the armchair, dropped into the couch opposite me, our knees almost touching. I was glad he didn't sit behind that desk. I can't stand it when men sit behind desks for the phoney authority it gives them. But I was unprepared to be so close physically to a man I didn't know.

"What do you do when you have a crowd?" I said.

He smiled. "I like to see people one or two at a time. There are folding chairs in the closet for emergencies."

"Do you have emergencies often?" I asked, glad to keep the real conversation from starting.

"My clients have emergencies."

He was examining me with those grey eyes. Was *he* thinking I looked like my father? Right now he's noticing I don't wear a bra.

The sun from the window was in my eyes. He got up, avoiding my knees, drew the blind just enough to block the offending rays.

"Thank you," I said.

"You seem," he said, "less . . ." His voice trailed off.

"Less?"

"Less upset than I thought you might be. You seem . . ."

I waited.

"Calm."

You expect me to be shrill.

"Have you seen the police?"

"Yes."

"Were they helpful?"

"No." *They were impossible.*

"You're seeing an analyst, a Dr. Koch?"

"Yes."

"What does he say?"

"He says hmmmmm to most things."

Thomassy laughed, a sharp, short, clear laugh. He was taking another look at me, as if something was contradicting the first impression he had formed.

"He said most women feel guilty about being raped."

"Do you?"

"No, I feel wronged. I want that son of a bitch in jail!"

I felt the heat in my cheeks, my whole body's instant rage. *Control yourself* was the one piece of childhood admonition that stuck like a flypaper echo I couldn't shake off. I took a lungful of air, watching him watching me.

"Did you say that to Dr. Koch?"

"Yes."

"What did he say?"

"He said he doesn't put people in jail, I should see a lawyer."

"Lawyers don't put people in jail. Why do you want the man in jail?"

"For what he did." *To me.*

"Miss Widmer, revenge is not one of the services I provide."

"Did my father tell you the man lives on the floor above me?"

"Yes."

"How am I supposed to go on living in that place, worrying about what he's going to try next? I can just see myself in bed, trying to fall asleep, knowing his bed is right in the bedroom above. When I hear sounds up there, is it supposed to mean that weirdo is banging his wife or that he's getting out of bed to come downstairs and have a go at me again?"

"Please, Miss Widmer."

"Please what, it's my house, what's the use if I can't feel safe in it?"

"Try to calm down."

"My body is not a public urinal for some loonie to go shoving his thing in!"

"Please calm down."

"I'll calm down when I feel safe. When he's in jail. Why are you looking at me that way?"

"What way?"

"You're staring at me."

"I didn't mean to stare. Please take it easy."

"I will when he's in jail."

Please help me put him there. If I knew how, I wouldn't ask for help. I closed my eyes, took a long, slow, deep breath. He thinks I'm hysterical. I have to somehow control myself. My father used to say we all have feelings—dismay, anger, rage—the difference is how we control those feelings. Letting go is weakness. Shrillness is foreign to us. Oh God, are we disciplined!

I opened my eyes, determined. This man is trying to help me. I need to help him help me.

"That's better," he said.

"I'm sorry."

"Understandable. Can we go on? There are facts I need to know."

I nodded.

"How many apartments in that house?"

"Six." *Control the voice.* "Two per floor."

"I gather you like it a lot."

"I've got a river view. The rooms are large. It's not expensive. It's convenient for commuting." *It doesn't belong to my parents.*

"Do you have a lease?"

"I don't want to move."

"How long is your lease?"

"Another two years. Is rape grounds for getting out of a lease?"

"I doubt it. Does the man—do you know his name?"

"Koslak." My image of him was the moment he opened his pants. *I could kill him.*

"You said something about a wife."

I don't see how anyone can live with him. "A wife and two kids that I've seen. At least two kids. You haven't answered my question. Will you help?"

The intercom buzzed. Without turning in its direction he said, "No calls."

"Thank you," I said.

Thomassy looked as if no one had ever thanked him for holding calls before.

"I won't require a retainer in your case," he said, "but I'd like you to settle once a month."

I nodded.

"It could get expensive. And I can't promise results."

What a wonderful line of work to be in, I thought. *Heads you win, tails you win.*

"How expensive?"

"Perhaps two thousand a month in the exploratory stages. If there's a trial, it might go to another five or ten."

That kind of money I can't afford.

"I'm sure your father will advance the monies if it becomes necessary."

I don't want to depend on anyone for money.

"Look," I said, "my father charges so much per hour. Don't you work that way?"

"Not really. I can't get involved in keeping track of phone calls and time sheets. If the client is a defendant, I usually get most of my fee in front."

"I'm not a defendant."

"I'm not asking for anything now. I'll bill you later. All right?"

What alternative do I have?

"You can trust me to be fair," he said. "I can't tell what'll be involved just yet. This isn't like a lawsuit. I can't file papers, that's something only the D.A.'s office can initiate. I know Cunham pretty well. The odds are he'll balk like hell. He'll decline to take it before a Grand Jury."

"On what grounds?" *Again, an edge of shrillness in my voice. I have to keep calm.*

"Truthfully? He'll see it as a threat to his work load. And other things."

What other things?

"You can leave those to me."

"I want to know."

"Cunham's a politician."

"What's that got to do with it?"

"Please hear me out. The way a fellow like Cunham thinks is: men have half the votes. Most men of voting age have come close to applying a little pressure in a sex situation. Cunham will figure that if he lets this come to trial, a lot of men, while they won't identify with the rapist, will be—consciously or not—protecting themselves. Some of the women will sympathize with you, more today than a couple of years ago, but middle-aged housewives think a young woman of today who, I'm sorry, doesn't wear a brassiere, is looking for trouble. That adds up to a majority of voters on the other side, that's what Cunham'll be thinking."

"Koslak raped me!"

"That'll have to be proven."

"Not to me!"

"You won't be on the jury. And first Cunham has to be convinced to prosecute."

"Oh this is so frustrating. Trying to map out how other people think."

"That's the only thing my experience is good for."

"But it's so straightforward. Koslak broke the law."

"If everybody who broke the law ended up in court, most of the population would crowd the docket for the next century trying to work off one year's case load. Look, Miss Widmer, suppose I succeed in getting the D.A. to prosecute, suppose the Grand Jury indicts, suppose there is a trial and the man is convicted—that's a lot of supposes—are you going to pay the rent and groceries for the wife and two kids?"

"Are you crazy?"

"I'm not crazy, and neither is Cunham. Send that man to jail and you're adding to the welfare rolls. Bad politics."

"You're a cynic."

"Well, won't we be polite about it and say I'm a realist? Look, doctors get malpractice insurance. Lawyers do, too. But politicians can't get it because almost all of them are guilty of malpractice. They say they want this or that. What they want is to get elected. Everything else is subordinate."

"Including the law?"

"Yes. They're supposed to represent their constituents. In fact they represent themselves. A few D.A.s practice law, but all the others are politicians looking to get reelected, and rape is not a good issue for a D.A. at this time. You live in the same world he does. I know only one way to survive in it. See it as it is. Find out where the short hairs on the other guy are. If my way of viewing things makes you gag—you went to Radcliffe, right?"

"Radcliffe women seem to make a lot of men feel insecure."

"Young lady, nobody makes me feel insecure. Naive people worry me. They've got a lot of rocks to carry around on their backs until they discover wheelbarrows."

I took it as a good sign that he was taking the trouble to lecture me.

"Mr. Thomassy?"

"Yes?"

"I don't suppose you've ever been raped?"

"I've been seduced a lot," he said.

"There's a difference."

"We'll talk about the difference some other time."

"If you'd been raped, Mr. Thomassy, you'd sure as hell not just put it out of your mind and forget it."

"Revenge isn't exactly a pure motive."

"I didn't know you were a purveyor of pure motives."

"I'm a lawyer. I win for my clients."

"Win for me."

"All I'm saying is I'm not sure I can."

"I'll help you."

"How?"

"I'm resourceful. You won't have a sheep-dog client waiting open-mouthed for the voice of God. I'll do anything to jail that cock."

"Anything may mean wearing a brassiere to court."

"I'll have to buy one."

"Okay," Thomassy said. "Start by telling me how it happened, step by step. The ground rules are you don't color things, you don't lie, you don't hold back, censor, or omit. I want to know as much as you do about what happened. What was the date?"

"March twenty-second."

"I don't suppose there was a witness?" he asked.

"Is there usually?"

"No."

"I thought you didn't need witnesses any more."

"The law's changed, but juries haven't. If you're going to sound convincing to twelve citizens who've never been raped, we'll need corroboration from objectively ascertainable evidence besides your testimony."

"Jesus! You mean women are no better off than they used to be?"

"Not in front of juries. Your father said you went to the hospital. Did they get a semen specimen?"

"Mr. Thomassy, when Koslak left, the first thing I did was take a long hot bath. I felt disgusted. I douched four times."

"What did they do in the hospital?"

"When I told the nurse I'd douched, they didn't bother. They put something on my wrists for the rope burns that stopped the smarting. They couldn't do anything for my face."

"What do you mean?"

"It's gone away now, but he slapped me so hard I had a red hand mark right here."

"Did they find any bruises?"

"The only bruise I had was not from him. It's a black and blue mark on my left thigh from bumping into an open dresser drawer."

"Did the doctor note the bruise?"

"I told you it wasn't from Koslak."

"Really? How badly do you want him in jail?"

"Boy, you're in a nasty business."

"The nasty business is what happened to you, and if you think fairness will get you anywhere in court, you're mistaken. We're not dealing with New England probity, Miss Widmer. We're dealing with a man who forces sex on another person. A normal human being doesn't chance getting locked up for a bit of sex."

You wouldn't, would you?

"It takes someone with an overriding compulsion."

"You don't have overriding compulsions?"

"Sure I do. Not about sex."

"It's just like a good meal. Take it or leave it."

"It's not just like a good meal. You're getting off the track."

"No, I'm not," I said. "We're talking about hiring you, and I'm finding out more." *I already know about the rapist.*

"Maybe your father ought to steer you to a lawyer with more time on his hands."

"Maybe."

We sat there in our discomfort, each waiting for the other to talk. His eyes avoided mine. *Look at me.*

Finally he said, "I apologize. I shouldn't have said that. I am interested."

"In rape?"

"In you. As a client."

"I won't lie about the bruise."

"I didn't ask you to lie. Did the doctor make a note of it?"

"Yes."

"Thank you. Did he give you a morning-after pill?"

"I refused one. I'm on the regular pill."

"Because?"

"Because I don't want to get pregnant."

"The right answer is because you don't know when you might have sexual relations and you want to be prepared, which means that you've had them in the past and expect to continue to have them."

"Don't you?" I asked.

"The defense counsel won't be trying to impeach my testimony by making me out to be promiscuous and enticing."

"I thought they're not supposed to do that any more."

"Oh, he could get cut down by the judge, but the jury will get the message, one way or the other."

"That's awful."

"That's realistic. What else did they do at the hospital?"

"They gave me a shot of penicillin, just in case."

"That's good."

"What do you mean?"

"It means they believed your story that you were raped."

Story! "This is hopeless."

"I don't deal in hopelessness, Francine."

"Oh?"

"Oh what?"

"May I call you George?"

"It won't get your fee reduced. Call me anything you like. Now then, can we start at the beginning, the day of the rape?"

The sun's rays were no longer in the window. Thomassy got up, drew the blind wide open again, turned his desk lamp on.

"How much time have we got?" I asked.

"You're my last appointment for the day. Well, next to last. I've got a dinner date at seven. Shoot."

Widmer

Who knows a daughter better than a father? Her suitors are afflicted with the nearsightedness of passion and the clangor of the chase. They meet a matured young woman. They lack biographical perspective, which is as much a failure in perceiving people as the lack of an historical perspective is a failure in perceiving events. A father knows his daughter as a child growing up, and can see the woman she is today through the gauze of all those years.

Even as a baby, Francine seemed more quickly exploratory of the world around her than her sisters had been. When she was six or seven, there seemed an aura of sexuality about her I hadn't detected in her sisters, though I must admit that when Joan and Margaret were that age, I was preoccupied with my career, and Priscilla carried most of the burden of their upbringing.

From school the reports were that Francine was aggressive. I went down to see the principal—he knew who I was of course—and it turned out that what Francine's teacher had characterized as aggression was pure precocious energy battling its way into the world. She was accelerated through school fast enough once they understood.

Francine was six when Priscilla told me the story of coming upon her and the little Crocker boy, who was younger than six, stark naked except for their socks and shoes.

"What were they doing?" I asked, stifling any visual image of the scene, knowing that I would think something far worse than had actually happened.

"They said they were playing doctor."

"What were they doing?" I was annoyed that Priscilla was taking it all so lightly.

"They were examining each other's orifices."

"Simultaneously?"

"Prurient interest, Mr. Widmer?"

"For God's sake, Priscilla," I said for the third time. "What were those children doing?"

"Well, at the very moment that I saw them, he seemed to be looking very closely at her private parts."

"Which parts?"

"Her vagina, if you must. Didn't you ever play doctor as a child?"

Of course I had. I felt absurd for having pressed Priscilla for the details. "I trust it won't happen again," I said.

Priscilla just looked at me. Finally she said, "They were just children playing. You're acting as if someone has trespassed on your lawn."

"That's a ridiculous comparison," I said, closing the matter, though when next I saw the Crocker boy my instinct was to throttle him. That very night I dreamt I was getting older year by year, though the years whipped by like minutes, yet Francine remained the same age as she was then, nine, and the growing gap between our ages seemed like a fault opening in the earth into which my child or I would fall if we attempted to reach across to each other. When I awoke I felt that I had been witnessing something obscene, and remember thinking that dreaming was an invention of Viennese Jews, a disease they had passed on to upset and weaken us.

In waking life, Francine also grew—too fast! What I noticed most was her quality of mind, quite different from her mother's. Priscilla's mind flits about like a hummingbird, poised before a flower for seconds, then off again for nourishment somewhere else. Francine in her very early teens seemed able to pursue a thought to its conclusion, in fact she had a relentless quality that to me still seems strange in a woman and something I more readily associate with a scientist or a trial lawyer building a case toward the making of a new law. Of course I realize that a scientist can be a woman as well these days, and a lawyer too. I speak from the perspective of what was customary in my own generation.

When Francine's breasts were no longer buds but of a size as to be apparent whatever she wore, it was more difficult for me to hug her to me when she accomplished something particularly pleasing. It was as if she wore a notice board warning me.

Of course she saw boys, and soon enough—too soon, alas—I'd meet the young men when she brought them by. She was very good about introducing them. The boys themselves usually struck me as handsome enough, though immature looking, you can understand that, and compared to Francine they seemed—what shall I say?—ordinary? I suppose the boys' parents might think Francine ordinary until they got to know her. It was about this time that I caught myself noticing the bulge in the young men's pants. In my day, of course, we wore quite ordinary trousers, and one supposed males had their apparatus at the appropriate location, but since this jeans thing, you not only know it's there, it's as if some special effort has been made to draw attention to the private parts. Oh I suppose a codpiece did the same long ago. All the boys Francine brought home seemed, in that regard, to be on display. I got used to it in time.

Because of her early acceleration, Francine was able to get into Radcliffe at sixteen and had her degree behind her at twenty. I frequently debated with myself about sending her off to Europe for a year—I could have easily afforded it then—but I weighed the experience of Paris, Venice, Florence against, well, it's not a myth that European men take advantage of young American women. Why should Francine have to experience a year of sordid attention from men who treated women as objects, Don Juans who expected to receive their meals and travel expenses in exchange for their sexual services? She pooh-poohed my alarms. I dealt with my doubts by way of a foolish compromise. Instead of a year, I sent her for six months. Her postcards told me nothing. When she got home, she could speak French better, and her Italian was quite passable. I noticed she would accept the offer of a cocktail before dinner more readily than she would before she left. Her appearance was strikingly changed. Perhaps it was the clothes she had bought in Europe, what they advertised about the figure of the person who wore them.

"Tell me about the people you met," I had asked her.

"You mean the men," she had replied, and went on to give us her observations of the museums she had visited, wickedly watching me from time to time.

I resigned myself to the fact that Francine had a private life knowledge of which was barred to me from now on.

I didn't want all the other ties cut as well, and interested myself in her plans for a career. But they weren't plans at all. She frivolously accepted positions, and as frivolously departed from them. In all, she spent nearly a year job-hopping through Manhattan, saying she was having a marvelous time, knowing how numb I made myself about it. In my day, you did not quit a job in a week or a month. You settled down.

The worst part of it, I thought, was taking a room in that brownstone floor-through in the East Fifties. Five young women in one apartment, blind-dating, the New York singles scene. Thank heaven she began to miss the countryside. The cacophony of traffic bothered her as much as it does me. I envy Thomassy that he can practice in Westchester instead of being involved like the rest of us in that highly unsatisfactory arrangement called commuting to work. The mindless hurrying of anonymous crowds is not the kind of thing our people were brought up for.

I was so pleased when she visited us one evening for dinner and announced that she had gotten a more permanent-seeming job at the U.N., and admitted that she yearned for Westchester, where houses are not always in sight of each other, and one can hear and watch and feed birds. In the summertime, we hear the occasional roar of a chainsaw or distant lawnmowers leveling grass, but on the whole, life here is so much better. I offered her a chance to move back in, which would help her put some money aside from her U.N. job, but she said that after sharing an apartment with four others, she'd prefer absolute privacy. I wasn't sure in my own mind whether that was true or whether she simply did not want us enmeshed in her life again.

I suggested it would be years before she could afford a house (the thought of a husband who could afford a house seemed even more remote). Nevertheless, she began to follow the real estate ads that led, each Sunday morning in a rented car, to disappointments, until she reluctantly accepted my advice—I told her it's all right to use one's father—and she got in touch with a certain real estate agent named

Phillips, called Well by his friends because of his habit of beginning every assertion with that word.

She reported that Well Phillips sat her down in his office—it's furnished and decorated solely in wood, like a New England cottage—and told her, "Well, you don't really need to run around to find a place if you use your head and my experience. You can't afford a house, young lady, and you don't want an apartment in a neighborhood where only bowling is spoken. That leaves here, here, and here," he pointed to the map, "if you want an easy commute by car. In the place last pointed to, there're a couple or three apartments, on the loose right now, three-story buildings that got their backs against the steep slope up from the Hudson, unbuildable, so there's woods and streams in back and the river in front. The Croton Aqueduct is great for walking on in that area, and it'll be years before the crazies tar it over for motorbikes, and by then you'll have gone somewhere else. Let's see now, if you want a living room, a separate bedroom with a view, and a kitchen that's a kitchen, there's a building I can get you a second-floor front apartment in for . . ."

He named a price less than she was paying for a fifth of the city flat. Of course, gas and parking would bridge the difference. She didn't want to pledge fealty to Conrail. Besides, I know she loved tooling around in the gearshift Mustang I had given her for graduation, not as a reward, but as an expression of my continuing affection.

Well Phillips had driven her to the place and it turned out to be better even than his description of it. The previous tenants had left the apartment in immaculate condition. The walls were off white, clean, even the windows seemed newly washed. She asked what the other tenants were like.

"Don't really know," Well Phillips had said, and checked with the man who had given them the key. I remember her description. Below the empty flat lived a couple, there since the building went up, and opposite a woman who keeps cats. Across the hall from the empty apartment two men lived together—can't avoid that any more—and upstairs, there was an Italian family with a baby and a grandmother. Just above the empty apartment lives a fellow who owned the nearest gas station, handy to know, I thought, if your car doesn't start some morning. He had a wife, a quiet sort according to Phillips, and two young kids. Young kids could clatter around on your ceiling, but then

Francine wouldn't be home weekdays and by her return from work, they'd probably be on their way to bed.

She asked if there were problems with burglaries in the neighborhood. The hippie janitor had told her, "It's not like that here. You're from New York. This is Westchester."

And so she paid the month's deposit and moved in under the gas station owner who raped her.

THREE

Francine Widmer

I wanted to tell it all in a breath, but Thomassy slowed me down immediately.

"What day of the week was it, Francine?"

"Monday."

"A work day."

"Yes."

"What time did you leave work?"

"About an hour earlier than usual, say four-thirty. I'd been fighting a three-aspirin headache. My work was finished. I decided there was no point in hanging around. If I drove home early, the traffic would be lighter."

"Go on. I won't interrupt any more."

When I got home, I told Thomassy, I stepped out of my shoes, pulled my dress off, slipped a caftan over my head, and stretched as if to let the acid in my arm muscles drain out of my fingertips. I sat staring across the Hudson out of the wide window. The choppiness of the water was barely discernible, ridges of tiny whitecaps undulating. The distant, rhythmic motion mesmerized me. On the long slope between my house and the water, I could see the lemon-yellow stalks of untrimmed forsythia hinting at spring. Now that the headache was gone, I could have dropped off to sleep. I was at peace.

The doorbell rang. I wasn't expecting anyone.

My mood slipped. With a shrug, I pushed my hair back and went to the door.

"Who is it?" I asked.

"Mr. Koslak."

The name didn't register.

"From upstairs."

"Oh, I'm sorry."

I expected to see the man who, when I passed him on the stairs, always wore black-grease-smeared striped coveralls—I thought of them as convict coveralls—with some name, his name?, over the pocket in red script. When I slipped the chain and opened the door, he was standing there wearing a white, horizontal tooth-smile, a white T-shirt, and jeans that looked brand new. He seemed younger, clean, thirty-five perhaps. I was struck by how short he was; this was the first time we were on the same level. His hand thrust forward an empty cup.

"Excuse me," he said. "This sounds nuts, but my wife's cooking up something and she's run out of sugar."

"Come in, come in," I said. "Of course," and as I went to the kitchen with his cup the thought flitted through my mind, "Why hasn't he tried the Italians across the hall?" Perhaps he had and they weren't home. Maybe his wife had quarreled with the Italian wife, you never know.

I handed him the cup, and then noticed he had closed the door behind him.

COMMENT BY MARY KOSLAK

I'm proud of the way Harry's made a real go of the gas station in just four years. I had no idea he'd turn into a terrific businessman. I've been in the office part of the station, watching out through the glass as all these people drive in, sometimes two and three waiting for a pump, and while the kid fills 'em up, they're talking to Harry, this and that, like they was friends not customers. I asked him how much he was making a week now and he said it'd blow my mind. I don't know where he keeps his cash. As long as I get my hundred fifty a week for shopping, I don't care. Truth is I'm putting some of that in my ha-ha rainy day fund. I keep the passbook in the bottom of the Kotex box in the drawer.

You'd have to know Harry for years to see how much he's really improved. When he worked for Pete's Sunoco, he'd blow up every other day, at Pete, at me, he just couldn't stand anyone telling him what to do. I'm glad he got the lease on the Esso. It's not just the money he makes working for himself, it's his temper.

He's not perfect, I mean I wished he was better with Mike and little Mary. They may be kids, but they're human beings, you gotta say something more than hello and goodbye. He ought to play with them like a father, you know what I mean?

Anyway, I ain't getting pregnant any more. The minute it shows, Harry changes. Instead of poking me every chance he gets, he just treats me as if I was off limits. He said he didn't like the idea of poking me with a kid inside. I asked the doctor. I told him the doctor said he can't do any harm, I'm only four months gone. I don't know what Harry does when I'm pregnant. Anyway, three kids is plenty, don't you think?

It's funny how quick the time has passed since I met Harry. I had this girl friend Roseanne who's going with a guy called Lefty and she calls me to double-date on this Saturday night because Lefty's got a friend named Harry, and I says sure, and she, Roseanne, says Harry's short, and I say does he look all right, and Roseanne says she seen him and he looks fine, just he's short. Well I'm not one to make a thing if someone's short, am I?

Harry's thing then was to tell jokes. He had a whole repertory and he told them good and Roseanne and I laughed a lot, though Lefty said he'd heard them. I could tell Harry took to me from the way he kept looking me over, not just when we were introduced but like afterwards. He referred to my tits as headlights, which Lefty and Roseanne thought was funny.

I could tell he was sensitive about being short. "Nobody's short lying down," he said that first night. He called me up the next day and asked for a date, just with me.

I never thought he'd marry me. That first time in his car when he bought that used car, I said I didn't want to, he said I was lying I did want to. How do you argue that? I didn't know what I thought. I said what I was supposed to say, no.

Then we were up in Lefty's apartment, and Lefty and Roseanne were in the bedroom. You could tell they didn't want company. We were in the other room necking, you know, nothing special, when Harry asks me to look at his thing when it was hard. I didn't have experience to compare him with, you know. It came up at an angle, the way they're all supposed to, and just a bit over to the side, that was what he said was different. He said the kids in high school had made fun of his dick because of the angle, and I said what were the kids in high school doing looking at his dick, and he said he and them, there were five or six, would get theirs hard, then corner some girl and all at once show her all those hard dicks, scare the hell out of her. Men are like boys about their things. I can't imagine girls doing the same, can you?

I liked Harry. I certainly didn't want him to feel bad. I said something nice about his dick, and he said could I touch it, and one thing always leads to another, doesn't it?

Well, he did marry me, surprise. I remember he looked shy and said "I love you" and I said "I know" and he said "How'd you know?" and I said "You made love to me, didn't you?" and he said "Oh" or something idiotic like that. When I was a kid I used to daydream about marrying somebody a lot taller than Harry, but you got to be realistic, don't you? Only I worry that Mike and Jean and whatever I got in the oven will all be short like Harry instead of tall like my father, but my mother said you got to be realistic, so I was.

Harry wanted us to go to Las Vegas. I said, "Las Vegas on a honeymoon?"

"What's wrong with Las Vegas?"

So I say, "You can't lie on the beach, you can't swim, you can't enjoy yourself."

He asks me didn't I like gambling.

I tell him we ought to get to know each other on a honeymoon, something like that.

"Okay," he says, "we'll go to the other place."

That's how we got to go to Miami. I got my first bikini to take with. Harry got used to the stares quick enough. I think he likes it when they stare. Even if they make remarks, he never picks a fight. My figure was like Ava Gardner's. I hadn't had the kids yet.

What I was really getting to was that first night, when it was official and okay. We'd sobered up from the wedding champagne on the ride to the airport. We ordered drinks on the plane, what the hell I'm scared of flying and who wants to be sober. Well, we're allowed two drinks each, so Harry orders four scotches, gives me one, and drinks three himself. He kept reaching across me for a magazine or a paperback out of the bag I was carrying, but what he wanted was a quick feel. Even though we were married I guess the idea of fooling around on an airplane surrounded by people was exciting, I don't know.

So we get to the hotel and he orders up a bottle of scotch, and I say what's that for, you could order a couple drinks but a bottle? He says it's cheaper by the bottle and you don't have to wait around for room service. I'm unpacking and he's drinking and pretty soon he's singing, you know, he's got a pretty good voice, and he tells me I should have a drink, and I tell him we have to go out to dinner, don't we, and before I know it he's flopped on the bed, sloshed.

"Come on," I tell him, "we got to go down to dinner soon."

He's not out, just sleepy, so trying not to get him mad I say, "Come on, you'll sleep later, Harry. Want to take a cold shower?" He mumbles but I can't make out what he's saying, if he's saying anything. I'm thinking *this is supposed to be our honeymoon.* Anyway, I figure he needs some time, so I take myself a shower, it was hot on the plane and in the cab from the airport, and I take my time dolling myself up, figuring it'll give Harry time to recover. I come out to the room and wouldn't you know he's out cold and snoring?

My mother told me to always be patient with a man, and I love him don't I, so I'm the good one, I undress him. Boy was that work. I try to get the new silk p.j.s on him—do you know how hard it is on an uncooperative nearly dead body? Well, I did it, and I decide it's no use my sitting there in the chair watching him, so I put the screw top back on the scotch, what's left of it, and stick it in the closet under some of my things, and then I go to bed too, thinking some wedding night.

In the middle of the night, I'm asleep, I wake up because Harry's corpse is awake and he's shoving it to me like a loan he forgot to pay, but before I can really wake up, bang, he's finished. It was like nothing, and he's snoring again. I hate to tell you what my thoughts were for the next hour, lying there, in Florida, wondering had I made the most colossal mistake of my life. When I woke up in the morning, he was dressed and shaved and had ordered up breakfast for me in bed, he kissed me on the cheek, told me how happy he was, okay.

We had a terrific day on the beach, Harry overtipped the blond boy who brought the deck chairs and towels, we ran into the ocean holding hands, we had clam chowder my favorite for lunch, then we walked looking in the stores, and I'm afraid to say I like this or that because if it isn't something super expensive he goes in and buys it for me and I think how stupid I was to worry.

My luck, by dinner time I got the curse. Here comes the second night of the honeymoon, the first really, you can't count what happened the previous night, I told him we should have gone with the wedding date I picked out because I had my days figured, but he insisted on the date his mother picked, she didn't know when my time was. His eyes are bullets. He doesn't want me criticizing his mother.

After dinner we get back to the room and he's coming at me, it isn't even bedtime yet, and I remind him, but he just pushed me down, practically pulls my clothes off, the blood excited him like crazy the way he went at it. What a mess for the chambermaid the next day!

From that time on it's like he waits for my time to get really excited and I got a new worry which is if I get pregnant I won't have my period for nine months. I actually talked to my doctor about it, but all he says it's perfectly all right to have sexual relations during the time if it doesn't bother either party. Bother? He loves it!

I don't want to make it seem that Harry is a kink or something. We have sex between times, too. But I learned quick that if I put on a sexy nightgown and strut around he won't take his eyes off the TV but if I want it, what I got to do is the opposite, make believe I don't want to, that I don't feel like it, try to talk him out of it, and he gets those raunchy twitches in his face and practically forces me, but try to understand. He's not really forcing me, I'm setting it up so he thinks he is because that's what he likes and as long as I'm in control of the situation, who cares?

Harry can be tender, like on my birthday he will pat my hair and kiss me and bring me presents, and now we got kids, he's a marvelous father to them, sweet, even if he doesn't spend time with them. He says when they get older he will, right now they're boring to him, he can't wait till Mike is old enough to go hunting with him. It takes a lot out of a man to own his own gas station, the hours are long, you got to keep open when it's raining or snowing, and I don't blame him for wanting to plop in front of the TV and not move except to snap open another beer can. It's just the romantic side of me feels left out now and then.

I knew he was in a mood when he left this morning, I mean the kind where he'll come home at night and get a bit rough and stick it to me. What I do is call the station to say some nice things, just friendly remarks, so maybe he won't go the black-and-blue route when he gets home, but when I called he said, "Oh it's you, don't have time to talk" and hung up. You see, when he's in this kind of mood, he doesn't take off his overalls when he comes home. He doesn't even wash the grease and dirt off of himself. He pours a shot glass, chases it with a beer, then another, then here we go. So you can imagine how glad I was when he comes home and goes into the shower and then puts on his brand new T-shirt and fresh pants and gets that cup out of the kitchen and goes out the door saying, "I'll be back."

I know lots of husbands what ain't as good providers as Harry. He's a terrific bowler. When October comes and he puts on his red mackintosh and goes off hunting with his guys, it's a week's vacation for me, too. I take the kids places he'd be bored to go. I see my mother. I buy myself things. He never complains about what I've bought when he comes home from hunting.

What would he want with a cup? I'm glad he took a plastic one in case he drops it. I'd hate to break the china set Aunt Louise gave us, it's not open stock.

I'll give him an hour before I get mad.

✹

"You've fixed up this apartment real nice," Koslak said to me.

"Thank you."

"I saw it previous, when the other people was here. You got a real eye for decoration."

Be neighborly, I thought. Don't look bored.

I said, "If your wife needs anything else, just let me know. If I've got it, it's yours."

Koslak laughed.

"I got the Esso station," he said.

"I know," I said. "You filled me up yourself the first time I was in there."

"Oh was you? I don't remember."

"It was raining. You were wet and looked like you wanted to be somewhere else."

"Yeah, inside," he said, laughing again. Then, "I got two kids

---

37

pumping gas now so I don't get to see all the customers the way I used to."

I wished I weren't wearing the tent. I felt naked underneath.

"You got a broom? I don't mean I want to borrow it, I want to show you something."

I brought the broom from the kitchen. He hadn't moved.

"Let me show you." He took the broom from me, stood on a chair, and thumped the ceiling once. "If you have any trouble from anyone, just do that and if I'm home, I'll come down and help, right?" He laughed. "I wonder what Mary'll think I'm doing banging on the ceiling like that." He looked sheepish for a moment. "Mary's the wife. Mrs. Koslak."

"I think I've seen her." *When will he leave?*

I turned to the window. I was going to ask him if he liked the view as much as I did since they obviously saw the same thing from their apartment upstairs, in fact they were higher, when I turned and noticed that he was still holding the cup of sugar in one hand but with the other had opened his fly and his cock in full erection was in his other hand.

"Are you scared?" he asked.

My heart was pounding. I had imagined other situations and how I might handle them, but I hadn't realized how much the fear choked off thought. *He wants me to be scared. Suppose I just calmly go to the phone . . .*

"What're you doing?"

What is he doing?

"No phoning," he said. "Just do what I say."

I waited.

"You're staring at it."

"I'm not staring at it." I noticed him putting the full cup of sugar down. He held on to the other thing.

"Go into the bedroom."

I could kick him just below it, in the balls. Or in the shin, hard. I don't have my shoes on.

I went toward the chair by the picture window where I'd dropped my shoes.

"Don't move," he said. "If I break your arms, I won't have to tie them."

"You don't have to break anything," I said. "Just tell me what you want."

"I want you in the bedroom."

Who would hear a scream through the closed windows? Maybe he wants me to be afraid. He could hurt me badly. He might kill me by accident if he's deranged. He's got to be crazy to do things like this.

I went into the bedroom. When I turned to face him, I noticed that he had let go of his thing and it had gone part way down. *He won't be able to.*

"Put it in your mouth," he said.

I shook my head vigorously. Did my disgust show?

"Put your hand on it."

Scream now. Why can't I scream?

He unfastened his jeans the rest of the way, let them drop. I went toward him as if I was going to obey, then darted for the open bedroom door, saw him scramble to get his pants back up, ran through the living room for the door into the hallway, got my hand on the knob, remembered I had to turn the latch he had locked, and suddenly he was behind me, grabbing my arms, forcing me back from the door.

"You'll be sorry you did that," he said.

"You're hurting my arms."

He fumbled in his pocket, pulled out a rope. *He brought it with him. He planned all this.*

I felt him get the loop over my left wrist, pull hard, then he tied it around my right wrist. I tried to wrench away. I had to keep my hands free. He forced me to the ground face down, put his knee in my back so hard I thought my spine would crack. He tied my hands together. I had to remember that the important thing is not to die.

I turned my head enough so that I could see him standing over me.

"Now you'll have to suck it," he said.

"I'll choke."

"Nobody chokes from sucking."

"I'll do it with my hand if you'll untie me."

"You tried to get away."

What would he believe?

"I just wanted to make sure the front door was locked so nobody would come in."

"I locked it."

"I didn't see you lock it."

"You saw. Now be nice. No use getting hurt, is there?"

"Can we talk?" I asked. My tied arms hurt.

"About what?"

"You want to . . . have sex, don't you?"

"I didn't come here to play marbles."

"I mean your wife upstairs, what about her, having sex with her, wouldn't that—"

"I don't want you talking about my wife."

"Okay."

"Get back in the bedroom."

"Sure." *Got to keep him talking.* "What kind of sex do you like?"

"What do you mean what kind?"

"You know what I mean. If it's different kinds and—" *Mustn't mention his wife.* "There are prostitutes who will do anything. I'll give you the money." I knew it was the wrong thing the instant I said it.

He slapped my face. "I don't need your money. I got all the money I want."

It came out of me like a wail. "Why me??"

He smiled.

He actually smiled. "I been watching you. You got class."

"There're supposed to be a lot of call girls with real class."

"Where'm I supposed to call them? The gas station? My house?"

"I'd let you use my apartment," I said eagerly.

"I'm using your apartment right now."

There must be something I can do. "You could go to jail," I said. "It isn't worth it, is it?"

"Let's find out. Take that thing off."

"I can't. My arms are tied."

"Unzip."

"It won't come over my arms."

"Lie down and pull it up. All the way up."

I sat down on the bed. "You don't want to go to jail."

He slapped me across the face, harder this time. "I'm not going to no jail."

"That hurt."

"Good. Nobody goes to jail if nobody talks. You're not going to talk. I live right upstairs. You do anything I don't like and you're finished, see?"

Koslak pushed me, swung my legs up on the bed, tugged at my caftan, pulling it up.

Kick him? Is it worth getting killed resisting? I pressed my thighs together.

"No you don't," he said, taking his pants off. "Spread. I want to see it."

"There're plenty of magazines with pictures," I said.

He pulled his T-shirt over his head.

He's not removing his shorts. His thing isn't hard, that's the problem. I'm safe as long as . . .

He had picked up the sewing scissors from the dressing table. "You gonna spread?"

I did as I was told.

"Real nice," he said, dropping the scissors on the table. He was rubbing his thing through his shorts, desperately I thought. Then he reached out with his left hand. "You're dry," he said.

The idiot expects me to be excited.

I had an idea. "I'll make it easier," I said. "See that jar?"

He glanced over at the dressing table, as if expecting a trick.

"The cold cream," I said.

He opened the jar, dipped two fingers in it.

"Not on me," I said. "On you."

He took his shorts off, put the cold cream on his thing.

"Rub it," I said. "Put your hand around it and stroke it."

At least, I thought, *I won't have to put it in my mouth.*

He stopped stroking when it was half erect again.

"Want me to help?" I said. *It might work.*

He smiled. A bit suspicious yet, but smiled.

"Untie my arms so I . . ."

"No funny stuff."

"Promise."

When he had untied me, his thing had lost most of its rigidity. *Have to go through with it,* I thought. *This way is better.*

I pulled the caftan completely off and let his eyes inspect me. The circulation was coming back into my hands. *Think of it like a chess game.* I took his thing and started stroking it. It was quickly erect, with that funny angling over to one side, as it was when I had turned from looking out of the window. With my left hand, I held his balls from underneath, stroking with my right.

41

"Okay?" I asked.

He nodded.

Find his rhythm and keep to it.

Suddenly he wrenched away from me. "You're trying to make me come!"

"Isn't that what you wanted?"

"Lie down!"

The scissors on the dressing table. Could I plunge it deep enough to kill him? Even if I stabbed him, it might not kill him. He could wrench the scissors away, kill me with them.

I closed my eyes. *Don't close your eyes, remember something to describe him afterwards.* The small tattoo on his right arm, what was it, why was it so small? *Mary.* No arrow, no heart, just *Mary.*

I closed my eyes again as he mounted me, thinking of the movie I had seen just a year ago when I had closed my eyes in the movies in the rape scene because it repulsed me so, and then I knew he was in me and thrusting, and I tried to think of him as something inanimate, a machine, it would only take a minute more, and it would be over, over, over. It was an accident that my eyes opened, just a slit for a second, and I saw his face. He had a desperate, wild, anguished expression. It was grotesque to call this making love.

I hadn't felt his orgasm, but when my eyes opened, he was standing at the bedside, detumescent now.

It was over, thank God, it was over.

FOUR

Thomassy

How many hundreds of clients over the years have responded to "Tell me what happened?" by proceeding to convince me of their inarticulateness. Most people use the language as if it were a grab bag of words, flinging them about in the hope that some will fit their meaning well enough to convey, loosely, what they want to say. Francine Widmer, to the contrary, strove for precision. If her first comment about something didn't satisfy her, she modified it. Her mind seemed to work the way I imagined a sculptor worked on a block of stone, chiseling away the debris until he got to the truth. When a client first tells me his or her story, I look for those small facial expressions—the tic of concealment, the eyes desperate to please—that sometimes tell you more than the words do. With Francine Widmer, one could concentrate on the words. During her recital of the events of March 22, I began to admire the inside of her head.

Which is quite a discipline considering how the outside looked, not just the strangely shaped eyes and the magnificent cheekbones, but also the curve of her long neck, the occasional pale blue vein under the skin, the way she sat tall like a dancer.

And though she must have been more distressed than she let me see, she didn't lose her sense of humor, which most people do the instant they are angry.

When she finished her story of the rape, I said "Thank you." One of her brows arched upward.

"What's the matter?" I asked.

"That's what he said."

"Who?"

"Koslak. Before he left he said thank you."

A thief acknowledging the donor. A point to remember about Koslak if we went to trial.

"A few more questions, Francine."

"Yes."

Most people would have said *All right.*

"What was the first moment when you felt there might be trouble?"

She thought. "When he exposed himself."

"Not before?"

"He was just a neighbor come to borrow something. He was friendly."

"Wouldn't the wife normally come for a cup of something?"

"Normal isn't normal these days. I did wonder why he hadn't gone to the people across the hall upstairs. It crossed my mind that perhaps the wives didn't get on."

"All right. When he exposed himself. Did you think of screaming, that a scream might scare him off?"

"I don't think I've ever screamed out loud in my life."

"Not even on a roller coaster?"

"I was never much for scaring myself. Look, I realized this was very weird behavior, but if you start screaming at every crazy you see, you'd better stay out of New York. I didn't at first feel it as a threat to me. He was a neighbor. I had seen him on the stairs several times. I had seen him at the gas station. Suddenly the neighbor behaves weird. I guess I hoped he was an exhibitionist, something like that. Do you understand? I didn't immediately see it as a threat to me."

"Did you think of screaming at any point?"

Francine put her long fingers to her lips. "Yes. As a matter of fact, twice. When he wouldn't let me telephone, for a second I was going to scream as loud as I could, and immediately thought they wouldn't hear me in the street, the windows were closed, a neighbor might or might not hear. Everybody hears somebody scream once in a while, they might or might not investigate. I doubt that they'd call the police. I guess what I thought was that if someone did come to the door, Koslak might make me say it was all right, or he might zip up and let them in, he had that perfect excuse, the cup he came in with, he'd lie about everything else. I'd feel ridiculous."

"Wouldn't it have been better to feel ridiculous than to be raped?"

"I wasn't thinking sensibly."

"You should have screamed."

"I wasn't sure anyone could hear me. I thought he'd get violent if I screamed. Okay, I should have screamed."

"And you didn't. All right, do you see what I'm getting at?"

"You're questioning me about things other people will be questioning me about."

"They won't be as friendly. They'll want to show that you didn't take advantage of early opportunities to scare him off, that maybe you were leading him on."

"But—"

"The courtroom, if we get there, is a very tough and dirty forum designed to protect the innocent."

"He wasn't innocent."

"He has the presumption of innocence in his favor. Did you at any point consider using physical means to stop him?"

"I said so."

"Would you have known what to do?"

"You mean like knee him in the balls, or a thumb in his eye, sure. I went to one of those consciousness-raising things. I saw a karate demonstration, one of those lethal blows, you know, the bridge of the nose, the Adam's apple. There was the scissors lying right there. Maybe I couldn't bring myself to kill him, I didn't know if I could, maybe all I'd do is hurt him and make him angrier and he'd kill me, you just don't think clearly under circumstances like that. I might have missed."

"The truth is . . ."

"I really thought I could outsmart him, talk him out of it."

"You know what others will see."

"What?"

"That you didn't scream, and that you had an idea of how to defend yourself and didn't do it."

She put her left thumb and forefinger in the inside corners of her eyes, sighing as if from sudden great weariness.

"Did you cry? When he left."

"I don't usually cry."

"Look," I said, "I'm sorry if this is trying for you. We're just fact gathering. We needed to assess our cards and their cards. It's better to know where our weaknesses are."

"Yes."

"Now tell me what happened immediately afterward."

"When he left, I—"

"No. Before he left."

"He went into the bathroom, it's just off the bedroom, left the door open, I heard the sink run, I suppose he was washing himself off so his wife wouldn't detect anything, I don't know."

"Did you put your dress back on?"

"It was a caftan really, not a dress. I just pulled it over me on the bed, like a blanket."

"You didn't think of escaping, or calling the police?"

"Actually, I didn't think of anything except would he hurry up and leave so I could take a bath."

"That was the worst thing you could do."

"They told me at the hospital. I just didn't think. I'll remember it the next time."

"I hope there won't be a next time."

"The son of a bitch could come down any time. He got in once, why not again? The odds are on his side, the damn law's on his side."

"The law is on nobody's side. It's a game."

"A game?"

"Like checkers. Like chess. Everybody starts the same. It's the moves you make that count. I'm trying to plan our tactics. Please try to understand."

She did that deep breath thing she does.

"Okay," she said.

"Now. He got dressed?"

"Well, he didn't leave naked."

"Did he say anything?"

"Like goodbye? I told you he said thank you. When I didn't answer he said see you around, something like that. For him it was normal."

"And then?"

"I bathed. I douched. I wanted more than anything else to talk to someone, to tell someone. It was too damn grotesque."

"Yes, I know."

"Well, I called Dr. Koch, my anchor."

"And?"

"He was impossible."

"I'm surprised."

"Think how damn surprised I was! Anyway, I went to the hospital, then to the police station on Wicker Street, then to Dr. Koch's. Bill drove me. He's a young man I know."

I hadn't thought about a boy friend. I may not have wanted her to have one.

"Finally, Bill drove me to my parents' home."

"Did he stay with you?"

"In my parents' house? Are you kidding?"

"It's a question you'll be asked. Tell me about the hospital."

"Nothing to tell. A bull dyke filled out a form. A kid resident examined me. He said he couldn't take a sample or whatever because I had douched and bathed. He said he saw no internal injuries. In fact, he said there was no sign that I had had sexual intercourse, much less forcible."

"Great."

"I told him I knew who did it. He said to tell it to the police."

"Tell me about that."

"Well, I knew where the precinct was. I went and asked the desk sergeant if I could see a police matron. He asked what was the problem? I told him. He sent me upstairs to talk to a detective and the matron. They filled out forms."

"Did they offer to go back home with you?"

"No."

"Did you tell them you knew who did it?"

"Of course!"

"What did they do?"

"They wrote it down and said it was a serious accusation. I could be sued if I charged somebody with something I couldn't prove. They asked if somebody had witnessed the alleged offense. They kept calling it that, alleged offense. I said no, it happened in my apartment, there was no one there. They asked about the hospital and I had to tell them it was no use. I told them I knew who it was, and they kept saying it wasn't enough, I needed proof."

"What were the names of the detective and the matron?"

"I don't know!"

"Well, we can get it off the report. If they filed it."

"You mean they might not have kept the form?"

"Anything is possible. Where did you go from the police station?"

"To Dr. Koch's. He wasn't helpful. I was angry. He was the one who told me to see a lawyer. That's when Bill drove me home to my parents."

"You told your parents."

"More or less."

"What does that mean?"

"There's a limit to what you can tell your parents. I told my father because Dr. Koch suggested I see a lawyer."

"Let's stop a minute. Understand this: you are the only witness we have."

"I know."

"We'll have to come up with very strong corroboration from independent sources for a jury."

"What kind?"

"That's the problem."

"What about Dr. Koch?"

"What he knows, he heard it from you. That's hearsay. That's the same story, not corroboration. However, we have a little time. My date's not till seven. I want to hear about your relationship to Dr. Koch, why you went to him, what you discuss. I realize that's private, but you see, if we succeed in persuading the D.A. or anybody else to take any action against this man, it's going to come out that you are seeing an analyst. That means—to the average person—that you have emotional problems, that you're neurotic, that . . . now don't get jumpy, we have to face the facts, that you could have made up some of the elements of this story. Or all of it."

Francine, who did not usually cry, was fighting to control her tears.

"Go ahead if you have to," I said.

"I'm not crying," she sobbed as I offered her a Kleenex.

She was crying uncontrollably when I said, "That's good."

Blowing her nose, trying to stop her sobs, she said, "What the hell do you mean that's good!"

"It'll be useful on the witness stand." I handed her another Kleenex.

"You bastard. You wanted to see me cry."

48

"I needed to know if you could. It's part of my preparation." I put a hand on her shoulder. "I'm not a bastard," I said. "I'm a lawyer. Now tell me about Dr. Koch."

FIVE

Widmer

It was over a year ago when I went to see Dr. Koch, an event fraught with the possibilities of embarrassment for someone like myself. On the phone I had said to him, "This is Archibald Widmer. I'd like to make an appointment."

I hadn't expected him to recognize my name—we travel in very different circles—but it seemed to me that if a man with a cultivated voice asks a doctor for an appointment, it should be a matter of simply finding a mutually convenient date and hour.

"Mr. Widmer," Dr. Koch said in an accent I took to be German—I didn't learn till later that he was Viennese—"I am not sure I can take on another patient at the moment."

I set him straight at once. "I'm not a prospective patient," I told him. "I merely wanted a consultation about my daughter. One hour is all I'm asking. When it's convenient."

I don't see why we are so intimidated by doctors, particularly specialists, and most particularly psychoanalysts. I was tempted to say they are people like ourselves, but that would not be true. First of all, so many of them in the New York area, frankly, are Jews, as I'm almost certain Dr. Koch is, and, actually, I think one would find a preponderance of them—I mean Jewish psychoanalysts—in Philadelphia, Chicago, and

Los Angeles, perhaps even Boston. They get an hourly rate for their services, which sets a ceiling on their income in an economy like ours, but lawyers like myself do also, theoretically at least, though I would be the first to admit that when I undertake an issue with important commercial considerations, my firm's fee, while ostensibly based on time, is usually altered upwards to more nearly reflect a percentage of the client's interest. The sophisticated client knows it. But an analyst like Koch, so near the end of his working life, is probably getting something between forty and seventy-five dollars per hour, while a considerably younger lawyer might make nearly twice as much. Please don't jump to the easy conclusion that I wonder about the preponderance of Jewish analysts because it would seem to be in conflict with the ostensible zeal of so many Jews to amass fortunes, or that I consciously value a person's advice by his affluence. I suppose what I'm really saying is that it would have been my preference to consult an American-born psychiatrist who had done his undergraduate work at Yale or Williams or Princeton, the pronunciation of whose name was never in doubt, and who practiced on the East Side of Manhattan, not the West Side as Koch did, in a neighborhood that had once been predominantly new middle class and now suffered shops with Spanish-language signs in their windows.

"Who referred you, please?" Koch asked me.

"George Thomassy," I offered. "But he didn't exactly refer me."

"I cannot place Dr. Thomassy."

"No, no. He's a lawyer up in Westchester. Someone I've known for a very long time. He passed on to me a reprint of yours, Dr. Koch, about the three types of human personality. Thomassy thought it brilliant—he practices criminal law—and when I read it, I had to agree. In my corporate practice, understanding the psychology of clients, self-made businessmen in particular, has always been of special interest. I thought your speculation extraordinarily acute, and the daughter I wanted to consult you about is a very bright girl who has the ability to run rings around her elders. I was once told that a very bright person needed a very bright analyst."

"That is not necessarily true," said Koch.

I had hoped to flatter him. His voice sounded as if he hadn't even understood the compliment and was merely responding to what he thought was an incorrect assertion of mine.

"It would be a very great favor, Dr. Koch."

"Sir, it is not a question of favor, it is a question of time." Then he said, "Did you think of asking your physician for a name?"

"The truth is I gave my physician your name and asked him to look up your credentials. Which are excellent, of course."

"I do not make a specialty" —he pronounced the word the way the British do, as if it had five syllables— "of children."

"My daughter," I said, "is twenty-seven."

"What is the problem?"

"Insomnia."

"Well, we all have sleepless hours from time to time . . ."

"No, no, no. She gets desperate from lack of sleep many nights in a row. And . . ."

"Yes?"

"She's got a Seconal problem now, I'm afraid."

"Does your daughter know you are calling me?"

I thought Dr. Koch rude. In retrospect I can see that he was not being rude at all.

"No."

"Psychotherapy has to be a voluntary process."

"I'm sure she'll agree."

"You seem to know your daughter better than most fathers do, Mr. Widmer."

He must have written down my name to remember it.

Finally he said, "I will give you an hour next Tuesday at four. Is that convenient?"

"I will make it convenient," I said, relieved and immediately wondering what meetings I would have to reschedule.

Tuesday at four turned out to be very inconvenient. I had to ask one of my partners, Whitney Armitage, to sit in for me at a meeting with the head of a foreign shipbuilding firm who would have been insulted to have met only with an associate, though the associate knew the matter better than I did and Whitney would have to take notes in silence as he had never been involved in maritime work, much less the particular client company.

I pleaded a personal emergency.

"You haven't got cancer, Ned?" my partner asked with his usual directness. He and I had both lost a partner two years earlier who had several "personal" appointments that eventually led him to Columbia Presbyterian and death.

"No," I said, wishing a witticism had come to mind.

"I did something very indiscreet, Ned. I leaned over your lovely secretary's shoulder and saw your calendar has a Dr. K. on it. Is that a cover for a new mistress, Ned?"

"Why of course," I said. *He looked at my calendar.*

"About time," said Whitney. "Keeping the pecker busy is a good way of pretending to stay alive."

Whitney was related to the Cabots by marriage, which in our circle at least gave him license.

"Don't worry, Ned," he said, "I'll go to your meeting. I can imitate anyone's style, including yours."

"Thanks, Whitney."

"Just keep a chit. One favor owed. I might want you to visit my mistress when my pecker's down."

It wouldn't be his nonexistent mistress. It was Alexandra, his queen of a wife, that I'd lusted after in the safety of my mind.

In some ways I wish Whitney were keeping the appointment with Koch for me, though I find it hard to imagine him entering the building on West Ninety-sixth Street that Dr. Koch apparently both lived and worked in. It had a doorman whose eyes were glazed in front of a closed-circuit security monitor. He responded to my tap on the glass of the locked front door as if I had interrupted him.

"Dr. Koch," I said.

"Got an appointment?"

Why that look? I nodded.

"Elevator on the right."

The elevator had initials scratched in the walls. Its operator, a dark young man with hair that hung over his uniform collar, nodded when I gave Dr. Koch's name and said something that sounded more Spanish than English. At the sixth floor, he let me out and pointed to a door down the hall.

The nameplate read "Gunther Koch." No mention of doctor. I rang the bell before I saw the small sign that said, "Walk in. Do not ring." I flushed with embarrassment.

Inside there was a waiting room with seven or eight identical plastic-covered chairs. I don't see why doctors can't have decent furnishings in their waiting rooms. Depends on their clientele, I suppose. If we had anything but leather in the firm's waiting room, some of our clients would be certain the firm had undergone reverses.

I had dreaded the prospect of finding several people waiting. Fortunately, the room was empty. Some doctors—not the kind I normally see—derive their self-image in part from the number of people they keep waiting at any one time. Dr. Koch was, in this respect, civilized.

Despite my having rung the bell, I sat ungreeted. No receptionist. Someone had to make out his bills, type his reports to other doctors. Did she occupy a back room somewhere? Discretion?

From the recesses of the apartment I heard the movement of furniture, voices, then the door opened and a man came out, forty or more, had a perfectly good suit on, vest as well, a watch chain with a key. *I thought they let patients out a second door?*

Then I saw a man I correctly assumed to be Koch, heavyset, a bit rumpled, a full head of disorganized grey hair. As the patient closed the outside door, Koch glanced at his wristwatch, then extended his hand to me. "Mr. Widmer," was all he said. His voice sounded much richer than it had on the telephone, or was this the mystique working? I followed him into a room where the drapes were drawn. The room was dark except for the light shed on his huge desk by a large lamp. There were four or five manila folders on the desk. Behind it was a high-backed leather chair of the kind that judges used in the days before our courtrooms were modernized. While I am not expert in such matters, I would suppose that the Persian carpet on the floor had once had great value. My eyes naturally wandered to the leather couch along the wall, the foot covered with a piece of transparent plastic to protect it from the shoes of patients. Somehow I had imagined that patients in analysis took their shoes off! The head of the couch was covered with the kind of paper headrest one sees in the economy sections of aircraft. I suppose he changed it from patient to patient?

For one awful moment I thought he was going to ask me to lie down on the couch my eyes had been taking in! Dr. Koch beckoned me to a chair across the room and sat down opposite me.

"I was flattered that you liked my paper, Mr. Widmer. I thought only other psychoanalysts read it."

"Mr. Thomassy's clients—he practices criminal law—are nearly all your category two and three people. The twos are small-timers who work for other criminals and get caught. The threes are the tough cases."

"Your clients are not like that."

"No."

"Not thieves?"

"No. Businessmen."

Dr. Koch laughed. "Tell me about your work, the essentials."

I gave him a three-minute summary. Why was he concerned about what I did?

"That will do," he said, I thought a bit brusquely. "As we have only fifty minutes before my next regular patient, perhaps you will tell me about your daughter."

I felt he was being unnecessarily quick with me, the way my father used to in my youth. Or was I imagining something that is part of this unnatural relationship?

I gave Dr. Koch a brief synopsis of Francine's life up until the point where her insomnia started.

"Very good," said Koch. "I mean you summarize well. Now tell me about yourself."

"As you know, it's my daughter I've come about."

"Yes, yes. However, she is the daughter of a particular set of parents. I don't often get an opportunity to consult with parents until much later and usually they are dead and I can't talk to them at all. Just a word or two about yourself and your wife."

I told him about Priscilla. When I finished, he said, "You left yourself for last. Very courteous."

I wondered if he was being sarcastic. I was not ducking. I tried to summarize myself.

"I could have read that in *Who's Who in America*," Koch said. "You have told me objectively verifiable facts. Now tell me the truth. How did you feel when . . ."

He probed deeper than any employment interviewer would dare, then said, "Mr. Widmer, have you ever considered analysis? For yourself."

"The thought never occurred to me. I'm not aware of any overriding emotional problems." I tried not to let my voice betray my annoyance.

"Understood," Koch said. He remained silent longer than people do in ordinary conversations. Then he wrote on a card and handed it to me.

"That is your daughter's appointment. Please have her telephone to confirm it. I do not know yet if I will take her as a patient."

I started to protest.

"No, no," he said. "It is perhaps that she should have a woman analyst. I think not, but maybe. I will direct her to another analyst if I am not right. However . . ."

He seemed to be trying to gauge my expression. People in my profession have had long experience in keeping their thoughts from intruding on the musculature of their faces.

"Mr. Widmer, from what you have told me, I cannot tell whether your wife or your daughter is the first woman in your life. You mention two other daughters, but you speak of this one in a way you do not speak even of your wife." He raised his hand before I could say anything. "That is natural, normal, nothing to suggest therapy. But you have said, perhaps not in so many words, that you have spent your life in a career that you stay in almost entirely because you are following the customs of a narrow class. You are an individual."

"I certainly like to think that I am."

"I don't know how well you know yourself as an individual."

I began a sentence in my head that I could not utter because my sense of protest blanketed any specific articulation I could muster.

"You are how old?"

"Fifty-seven," I said.

"And you have not yet led your life. Or do you maintain that you elected to be an affluent slave?"

The impertinence of the man! I knew I should not have come to the offices of a West Side Jew!

He smiled. "Good," he said, "very good. You have a high color in your face now. You are angry at me. If you were in analysis, one day you would tell me the sentence you just thought and we would both begin to find out who you are. No, Mr. Widmer, I am not soliciting you as a patient. I have enough. If I take your daughter, I will have more than enough. But if your daughter is eccentric, as you say, and forthright, as you say, and conducts her life in a manner undreamt of by her parents, as you say, she has done so without a model in her immediate family, she has had to shape her own life outside it. If her life

---

56

style deviates greatly from her parents', she may be suppressing the guilt she feels about her rebellion. We shall see. I am not surprised that she has insomnia. Please have her call me. I will send you a separate bill for this time."

He saw me to the door. Then he said something odd.

"The unexpected can be interesting."

What did he mean by that?

As I pressed the button of the elevator I glanced at my watch and noticed that he had given me only forty minutes, not fifty! I caught the absurdity of this reaction instantly, as if I had been shortchanged in a meat market. He hadn't given me short shrift. He had opened my head with a cleaver. Did I dare put Francine in the hands of a man like that?

SIX

Koch

A first meeting is for me always a difficult acting role. I spend so many of my working hours being passively sympathetic. As the patient explores his thoughts, I grunt neutral sounds. I listen the way a neighbor or a friend does, forming my own perceptions. I remember the Baumgarten woman telling me I sounded like a big teddy bear, a larger version of the stuffed animal of her childhood to whom she talked for comfort. We are so lonely in our anguish that talking to a willing listener is itself therapeutic, and if the listener is a priest or a doctor, who knows, perhaps his experience of listening to so many private torments that are, at heart, so similar, perhaps the listener will have something useful to say in the end.

Yet if the person I am seeing for the first time is another doctor's patient upset at his transference, ready to switch allegiances, interviewing me to see if I am acceptable, I must seem to be harsh, cold, uncaring, a stone wall that talks back. And if the person who has come to see me is not the patient, but a father like Mr. Widmer who acts as if he knows his own high place in the world and has come to deliver his daughter over to the psychological zookeeper, I am an actor again. He is used to businessmen who smile when they feel derision, but he is not used to the idea of a doctor who sees through his great surface calm. A Jew, a

Greek, an Italian would have wailed about the plight of his daughter. Widmer speaks calmly—I would like to know what his pulse was, I would like to have seen his electroencephalogram. He flatters me, he says he comes to me by reading a piece of my work, am I to believe that? Somewhere in his mind, when he comes to visit me, he is trading down. His child has fallen from grace. She has terrible insomnia. She has betrayed the Wasp ethic of control. Am I to do some Freudian hocus-pocus so that she will become acceptable again to her mother and father?

In three minutes Widmer reveals that he is a lawyer who is not a lawyer. He is not a Clarence Darrow spellbinding a jury, he is a businessman who takes money for writing the same contracts over and over again, changing the names of the parties, the terms, it doesn't matter, he will never shake the Supreme Court's interpretation of the Constitution, yet he lusts after that excitement in the law and hangs on to it by a vicarious thread to an Armenian who is a real lawyer! Then, in the next few minutes, he betrays that in his mind—where else does man fornicate except in his mind?!—he is a lover to his daughter and a pastor to his wife. Is this none of my business except that it arms me now to deal with the girl?

I come out to the waiting room for my first look at Francine Widmer.

"How do you do?" she says, standing.

She is as tall as I am, blond, with unusual bone structure in her face. I wonder what her father thinks of the touch of oriental in her eyes. A distant ancestor? A mutation?

"I am pleased to meet you," I say, shaking her hand. "Please come in."

She has looked directly at me. Good.

We are standing in my study at the moment of greatest discomfort. "We will have a talk first," I say.

"Shall I sit here?" she says, pointing to the chair in which her father sat during our interview.

"Yes, please."

Am I imagining she slides her body into the chair as if it is an intimate act? I notice the naturalness of the shape of her breasts. Marta wore a brassiere always, a girdle always. It was the times.

She crosses her legs in defense of the flower. Better than the subway-riding women, sitting legs apart, unwanted. She tosses her hair. I expect it is lovely to touch.

"Our actual sessions," I explain, "will be with you lying down."

I have said this so often, and yet this time the words *lying down* simmer with an expectation that sounds sexual. What is this, Gunther?

I know of an actual case, a father who was himself a doctor, who had a heart attack at his beautiful daughter's wedding reception. Everyone thought of him as the happy father giving her hand in marriage, but he was in the darkness of his mind the dismissed suitor, haunted by the guilt of his illegitimate claim, now seeing his daughter's body claimed forever by a legitimate lover. What a heart it takes to adjust to that! But that was long ago. Marta and I thought of ourselves as brave revolutionaries, having intercourse four months before marriage, mingling in a sweat of excitement that would have brought apoplexy to our parents. Now Widmer and I live in a world where children—why do we still think of them as children?!—openly fornicate, shocking even those of us who were trained to think that our lusts are natural and the restrictions of society unnatural.

If I think *poor Widmer* am I not also thinking *poor Koch?* Isn't Widmer a warning to myself? I, too, walk around in camouflage, showing the world what?, a passive teddy bear listening?

I am older than Widmer by three years at least, a widower who sees no one, who rolls on the screen of his mind nostalgic movies about his dead wife, who sublimates by immersing himself in helping other people realize themselves, and who has talked himself into believing he no longer lusts, this man, Koch, sees a twenty-seven-year-old girl and feels his loins tingle for the first time in how long? How can I say of Widmer that he confuses his wife and his daughter when his daughter has the same effect on me? With less cause. Widmer has seen this Francine since a baby, watched her naked body grow lean, her legs lengthen, her breasts develop into pearls, her hips widen, her childhood lope become that walk she had when she walked into this office. I accuse Widmer's accuser of carnality! Of being human still at sixty!

How many patients have I seen in my lifetime, a thousand, and at the center of how many, most, yes most, it is the urgency of the testicles, the hungry labia that we come to. They say they have come to therapy because they have difficulty communicating with people, they have trouble keeping jobs, they have trouble keeping wives and husbands, they have nightmares, they take pills too much, and when we peel the onion away, we are left God's clever little motor for forcing us to procreate, a penis looking for a home, a home looking for a penis. The rest is culture.

"You have insomnia?" I ask.

"Very bad, I'm afraid."

"We must probe for the cause," I say.

Probe. Another word invested with meaning. What is this?

I have friends among analysts who talked seriously for a while that the sexual revolution was going to put us out of business. I laughed at them! The open ambiguity of our sexual natures now gives us more cases to deal with, the closet doors are opening up not to admit a minority into the light, we are finding out that almost all of humanity was packed in there, behind some door. What is our own Freud become, a blind genius who thought women envied him his penis! We are always beginning all over again.

I, at sixty, must take time for a new patient, myself, to find out why for the years since Marta died I have pretended to be a eunuch, my sexual life over, why it took this other new patient, Francine Widmer, to in one minute make God's little motor in my groin start humming? We are the physicians, the patients trust us, they put themselves into our power for therapy, we cannot abuse our power, we cannot involve ourselves in their sexual lives! Yet that is a lie, we do, we do!

COMMENT BY FRANCINE WIDMER

For my generation, psychoanalysis is a last resort. My friends get involved in things like transcendental meditation. Some of them have gone for weekend retreats at one of these places where you purge your soul in groups, but I can't think of one that took up the couch. Why waste the time and money? I wasn't interested in getting into a maze to find myself. I was into other people from the moment I got to Radcliffe.

My parents' idea of Cambridge and Boston comes from old books. What a difference! With all the colleges up there, including my own, it was a great place to find exotics, by which I mean people who weren't like Mom and Dad. My mother's melting pot consisted of Republican ladies. And my father joined clubs where they didn't let the other kinds in. In a big zoo like Boston, you want to look at what's in the other cages.

When I was a kid, whenever we were someplace my mother used to call "public," like a public swimming pool, and some kid would get up on the high diving board and cross himself before take-off, my mother would look at my father as if she were tolerating somebody who picked his nose. Well, the Cambridge they sent me to was littered with some of these cross-yourself Mediterranean-type Catholics, some of whom went to churches that were decorated on the inside like pinball machines. Our Presbyterian church, even when it's got people in it, looks like it needs dusting. I met Jewish kids at Harvard who kept running off at the mouth with an intensity that scared you till you got used to it. They didn't know that intensity was not nice, that if you had anything to say, you ought to say it quietly, using words that won't upset anybody. I don't mean there weren't Protestants at school who weren't into this and that with feeling, but the Jewish kids, hell, they were into everything as if being into was the thing and not the subject matter. Also in Cambridge I met a lot of et ceteras, Greeks, Irish girls pure enough to have freckles all over and real red hair.

It was exciting being in a big pond full of strange animals. The variety itself kept my adrenaline up through those late-night rap sessions, but late hours and insomnia are a poor mix. It was at Radcliffe that I started envying people who slept all night, or who could sleep in the mornings. I couldn't even sleep into Sunday mornings. I marked a passage in Kafka's *Diaries*: "Slept, awoke, slept, awoke, miserable life."

After graduation, my father gave me a blessed six months in Europe and I didn't miss a single night's sleep. Was that a clue?

I roomed with some girls in New York, drifted from job to job, and the insomnia came galloping back. I needed an anchor. A job or a man or both? My interests had something of an international flavor even then, so I put on a dress, poked around the U.N. and, to my surprise, getting a good job was easier than I thought because I looked so straight, Wasp nose, Ivy League references, accent okay, I was a lady!

With insomnia.

The U.N. wasn't at all like Cambridge. All those exotic types straight out of the *National Geographic* were *actors*, I mean they didn't behave the way they must've at home, they all acted like they were trying to be Henry Cabot Lodge. Sure there were real ones here and there, like that Russian sun freak from Moscow who used to take his shirt off in fur-coat weather if the sun was out. He kept complaining that the U.S. wouldn't let him go to Florida when he had a weekend off and wanted to know when we'd become a free country! I once asked him if he was an MVD agent—what the hell, there's no harm in asking—and he said he was the only member of the delegation who wasn't—I mean he had a sense of humor. I was also amused by those bucks from Africa who used polysyllabic English tongue-twisters incorrectly and frequently, you couldn't get a straight, simple sentence out of them. And real Arabs, no American girl should skip the experience of one date with a genuine Arab, especially one who's super polite and is desperate because he hasn't gotten laid since Saudi Arabia, that is an experience. Growing up in Westchester sure doesn't prepare you for living in the world.

I am not cynical. I am trying to nail down for myself what's real. It is one hundred percent true that the guys who make the speeches in the Assembly are Charlie McCarthys who don't believe most of what they move their lips with—listen, I know the guys who write their speeches. What you have in the General Assembly is like a Hollywood cocktail party where everybody *knows* everybody else is lying but they've got to make believe with each other, it's their thing. What most of my friends' bosses at the U.N. are into—wherever they come from—is having a good time in New York for two or three years, being called Mr. Ambassador by head waiters, having DPL license plates that enable you to park in the middle of traffic and get away with it, where can you get that kind of power back in the jungle where everybody else is like you? It's the fastest race for class mobility I know. The U.N. is packed with monkeys hurrying to get their nuts off, their booze drunk, and some money squirreled away before they are crated up and sent back to Stink, or whatever their country is called.

I was doing fine, enjoying myself, especially after I got myself transferred to X. X is what he was called. His real job was not writing speeches for the American Ambassador to the U.N., but drafting a so-called political memorandum that was used by the speech writer. X was the Mission's contact with the intelligence services, which is why I had to wait all those months for a clearance though I was really working for him in the meantime anyway, unofficially but getting paid. Even the Ambassador called him X sometimes, jokingly of course. I was his assistant, which meant I did his shit work. X said that I didn't have what he called a proper command of the language but since nobody under thirty did according to him and he thought I was smart, he would give me a batch of stuff that had come in and say something like, "Pull out the content." Five thousand words of garbage and he'd trust me to find if there was anything of substance and I'd give him three or four items, one line each, and X would say, "Smart lady" and pat me on the head, the pig. I did the digging, I did the choosing, and he dictated it to his secretary and claimed the credit. Of course I resented him, making three hundred and twenty percent of what I make. Yes, it's my first real job, yes he's older, yes he's got a wife and two kids to support, but why three hundred and twenty percent for what I do? If the crunch came—Washington is always threatening cutbacks in staff—he'd can me politely. But the work would still have to be done. He'd have to hire another me eventually, security clearance and all, so he might as well hang on to the original. That's my job security.

Once after a day of doing X's bidding only to find out he'd forgotten one significant part of his instruction and when he told me, sorry, I'd have to wade through that crap all over again, I let out some expletive and he said, "Why do you resent being a woman?" and I told him wearily, "Because I can't pee standing up." I'll find a way of telling him how I feel about that three hundred and twenty percent and a lot of other things the moment he makes that first pass, and he will, he will.

Well, here I was being X's digestive system—I have to admit I liked the actual work—and everything's going fine except the insomnia I had in Radcliffe comes back in spades. I'd go to sleep and within an hour, sometimes within ten minutes, I'd be awake, tired, blood-eyed. I tried reading things I hated, I tried hot cocoa, I tried some Indian system where you relax one muscle at a time. I began to wear dark glasses indoors to hide my eyes.

One weekend my friend from Radcliffe, Betsy Thorne, stayed over. At two in the morning I was sitting on the edge of my bed, nodding but not enough to sleep, desperate, when Betsy awoke. She came over to sit beside me.

"What's the matter, hon?" she said.

I told her it was nothing new, that it'd been going on for months, that I'd had it for a while in school, but now it was much worse.

"You'll kill yourself fighting it," Betsy said.

"I don't know what to do."

Betsy rummaged around in her bag and came up with the bottle of reds. I knew what they were.

"Try one," she said. "It works for me."

I took it with me to the bathroom, saying I was getting a cup of water, but my intention was really to flush it down and pretend to have taken it. When I saw my face in the mirror, the purple circles under my red eyes, I thought what the hell and swallowed the capsule.

We talked for a bit. Betsy said there was nothing to worry about as long as I didn't drink alcohol before taking them. Twenty minutes later I was yawning, and when I fell asleep I slept straight through. In the morning Betsy was gone but had left me three or four reds on my night table.

I had to scramble to find a steady source. My damn so-called doctor was the family's doctor and I knew he wouldn't approve. I thought of going to another doctor, *please can I have some Seconals*, and decided I'd rather pay more and skip the hypocrisy. Soon I was into two a night, then two when I went to sleep and one more when I woke up after a few hours, and once I found myself taking two more when I woke up, and I knew I was in trouble.

I was at my parents' house for one of my rare sleepovers when my mother, doing me a favor and unpacking my canvas duffel while I chit-chatted with Dad down below, saw the downers and told me, away from Dad's hearing, about the time she was on them. It was as if she was confessing to having been a streetwalker or something. We just can't imagine our parents into drugs a long time ago.

"Your father was away at a convention for a week. When he re-turned," she said, "he didn't, well, he wasn't loving the way he usually was after a time away. He kept to his side of the bed. I stayed awake longer and longer, unable not to think. The doctor prescribed the Se-conal. He cautioned me to take only one. But I'd wake in a few hours and couldn't get back to sleep, so I'd take another. Then one wouldn't get me to sleep, so I took two, and then another one when I woke in the middle of the night, and if I woke toward morning, I couldn't take just lying there in bed with your father asleep, and I'd take another, and then when it was time to get up I was foggy, and then when I told the doctor, he suggested I try Benzedrine in the morning, and it drove me nearly crazy. I decided I had to quit all of it. I had the most awful withdrawal symptoms. Your father was very sympathetic. He used to cradle me in his arms at night. As it turned out, his affection was my cure. The pills camouflaged the problem."

It was a short road from that conversation to Dr. Koch. Those early sessions were like root canal work, except the canal was my memory. Dr. Koch wanted me to see if I could remember the very first time I had awakened and couldn't get back to sleep. Had I been dreaming? I didn't remember. What were you thinking about before you went to sleep? How could I remember, it was so long ago? You will remember, he said. Be patient.

The first time I was really glad to be in therapy was when the rape happened. People don't understand that when something like that hits you, what you want to do is get rid of the disgust by laying it on the table in front of someone. I never expected Koch to be a son of a bitch the way he was that night. He was supposed to be helping me!

When I was a kid I always expected doctors to look like my father, World War II type haircuts, narrow ties, how-do-you-dos every time they saw you. Not that they really looked alike, but they all seemed to have noses that were going to turn into those long thin ones on Modigliani's sculptures, breathing tubes, no bridge, barely visible except as a line down the middle of the face. I'm not exaggerating. If you listened to them talking to my father it sounded like they had all taken speech lessons in the same class. Well, when you get used to doctors looking or acting in one particular way and then you go to see a doctor who looks like Koch, it blows your preconceptions.

Dr. Koch was a big old blob of a man, shaggy hair bushed up, and his nose was more W. C. Fields than Valentino. Maybe that sounds unfair, because all of his pieces fit, and I've got to admit his eyes, with those bushy grey brows growing in all directions, were all soul. I did look him over that first time. He wore a tie as if it was an impediment to free breathing; he kept the knot an inch or two from his neck. He wore sandals. Whoever heard of a doctor wearing sandals?

He stonewalled me the first time, just at the beginning, as if it was a technique, keeping his distance, but he noticed I was looking him over as a person, and before the hour was up he relaxed, smiled, like an instant friend saying okay, let's talk.

It was the second hour when I sensed him looking at me. I don't mean my face. I mean all of me. Do people that age fuck regularly? I guess we always think people stop at some point until we get to that point. Betsy Thorne fucked a much older man when she was a sophomore, some friend of her father's she met in the street when she was in L.A. and he said aren't you Betsy Thorne, what are you doing so far from home, and she said what are you doing so far from home, and then he asked her to dinner, why not, what kind of dinner, she doesn't care, he takes her to a topless place on the strip, and Betsy thinks so that's what Dad's friends do out of town. The food, Betsy said, was yuch, but the drinks were okay, and the show was something else, much better-looking girls than she'd expected to do that kind of thing, and he said some of them go to UCLA, and then she wonders why, when the meal's over, he doesn't put the napkin on the table, has he got an erection, she's thinking, and anyway, they end up in his hotel, and she said it was miles different than the guys at school, slow, you know what I mean, a fantastically long build-up. She got me going just talking about it. Of course it intrigued me, I think it does most girls who aren't cheerleaders chasing jocks. Someone else's old man might satisfy my curiosity. You see, it's Koch looking at me that way that got me thinking about it all again, because with all my previous thinking I never fell into the circumstance, and it didn't seem something I wanted to pursue especially. What we do is try to retailor life. I would have wanted Koch to be just a bit younger, maybe just less round in the middle, I have a strange feeling about a pot, as if it's just a little obscene. And I worry suppose he couldn't get it up, it would be awful. I wouldn't feel it was my fault, but you never can tell how you feel until something like that happens. Anyway, Koch never made a pass at me that whole year. I thought about him from time to time when I was lying there on the couch. I censored at first, I'd tell him what I was thinking, but I'd skip the things I was thinking about him, and then, shit, I told him because he said always tell everything, that's what analysis is, following the meanderings to find out what it's all about. I wish I had seen his face when I told him the first time, but he sits in back of me, you know, and he's just a voice grunting now and again.

The truth is that telling Koch about my thinking about him wasn't as bad as telling him the details when I was having that affair with the French interpreter at the U.N. What I wanted to say was I'm involved with this French person who works where I do and let it go at that, but it doesn't work that way because you talk about yesterday. Yesterday I did this and I did that, and I thought, I'm making Koch jealous, it's cruel to him to tell him about my being in bed with someone else when that's probably where he wants to be, and he just takes it like he takes everything, yes, go on, and then what happened? God you have to be like God to be an analyst sometimes! He wants me to tell him everything that's on my mind, and if nothing's on my mind, he says well yesterday, what did you do, and we're off and soon I'm talking about Bill.

Bill Acton, I regret to report, is the son of an old friend of my father's from Yale. We met under the worst of circumstances, my parents were throwing a between-Christmas-and-New-Year's party at the house and it's their idea of conviviality to have young people—that's what they call us, young people—invited also, so it's a familylike party. Only what happens is that the parents congregate together getting sloshed and the young people, if they can stand each other, smoke dope in an upstairs room. What struck me about Bill was his shyness. The other fellows who were about my age were all coming on the same way they used to in college, jocks-with-cocks looking for an opening, and Bill just sat there. I don't like wallflowers, female or male, but I happened to ask Bill something and his answer was a quote from Auden. I mean he didn't say it pretentiously, just as if it was the right answer. I guess I was also flattered by the fact that he assumed I'd know, that I wasn't just an opening for his oil rig, I was a person with a brain.

Well, we talked a lot that evening, and when the adults were ready to go home, Bill didn't offer to take me somewhere for a drink, meaning something else of course, he *shook hands*. Sure there's something terribly square and old-fashioned about that, and I guess all I thought at the time was that Bill was not boring and he's the kind of guy you could bring home if you had to (can you imagine my bringing the Frenchman from the U.N. home? My father'd have had a heart attack!). So when he was leaving I said call me. That's all.

Well, of course he called my home and Mom told him I don't live at home and gave him my phone number, and we got together for the movies, we went on a picnic believe it or not, I found out he liked rock and classical just like me, and then one Saturday we had dinner at Adam's Apple, which I sometimes go to to get away from the U.N. crowd at lunch, and we had no particular plans for afterwards, so we walked downtown and then West, and before you know it, we're in pornsville, and when he realized it, I swear he blushed. The theater right in front of us was playing *Behind the Green Door*. He asked me did I know what kind of a film it was, and I said yes, Betsy Thorne described it scene by scene to me. The box office was manned by a Puerto-Rican-looking woman. We were about five feet from her, and she was looking Bill right in the eyeball when he said to me, "Let's not."

I could hear the woman whisper "Chicken shit."

Bill walked closer to her cage and said, "What did you say?"

"Nothing," said the woman.

I took Bill by the arm and said, "Let's go." We walked quite a while before he talked. He said he'd seen a couple of films like that some time ago and really didn't care for them, they made sex seem mechanical and impersonal.

"But did you find them exciting?" I asked.

"Sure," he said. "It gets you going and stops you at the same time because it's so crude. Did you ever get a tan from a sunlamp?"

I hadn't.

"Well, I have," Bill said, "and it's not the same as getting it from the sun. It feels artificial. That's what I'm talking about."

I knew all about his ambivalence because I was churning over some of my own. A fellow couldn't be nicer than Bill. Bill was reliable. A friend. A nonthreatening friend. I asked him did he ever lose his temper, and he said he tried to control his temper. I told him about my insomnia, and he looked at me as if I were reporting on outer space. He always slept. It's not that I'm afraid of perfect people. I'm leery of my reaction to them.

Eventually we wound our way back to Bill's car. When we got to my place, I invited him up for a drink, and for a moment I thought he was going to beg off, but I said, "There's a parking place right in front. A New Yorker can't turn down an empty parking place, can he?"

Upstairs he hung his jacket up on a chair. I put a record on and brought out a half-gallon jug of Gallo's Hearty Burgundy and a couple of glasses. Bill did the pouring as if it were his role.

I tried to get him to talk about himself, and finally he told me about his year-long leading-to-marriage kind of thing that broke up. She sounded like a very nice person, a perfect match. She took up with someone Bill described as mean. Isn't that the way the ball bounces?

I asked him if he'd ever smoked dope. He nodded. I wanted to say *Good for you.* So I went to my stash and brought us a joint. Neither of us was a cigarette smoker, and we had a lot of trouble inhaling. It was a bit comical. He seemed happy that I was sharing the embarrassment as well as the joint. It relaxed him, I could tell, and I felt he was making something erotic out of passing the joint from his lips to my lips, back and forth. Suddenly he excused himself and went to the john. When he came back his breath smelled of toothpaste. I knew Bill was the kind of person who would never use someone else's toothbrush. What did he use, his finger?

When I offered a second joint, Bill volunteered to reimburse me for it and I told him not to be silly.

"It's funny," he said, not looking at me, "before the wine and dope I was wondering what a person like you saw in a person like me, but now I'm feeling pretty good about myself," and he tried to put his arms around me.

"No," I said.

He took his arms back immediately.

"I like you," I said. "But not that way."

He looked so crestfallen I wanted to take his face in my hands and kiss it, but anything physical at that point could have been misinterpreted.

I didn't pass the joint back. "Not if you're driving soon," I said.

"I better go," said good Bill.

"Yes. I enjoyed your company."

"Thanks for the wine. And the . . ." He pointed to the joint I was still holding. Then he fled.

I felt like a shit. What would have been so awful if I had gone to bed with him? The Frenchman didn't misinterpret it, a fuck was a fuck. But Bill would have, wouldn't he?

The following afternoon, lying on Dr. Koch's couch, I described the evening with Bill in minute detail. I am listening to myself tell it as if I'm a Christian martyr. I felt I was inches away from grasping something about myself. Dr. Koch interrupted my silence to say, "What are you thinking?" and I said I was reciting the evening with Bill to make Koch jealous.

I could hear the clock ticking in Koch's study.

For a long time he said nothing. Finally, I heard a deep sigh.

"Do you feel guilty about what you said?"

I didn't answer.

"You did nothing terrible," he said.

I come here for insight, not for absolution. I didn't want to talk.

"What are you thinking?" he insisted.

"Nothing," I lied. "Nothing, nothing, nothing."

❖

Before Marta died, for almost all of the thirty-four years of our marriage, every Saturday morning when weather permitted, we would go out shopping together. In the early years it was often just window shopping, discussing with high seriousness which of two armchairs we would buy for my den, knowing we would never decide between the two and have to look for a third because there was not enough money to buy something as frivolous as a comfortable place for me to sit. But when I had paid off my debts from medical school and from the early years of transposing myself to this country, we used whatever was left after food and rent not to save—how could we save for the future when we had so much to make up for the past?—but to spend with a vengeance against the forces that had denied us!

When we go on a shopping spree not for what we need but for what we want, we find we still have the reckless joy of children somewhere inside bursting out. I remember the day Marta and I splurged—we felt like kings—buying our first wall-to-wall carpeting for the living room and hallway to replace the second-hand rugs, threadbare from the feet of our only son, Kurt, and his friends, and our friends, and our own feet, and from the feet of patients without count, coming and going.

I remember the crazy delight we took in buying an electric orange juice squeezer—this was before the days of frozen juice—because I drink orange juice the way Americans drink Coca-Cola and it pained me to see Marta squeeze each orange half, the palm of her right hand turning it against the serrations of a glass squeezer that had cost twenty-five cents in Woolworth's when we were first married. For Kurt, when he was eight, we committed the ultimate extravagance. We bought him a new dress coat and a new lined jacket for playing street hockey, even though we knew he could wear them only one season before his limbs were too long.

These Saturday-morning escapades into department stores were our chief form of recreation. Never once in all those years did I think of patients during the time that Marta and I were out. Only when we came back home, exhilarated and exhausted eye-consumers, did I slump into my armchair, put my feet up on the ottoman, and think of my Worry Number One, Higgins, the only patient I had who could be a murderer in fact and not just in heart. Three times a week I would wait for his first words on the couch, wondering had something finally happened, had he been unable to control his desire to beat another human to death with his bare hands. Higgins was a strong man, capable, quick-tempered, a boss of truck drivers. Thank God he found a prostitute with well-padded buttocks who let him spank her with his hand till relief came. I told Higgins he should save the money he spent on me and just see that woman as often as he needed. When you think of the millions of aberrant and lonely persons over the course of human history who have found some release among prostitutes—those great actresses who understood human aberration long before Sacher-Masoch or Krafft-Ebing, we have cause to be grateful. It is possible that prostitution has done more than medicine for mankind, and with fewer mistakes that have converted a minor affliction into death by surgery and malpractice.

All right, I am meandering. Since Marta died, the Saturday shopping ritual continues without heart. What am I to buy, new carpeting when the old will outlive me? And so I buy light bulbs, Kleenex boxes, toilet tissue, soap, all with the excuse that it is very inconvenient to run out of such things, but what would another analyst make of my collection of such items? Of my need to pretend to shop when there is nothing I really have to buy? Why do I not go on weekends to visit my grandchild? Because our son Kurt married a young woman who had already had a needless hysterectomy, and I have asked was this to spite us, a willful attack, to deprive me of grandchildren?

The truth is that I have developed Worry Number Two, a patient who occupies my thoughts on weekends, not a murderer, not a suicide, but Francine Widmer, whose source of difficulty I now understand and am possibly postponing, dragging out her own understanding of the problem, because I do not want her to stop coming to me because I am infatuated with this baby of twenty-seven. Please understand, ever since Marta's passing, I go to dinner parties, pushed by friends to meet eligible widows, it doesn't work, it would be a housekeeping arrangement, I would constantly be making comparisons to Marta, whose shadows are still in every corner of my mind. But this young woman, Francine, is not in any way like Marta, and I have tried to tie off the waves of stimulation that flow from her without success. I daydream that I am licking the palm of her hand, it is a disgrace for a man my age, I must control this urge, I must arrange for her to see another analyst even though we are on the verge of success, I cannot give her up. I ask myself, does she know? Of course a person always knows. It would be easier for me to marry one of the widows than to act out my fantasies for this young woman.

I have a confession. Not too long ago—why do I say that? I remember the exact date of course!—I was at a matchmaking dinner contrived by my friend Herman, when he is called to the hospital—his wife says it always happens—to deliver another inconveniently timed baby, and when Herman stops talking, the dinner party died. I tried to keep the conversation flowing, and finally the widow says we had better say good night, would I drop her off, so we walk the few blocks to her apartment, and she says come up, so I go, and when we get there, without fuss, she takes me to her bed. The widow is an ordinary woman of her age, fifty-something, not too bad looking, a bit thin, she is on estrogen, full of hope, my testicles are as full as those of a stud bull whose farmer has closed the fence and thrown the key away. So I do what is asked, and all the time I am thinking of Francine, her face, what her body must look like, what it would feel to be doing this and that to her. The widow asks will I see her again, I am a careful lover, her face shines, I have provided her as well as myself with relief, and I promise to call, knowing I am not likely to call because the widow bores me and I am a poor actor who cannot sustain a role for too long.

Within a week, I am rumbling about the house, looking through old books read long ago, when I get a phone call after my last patient has said good night, and I think aha, it is the widow, but when I answer it is Francine, she is half talking, half sobbing, and she tells me that a man has violated the orifice I coveted. This is not what she tells me, of course, this is what I think. I try to reassure her, but my heart is pounding wildly as if she is telling me about a crime against myself. I ask her if she has gone to a hospital, I tell her to go, I ask her if she has called the police, I advise her to do so after the hospital, and to please call me afterward, I will wait for her call (what else do I have to do?).

She asks me to go to the hospital and the police with her, she wants to come see me now, first, and I tell her, coward that I am, that I cannot, has she told her father, she says she can't, and then I think of that young man she has been dating—whom I despise out of sheer jealousy of his age—and she says in anger yes, that is what she will do, slamming down the phone.

Years ago I devised a quick remedy for when tension ties my insides into knots. On my desk I keep three well-balanced English darts in a holder. When I open the closet door in my study, hanging on the back is the same dart board I have been using as long as I can remember. When you pick up the darts and take aim, your concentration is one thing only, moving the right arm forward with a snap to release the dart headed for as close to the bull's-eye as you can. And then there is the second and the third. You see your score, and in a moment you are plucking the darts out to show yourself that you can improve the result. Darts are addictive. You never throw just one. And before you know it, you have recreated yourself. And there is not, as with other recreations, a mess to clean up afterwards; just to close the closet door, and put the three darts back in the holder on the desk.

This evening my throwing of the darts is not entirely successful, because as I throw I cannot put completely out of my mind a petition to the absent Francine. I don't want her to continue her anger at me. Long after I have put away the darts, the phone rings again. It is the young man calling for her, I agree to see her though it is very late. It is in this moment of crisis that the cause of her insomnia comes surging into her memory. I am delighted, even though the cost of the revelation is this hideous thing. It is out in the open, and what do I do? I find myself lecturing instead of soothing her. Is this a form of attack because of her unfaithfulness to me, with the boy Bill and with the rapist?

In the silence after she leaves, I sit in my bathrobe into the night, trying to define my worthlessness this evening. I am not her father, her lover, I am her therapist, I must help her, I hope I do not love her, she has become a sexual affliction for me, I am afraid I adore her unreasonably, I must give her up as a patient, I cannot give her up, I must have the help of the Deity now in exchange for whatever promises will buy surcease.

SEVEN

Francine

All those wasted hours Koch the Coward sat behind my head listening, when he has to *do* something to help, he waddles out of it like a fat chicken, refusing me!

Oh I know what mother would have said, you need a best girl friend to turn to, as if I were a ten-year-old.

My best girl friend was a boy, the one sweet man who, even if he couldn't possibly understand what rape was like, would be a presence, a friend. I dialed Bill's number, still seeing Koch's fat face in my mind, wanting to pummel it with my fists. When Bill answered, my voice was quivering.

"What's the matter?" Bill said.

I told Bill what had happened. No details, just a man forced me.

"Oh nooo," he said. He sounded as if I had just told him his mother and father had died in a car crash.

"Are you all right?"

What does that mean?

"Are you hurt?"

How can I answer that?

"Please, Francine, say something!"

I became aware of my silence. I couldn't connect my rage and my voice.

"Are you there?!"

"I'm here," I managed to say, my voice a dry rasp defying me to control it.

"I'll be right over," he said.

I gentled the receiver back onto the cradle, not letting it go, then felt it shivering, ringing in my hand, and I picked it up again to hear Bill saying, "It'll take me nearly an hour driving fast."

"Don't drive fast. You'll get a ticket." *There's no point getting killed coming to me.*

When Bill walked in, he looked at me as if to see how I was different.

Don't look at me, I am a violated person.

"Are you hurt?"

He's not looking at me.

"Your cheek is very red."

I put my hand up to where Koslak's hand had slapped me hard. It hurt to the touch.

I turned my wrists up so Bill could see where the rope had burned in.

He was wondering about the rest of me. "I hurt inside," I said.

He was looking at me as if to define "inside."

"In my head," I said, "and everywhere else. Please drive me to the hospital."

When we arrived there, Bill double-parked—I was sure he'd get a ticket, I said—and accompanied me inside the double doors marked "Emergency." We went up to the nurse's desk.

Before I could speak, the nurse said, "Which one of you is the patient?"

My mouth felt too dry to talk. I pointed to myself. I wondered if my breath was bad.

"Are you her husband?" the nurse asked Bill.

He shook his head.

"Then step back behind the white line."

Bill blushed, moved back fifteen feet to the white line he had not noticed. I could feel him watching me.

"Name?"

"Francine Widmer."

"Spell it. Do you feel faint?"

"No." I spelled my name, gave my address, said I had Blue Cross coverage, signed the form the nurse pushed at me.

"What's the complaint?"

"I have an internal problem."

Bill, watching my lips, heard.

"What kind of internal problem?"

There were now two people in line behind Bill, impatient to get to the nurse.

"I don't know," I said.

"We can't admit you without a doctor's authorization and without a specific complaint."

"You mean I have to go away."

"Unless there's something specifically wrong."

"I'll go," I said, but in a second, Bill had crossed the line and was saying to the nurse, "She's not telling the truth. She was raped."

The nurse looked at Bill and then at me.

Into the silence Bill said inanely, "It wasn't me."

"Step back behind the white line," said the nurse.

"Why didn't you say so?" asked the nurse.

"I don't know," I said.

"Alleged rape," the nurse said slowly, out loud, as she wrote the words on the form.

"Go to the second floor east waiting room. Give this to the nurse. Next."

I took Bill's arm. "Thank you," I said.

"He has to wait down here," the nurse yelled at us.

Upstairs, the nurse on duty had a blank expression when she took the slip.

"When did this happen?"

"This evening."

"Have a seat over there. I'm going off duty in a minute. Another nurse will come out for you."

The wait seemed endless. Then I was ushered into a cubicle, told to remove my clothes from the waist down, to get on the examination table, put my feet in the stirrups. I did as I was instructed.

The doctor was a resident. My age. I felt hideous in that awkward position. He glanced at my cunt without a flicker. Then at my face. Then at the paper on his clipboard.

"What happened?" he said. He sounded as if he was in a hurry.

I showed him my wrists. The pink striations were less now than when I had shown them to Bill.

"Your hands were tied?"

"Behind my back."

I showed my left cheek. "From a slap," I said. "A hard slap."

The doctor handed his clipboard to the nurse.

"We'll do an internal," he said.

"I took a bath," I said.

"You what?"

"I felt awful. I had to take a bath. I douched several times."

"Jesus!" the doctor said. "We couldn't get a specimen that'll do the police any good."

"What are you doing?" I asked.

"Combing your pubic hairs to see if we find any of his."

He came away with three or four.

"These look like yours."

"If you pulled them out, they're mine."

"I didn't mean to pull any. The loose ones are probably yours, too." He put them on a piece of waxy-looking paper, folded the paper over, and gave it to the nurse. "I'm sorry," he said, "but I'm going to pull one on purpose now, for comparison."

When he had plucked the hair and put it into a second piece of waxy paper, he said, "What about inside? Are you hurt?"

"It aches a bit, too."

"I'll take a look."

It was embarrassing.

"No evidence of trauma," he told the nurse, who wrote it down. To me he said, "Did you resist?"

"I didn't want him to do it."

"Did you resist, though?"

"I tried to get away but he grabbed me at the door. I tried to talk him out of it. And other things."

"What other things?"

I looked at the nurse, ready to write.

"Nothing," I said, pulling my feet from the stirrups and getting off the table.

"What are you doing?" asked the doctor.

"Dressing."

"Here," he said, giving me a card on which he penned something. "This is your case number. The police will need it."

In the car with Bill I said, "The doctor was just about your age. He was awful."

"I'm sorry," said Bill, putting his arm around me.

His arm felt mechanical, as if it didn't belong to him, just an arm he put there because he was supposed to.

"I don't think he found what he was looking for."

"What was he looking for?"

"Semen and pubic hair," I said. "Doesn't it disgust you?"

"What do you mean?" said Bill, taking his arm away.

"Doesn't it change your attitude?"

"About what?"

"About me?"

Bill was shrugging his shoulders, groping for words.

"It does, doesn't it?"

"It's like anything. You have to kind of absorb it, right?"

"I didn't do anything. It was done to me."

"I know."

"It wasn't as if I went to bed with someone else, don't you understand?"

Bill, his hands folded helplessly in his lap, seemed to find conversation impossible. He looked like I feel when stomach acids back up into my throat. Finally, he said, "Where do you want to go?"

"The police station on Wicker Avenue."

When we arrived, Bill accompanied me inside. I told the desk sergeant I wanted to see a police matron.

"What for?"

"I want to report a crime."

"What kind of crime?" asked the desk sergeant.

"Rape." *Does one ever get used to the word when it's about yourself?*

"One flight up, turn left at the head of the stairs, door marked 'Detectives.'" A ticket taker saying "next."

"I'll wait down here," said Bill.

"You won't go away, will you?"

"I'll be here."

In the room marked "Detectives," as soon as I said the word again, the detective, a very freckled man of forty, pulled a form out of the drawer and said "Sit tight" as he went to get a police matron. The matron was older than the detective. *Why is it,* I thought, *in a police station nobody says hello to you, nobody shakes your hand?*

The matron said something to the detective that I couldn't hear and the detective nodded. They led the way into a private room and shut the door. The detective offered me a cigarette. I shook my head. The matron sat at the side of the table.

"All right," said the detective. "When did the alleged offense take place?"

I told him.

"Where?"

I told him.

"Can you describe the alleged assailant?"

"I know who he is."

The detective looked up at me, then at the matron. "Before you give us the name, I have to make you aware that if you accuse someone, you could be subject to a suit for false arrest."

"Even if he's guilty?"

"Well, not too many allegations of rape draw convictions, miss."

The green walls of the small room had not been painted for a long time. There were marks where the backs of chairs had scraped against the paint. A two-year-old calendar had not been removed. Near it, some flakes of faded paint had fallen from the wall.

"Well, give us the name, miss."

I looked at the freckled face that was anxious to get this bit of work out of the way.

"Isn't rape a serious crime?"

The detective flicked a look at the matron. "Oh yes, miss," he said, "it always goes with the major crime statistics. The problem, please understand, is that nobody reports an armed robbery that didn't take place. Or a murder. But a lot of the alleged rape cases that walk in here turn out to be, well, borderline seduction, or fantasy, or won't hold up because there are no witnesses, no proof, and nowhere to look for it."

"I am not a rape case," I said. "I am a person reporting a crime."

The detective moved his bottom on the chair, squirming. He seemed the type that always felt uncomfortable with women he didn't know.

"Please spell his name."

I spelled Harry Koslak. "He lives in the apartment above me. I think he owns an Esso station in the neighborhood. At least he seems to be the boss there."

"Did he force his way into your apartment?"

I thought *Should I have a lawyer with me? I haven't been accused of anything. I'm filing a complaint, why do I feel trapped?*

The detective was waiting for an answer.

"I let him in."

The detective glanced at the matron again. *Another one of those.*

"He came to borrow a cup of sugar."

The detective started to smile, then stopped, a checked swing. "Do the neighbors in that building come around to borrow things often?"

He wasn't writing answers now.

"That was the first time."

"Didn't it strike you as strange that a man would come around for a cup of sugar?"

"No. He said his wife was cooking something and had run out."

"Okay. Tell me what happened. Keep to the facts. What you saw. What you said, what he said, what you and he did. No speculations."

I told him, eliding a few of the details.

"Did you go to the hospital?"

"Yes."

"What did they do?"

"Can I talk to the matron about this?"

"You're talking to both of us, miss."

"I mean can I talk to her with you out of the room?"

The freckled man lifted himself from the chair, closed the door behind him. The matron sat at the desk where the detective had been. She picked up the ball point pen he'd been using.

"They combed for pubic hairs."

"Semen test?" the matron asked.

"No. I'd douched. Took a bath first, then douched four times."

"Never do that!"

"I didn't know. I hadn't had the experience before. Nobody warned me."

"We'd better call him back in. He knows these forms better than I do. He'll see what I write anyway. Okay?"

I nodded.

"All right," the detective said, resuming his seat, and glancing at what the matron had written. "Is there any way you can identify the alleged assailant?"

"I've seen him around. I've passed him on the stairs. I've been to the gas station."

"Are you friendly?"

"With him? No, first time we spoke was when he came for the sugar."

"Can you identify anything about him that somebody wouldn't ordinarily see?"

"He's got a tattoo."

"What kind of tattoo?"

"It says Mary. It's on his upper arm."

"Anybody could see that."

"He wears overalls going to and from work."

"Well, you might have seen him in summertime with a short-sleeved shirt."

"I didn't live in that house in the summertime."

"Anything else?"

I thought of the strange curve of his erect member, the point he had made about it.

"No," I said.

"If you saw nude photographs of six men, just the torsos, could you pick him out?"

"I don't know."

"You saw him naked didn't you?"

"I wasn't making a study of him. I was scared."

"Sure, sure. I understand. I just want to know if there's anything that will interest the D.A."

"Is there?"

"Truthfully, hardly anything."

"There must be something that can be done!"

"Keep cool, miss. We could pay a visit to this Mr. Koslak. See what he says. He'll deny it, of course. No reason for him not to."

"He'd know I'd been to the police. He'll kill me unless you do something about him."

"Like what?"

"I suppose you can arrest him."

"I don't think there's enough to go on here."

"What am I supposed to do?"

"You've done it, miss. You've filed a report. If it happens again—I see on this report—well, don't douche or anything, go straight to the hospital."

"Is that the only kind of proof there is?"

"You could scratch, get some skin under your fingernails."

"He's strong, he could—"

"Well, you shouldn't ever do anything that would endanger your safety."

"You mean let him do it."

The detective said nothing.

"I know what you mean. Then I wouldn't be resisting, so it wouldn't be rape, would it? *What the hell can you do?!*"

The matron came over and put her hand on my shoulder. It wasn't the hand of a sister. It was the hand of a policewoman.

I found Bill downstairs, thumbing the pages of a beat-up police magazine.

"Finished?" he asked.

"Let's get out of here."

I sat in Bill's car shivering.

"Are you cold?" Bill asked.

"No."

"You look," he said, trying to keep his voice light, "like a machine about to self-destruct."

I didn't respond. We sat in silence for a few minutes.

My voice was a near whisper when I spoke. I could see Bill straining to hear and to understand.

"It's like one of those nightmares, you go to one place and then another and another trying to get some official to understand what you're trying to say, and you just get shunted about, and nothing happens till you want to scream doesn't anyone believe me!"

"What would you like me to do?" asked Bill.

"I didn't mean you. I meant the police, the authorities, somebody."

"You're still shaking."

"Would you do me a favor?"

"Anything."

"Call Dr. Koch. Call this number." I wrote it down on the back of a grocery receipt from my purse. "Tell him I'm coming down. You don't have to drive me. I'll take a cab."

"I'll drive you." Bill slipped out of the driver's seat and called from a pay booth on the corner.

"Dr. Koch wasn't very friendly."

"Oh he's friendly. He probably just doesn't like to see people at this hour of the night. Did he say okay?"

Bill nodded and turned the ignition on. He didn't tell me till later that Koch seemed very concerned until he asked who Bill was, and when Bill identified himself, it was then the coldness came into Koch's voice.

When we arrived in front of Koch's apartment building, I didn't get out of the car immediately. "Thank you," I said, putting my hand on Bill's hand.

"I'll wait for you," he said.

"Oh it could be such a long time."

"You won't get a cab to take you to Westchester. It'd cost a mint. Besides you won't find cabs cruising in this neighborhood that late. I'll wait. You don't need any more trouble."

Koch answered the door wearing a grey, cable-stitched cardigan instead of his usual jacket or suit.

"Come in, come in," he said, looking at my face for signs of distress.

I followed him into his consulting room. Out of habit I headed for the couch until his voice stopped me. "No, no, please, sit here so we can talk."

He gestured not to the chair beside his cluttered desk but to two armchairs at the other side of the room. The chairs were too close. I wished there were a coffee table between us.

"I'm sorry to come so late," I said. "I'm keeping you up."

"It's all right."

"I needed to talk to you." I was used to talking to him as an unseen presence behind me, not a face in front of me like other people.

I looked at my fingernails. I didn't know where to start.

"I guess one always thinks of rape as happening to someone else," I said.

"Yes," said Koch. "Like death."

Suddenly I wished I hadn't come to him.

"Take your time," he said.

When I didn't say anything, he said, "Would you rather lie down? As usual?"

Oh what a relief to be able to lie back on that couch with its familiar leathery smell, with my eyes closed. "I could sleep," I said.

"Sleep if you wish."

I thought I couldn't do that, fall asleep with the old man watching me. I was keeping him up. Yet, tired beyond belief and drifting, I tried not to think, to wash my mind of people and buildings and just see a horizon, the sky meeting the ocean, an infinite expanse of tranquil blue. Suddenly the blue of the ocean was dark and roiling with dangerous white-capped waves coming toward me.

I must have screamed.

I was sitting up on the couch, panting, sweat on my face.

"Tell me," he said. "Lie back down."

"I can't."

"You're afraid."

Oh I was, I was.

"Afraid of what?"

Though I felt drenched in sweat, my mouth was dry, parched.

"What woke you?"

"The water," I said, lying back down, exhausted.

"What water?"

"The water you drown in."

He was silent for a moment. I could hear his breathing. No, it was my breathing. My chest was heaving as if I'd been running.

"Tell me about the water."

And so I told him. "When I was very young, three or four, Mommy and Daddy took us—my parents, I mean, took my sisters and me—to Texas, to visit Uncle Jim in Texas. I remember the long, long train ride to St. Louis and then another train south. Texas seemed like a desert, with dry gulleys and small crevasses in the ground, and I had to hold Daddy's hand when we explored. I remember thunder very loud and then the rain came down, tons of water all at once. We were out walking far from my uncle's place, and suddenly we were drenched, and I remember Uncle Jim yelling at my father, and my father told my mother to carry me and he took my two sisters—they were bigger—and then there were like small rivers where minutes before there'd been just dry runnels, my mother stumbled, dropped me, then scooped me up and I wanted to be with my father, but he was up ahead with my sisters, and suddenly it was so bad we couldn't see him, I was frightened of my parents getting separated, and of all the rushing water. I was sure somebody was going to die, and I didn't want it to be me, or Daddy, or my mother and then just as suddenly as it had started, the rains stopped, and there was just the water rushing over the ground so fast, looking for places to run in, and we were trying to stay out of those places, and then, thank God, we saw up ahead Uncle Jim who had run to bring the pick-up truck, and he had already gotten my sisters aboard, and my father was running toward us to get my mother and me. Four people died in that area in the one flash flood, three of them from one family, but we were okay, wet and shivering and breathless when we got into the house, but okay. I couldn't get it straight in my head that the earth could suddenly turn into rivers."

Dr. Koch said nothing. I could hear a clock ticking.

"What are you thinking now?" he finally said.

"If I am awake . . ."

"Yes?"

"If I am awake, I cannot drown."

"To be asleep is dangerous to life."

"Yes," I said.

"Hence insomnia."

I remembered my mother singing me to sleep that first night after the flood at Uncle Jim's house. I remembered desperately not wanting to go to sleep.

"That is a terrible fright for a child," he said.

"For anyone," I said. "My mother talked about it for years."

"That didn't help. Yet think of when your insomnia came on badly."

"When I was away from home for the first time."

"When you didn't have Mommy or Daddy to pull you out of the water."

"It sounds ridiculous."

"All of our recurrent nightmares are ridiculous in one sense, and re-vealing in another. I am so happy."

"Happy?"

"For you. Now that this has come out, it should be better at night. You have let the genie out of the bottle. Sometimes the shock of some-thing else, what happened to you today, helps open the gate of memo-ries. Your insomnia was for a purpose, in the curious logic of the unconscious, it was for your safety so you would not drown."

"There's a difference," I said.

"About what?"

"I didn't drown. I was just afraid of it. I was raped. I didn't imagine it."

"You will not have insomnia about rape."

"How do you know?"

"Because it is not a source of severe anxiety for you. While rape can be very traumatic for some, for you, well, you are strong."

I am not strong.

"May I say how I think you should think about it?"

I know how I think about it.

"Why do you seem upset now? You should be relieved."

I am furious.

"I know how you feel about it. Awful. Terrible. Those are just large canvases of feeling. You must think about it like an unpleasant sex ex-perience that must be brushed out of the mind."

I could kill that man. "You don't understand!" I was sweating all over again.

"Oh I do, I do. All this past year I have felt your strength grow, your security, I think now is perhaps the time for us to begin, gently, slowly, discussing something I have wanted to explore with you before this came up."

Stick to the subject. You are supposed to be helping me.

"I want you to relax. Here, sit up. That's it. Look at your knuckles. Open your hands."

He took one of my hands and opened my fingers. *Don't do that. I don't want to be forced to do anything.*

"Now," said Dr. Koch, giving me back my hand, "you have reached a turning point. Your talking about the flood, it will be a catharsis for the insomnia. You can turn from the demons of the night to the opportunities of the day. You see, my dear, I have long thought that if you were an artist, say, or a dancer, something like that, a person trying to release a talent from your soul, you would know what vocation is."

What the hell are you talking about?

"If you had a special talent with your hands even, you would know what a craft is. You would feel driven."

I feel driven to claw your face right now.

"You would know the meaning of work in the highest sense given to man. But alas, because of circumstances, you lack even an economic stimulus. Your family is well-to-do, work is a hobby for you. Neither money nor talent drive you toward a vocation."

I deliberately picked up the fragile ashtray and slammed it to the floor.

He pretended not to notice! He just said to me, "What are you thinking?"

"I'm thinking you are one first class son of a bitch. I came here for help. What does all that garbage have to do with the way I feel?"

"Everything." He stooped to pick up the pieces of ashtray.

"I'll pay for it," I said.

He dismissed that with a wave of his hand.

"What happened today," he said, "is a transitory matter. A wound that will heal."

I felt as if I were dissolving. "I haven't even told you what that man did to me today."

"Please tell me," he said.

I bit my lip. Suddenly I didn't want to talk.

"Please," he said. "You must talk it out."

I shook my head.

"I'm trying to help you."

You're not helping me.

"Say it."

"You're not helping me."

"Tell me what happened. How did it start?"

"A knock on the door." My voice sounded like an automaton to me.

"Then?"

I told him about the cup of sugar. About the broom, for banging on the ceiling. Then about when Koslak exposed himself.

"What did you think about that?" asked Koch.

I didn't want to hear my automaton voice. I didn't want to talk any more.

"What did you think?"

I forced my dry throat to speak. "He wanted me to be frightened. I knew that."

"Were you frightened?"

"Of course I was."

I exhausted myself in the telling of the rest of it. Finally, he said, "Do you feel better now?"

"I don't know."

"You will feel better when you come to grips with one thing. Your rootless brilliance."

What the fuck was wrong with this man? "Are you talking about my job again?"

"I thought tonight it might distract you. We can talk about it some other time."

You started it, finish it. "Talk about it now."

Koch sighed. "You are young."

You are old.

"There is time. A job," he said, "is not a vocation. A vocation is like an engine that burns out only when you burn out. You desperately need roots for your brilliance. And the handicap you have is that you are a second generation vocational foundling."

"Now what does that horseshit mean."

Koch stared in surprise.

"You said I could talk as uninhibited as I wanted to in these sessions. I said horseshit because that's what it is. I don't understand what you're talking about."

"Don't get so worked up. Your father is a vocational foundling."

"He's a lawyer."

"He has no vocation as a lawyer. He is filling a role out of strange reasons. I have heard him. He has the same problem as you have."

I was standing now. "I was raped today."

"Yes."

"Rape is a crime. It's my body was violated. I was tied up. I could have been killed."

He did not get up. It was as if by remaining seated, he was forcing me to sit back down.

"But you were not killed. You must deal with reality."

"I am! For Christ's sake, I went to the hospital, I went to the police, I thought at least here I would find some sympathy, some understanding."

"Please sit down."

"I feel like I'm in enemy territory. Just like in the police station. Don't any of you men understand?"

"What have you against men?"

"Oh shit, let's not start that kind of thing. Let's talk like normal human beings. If I'd been robbed, if I'd been burglarized, you'd be sympathetic!"

"I am sympathetic."

"Like hell you are. You started criticizing my whole way of life. Tonight. When I came for help."

"I was trying to direct your attention to your deepest problem now that we have found the source of your insomnia. You will not have it again, I promise. Please sit down."

"I'm not going to sit down. I'm going to get the hell out of here."

"Please, please." He was standing now. "You've never done this before."

"You've never been this obtuse and cruel before."

"I think you should come back tomorrow when you are feeling calmer."

"I hope—"

"Yes?"

"Something happens."

"To me?"

"Yes to you. So you'll understand what I feel like."

"You mean I should be raped."

"Something like that. Something that takes you out of this padded cell you live in."

"I hurt you because I talked of you being a vocational foundling."

"You hurt me because you are not helping me to understand what happened to me today!"

"If you feel such injustice, perhaps you should see a lawyer."

"I don't know any lawyers."

"Your father might help you."

"You said he wasn't a lawyer."

"He might know somebody."

"Thanks a lot."

I tried very hard not to slam the front door.

"Where to?" said Bill.

"I'm not going back to my apartment. Not in that building. Not with that man still there."

"Want to stay at my place?" Bill asked.

"No," I said.

"I'd sleep in the living room."

I shook my head.

"Where to?"

"My parents' house."

He released the parking brake, and we were off. In a moment we were on the West Side Highway, headed for the county to the north.

EIGHT

Widmer

People refer to our home as the Widmer House, we've been in it so long. It's in the village of Briarcliff Manor in the western part of central Westchester. If you're driving up from the city on any of the parkways, you'll eventually end up on 9A, a four-lane, poorly engineered, twisting road that has been host to countless fatal accidents. Over the years, the State Department of Transportation, corrupted no more than most government bureaucracies, eventually responded to the clamor about fatalities by erecting median barriers here and there. When guests come up the first time, I suggest they take 9A in order to avoid getting lost, but until they arrive I feel that I have consigned them to danger and I worry until the doorbell rings.

That night I was expecting no one. After dinner, Priscilla and I played cribbage in front of the living room fireplace, not that we needed its heat. As the winter season draws to a close, we know that soon the damper will be shut for half a year, and the logs will be carried back to the lean-to behind the garage where they are protected from the rain. The fireplace, when it splutters from green wood, has an aph- rodisiac effect on Priscilla, and that evening I had mischievously put a branch from a recently fallen pine in with the seasoned hardwood. I had offered, and she had accepted, some port, and Priscilla won the first time around the cribbage board, all of which contributed to her confidence, and when she feels confident, she radiates the sexuality that had first attracted me to her many years ago.

And so we were in the bedroom in each other's arms when I heard the clear sound of a car leaving Elm Road and heading up our driveway. It stopped far too soon. In the countryside you become attuned to interruptions of the familiar outdoor sounds, and when, distracted, I said to Priscilla I thought the engine of the car had been turned off, she and I both thought of the burglary at the Watsons just a week ago. We listened. I went to the window. I could see nothing in the driveway at the front of the house and the trees obscured the rest of it. Whatever car had come halfway up the drive no longer had its lights on. Were we now to wait for the tinkle of broken glass?

I keep my rifle in the closet in the dressing room behind my row of suits. I put it against the foot of the bed and then put my dressing gown on. Priscilla got out of the opposite side of the bed. Her nakedness, which had held my attention just a minute earlier, seemed so inappropriate now. I was glad when she drew her robe around herself.

When I opened the window a crack, I felt like an animal perking its ears to catch sounds humans do not ordinarily hear. Priscilla and I both heard a male voice. Quickly I went to the bedroom phone and dialed the police. The desk sergeant said he'd send a car right away, and I went down with the rifle, to sit on the last turn of the stairs from which vantage I had a view of the front windows and the door but would not be seen immediately by anyone who did not look up. I make it a rule to leave one small table lamp lit the night long, and this night I was grateful for it. Priscilla sat down just behind me.

At that moment I heard the key in the lock. Immediately my thoughts were of housekeepers we had had in the past who might have copied the front door key for a friend or someone who paid a commission on his thefts.

Naturally I was stunned when the knob turned and the door swung open.

"Francine!"

"Father. What are you doing with that rifle?"

"Oh Francine," said Priscilla, coming around me and rushing down to her daughter.

It was then we all heard the sound of more than one car, a screech of brakes, raised voices, and in a moment a patrolman was leading young Bill Acton up to the house.

"He was backing his car down to Elm Road," said the officer. "Do you know him?"

I had them both come in and shut the door behind them to cut off the night air.

"I'm sorry," I said. It was at Francine I was directing my words. "We heard a car come part way up the drive and stop. The Watsons were burglarized just last week and I thought—why didn't you phone?"

"It was late," said Francine.

"You always phone," said Priscilla.

"Well never mind," I said. "Officer, we know this young man. He's brought our daughter here. I'm sorry to have called you out."

"It's okay, Mr. Widmer. Better safe than sorry. Good night."

"I'd better go," said Bill. "My car's blocking the end of the driveway."

"We're not expecting any more visitors tonight," I said, trying to lighten the awkward tension we were all aware of.

"I've got to talk to you," said Francine.

"I'm going," said Bill.

I saw Francine whisper thanks to him, and kiss him on the cheek, which seemed unnecessary to me at the time.

As soon as Bill was gone, Francine and Priscilla and I went into the living room, and I turned on the lights. Francine noted our garb and said she was sorry to have gotten us out of bed.

"I'm planning to stay the night," she said. "But I may want to stay a few days, would that be all right?"

"Of course," I said.

"It's just until, well, something is resolved."

"You wanted to talk to us," Priscilla said.

"Yes."

I experienced the kind of preparatory silence during which, out of courtesy, one should not speak. Of course I knew Francine was distraught. She was breathing deeply in what I thought was a conscious effort to control her nerves.

"I've been to Dr. Koch, the police, and the hospital this evening."

"Are you sick?" asked Priscilla.

"No. Yes. Not really. It's very hard to talk about."

"Would you rather I left you with your mother?" I asked, thinking it might be some female trouble she wanted to discuss.

"No. In fact the main reason I came was to get your advice, Dad. It was suggested I see a lawyer. You're the only lawyer I know."

I didn't know quite how to interpret that.

"I've been raped," she said.

Priscilla's face went white. She stood up, her fingertips at her lips.

"By whom?" I asked, standing. "By Bill?"

"No, no, no, no, Dad, please sit down."

I must admit that at that moment I was not thinking clearly at all. I felt anger to the point of outrage as if *something of mine* had been violated. That was so wrong. I should have felt instant sympathy for her. If she had been hit by a car or fallen from a kitchen chair while reaching for something, I would have thought only of her. Why did I feel as if something had been done to me?

I found myself picking up the poker and stoking the embers in the fireplace.

"Dad?"

I looked directly at Francine, avoiding her breasts. It was as if I was steeling myself from looking further down, as if some great wound might show where her legs met. How absurd our thoughts are!

"Please sit."

I sat back down.

"It was a man who lives in the apartment above me. A married man with kids. He came, pretending to want to borrow a cup of something."

"You fought him?"

"I tried to outsmart him. Then he tied my arms behind my back. There was nothing I could do."

"Are you hurt?" Priscilla asked. "Anywhere."

"My face smarted a lot for a while from a hard slap. My wrists hurt. Nothing serious."

"Thank heaven," I said.

She told us about the hospital, what happened at the police station, and then the strange experience with Dr. Koch. I couldn't believe a psychoanalyst could be so insensitive.

"I'm going to fix up your bedroom," said Priscilla. "Won't be a minute."

"Oh I'll do that, Mother."

"We don't use the linen closet any more. We had a bad roof leak that kept getting everything damp in there. I'll be right back."

When we were alone, Francine said, "Could I have a drink?"

"Of course. What would you like?"

I prepared a scotch and water.

"Thank you. I'm afraid to go back to the apartment. He might try again. There must be some legal way of protecting me."

I was thinking of ways that weren't legal. The poker that I still held in my hands. The rifle leaning against the stairs. I am not a violent man, yet I felt rage.

Though drink late at night doesn't agree with me, I poured myself a stronger scotch than I had poured for her. I wanted to go over to Francine, take her hands, raise her to her feet, enfold her, restore her. Yet the truth is I was thinking she was soiled.

When Priscilla came back down, I thought there might be something the women would want to talk about alone, so I excused myself and went upstairs to put the rifle away, hoping I could put my anger away with it. When I did, I knew I had come upstairs for another reason. It was a vicious thing to do. I felt governed by necessity when I reached among the few books I keep in the bedroom to the volume of outdated procedures that I knew Priscilla would never pick up, and from its pages I took the small envelope that was sealed and marked "private" in my own hand. I put it in the pocket of my dressing gown and returned downstairs.

Francine seemed to have calmed somewhat, whether from the drink or the conversation with her mother I did not know.

"Thomassy," I said. "That's the name of the lawyer who might be able to help you. I don't know how these things work, whose arm has to be twisted, but he'll know. I'll speak to him. I hope he can see you. Meanwhile, you must stay here."

It'd been many years since I'd seen Priscilla kiss Francine good night.

"I'll be right up," I said to Priscilla, but I knew I could never resume what the sound of the car had interrupted. Francine was about to follow her mother up when I said, "Could I have a word with you?"

I sat two or three feet away from her so that I would not have to raise my voice.

"Thomassy is a very busy man, mainly because he's the best we have in this county at his kind of work. I mean criminal law. You'll have to be very candid with him. Are you prepared for that?"

"I was candid with the hospital and the police and it got me nowhere."

"That's not what I mean. Francine, the man who—that man, is it possible you did something to entice him?"

"Of course not!" Her face flowered in a blush.

"Are you sure?"

"Oh, Dad, what do you think I am?"

"I once thought I knew."

I took the envelope out of my pocket, opened it where it'd been Scotch-taped down, and took the photograph out. It was a Polaroid picture of Francine completely nude, stretched out like an odalisque, posing.

"Who took this?" I asked, handing it to her, remembering both the anger and excitement I had felt when I first came upon it.

"Where did you find this?"

"Thank God I found it and not your mother. Who took it?"

"It's really not your business."

"You are free to do whatever you like, Francine, but anyone who will pose for a lascivious photograph like that could have a very difficult time persuading the authorities or a jury that she was innocent of enticement. It wasn't taken by a woman, was it?"

"No."

I had expected her to hand it back to me. Or tear it up. She did neither.

"I'm going up," she said. "Good night."

Those words were in the coldest voice she had ever used with me. Might she be thinking why had I not destroyed the photograph when I found it wedged behind a drawer of her dressing table when I moved it into the attic? Might she be wondering how often I had looked at it? I had produced something unspeakable. And the worst was I wanted that picture back.

NINE

Thomassy

The line of Francine's neck was a stretched, soft "s" from below her earlobe to the delicate indentation just above her collarbone. Was it that, or the high cheekbones and the almond eyes? I was used to observing the details of appearance the way a detective looks for clues. I observed Francine, however, the way one reacts in a museum when you turn a corner into a room and suddenly see an exquisitely beautiful portrait of an unknown woman and begin to wonder what she was like to the man who, in life, touched her. Thomassy, I told myself, you are not a gallery goer; your natural habitat is the raucous courtroom full of thieves, adversaries, and spectators. She is not your scene. This is not your type of woman.

Like most men of my generation, I was accustomed to admiring the shape of a woman's calf when she crossed her legs. If a woman wore décolletage, I was aware of the part of her bosom that showed and of the part that didn't show. If a young lady was walking ahead of me, I'd notice the tuck at her waist or the way the halves of her buttocks alternated as she walked. Then all of a sudden kids were all over the streets saying *This is my body, so what.*

In my peek-a-boo generation, even the best of women were brought up as cockteasers. Now that they're older and hear the clock running, they're as determined to get under the sheets as any man. That's your type of woman, Thomassy. You go to dinner, a movie, then fuck. If she's married, you meet someplace safe and fuck. It's a simple program. What the hell are you doing watching that undeniably erotic line of Francine Widmer's neck as if she were an eighteenth-century painting? She's a braless kid. A client.

I had a mentor in law school who said, *Don't put your penis in your pocketbook. Leave clients alone.*

"I don't think you've got a case," I told her.

She didn't expect me to say that. She thought she'd been convincing.

"We don't have the ingredients," I said. "When you're cooking, you lay out the steak, the potatoes, lettuce and tomatoes for a salad, right, and you know you've got a meal in the making."

"Don't condescend to a woman by using kitchen examples. In the kitchen, I improvise. So can you."

"What I meant was I don't see the ingredients of a case a D.A. can go into a courtroom and prove. He needs to say that a certain individual did so-and-so. This is the evidence. And he's got to know opposing counsel won't upset his prima facie case. He can't just wing it. Too much would depend on how he delivered his testimony, how well you stood up under cross-examination in very tough territory."

"And you wouldn't want the D.A. to risk his reputation on me as a witness?"

"We don't have any other witnesses. And not much in the way of corroborative evidence."

"You don't want to take this on."

"I'm not prepared to make a commitment," I said.

She looked at me, then said, "I won't let you down."

"I didn't mean that."

"I'm a good student," she said.

"I'm sure."

"How good a teacher are you?"

In the courtroom you learn that a witness who's a rug is no fun, you need the resilience, the springback of a witness who tries to parry your questions.

"I can't work with air. I need provable facts. Evidence."

"If I were dead, that would be the kind of evidence you're looking for."

"That's evidence only that you're dead. The body might show how you came to be dead, and if it wasn't from natural causes, we'd still need evidence as to who did it. Rapists don't leave fingerprints on their victims."

"I get it," she said. "Rape is an inconvenient crime. It's hard for whiz-bangs like you to lay out the meat and potatoes and know how you're going to win your case before you start. You don't like to take chances!"

"Miss Widmer, it's you who'd be taking chances. You're the one whose life is going to get pulled apart on the witness stand. Do you know how many rape cases end in conviction? Very, very few."

"It's your conviction I want right now."

"I'm not the jury."

"Juries are audiences. You're the actor who convinces them, aren't you?"

Why am I sitting around taking crap from this kid?

"Mr. Thomassy," she said, "I bet you feel more comfortable with robbery or murder . . ."

"Yes I do!"

"You men are capable of working both sides of that street. You can rob and be robbed, you can kill, and you can be killed. But when it comes to rape we're not equal because you can rape us and we can't rape you and that's why you don't know how I feel!"

"Now take it easy."

"Easy? What are women to do? We've got this opening a thousand loonies out there are trying to get into, and most of them aren't afraid to try because men have been getting away with it for centuries. She was seducing me, they say. Look at the provocative clothes she was wearing, they say. Look at the way she was walking around half-naked, she was asking for it, they say. Right? All women ask for it. Right Mr. Thomassy?"

"Some do."

"Even supposedly nice guys like you believe those arguments. Next you'll tell me there are SM freaks who say they like to be forced. That's another lie. They like to *pretend* to be forced. If one of those scenes turns into a real rape, I mean an uncontrollable rape the woman can't do anything about, you'll see how quickly her kink unkinks. Nobody likes real violence done to them! And besides, we're not talking about an occasional freak with special tastes. We're talking about the great majority of women who thrive on tenderness and affection and can't get the message through to male lunkheads that we don't want to be raped any more."

"Men get raped, too," I said.

"In jail."

"Right."

"Well at least those rapists are in jail, and that's where I want Koslak!"

It was then, behind her strident syllables, I began to remember my father's voice.

Francine continued, "What do you men expect us to do if we live alone, get behind double locks on the door, not let anyone in where we live, put a sign on the door, go away, no soliciting, no neighbors, no visiting hours from anybody? Should I buy a gun? Should I use it? Or is it that you guys want me to be tempted to marry some idiot just so I won't be a vulnerable woman living alone?"

George, my father had said, *you have hair above your privates, there is something you must know. Wait till your mother goes to sleep.*

"And," said Francine, "what are we supposed to do out in the street, carry a machine gun?!"

I was thirteen when my father decided to have that talk with me. My mother, complaining of a headache, drifted off to bed soon after dinner. I remember I was whittling something in front of the fireplace when Papa touched my shoulder—I hadn't heard him come up behind me—and I dropped the knife with a clatter.

"Pick it up," he said.

I picked up the knife. My instant fantasy was to stick it into him.

"Close the blade," he said. I felt he could read my mind.

"Put it away, George," he said.

I pocketed it. Only then did he pull the rocking chair so that we were sitting side by side, staring into the fire, more comfortable for both of us because we could look at the fire instead of each other.

"I am going to talk to you about sex," he said in that smoke-dry voice that resonated with authority.

I waited.

"Sex is very important. Like horses."

This was before he had given up on me and horses.

"Men," he said, "have a thing like a stick."

I could feel him glancing sideways at me.

"A woman," he continued, "has in front a hole for the stick, you know this?"

I nodded.

"That is sex," he said.

I heard no further sound, not even his breathing. After a bit, I turned just enough to glimpse his leathered visage. He was floating in a memory somewhere. Suddenly he sensed my intrusion and turned toward me. I quickly averted my gaze back to the fire. I felt I had embarrassed him.

"I have more, George."

My mind whirred with the possibilities: more about the stick and the hole? How women get pregnant? How masturbation can bring on blindness?

"Your mama," he said, then stopped.

I imagined his leather face over my mother's, her submissive expression, he with his nightshirt pulled up exposing his flat buttocks, she with her nightgown pulled to her waist.

"Your mama was not my first wife."

At thirteen I was a champion of overheard conversations. With my ear against the bedroom wall I had heard snatches. And the jangling of the brass bed that had given me my first guilty erections.

"You did not know this?"

"No," I lied.

From the depths of his chest came a sound of remembered regret, a sigh of such profound dimensions that I couldn't imagine what words were to come after.

"In my sixteenth summer in the land of Ararat I took in a Catholic ceremony a girl named Shushan Harossian as my wife. She was a cousin of a cousin from Zeytoon, very beautiful dark hair, a face like an olive blossom. Her three brothers and her father and mother were taken from Zeytoon by the Turks into the desert and that was that. She was hidden by a priest who arranged for her to be taken by a merchant to us in Marash for safety.

"When we see each other, it was an explosion of love, and everyone believes that living in the same house we will not be able to keep from each other, so we are quickly married.

"Our marriage was not a week old when the Turks come, three thousand soldiers crying out *La ilaha ill-Allah uhammed Rasula-llah*, There is no other God but one God and Mohammed is his prophet. The Turks let it be known that any Armenian who deserts his Christ will be spared. Perhaps there were cowards. I knew none. We prayed, we offer our devotion to God, then my father hurries my mother and the younger children to the church, it is a sanctuary he says. But I have heard of the burning of churches. I plead with my father to let Shushan and me hide in the cellar, where the small treasures of our family are hidden away under rugs. My father calls me a fool of love, he says we will die at the hands of the Turks, and he slams the door so that it shakes the house, as he runs after my mother and the younger children to the church of their salvation.

"Shushan, obeying her bridegroom's instructions, puts bread and cheese away in the cellar. Then, when the shouting is already very near, Shushan suddenly says we have not locked the door behind my father! I say they will break any door that is locked. But Shushan, without my permission, leaves the sanctuary of the cellar. I can hear them, I shout 'Come back, come back!' but it is too late. A Turk pushes open the door. He is tall and has a pock-marked face. He sees Shushan and she scurries away from the direction of the cellar door in order not to reveal my hiding place. The Turk cries to his comrades that the infidels have left an angel behind. They come, six or seven of the beasts. Two of them hold her on the floor as she struggles, my heart bursts because I can see everything from a crack in the cellar door, and the leader opens his pants, his stick is curved like a scimitar, and he falls to his knees, and Shushan screams as he leans forward, shoving his stick like a madman."

I cannot look at my father when his eyes are wet like a woman's. My hands are clasped white until he speaks again.

"That is sex," says my father at last. "All the Turks—may they rot in hell—have sex with Shushan, who a week before was a virgin. Should I not have risen from my knees and with my bare hands raged at them with their swords? Am I a coward to have stayed in the cellar?"

Papa now looks toward me to forgive him. My mouth is dry, as if I am choked with sesame seeds.

"You couldn't do anything," I say.

He continues, "That is not the end. The leader goes to the door to call other infidels. My pearl, Shushan, struggles to her knees, begging 'No more, no more,' the Turk who was first draws his scimitar and with a cry curves it over his head then down with the yell of a beast, beheading her."

My father, the horseman with infinite strength, now cried from the depths of his chest an agony that had been carried within him for more than half a century, from the world of Ararat to America. I was then three years younger than he was as a bridegroom. In his place, I would have wanted to fight, not to lose but to win! It was at that moment I have since felt that I swallowed the seed of a Maccabee.

"Those who fled to the church lived?" I asked.

"For an hour. They died in the flames. I was the only one left."

I got up and put my arms around Papa's hunched shoulders, and we cried together for his lost love, for the confession of his cowardice, and for the absence of justice in the world, and for the new burden of the vocation I had found.

"Men don't understand rape," Francine was saying. "They never have."

I was silent for a moment, but she wanted a response from me, so I said, "They never have. Look, can you come back tomorrow at the same time?"

When she left, I sat in the near-darkened office, knowing it would be a half hour before my date would arrive. Geraldine would expect dinner, which we would have, and bed, which we would not have this evening, for with my father's memories thundering in my head, I was not seducible.

TEN

Koslak

I ain't seen the girl around. She must be keeping to herself. Fuck her, I got Mary.

Mary's out, dropping the kids off at her mother's. She likes partyin' better when the kids aren't in the house.

Wonder what's taking Jason so fucking long, he must have a single-pole switch down in the basement somewhere.

I get awful restless just waiting so I called the station. When the kid answers, I said, "Jim, you handle things, I won't be back today. Just remember the pumps show the number of gallons pumped since I left. Don't take the money home with you, ha, ha. Just stash it you know where. Yeah, I hear them honkin'. See ya tomorrow."

The doorbell rings and it's Jason, holding a switch in that left claw and a screwdriver and tape in his right.

"Hi," he says. "Which room?"

"Bathroom," I says.

I really had to get used to him bein' superintendent, you know. It used to be old guys was superintendents, but Jason had to be no more than thirty or so, like a grown-up hippie sort of, a good-looking guy, beard, wears jeans instead of coveralls, and that clamp is really somethin'. I tried to get him to talk about it once or twice. All I learned is that the government paid for it and he works the mechanical arm off straps around his shoulders.

He was taking the old switch out of the wall and I says, "Don't you turn the fuse first?" and he says, "If you do it right, you don't get no shock."

I'm sittin' on the edge of the tub—I mean I'm not going to sit on the pot watching him, am I?—and I say, "Hey, Jason, how come you sometimes wear the arm and sometimes not?"

"That's a very personal question," he says. Then he laughs. Every time that guy laughs I think he must be on somethin', just when he laughs I mean. "My turf," he says, "is two more buildings sides this one. You know how many women in this old parking lot got husbands go to work?"

"Plenty."

"Well, they get put off some, some of them do, by the mechanical thing, it just takes too much of their attention, so when I'm sniffing round the lot for today's pussy, I take it off. You know something?" And he says this like he's telling me the world's number one super-secret. "When I'm naked, they find that stump real attractive. I mean it's healed perfect, and the skin around the end is real smooth and sensitive like the end of a big cock. Some of them ask to feel it, you know. Most people don't understand women, they're much more freaky than people think. And something else. Women want it a lot more than their propaganda lets on. All you got to do is let 'em get past the propaganda, and you're home."

While he was wrapping black plastic tape around the wire where the old cord was frayed, I was sure he was gonna get a shock, but he didn't.

"You get a lot of pussy in these buildings?" I ask.

"You know how many times I get called for the sink's stopped up and it's nothing, or the light won't work when it's just the bulb, and there she is in a housecoat saying thank-you-very-much-don't-you-want-a-cold-drink and I know I've got a new pussy on the block. The old ones don't bother with the jazz, they just call up and say do I got a minute. That minute sometimes takes half an hour. It's a goddamn good thing I don't have a boss looking over my shoulder on this job. He'd wonder where I was sometimes. There."

The plate was back on the box. He flicked the switch. "All set," he says.

I reach in for four bits to tip him and say, "You ever get to the one downstairs?"

"Widmer?"

"Right below."

"That's Widmer. She's not home daytimes. She works."

"You don't play your parking lot on Saturdays and Sundays?"

"It could get tricky. I rest on weekends, except for emergencies like stopped-up toilets and the like."

I went to the fridge and got two beers. "Have a Bud."

"Sure."

"Sit down."

"Don't mind." He plops down on the sofa.

"You ever tried my wife?" I look him in the eye.

"With those little kids around? Sides, she wouldn't give me the time of day, would she?"

I just smile at him. Then I say, "How come you never get any of those women pregnant?"

"Christ, man, where you been? All you needs to do what I do is a vasectomy. It's easier'n pulling a tooth."

"Didn't bother you none?"

"I had to pay for it. I mean I couldn't talk the VA into paying for a vasectomy!" and he laughs that strung-out laugh.

"I'm disappointed," I said.

"About what?"

"That you didn't have a go at Widmer. She's terrific."

"You don't say."

I couldn't tell if he was believing me. If he had a go at Widmer, if she was that available, she couldn't complain about me. I like the way she fought back, just enough, not too much. The next time it'd be easier and quicker.

Jason was just finishing the Bud when the key turns in the door and Mary comes in. Jason starts to get up. I say, "You know Jason, Mary," and she says, "Sure," and I say, "What do you mean sure?" and she says, "He's the super, ain't he?"

Mary vanishes into the kitchen and Jason says, "I got to go."

"Hey, Mary," I yell, "kids gonna be at Grandma's rest of the afternoon?"

She comes in, drying her hands, and says, "Till six. Wasn't that what you . . ."

"Yeah," I says quickly. "Hey, want to see what Jason did?"

I take her by the arm into the john and say, "Jason put that wall switch in without the fuse being off."

"Really?" she says, not knowing what is going on.

"Hey Jason," I yell into the living room, "Mary said she was gonna take a shower soon's she got home. Want another Bud? Help yourself in the fridge." That's when I'm just behind Mary and butt her from behind. She has got a very sensitive ass, let me tell you. If I come up behind her and just squiggle a little . . .

COMMENT BY MARY KOSLAK

When I walked in the door and saw Jason I could a died. I immediately thought Harry's found out and there's been a scene. Harry would kill him if he knew, wouldn't he, but Jason'd said nobody ever really knows unless they actually see you doing it. They're just sitting around beering, but my heart, I tell you, was like bongo drums.

Jason is the most sensitive love-maker. There isn't a part of your body he doesn't touch and kiss first. Not like Harry.

❀

I put my hands around on Mary's tits while I got her from behind and she says, "He'll see," in a kind of whisper. And Jason comes out of the kitchen with two Buds, one in the claw, and he sees all right, which is what I intended.

"Okay," I say in an extra loud voice, "you can take your shower now."

I mean what can Mary do? I try to imagine what's going on in her mind, but she does like I want and starts takin' her things and hanging them behind the bathroom door while I stand on the sill with my back to her so she can't close the door completely. Or lock it. Jason brings me the beer, looking funny.

"I gotta go now," he says.

"You don't want to walk around with a full bottle of beer. Afterwards."

I say the "afterwards" in a special voice, hoping he catches something from it.

I can hear the water running so I turn and look because I know that Mary always stands outside the tub mixing the hot and cold in the tub part before she switches the water to the shower and gets in. She's bending over, looking terrific, and I say, "Ha, ha, I think I'd better take a shower, too," and I take a swig of the Bud and put the bottle down next to the wall so it don't get knocked over by accident. I kick off my moccasins and pull my socks off because Mary laughs at me if she sees me with socks on after I'm undressed. It's a habit with me to start at the bottom, so I slip my pants and boxers off and throw them on the couch where Jason is sitting down. Men don't pay as much attention to the angle of my cock the way women do, that's my belief, and I wasn't bothered by Jason's staring just a second before he turned away.

I unbutton my shirt because it's funny standing there like that, you're more naked with a shirt on, aren't you? I pull the undershirt off and say to Jason, turning my back to him for politeness, "I guess it's shower time for me, too. Why don't you join us?"

I turned because I wanted to catch the expression in his face just then, but I missed it because he had the Bud bottle up and gulping as if to pretend he didn't see nothin'. Well, I'm into the bathroom, she's got the shower curtain pulled, and I pull it back a bit and say, "Soap, madame?" and she points a finger hard in the direction of the open door, and then down at my stand-up situation. I just shrug my shoulders as if everything is just normal, right, casual, but I poke my head around the door just to see, and there's Jason with his shirt off, taking the straps from around his shoulder, removing the arm, and laying it on the coffee table. I don't know, that was a real turn-on to see.

I pull the curtain back—I don't give a damn if the bathroom floor gets wet—and I climb in. I take the soap and lather up in my hands and then smear the lather all over Mary's tits, and she's saying kind of desperately, "Shut the bathroom door," and I pretend I don't understand, so she points fiercely like, and I just put my arms around her, but she's tight as hell, blushing, but I know nothin' is going to stop this now unless Jason chickens, which he doesn't, because there he is, standing in the bathroom door, naked as a bird, with three heads of hair, on his head, on his chin, and a bush just above where his shlong hangs down. I can see what he means about the shiny end of his stump when the apparatus is off. "Plenty of room in here," I yell. I'm having one helluva good time just anticipating.

I motion to Jason and he steps into the tub. It's pretty hard not touchin', three people standing up in one ordinary-sized tub, and I say to Mary, "Don't mind his arm, he says women find it sexy." I swear Mary looks like she's gonna have a heart attack or something, so I kiss her wet lips and say, "Look at his poor shlong, why don't you touch it for encouragement," and she grabs her right hand with her left as if to lock it back, and I say, "All you got to do is like this," and I put my soapy hand on Jason's you-know-what. For a second, he twitches back like he was stung, saying, "Hey what are you doin'," and so I say, "Just partyin', right?" and I take Mary's wrist firm and put her hand on Jason. She tries not to move her hand, which is pretty hard considerin' how we're all tryin' to keep from slipping, and I notice his thing is activating fast, and I'm excited, I tell you, saying, "Whoo, this is a party all right," and "Who's gonna do what next?" and Jason, he moves around me and caresses Mary's arm, I mean long strokes from her shoulder to her wrist, all with the one hand, and then her other arm, and then like some Oriental he sits down in the tub cross-legged and does the same feel thing down her one thigh and leg and then the other. I never seen a technique like that, I mean I usually go for the box right off, but I notice that Mary is not tight the way she was, she is liking all that smoothin'. "Can I do that?" I says, not waiting, and I do the same thing on her arms and legs and I'll be damned if Mary is looking like, well, terrific, and she takes each of our dongs, one in each hand, and starts stroking. I feel my nuts come up and tighten like I'm ready, but Jason stops her, and I want to know what he's stopping her for, and he says, "She's not ready," and then he gets in position and starts kissing and lickin' and sucking her like he knew what he was doing, which he must have, because I see Mary start to shake and suddenly she's ooh, aah, ooh, and pushing his head away as she hangs on to the towel bar, coming like it was the end of the world.

It was somethin' to see, I tell you. When she's finished, her head flops forward exhausted, and we both ease her down into the tub, where we're all tangled up good, laughing cause the shower is still coming down on us. I turn it off, careful to turn both handles at the same time so no one gets scalded or ice water on them, and then she finishes him off and then me, one of the best times I ever had in my life.

ELEVEN

Francine

Question: Describe what it feels like moving back to your parents' house even temporarily.

Answer: Perfectly not at home.

Sure, the physical surroundings are supposed to be comfortable because they're familiar. My room's as it was when I left, a monument to my not growing up, preserved by my mother the caretaker. Of course I love them both, but when you leave, you've left. For instance, I watch my father loosening his necktie after he comes home from the office— something he would never do in front of anyone but the immediate family—and I think put your tie back up in place, I'm an interloper, don't act familiar with me. What was he keeping that picture of me in the buff for, inspiration? And showing it to me when I could still feel Koslak pumping me, what the hell was that supposed to be, considerate? *I don't feel at home here with you any more.* My place is in my apartment. Under Koslak. The key in my handbag's no damn use till that lawyer gets Koslak arrested. How will I feel with the wife and kids still living above me? Jesus, I am being forced to move like the Jews in Germany, my poli-sci voice tells me. Studying political science is like studying an incurable disease, why did I do it, it tells me nothing about *my* predicament.

Question: In the daily bullshit at the U.N., who thinks of Matthau-
sen, Bataan, Singapore, or Guernica?

Answer: Nobody.

"What did you say?" my father asks.

"Just talking out loud."

His puzzlement shows. "How did you get on with Mr. Thomassy
today?"

Thank heaven, a question I can field.

"He's tall," I said.

Ah, that look. My daughter is off on her irrelevances, the nonconsec-
utive thinking of an ex-student who bypassed Latin and logic. He loves
me anyway.

"Does Thomassy think he can do anything for you?"

He can be prejudiced in my favor.

"I don't know. I see him again tomorrow."

He lights up. "Good," he says, having elicited a rational answer from
his twenty-seven-year-old unmarried, slightly tarnished daughter.

Mama comes to the rescue. "Are you with us for dinner tonight?"

It depends whom you're eating. "Yes, I'll be around for dinner."

My mother, always on the side of sanity, says, "Why don't you give
that nice young man Bill a ring. Perhaps he'd like to drive up and join
us or take you to a movie afterwards."

"I don't think so."

"You're still upset."

"Mother, I'm not getting over a tummy ache or the flu. I was
raped."

"I know," my mother muttered, both of them staring at me.

"You'd know if you'd been raped once. You're both more concerned
that I'm raising my voice than what happened to me."

"That's not true," Mother said.

My father leaned forward as if he wanted to take my hands. "I'll give
Thomassy a ring in the morning," he said, "and see if he can't speed
things up."

"You keep out of it, Dad. I mean you set it up. That's enough."

There was a lot of silence during dinner.

I retired to my room and lay down on the bedspread and talked to
my teddy bear as I had all the years I had lived at home. What a great

audience he was, every question I asked reduced him to perfect speechlessness.

If I'd been married at the time of the rape, would I have felt different about it? Consoling my husband because his exclusive vessel had been used? Would a husband have quelled my rage by taking a club to Koslak? A good husband would have had my rape covered by insurance under some property damage clause.

I put my hands around the throat of my beloved teddy bear. He didn't change expression. He was just ready to hear more, like Dr. Koch, the listening machine. I need to see him, my rocker is rocking.

As I drove to my appointment with Thomassy the next day, the foliage streamed past, spring is coming, spring is coming. Thomassy is waiting for *me*, the ultimate temptation, a client with a brain. If the case is difficult, so much the better: a long involvement, leading to mutual triumph. *Oh Miss Widmer, we've won our case, I'll miss you, come back soon on any pretext. Don't get raped again, do something else, commit a minor crime against property, I Thomassy will defend you to the Supreme Court if need be.*

I expected to find Thomassy leaning against the door jamb of his inner office, as if that were his receiving station to welcome me.

What do you mean he isn't in?

There were two people waiting, a woman and a scruffy teen-age boy. I told his secretary I had an appointment for the same time as yesterday.

"He didn't tell me. He didn't put it in his book."

"I'll wait."

"He's still in court."

"I'll wait."

"Those people have an appointment." The secretary beckoned me closer. She put her mouth next to my ear. Secret coming up. "It's a manslaughter case. First visit after bail was set. Likely to take time."

"That kid?"

The secretary shrugged her shoulders, then looked past me at the outside door.

Enter Thomassy, harassed. Quick glance at mother and boy, then at me, "Good God, I forgot about you."

At fourteen, a high school sophomore stood me up. The agony of waiting was still remembered.

"Come in a minute," Thomassy said, and motioned me into his office, then said to the mother, "I'll be with you in two minutes, Mrs. Tankoos."

"Oh thank you, Mr. Thomassy." Mrs. Tankoos's head bobbed gratefully.

Doctors and lawyers, medicine men.

When he closed the door, he said, "I'm sorry."

"I'm sorry I wasn't more memorable."

"It's not that, it's . . ." Truthfully, he looked at a loss for the reason. Lawyer's block. If he forgets the client, it means he doesn't want the case.

"I'll call your father."

"To say what?"

"I'll get someone else to take your case. I'm really jammed."

"You didn't seem jammed yesterday evening."

"I was distracted."

"By me?"

He went to the phone. "I'll get him at his office."

"I can call him. You take care of your manslaughter case."

I shouldn't have given away his secretary's indiscretion. But what did I have to lose? So I said, "If I kill Koslak, that'll make it manslaughter. Maybe you'll take my case, too, Mr. Thomassy?"

I put out my hand. There was a reluctance in his grasp.

"I feel like a fool," Thomassy said.

"Your witness," I said, and left.

Dear God, please grant me a thicker skin for Christmas. Except give it to me now, and you won't owe me anything for Christmas.

I decided to drive back to my own apartment. This is the age of self-defense. I double-locked the door and phoned my father.

"He's in conference, Francine dear," said Bette Davis (whose name I could never remember, with cause).

"Fuck his conference and put him on."

That'll give her something to sprinkle on her bran flakes.

"What is it, Francine?"

"Just give me the name of another lawyer I can see."

"I thought you saw Thomassy."

"He's busy."

"I don't understand."

"Who's second best?"

Long pause.

"I'd stick with Thomassy, however busy he may be."

"Thanks. Go back to your conference. And please apologize to Bette Davis for me. I know she's doing the right thing protecting you from me."

Billowing clouds drifting in from the west brought darkness early. The minute I saw Thomassy headed for the Mercedes surrounded by empty spaces in the deserted parking lot, I ducked down in the back seat. I heard him unlock the trunk, heard the clunk of his briefcase being thrown in, and I could feel him slam the lid closed. I held my breath as he slid into the driver's seat in front of me.

Lowering my voice and stretching out each syllable, I said, "Don't turn the key. It'll blow up."

His head didn't move.

"Now raise both hands," I said, losing control of my falsetto.

Thomassy's head whirled around. "What the fuck!" Then he saw me crouched foolishly behind his seat.

"It's you," he said.

"It's me. Sorry if I scared you."

"What a damn fool thing to do! Get up out of there! What the hell do you think you're doing?"

I hadn't expected him to be this angry. It was only a practical joke.

"Don't *ever* do that to a man who's had his car wired!"

"What does that mean?"

"Don't do it to anybody. You could kill someone with a weak heart."

I could see the tremor in his hands. "I'm sorry," I said.

"Even after the police disconnected the bomb and removed it—it was from this car the first year I had it—it took all the resolution I could muster to turn the ignition that first time. It seemed an age before the engine caught and nothing happened. All that went through my head when I heard you back there."

"I'm sorry. I mean it. Who tried to blow you up?"

"You look ridiculous back there. At least sit up on the seat."

I did as instructed.

"I was defending a trucker who'd been into the loan sharks. He had good connections. When they sent an enforcer around, he'd been warned. The trucker had two of his teen-age sons, big fellows, with him, and they beat the daylights out of the enforcer. The loan shark couldn't go to the cops and charge them with assault, so they framed the man for a truck hijacking job he didn't do. When he hired me, I decided the easiest way to prove he didn't do it, was to prove who did. My mistake. Fortunately, my client's connections tipped him that my car was being wired right while we were in the courtroom." Thomassy looked at me. "Jesus, don't ever do that to anybody."

"Did you drop the case . . . ?"

"Of course not! I won it!"

". . . like you dropped mine?"

"How did you know this was my car?"

"Deduction. Your office light was on. This was the only one left in the parking lot. It looks like it ought to be your car. It's neat."

"Thanks. Where's yours?"

"Around the corner."

"I'm sorry about the mess-up this afternoon."

"I got even. Can I come around to the front seat? I've been thinking about what I could do."

"Do?"

"About the case."

"I'm afraid I've got a date."

"We could talk while you're driving there, and I'll take a cab back. It won't take any extra time. Please?"

I got out and slipped into the front seat. He glanced over at me, then started the car.

"Your . . . date . . . someone important to you?"

"This evening, yes." .

"Otherwise? I hope you don't mind my asking."

"She's married."

"I see. Did her husband let her out tonight?"

"Her husband's on a business trip. We've got three more days."

I wondered what a woman of his was like.

"My father thinks you have no second best."

"There are a lot of good lawyers around."

"You're just saying that."

He laughed, and looked over at me with an expression I remembered from our first meeting.

"Well," he said, "there're a few good lawyers around."

"Name two."

"Your father and me."

"He doesn't know anything about this whole area. Besides, I get a feeling there's something in your arsenal he's never had."

"Oh?"

"Guts. The great missing ingredient. I'm not knocking my father. He's got pluck. It's not the same. I'm thinking of the place where I work. Forty-six languages and not an ounce of guts. What's the matter?"

"I've been looking for a taxi stand. We're nearly there. I guess we can call one from her house."

"I'd like to meet your friend."

"Looks like you're going to."

The woman lived in Elmsford in a white frame house just a block off Route 9A. As we pulled up, I said, "She must like highway sounds."

Thomassy looked at me. That was the third time by my count. "She sure is going to be surprised to see you."

I said lightly, "Surprises keep our interest in life."

"Okay, philosopher," he said, "let's go."

When he rang, she didn't ask who it was, just yelled, "Come on in," and we both did that. She was coming toward the door with a drink in each hand.

"Perfect tim- . . ."

"This is Miss Widmer, Jane. A client. We were discussing her case. I'm afraid I messed up her appointment today."

"Now she's messing yours up."

"I just need to call a cab to get back to my car."

The flush in her face ebbed. "I'll call for you, honey. Where you headed?"

"Back to my office," said Thomassy.

Jane handed me one of the drinks, saying, "You might as well have this while you're waiting." She gave the other drink to Thomassy.

I could hear her at the phone in the other room. When she put her head in the doorway, she didn't seem happy about the news. "It'll be at least twenty minutes," she said. "Relax while I make myself one of those."

Thomassy tapped his foot restlessly.

"I'm afraid I've botched things up," I said.

"Forget it."

When she returned, it was as if nothing had happened.

"Skoal," she said.

"Skoal," said Thomassy.

I raised my glass.

Quietly she said to him, "We have a reservation?"

"We'll leave as soon as the cab comes," he said.

"What kind of client are you, dear?" Jane asked. "You look kind of sweet to be a criminal."

I would have guessed Jane to be thirty-eight, maybe forty. She was pretty, a little too much lipstick, winter suntan from, a lamp? A lot of time spent on hair. "And too young," she added.

"Most criminals," said Thomassy, "are younger than she is."

"Is that so?"

"That kid who was in with his mother this afternoon," he turned to me, "is fifteen."

"What'd he do?" said Jane. She was looking at my body instead of my face.

"Oh, the last snow of winter, last chance for sledding. Another kid went down dead man's hill out of turn. They had an argument. Buster knocked the other kid down. The other kid called him a shit. Buster picked up the kid's sled and rammed the point of the runners into the kid's gut. The other kids ran away. By the time somebody came, the kid had bled too much. Manslaughter."

"You associate with nice people," I said.

"This evening, yes."

"What will he get?"

"Juvenile delinquency. A year in reform school, out in three months."

"Easy."

"Usual."

"Why'd you take him on?"

"Another lawyer turned him down. He was in Woodside Cottage three days before the mother got to me and I worked out bail."

Jane spoke up. "Maybe he shoulda stayed in jail."

"It's just a holding tank. Some wino tried to force the kid to get down on his knees."

"Ah," I said. "Rape."

"This is a pretty tough kid and—"

He stopped when he realized what I was getting at. Jane looked from him to me to him. I nodded.

"Francine is a rape victim."

"Tell me about it."

"I'd rather not," I said.

"I mean," said Jane, "I always thought if you crossed your legs and scratched and yelled . . ."

"He had a pair of scissors."

"Oh? Did he use it?"

"He threatened to."

"Oh lots of them do."

"I didn't have lots of experience."

"Ladies," said Thomassy. "Why don't we have another drink while we're waiting. Just a light one for me. I have to drive."

"Look," said Jane, "I don't understand why she's here. What the hell is going on?"

I thought I'd better explain. "I'm not after his body. I'm seducing his legal talents. I want him to take my case."

"Well, honey," she said, "why don't you just agree to take her case so she can take the cab in peace."

Just then the phone rang. Jane excused herself and went to take it in the bedroom.

"It's probably her husband," said Thomassy. "He checks in with her every evening about this time."

"My father said you're very good in the courtroom. He didn't tell me about your technique of setting your opponents against each other."

Thomassy laughed.

Jane came back in. "That's done. What time is our reservation for?"

"We won't lose it."

"You wouldn't care to have your client join us so dinner'll be deductible?"

"Okay," I said, getting up, "I can wait for the cab outside. I can take care of myself."

"Good for you, dear. I prefer to be taken care of. Three-finger Italian isn't as good as old George here."

I caught the sting of embarrassment on his face.

I said goodbye from the door and went out. I could hear raised voices, hers then his, from inside. I walked down the path to the sidewalk, noticing the crocuses pushing through the thawed ground. I looked left and then right, trying to decide which way the cab would come from, when I heard his footsteps. I turned. Jane was at the door. "You'll be sorry," she said and slammed the door.

Thomassy opened the door of his Mercedes. "Get in." It sounded like an order.

He got in on the driver's side.

"What about the cab?" I said.

"It'll serve him right for taking so damn long."

We drove for a while before he said, "No use wasting that reservation. Dinner?"

"Mixed singles. How many sets?"

"You're a tennis player?"

"No. I play the same game you do."

"Oh? What's that?"

"Words."

TWELVE

Thomassy

When we walked into the restaurant, Michael waved from behind the bar and came around to show us to my place, a corner table away from the chatter up front.

Michael Diachropoulis moved like a younger Sydney Greenstreet without the menace. His corpulence, achieved through an insatiable affair with his own cooking, slowed him down, but his dark eyes had the frantic rhythm of a proprietor intent on fulfilling the wishes of his customers.

As he good-evening'd us, Michael's eyes inspected Francine. He would be noticing that she was a lot younger than the women I usually brought. "Welcome!" he said to her as if he had been waiting all evening for her appearance. He held her chair in readiness for her to sit, and when she did, he slipped it under her as if the chair were his hands.

"This is Miss Widmer, Michael, a client of mine."

"I am glad she is now a client of mine as well."

At that moment the attention of Michael's darting eyes was caught by a party of three couples coming in the door, and he was off, promising to return as soon as he attended to "his customers." We, of course, were guests.

I told Francine that Michael had named his place the Acropolis, he said, because he thought that even if Americans could never remember his name, they would remember the name of his restaurant. As it turned out, to Michael's dismay, most of his steadies called it the Annapolis.

I have always had curiosity about what draws people to certain occupations. Some restaurateurs, in private, will claim only an economic motivation; it is a depression-safe business, people have to eat. There is a fallacy there, of course, in that people do not have to eat in restaurants, and, in fact, when there is a downturn in the economy, restaurant business can fall off precipitously except for the fast-food chains that sell spicy garbage cheap. The real restaurateurs, the ones who develop a clientele, are like their cooks, comforted by the atmosphere of food, preparing it, serving it well, seeing that people enjoy it. These Greeks and Italians are the Jewish mothers of the food world: *eat, eat,* they remonstrate, I made it especially for you. Think what the Middle West would be if the immigrants had not descended upon it, a wasteland of slab steak, baked potato, and a crisp, sugared salad served as an appetizer!

When my attention returned from its ruminations, I observed Francine listening intently to the bouzouki music in the background. I studied her head, the grace of the way she held it.

After our waitress brought drinks, Michael's formidable roundness reappeared, his benign face beaming with a secret to be shared.

"All right, Michael," I asked, "what is today?"

"Today," said Michael, "is ambrosia of the sea."

"You sure it's not left over from last Friday?"

Mock-shocked, Michael said, "Would I ever offer the greatest lawyer in America five days leftover fish? Am I looking to go to jail, to lose my reputation?"

"Michael, has anyone ever sued you?"

"Never!"

"Has anyone ever complained that your food was not good?"

"They only complain that it is never enough!"

"Michael, tell us about your ambrosia."

"Yes, your honor."

"That is for a judge, Michael, not a lawyer."

"A great lawyer must become a great judge, right?"

"Wrong," I said, turning to Francine.

She looked past me and said, "Michael, isn't it better to be a base-ball player than an umpire?"

"Aha!" said Michael.

"A judge," Francine continued, "never wins a game."

Our host, Michael Diachropoulis, sensed that there was more going on than even his dancing eyes could take in. He put his hands together as if in prayer. "I explain ambrosia of the sea. It is my own recipe pom-pano. The sauce is," he smacked his fingertips, "with little baby shrimp, abandoned by the sea, and given by Michael a proper home, next to king pompano."

Michael looked to Francine for her reaction. She nodded her assent to the ambrosia.

"One cannot refuse," Michael said. He scorned customers who or-dered from the menu. "Tourists," he called them, even if he had served them a dozen times.

"Make that two," I said. "I hope your free chablis is good and cold."

"My chablis is six dollars fifty cents the full bottle, special tonight for all who have the good senses to order ambrosia. Would I spend hours preparing my special and not have some bottles of chablis on ice? What do you think I am, McDonald's?"

That remark was not without an edge of bitterness. Michael used to have a crowd of young people drop in early in the evening for cold draft beer and his blue cheese sirloinburgers ("You don't need me for ham-burgers," he would say). He knew how to rap with the kids, and left them alone when they wanted to be. Then McDonald's opened down the block, and while it could not supply conversation like Michael's or food as good, the prices were unbeatable; two and three at a time, his regulars among the young people stopped coming except for special occasions. They ate less well in a poorer ambience for a lot less money, but there was a recession on. To Michael the defection of the young was a further notch in the unending decline of civilization since the first Acropolis.

"Anything to start?" Michael asked.

"First we'll talk a little over our drinks."

"Signal when ready."

Michael went home behind the bar.

Looking at Francine the Unexpected, I thought of Jane. This eve-ning had been designed with a different plan for a different woman. I had been prepared for Jane's conversation about what was wrong with

the world, her world consisting of cars and clothes, and all of it pro-
logue to bedding the animals, hers and mine. That woman could have
gotten a Ph.D. in lovemaking. Most women, I have found, know only
half of what there is to know about what to do with a man once they've
turned him on, which is probably a higher percentage than most men
know about women. Jane had a hooker's skills without the liabilities.
She didn't put on an act, she wasn't a man hater. She didn't even dis-
like her husband. It's just that he had to be on the road a lot, and Jane
was greedy, a consumer of sex who didn't want to do without. I served
a purpose for her and she served a purpose for me, like two immigrant
checker players who knew only a few words of English in common but
who met in the park on a regular schedule.

Francine the Unexpected wanted me for my alleged ability to win
what I then thought truthfully to be her hopeless case. What use was
she to me?

She was ready to talk back in a high-risk way, a convenience women
like Jane would never dare. In fact, wasn't I having dinner with Francine because she, not I, had wanted it?

"I'm sorry about goofing the appointment," I said.

"Conciliation accepted," she said. "I'm sorry for goofing your evening this evening."

"You haven't yet."

"I've been thinking. How come a fellow like you isn't rich?"

"I do okay," I said.

"I don't mean okay, I mean real rich like F. Lee Bailey, lawyers like
that. Wouldn't you like to have a fancy pad with an indoor-outdoor
swimming pool, a wine cellar, a game room, a mirrored bedroom with a
revolving circular bed, you know?"

"Does crap like that turn you on?"

"No."

"Why'd you think I'd want things like that?"

"You're a bachelor. You don't have a mess of kids to support."

"I have all these women."

That stopped her only for a second. "You ever buy them presents?"

"Not often. Sometimes they buy me presents."

"In gratitude?"

"I think I'm a respectable lover." Quickly I added, "I'll tell you why
I'm not rich like some criminal lawyers. I have a few rules."

"Scruples?"

"I said rules. Those lawyers are like cruising Cadillacs. Anybody with a lot of dough and a highly publicizable case can flag them down. I pick my cases. I never make a final judgment based on the client's ability to pay or to draw the newspapers."

"You're a socialist."

"Fuck that. I do what I like to do. No corporation tells me what to do with my work. I don't have to compromise with a lot of law partners. And I'm not for hire to a mobster with a hundred grand in his pocket. Unless, of course, his case intrigues me beyond my capacity to resist."

"What kind of case do you find irresistible?"

"This is going to sound egotistical."

"I'll bet you won't let that stop you."

"I like a case to depend more on me than on the evidence. The same way a specializing surgeon will take on even a charity case if it's the kind that scares off the other surgeons. Showing off."

"Not money?"

"I never knew an interesting professional who'd choose mere money over a chance to display his tail feathers."

"I'm not convinced. You know how men love to test out women—would you screw so-and-so for a thousand dollars, ten thousand dollars, a million? And when he finally names a number you say yes to, he says 'I knew you were a whore, I just wanted to establish the price.' What's your price, Mr. Thomassy? Would you take a six-week case in Las Vegas for six hundred thousand dollars?"

"You offering?"

"Just testing."

"I don't take tests."

"How about one week's work for a Howard Hughes or an Onassis for a million even?"

"What's the case?"

"Mr. Virtue. Would they pay a million if the case didn't stink?"

"I'll tell you something, Francine. Those guys didn't get rich overpaying lawyers or accountants. They know where to find footmen with accounting and law degrees. The world is full of ass kissers. I thought you'd have noticed in that zoo where you work."

"I am not an ass kisser."

"I didn't think you were. Neither am I. I take what I want. I make what I make."

She seemed embarrassed.

"Can you say the same?" I asked.

"Not yet."

"Take your time. You're still growing up."

"I'm twenty-seven."

"That's what I mean, a very bright kid. I'll give you a piece of nonlegal advice. Don't ask a middle-aged man why he's not rich. He's either rich by then or doing something different."

"F. Lee Bailey and Edward Bennett Williams are famous. Doesn't that attract you?"

"I've got enough clients."

"You don't want to be well known."

"To headwaiters? To people in the street? The judges know who I am. I know who I am."

"Thomassy the Unshakable. Don't you ever get thrown by events?"

"Sure."

"Like what?"

"Like now."

"Meaning?"

"Catching myself fencing with a twenty-seven-year-old kid."

"Want to go?"

"No."

"That's the nicest compliment I've had in ages."

"I don't compliment people. Let's get this straight, Francine. I'm the only rank in my business. I do my thing my own way at my own pace."

"As if the rest of the world didn't exist."

"Bullshit. I know it's there. It can do what it wants. I just don't want it poking its finger in my eye. Most people would like to stay out of jail. All people would like to keep from being jammed into a concentration camp, yet they live their business lives part of the time as if they were being regulated by blackshirts."

"White shirts."

"Same thing," I said.

"What do you know about concentration camps?"

"A lot," I said.

"You're not Jewish, are you?" Francine asked.

"Would it matter?"

"I don't know. I hope not."

"My father's an Armenian. They're the ones the twentieth century practiced on before they got around to the main act on the Jews."

"You're more political than I thought."

"You operate out of a whole garbage bag full of prejudices. You think 'political' means the kind of cloakroom crap your U.N. is full of? I run my own life. That's political."

I could see the waitress coming out of the kitchen with a full tray, headed in our direction. "Want to go?" I asked.

"No," Francine said. "But I don't want to impose on your freedom."

I could face sending the food back. I could even face Michael. It was time to confess. "I'm electing to be here," I said.

Francine was blushing. Without thinking, I rested my hand on hers, just a second, but it was enough.

"What's the matter?" I said finally.

"I started the evening as an imposition. I guess I'm very pleased to have turned into an elective," she said.

My apologies, Michael, for not paying full attention to your ambrosia as I ate. I used your meal the way I use a distraction in the courtroom that doesn't involve me: to think of my next step.

I like to know where I'm going. I like to plan my moves. Great actors, it is said, plan their most extemporaneous-seeming bits of business most carefully. I wasn't an actor. I didn't know where this script was leading to.

Francine said something complimentary about the food. I smiled a shit-ass smile. I hadn't been paying attention.

"Francine," I said. "There's no point in starting anything—I mean your case—unless I can see my way clear to a successful conclusion."

"You don't wing it?"

"That's unprofessional."

"Do you play chess?"

"I used to. As a kid."

"You stopped?"

"Yes."

"Because you couldn't count on winning all the time?"

"You trying to goad me?"

"It was a real question."

"Okay, a real answer. There's not enough at stake in chess. In my game, losers go to jail."

"In that case, you don't go in for any sports?"

I had to confess I didn't.

"Neither do I," Francine said. "Maybe we can take tennis lessons together. On second thought, you'd probably spend your time trying to psyche me instead of learning to play well."

"Not true. I can't psyche anybody successfully in or out of the courtroom without ammunition, facts, background. For instance, I don't know half enough about you to handle anything as personal as a rape case always turns out to be. I'd like to get your permission for me to see your Dr. Koch."

"Oh?" She didn't seem to warm to the idea. Then she said, "When do I get to talk to *your* shrink?"

I laughed. "When you're handling my case."

"Have you ever seen a shrink?" she asked.

"No."

"It might help you see between the interstices."

"What the hell does that mean?" I asked.

"You go from point to point in a preplanned way. A little free association might help you see the way life is. The elusive thoughts are sometimes the most interesting."

"You don't like my style."

"I like winners."

"Well," I said, "do I get to see Koch?"

"I was just thinking that while you were talking to him, I'd be paying for your time and his time both."

"How else am I going to learn about the interstices?"

"Okay," she said.

Was I more curious about the woman or the case? What could Koch tell me? "You'll have to phone him. Does he see people after normal working hours?"

"His working hours aren't normal. Some people probably call him at three in the morning with a pill bottle in hand. When can you make it?"

"After hours, almost any time."

She got up. "Excuse me." She headed for the phone booths in the back.

The coffee was just being served when she returned, slid gracefully into her chair as I half stood.

"He was very pleased to hear my voice," she said, "until I told him I was calling to make an appointment for someone else. He's got you down for Friday at seven." She wrote the address down on the back of a pack of matches. "Allow yourself time to park. It's Manhattan, you know."

Michael reappeared to chastise me for not ordering the mandatory sweet.

"Too much," I said, patting my midriff.

"Perhaps the lady?" Michael said.

"Next time," she said to Michael. Grateful for the promise, Michael waddled off, returning in a moment with an inch of marzipan on a small plate. "On the house," he said, "for a lovely lady."

I signed the check. Francine broke the marzipan in two, put a half between my lips, then nibbled at the second half. The bouzouki music seemed wild now, a dervish of sound.

Outside, in the car, I opened the door for her. She looked as if she hadn't expected me to do that. The truth is that I usually don't for Jane. Or the others.

I got in on the driver's side, strapped myself in, shoulder harness and seat belt. Francine, who hadn't used the seat belt on the way to the restaurant, followed my example.

"The car makers call it a restraining harness," I said.

She laughed.

I put my hand out and found hers, just for a second. She didn't pull it away, just disengaged it gently, and said, "We sitting here or going somewhere?"

I put the key into the ignition, but didn't turn it. From our darkened car we could see a middle-aged couple come out of the restaurant, walking in the same direction as if they didn't know each other.

"I'll bet they're married," I said.

The woman got into the driver's seat. The man slid in from the passenger side.

"I wonder why she's driving," said Francine.

"He's lost his license. Accident. Drunken driving."

"Maybe she's the better driver."

"He'd still drive if he had the license."

"Maybe he never learned," said Francine.

"If he's American, he learned," I said.

"You're very sure of yourself."

"On some things."

"On what not?"

"You," I said.

I turned the ignition key back a notch and switched the radio on to WQXR.

"Brandenburg," she said.

"Which?"

"I don't know," she said.

"I don't either," I admitted.

"That was a very nice meal, thank you."

"Michael's a nice man," I said. "I enjoyed your company."

Encapsuled in the car, we listened to Bach. And to our separate thoughts. I wish I knew hers.

Finally she said, "Feels funny strapped in like this and going nowhere."

"Shall I drive you back to your car?"

"It'll keep overnight. It's silly to go all the way back there now. I'm staying with my parents. My mother can drive me there after she drops my father off at the station."

"Which means you want a ride to your parents' house now?"

"I'd stay at the apartment if I had an armed guard."

"I have no arms."

"Not true."

"You like to play with words."

"I do. You do."

"Sounds like a marriage ceremony."

"See," she said. "You do." Then, "Have you ever been close to getting married?"

"Only in the very old days once, when abortions were hard to come by and dangerous."

"What happened?"

"She met another guy and they went off somewhere and got married."

"Does that mean you may have a child somewhere?"

"I don't know what happened."

"Don't you care?"

I started the engine.

"You've built a lot of insulation around yourself," she said.

"It doesn't keep me warm on cold nights."

She held her left hand in the air for a moment as if she were going to touch me with it.

"That lawyer you wear," she said, "may be hiding a nice man."

"I doubt it." I snapped the radio off.

"Please leave it on."

I turned it back on a bit too loud. Which I suppose was childish.

"Do you know where my parents' house is?"

"You'll have to direct me."

"When we get there, will you come in?" This time her hand touched my hand, just for a second.

"It'd be awkward," I said. "You wouldn't care to come up to my place first. For a drink?"

"I'm not a prude," she said. "But that thing was much too recent."

"What thing?"

She seemed suddenly angry. "The thing I came to you about."

"Koslak," I said.

"Yes."

"And you're angry at all men?"

"In a way."

"Is that fair?"

"It isn't a question of being fair."

"You mean that if it wasn't for what happened, you might come up tonight?"

"I might."

Brandenburg seemed loud against the silence of the parking lot. "You're very hard to figure, Francine. You seem very smart-ass at times."

"And?"

"And at times very vulnerable."

"That's right. That's me. Smart-ass and vulnerable. Don't you think they go together?"

"I know they do."

"Are you ever vulnerable, counselor?"

"Yes."

"When?"

"Right now," I said, turning the engine on, backing out of the parking space, zipping out of the lot too fast, tires squealing, heading for the parkway.

"You seem in an awful hurry," she said.

I didn't answer.

After a while she said, "You're afraid of your feelings, aren't you?"

"Aren't you?"

"You sound angry."

"I didn't mean to sound angry."

I slowed down some. I followed her directions. When we pulled up in her parents' driveway, I felt an exhaustion in my chest. I saw the foyer light go on.

"You want to get away fast, don't you?" she said.

I kept both hands tight on the wheel.

She got out of the car. Before the door of the house was opened for her, I was pulling away.

I felt as if we'd had a lovers' quarrel and we weren't even lovers.

THIRTEEN

Koch

I think about this name Thomassy. Never have I heard a name like that exactly. George could be anything, Georg, Georgio, Jorge, Georges, the English had kings named George. Everywhere the Tigris and Euphrates fertilize, the land is rich with Georges. In the thirties, if this Thomassy was to be an actor, the movie people would call him what? George Thomas? Now they keep their names. George Segal. They put foreign flags on their bumpers. My forebears came from somewhere else, *make something of it*, a challenge to the Wasp world whose daughters run loose among Greeks, Italians, Jews, whatnot, seeking interesting genes. Almighty, You are manipulating us for some plan that will give us again a Jewbaby hidden in the bulrushes by a shiksa of high station. In the Sistine Chapel the fingers still almost touch. Scientists bring their children to look up at God and Adam. Do they laugh? Do they say it is a good painting period? They do not? They are in awe.

Gunther, Marta would say were she still alive, you are about to declare yourself a failure. You still think of yourself the way your mother thought of you: Go out into the world and make a name for yourself, meaning that if your mind leads you to interesting speculations, put them down, make an article, a book even, pass them on. Success she demanded, meaning the name that she gave you will be recognized.

Gunther, Marta would say, it is permitted to be a dilettante if that pleases you, it is not a failure to depart the world leaving no grandchildren and no books. Passing through is okay. Marta, my heart cries, it would be a comfort to believe you! It is not my mother who is nagging me now, it is myself telling me that I am sixty and there is not much time to leave a mark.

I was meandering in thoughts like these when the doorbell rang and I went to greet this Thomassy. We shook hands. I do not want him in the study where I see my patients. I show him to a comfortable chair in my living room. He looks at me, I look at him, two animals of similar but different species inhabiting the same forest and meeting for the first time.

I would say he is in his middle forties. No accent, therefore probably American born or arrived before the age of twelve. Perhaps Greek-looking, but taller by far than Greeks, and in his movement strength, in his face I see what I envy, a man the world will not abuse easily. I wish I had a Rorschach of him!

"How much time have we got?" he says.

"You have twenty-five years, I have ten."

It takes him only a second to see that I am subtracting from three score and ten, and he laughs.

"You have a good laugh," I tell him.

"As distinguished from?"

"A bad laugh is a form of manipulation. I laugh to show I despise what you have said or what you are. I put you down. A good laugh is a quick, uncontrolled reaction, finding amusement or joy. Yours was a good laugh."

"Thank you," Thomassy said. "I suppose we get to think of analysts in terms of fifty minutes. We may need more. I have quite a few questions."

"Take all the time you need. Have you ever been to an analyst yourself?"

"No."

"Forgive me," I said, "I didn't mean to intrude on your private life. It's just I wanted to know if I may use the terms of reference we have. You are familiar with them?"

"Oh yes," he said. "Even the uneducated witness in the box now recognizes his unconscious slips have meaning."

I nodded. "Before we begin," I said, "I wonder if you would satisfy a small point of curiosity. I have not heard the name Thomassy before."

"It's Armenian. Thomassian. I shortened it."

"Why?"

"To keep people guessing. Koch is German?"

"I am a Jew," I said.

"I knew someone once who spent months trying to find a Gentile psychoanalyst."

"An anti-Semite looking to avoid a transference?"

"I guess he thought a Christian would be more forgiving."

I could not help laughing.

"I guess that was a good laugh," said Thomassy.

I was liking the man, which surprised me. I expect lawyers to be like lawyers the way the inexperienced expect Jews to be like Jews.

"Armenians suffered a great deal," I said.

"Most people don't know they exist."

"They were the first Christians. They carried their cross into the twentieth century."

"My father left his at Ellis Island."

"Too much was left at Ellis Island. We are beginning to reclaim it." I sighed. "The Turks were as bad as the Nazis."

"No," said Thomassy. "They weren't hypocrites. No Beethovens, Kants, no claims of high civilization. They hated us, they wanted us all dead. Straightforward. Anyway, I'm not here to right the wrongs of the world, doctor. I just want to see if I can be of some help to . . ."

"The Widmer woman, of course."

"Francine."

"Yes, let us call her Francine. She has asked you to pursue her assailant until he is punished for violating the one orifice that requires permission for its senses to be activated."

Thomassy seemed puzzled.

"The ears hear whatever sounds strike them," I explained. "The eyes, when open, see. The nose smells full time. The vagina requires an admission ticket."

"Dr. Koch, if you talk like that, I promise I'll never call you as a witness."

"Splendid. Already I have accomplished something."

"Francine feels she has been the victim of a serious crime some men don't understand."

I could not help sighing again. Francine had been working on him. "There are a thousand ways in which we rape each other, including ways that cause death sooner or later, yet there is only one form of rape that is categorized as a major crime. I think women have had greater influence on the law than they think."

"You think, doctor, that she is making too much of what happened to her?"

"No. But one must understand the woman to understand what this particular event meant. Can I get you some coffee?"

Thomassy said he preferred a scotch and soda. "I will join you," I said, "though I am not a drinker really." Then, settled once more, I said, "Francine is a zealot, which means she will try to pursue an idea till its end. She has courage, what we men chauvinistically refer to as 'balls.' "

"Would you explain?"

"It is my lifelong adventure to explain. It is my ego's flower. She has political interests, in the broad sense, as do many young women of this period. Where does she find employment? In the most conspicuous place where power does not work at all. In the enemy camp, in the United Nations. She is probably a disruptive force there, or could be. Do you find her disruptive?"

"Yes. I also find her attractive."

He too? "That can be a handicap with a client as with a patient."

"Yes," said Thomassy.

"What attracts you?"

"I don't want to bore you."

"No, no, go on."

"Spunk. What you said, balls."

"An aggressive quality normally associated with males. We analysts sometimes pay close attention to words. You know the other meaning of spunk?"

"Semen."

"Yes. Now how do you think I might help with this case of hers?"

Thomassy lit up his pipe, giving him a moment to formulate. I'm sure he does not enjoy this luxury in the courtroom. There would be other devices. Going to the counsel table for a pad. Pacing.

"Let me outline the problems I see," he said. "I will have a hard time convincing the District Attorney to press the case, even to the point of taking it before the Grand Jury."

"Why?"

"Because there is no external corroborating evidence. So many rape accusations come to nothing because rape is almost impossible to prove."

"Like love. Have you ever been in love?"

Koch, Koch, don't flirt with dangerous questions. "Go on," I said, "I didn't mean to interrupt."

Thomassy continued. "If you have property and someone takes it from you, if you can prove the property was yours, that you no longer have it, and that the accused now has it, and you say—even if there are no witnesses—that you did not give him permission to take it, then there is an easy basis for a juror agreeing."

"I see the problem with rape."

"I cannot take this case before a Grand Jury. I have to convince a district attorney to do so. And the prosecutor knows that if he gets the Grand Jury to see that there is sufficient evidence that a crime may have been committed, he will then have to face the choosing of twelve citizens who will decide. The prosecutor will want women on the jury because they share the fear of rape and they may be sympathetic to Francine. But the defense counsel will want men, many of whom will have a touch or more of coercion in their past. The prosecutor will give in on men who have a daughter Francine's age. The defense counsel will try for the older, conservative male—preferably without daughters—who will automatically react adversely to the fact that Francine is physically attractive, and therefore tempting, that she does not wear a brassiere, which is a provocation, that she is not married yet at twenty-seven and the jury will get the idea she's been around. Under the new law, the defendant's lawyer can't cross-examine her about her sex life without risking a contempt citation, but so what? Her life style will be apparent, and that's enough to condemn her in a lot of eyes. For me, the most difficult aspect is that I will have to do whatever I can from backstage, as it were. It is the prosecutor and the defense counsel who will be adversaries in the arena, the people versus the defendant. As her lawyer I have no role except to shore up the reluctant prosecution as best I can. You see the problems?"

I nodded.

"I see the game plan as follows," Thomassy continued. "A minority of men," he looked at me, "are attracted to smart, even aggressively smart women."

"An equal combatant on the field of life."

Thomassy liked that. "However," he said, "the chance of getting more than one or two such men on the jury is poor. On the contrary, there will be some men—the defense counsel will fight like hell to get them on—who are working class, or middle class with a working-class orientation. Men who feel safe with women who are in every respect, and not just in bed, beneath them."

"Yes," I said, "but such men are not psychopathic rapists. This Koslak man is a clear type. He must defend his ego by forcing a superior-seeming woman. It is as old as the world. If I put my penis in the queen, she is no longer my queen but an equal. I have raised myself by putting her down."

"If I were prosecuting the case myself—and I wish to hell that were possible instead of relying on whatever jerk is going to be assigned this—I'd have to try to make the jury feel repulsed by Koslak's act."

"The fact is," I said, "that they will be intrigued by it. As we are."

Thomassy had not expected that. "Come," I said, "in the privacy of our conversation, we have to be precise. Koslak's penis has been where yours and mine would like to go. It has to intrigue us that this strong-arm idiot made his way, while we are inhibited by all the things we think make us civilized. Including affection."

He was silent, so I offered to refresh his drink. He shrugged it off.

Finally he said, "I have a reputation for liking difficult cases."

"One does not like to play chess against checker players. You see the conflict? One wants strong opponents, and one wants to win against them, so that we will think of ourselves as even stronger."

"Do you usually win, Dr. Koch?"

"At chess?"

"With patients."

"I am in the curing business. There is nothing to win."

"Do you always cure?"

"No, one always hopes."

"I don't like to depend on hope."

"Do you always win, Mr. Thomassy?"

I noted that he did not answer me. Then I said, "May I give you a word of hope then? Let us reflect a moment on Francine's psychology. We have no proof that she did or did not want relations with this Koslak man. Why would she want to have intercourse with a man like that?"

"She wouldn't."

"Ah, but some intelligent, educated, strong women at every time have sought out the gamekeeper. They are fed up by our civilities, our circumlocutions, our gentleness even."

"I don't think that's true of Francine," he said.

"Ah," I said, "that is the point. If we can prove somehow convincingly that this particular individual, Francine Widmer by name, would not want to have sex with such an individual as Koslak, and if he admits to having sex with her, then you have proven rape."

"The world I function in demands hard evidence."

"If you don't think psychological fact is hard evidence, you have come to the wrong place."

"I'm listening. Go on."

"Can she, on the witness stand, be asked questions that make it evident she would not have interest in a brute like Koslak?"

"I don't know how much of that a judge would allow."

"The judge cannot have a Polaroid photo of the act."

Thomassy laughed. "Wouldn't help. It would have to show her resisting."

"She says she did. For a while."

"She says, that's the problem. Her word against his."

"Surely she would make the better witness."

"It depends on whether his lawyer is better than the prosecutor."

"Not the facts of the case?"

"Not usually. And in this matter, there are pitifully few objectively verifiable facts."

It seemed time for me to say what I had planned to. "Mr. Thomassy, you have an option not to pursue the matter any further."

He was without response, so I said, "I do not have that option. She is a patient of mine. She was before the event, she continues—I hope she continues—after the event. My role with her will be very difficult if she is to spend her emotions in rage that justice could not be had. Both of us are dependent on you."

It was at that moment that the telephone rang. Service should answer, but they did not. It rang again and again, and so I excused myself, and went into my study to find that it was service calling.

Thomassy rose from his chair when he saw the color of my face.

"Service took a call from Francine Widmer."

"Saying?"

"She had to cancel. But she didn't have an appointment this evening."

"She knew we had."

"She said she was having a repeat of her problem. She said she needed *au secours* urgently. Help."

"She's gone back to her apartment."

"And what's-his-name is after her again."

Thomassy went for the phone. He flipped through his wallet for a card of numbers, dialed. To me he said, "Get me her address." As I looked, I could hear him identify himself and say there was a crime in progress. He spelled Francine Widmer. I gave him the address from my records. He was like a man on fire when he hung up. "I'm driving up there now. Will you come?"

"Yes," I said.

When I was in Thomassy's car, racing like a maniac eighty miles an hour up the West Side Highway, I said only one thing to him. "You didn't tell the police it was a rape."

"You're damn right," he said.

FOURTEEN

Koslak

I wasn't gonna let Jason get too familiar with Mary and me. That bath-tub scene was okay once, I mean watching Jason giving head and Mary going off like July Fourth was an experience, but I felt a bit like queer afterwards, you know what I mean, three persons, two of us being men? I don't want Jason getting familiar with Mary when I'm at the station because if I caught him at it without my permission I'd *have* to do something about him, wouldn't I?

I figured the best way to get Jason's mind off the bathtub party—I almost said bathrub party, isn't that funny?—I reminded him about Widmer. Jason, he wasn't too sure, but I invented a whole ton of stuff about how being a queen bee made her an expert in all kinds of things Jason might like to try, and I guaranteed him she'd appreciate the way he gave head.

Jason was no pushover. "You sure you made it with her?" he asked.

"Would I lie to you?" I said to him.

"She wasn't any trouble, was she?"

"All women are a bit of trouble," I said.

"Mary wasn't."

"Oh Mary can be trouble sometimes."

I really wanted to get his mind off my turf. From all the hours rap-ping at the station I've gotten pretty good at talking up a hard on, and Jason finally says okay, he'll join me the next time I have a go at Widmer.

I explained there was one problem, she hadn't been home for a few days, but I'd let him know when.

When came right away. It was only a couple of minutes later when I see lights in her window, I go racing downstairs to Jason's place and say, "Come on, man, now."

FIFTEEN

Francine

Of course I had no intention of staying the night. The minute I came in the door I knew I could not go on living there while Koslak was still on the loose. All I wanted to do was to stuff a few things I needed into a canvas duffel and get the hell out of there fast. I was jumpy about Thomassy's meeting with Dr. Koch that evening, and I thought I'd just keep myself busy after work by driving up to the apartment, getting what I wanted real quick, and scramming. I planned to drive up to Mom and Dad's. By the time I got there, the meeting with Dr. Koch would be over. I had asked each of them to call me afterwards, and I hoped at least one of them would.

The doorbell ring had the same effect on me as sticking a hairpin in an electric outlet. I'd done it once at the age of three and still remembered. *Who could it be?*

At first I wasn't going to answer at all.

It rang again. Then a voice said, "It's the super."

At the door I said, "I didn't call you."

"There's a leak in the ceiling in the apartment below. I have to shut your kitchen water off."

He'd been in the apartment several times for various things and had never given me any trouble. I had to let him in, didn't I?

I slipped the safety chain, unbolted the deadlock, and opened the door. At least with him there, I'd be safe from Koslak. I noticed he wasn't wearing his prosthetic arm. He went right into the kitchen, carrying a big plumber's wrench in his good hand, and I went into the bedroom to finish putting my extra underthings, pajamas, and et ceteras into the duffel I had gotten down from the closet. I was almost finished. I figured I could tell him I was going out and just go. He could lock up on his own if I left him the key to the deadlock. On second thought, that wouldn't be a good idea. It never occurred to me to go into the kitchen to watch him turning off the water under the sink. I find it embarrassing to watch any repairman because I don't like people staring at me while I'm working.

Then I heard the super in the living room. He must have finished.

He was already at the door, about to open it, and I said, "Did the water do a lot of damage?" and he said, "Not too bad." Then I asked him when he would be able to turn the water back on because I was going away and he couldn't get into the apartment if the deadbolt was on. I didn't want to hang around.

"You've got water now," he said. "I found the problem."

It didn't sound right to me.

"You sure?"

"Sure."

"Well, thank you," I said, and watched him unbolt the door. He opened it, but instead of going out, well, he let Koslak in. Koslak quickly locked the door behind him, and they both just stood there, staring at me.

I said, "I was just getting ready to leave." *They mustn't see how terrified I am.*

I went to the bedroom, zipped up the duffel, and came back out to the living room. They were still in front of the door.

"Excuse me," I said. The super was about to step aside when Koslak put his hand on the super's good arm.

"You know why we're here," Koslak said to me.

"I'm late for an appointment," I said.

"We won't keep you too long," Koslak said with that tight grin.

We. Both of them. Oh no.

"It's a doctor's appointment," I said.

"Oh, you sick?" asks Koslak.

I didn't answer. He said, "Is it catching?"

If I said I have the clap, would that put them off? I could feel the constriction in my throat.

"Please," I said to the super, "the doctor charges fifty dollars whether or not I show up."

The super looked at Koslak. Koslak said, "What kind of doctor charges fifty dollars, a shrink?"

I nodded.

"Well, that's easy. If you get laid enough, you won't need a shrink."

The super laughs at this.

"Please let me call him."

The super looks at Koslak again.

"No calls." Then to the super, "Don't want to spoil the party, right?"

The super looks uncomfortable. Is it possible he didn't know Koslak intended to force me? I appealed to him. "Please?"

Koslak's worrying about the super, I can see that. He said, "Everybody stay calm. Just give me the number, I'll call."

I tell him Koch's number. Koslak goes to the kitchen phone. The super remains at the door.

Koslak yells from the kitchen, "Give me that number again, doll."

I repeat the number slowly, trying to control the tremor in my voice.

"Where are you going?" he snaps at me.

"I need a glass of water." My throat is tightening.

I run a glass of water from the tap. I swallow once or twice. I just cannot drink it all. It's as if my throat had narrowed to the closing point. *Think fast.*

"Tell the doctor . . . " I said.

"I know what to tell him," Koslak snapped.

He dialed, then put his hand over the mouthpiece. "Shit," he said, "it's an answering service."

"Tell them to give Dr. Koch a message."

Koslak said, "This is a message for Dr. Koch." Then to me, "What message?"

"Tell them it's Francine Widmer. Have to cancel. I'm having a repeat of my problem. I—"

"Hold it?" Koslak shouted. "I can't remember everything."

"Let me tell them."

"No!"

"Tell them to tell Dr. Koch I need *au secours* urgently."

"What the fuck's that?"

"My medicine."

"You don't have any?"

I shake my head.

"Say it again."

I repeated it. Koslak said to the service, "This is some damn medicine she needs. Osekure." Then to me. "They want me to spell it."

"A-U-S-E-C-O-U-R-S."

He repeated each letter after me, then hung up.

"She got it. Now you're going to get it. There's a little medicine old Jason here and I need."

Koslak pointed to the bedroom.

Think. Will Koch understand my message. Even if he does, will he know what to do? Maybe Thomassy'll know what to do. If they get the message. In time. Anything to delay. This is a new experience for the super, he's looking hesitant. *Take a chance.*

I took several steps in the direction of the super. Not too close. "Please," I said to him, "don't make me do anything I don't want to."

Koslak's shout cut across the room. "This is my show!" he bellowed. I threw my arm across my face because I could see the slap coming as he rushed at me. The flat of his hand hit my arm, which only made him more angry as he grabbed my other arm, twisted it hard behind my back just like the last time. *Stay on your feet.*

He pushed and pulled me by my arm, twisting to get me to my knees. I must try to scratch, get some skin under my fingernails. I must try to get at least one hair. I must try to tear some clothes. I must not douche afterwards. The hell with proof, I didn't want to let it happen!

That's when I started screaming. I screamed and screamed and screamed, as he twisted me down to the carpet.

I remember his slapping me across the face once or twice to stop me, but it was I who stopped myself, exhausted. He had let me go.

I lay there looking up at both of them.

"That did you a lotta good, didn't it?" said Koslak. "Nobody heard."

Somebody must have heard.

I listened. If anyone had heard, no one was doing anything about it. Nobody wants to get involved.

"What if somebody comes?" I heard Jason whisper.

Koslak didn't bother whispering. "We heard the screaming, too, didn't we? We came to investigate, to see what we could do, right? It's our word against hers, and there're two of us."

I said to Koslak, "Can I stand up? I want to talk."

"I came here to fuck, not talk."

"I want to talk to you about that," I said.

"I'm gonna ram it so hard you'll feel it come outa the top of your head. What have you got to say about that?"

I started to get up. My arms hurt. My face hurt. "I want to talk about what turns you on."

Koslak turned to the super. "Knocking her on her ass is what turns me on."

"Do you ever look at those magazines?" I said.

"What magazines?"

The super, the quiet one, said, "Skin."

"Is that what you mean?" said Koslak.

I nodded.

"So what?"

"You want to see my skin?" I said.

The super was looking very unhappy. Koslak gave him a pat on the ass, saying, "This is going to be all right, man."

"If you like to see skin . . . " I said. I opened one button of my blouse.

"Listen," said Koslak. "Who the fuck you think you're kidding? Take your clothes off before I rip them off."

I opened another button. How long could I keep this going?

"Come on!" Koslak yelled, coming toward me.

"Okay," I said, "okay," and opened my blouse all the way. The super is looking. Koslak is looking.

"Don't that make the gism tighten your balls, man?" Koslak said to the super. "Great tits."

I am watching them both.

The super is watching me as if he's appreciating a statue. If the circumstances were different, it might be a compliment.

"We ain't got all day," said Koslak. "Take it all off. I want to see the beaver."

I let the blouse slip off my arms.

"All of it," he yelled.

I don't want him to touch me.

"Hurry up. If you don't want to go into the bedroom, lie back on the couch and spread it."

He sees how frightened I am. He's feeding on my fear.

"Just a minute," I said, and I went for the kitchen, with Koslak following right behind me fast, saying, "What's up? Where you going?" but he didn't do anything to stop me till he saw me reach up to the magnetic knife rack above the sink and then it was too late. For a split second I almost took the meat cleaver. I'd cut chicken into parts with it, whacked fish heads off, but using it against a human being? It was self-defense, wasn't it? The knife I took was the bread knife.

I thrust it at him foolishly. He was too far away.

"Wait a minute," he said. What frightened me was the twisted pleasure of his smile. *He likes the possibility of violence.*

"Don't come near me," I said, holding the knife out in front of me, point toward him. I wished I knew how to use it. I knew I was doing it wrong.

When I moved forward, he moved back. He was looking to grab my arm.

I had walked him back into the living room. The super saw the knife. "Hey, Harry," he said, "this isn't my scene."

"It's your scene now," Koslak said. He had that commanding shake in his voice. "Get behind her," he said. "She can't take on two of us."

I was backing toward the front door when I thought I heard voices outside. I screamed with full lungs. The super really looked frightened, but Koslak lunged for my arm. I tried to strike at him with the knife, but he grabbed my wrist and twisted so hard I felt the pain shoot up to my shoulder. I dropped the knife. Instantly he stooped and picked it up.

The doorbell rang. "Open up," a voice said. "Police officers."

Koslak was standing there with the knife when the super stepped behind me and unlocked the door. The two policemen had guns in their hands.

SIXTEEN

Thomassy

Koch sat scrunched up in the passenger seat, obviously alarmed at how fast I was tooling up the West Side Highway. I wonder what kind of teen-ager this psychiatrist had been.

This got me thinking about Papa Thomassian, who sometimes thought he was a psychiatrist to his horses. He'd mother them and father them, a taskmaster, trainer, and in the case of that crazy stallion that should have been shot, Papa behaved like a head doctor trying to reason and cajole a berserk animal. I was fourteen when the stallion responded to Papa's ministrations by kicking him unconscious.

I remember Mama screaming out of control as if I could hear it right now.

I did what I had to do. I hauled the limp sack of old man into the back of the antique car. Every kid my age in Oswego knew how to drive, but I didn't even have a learner's permit. I drove the distance to the hospital in Binghamton, Mama crying her widow's wail, sure this was the end. I had to tell her that if she didn't shut up, I'd crack up the car and we'd all die.

I got the old man into emergency—the intern said it was in the nick of time—and the cop who wrote up the report said to me, "How'd you get here, kid?" and I said, "I drove," and that was that because if you won, it didn't matter how you won.

Which didn't get me a driver's license before I was sixteen. We had to take the bus to Binghamton to visit the old man. The wheezing had turned to breathing. Then he was sitting up in bed.

"Mama," he said, "give me a dollar."

"You can't spend no money in the hospital, what for you need a dollar?"

The patriarch's authority had come back to his eyes. She gave him the dollar.

Then he turned to me and said, "Georgie, you save my life the doctor says. Here."

I shook my head. I didn't want the dollar.

"You see how he turns away from my dollar, Mama? The only reason he saved my life was because he don't want to take care of you."

Gratitude, I learned, is like love. Don't try for it. If you get it, it won't last.

"What did you say?" asked Dr. Koch.

"I was thinking gratitude is like love. It never lasts."

"Not true," said Koch the curer.

We knew we were at the right building because people had clustered around the empty police car, its light whirling. "Follow me," I yelled to Koch, and went up the stairs two at a time.

The apartment door was open. Inside, an unbelievable scene, the cops, Francine, and *two* guys, all of them trying to talk or shout. Francine had some kind of wrap around herself. Her hair was wild. I kept my eyes averted from her. I identified myself to the police as her lawyer, by which time Koch had come up the stairs, puffing, and I said he was Miss Widmer's doctor, that there'd been a call asking for help, and, yes, I was the one who had called the police.

The older, heavyset cop said, "This guy," pointing at the man I assumed to be Koslak, "is threatening false arrest."

"You're damn right," Koslak's strident pitch cut at me.

Francine allowed herself to be engulfed by Koch's arm. Permissible for a doctor, not for a lawyer.

"He says nothing happened."

"That's true," said the man with one arm. "Nothing did."

"You let him in," Francine screamed. "He's the man who raped me."

"Nobody raped anybody while I was here," said the super.

"Last week! Last week!" said Francine.

"Who called the cops tonight?" said the cop.

I repeated that I had. "I was in Dr. Koch's office. He got a message from his service that Miss Widmer needed help."

"Let me tell you something, mister," said Koslak, "she don't need no help. She *offered* to put on a show."

I looked at Francine.

"This girl was naked from the waist up when I come in," said the cop. He turned to Francine. "You live here alone?"

Francine nodded.

"Did you invite these men in?"

"The super said he had to turn the water in the kitchen off because there was a leak down below."

"That's right," said the super.

"Then what happened?" asked the cop.

"He let the other man in, I told you," said Francine.

"She offered to put on this show," said the super. "She wanted twenty bucks, and I asked Mr. Koslak in so we could split it ten and ten."

"That's a lie." Francine was appealing to me to take charge.

"Officer," I said, "what did you see when you entered?"

The younger cop answered. "I was in first. This fellow—" he pointed at Koslak— "was holding a knife, the other fellow was just standing there, the girl was—"

"Why was he holding a knife?"

"It wasn't my knife," said Koslak. "It was her knife. I had to take it away from her."

The cop said, "She admitted it was her knife."

"She pulled the knife," said Koslak, "when we said we'd pay after the show. She wanted the cash in advance."

"They were threatening to rape me!"

"Hold everything!" I said. "Officer, my client is employed as an executive in the United Nations, comes from a socially prominent Westchester family, earns a good living. Why would she be interested in exhibiting herself for a few dollars?"

"I don't know," said the older cop. "Hey, honey," he said to Francine, "why would you?"

Koch was trying to calm her.

"I wouldn't!" she yelled. "I was screaming before the police came in."

"Was she in fact screaming?" I asked.

"She was," said the cop.

"Because I took her damn knife away from her," said Koslak. "Listen, anybody going to make charges around here, it's me. I'm a respectable married man. I got a pregnant wife and two kids upstairs. I only came in because she was going to put on a show, right?"

"Right," said the super.

"Anybody'd want to see that kind of a show. But if she's going to scream rape or whatever, I'm going to charge false arrest. I'm a businessman. I own the Esso station on Hertford. I know my rights."

"Officer," I said, "can the doctor talk to my client in the next room for a minute?"

He looked hesitant.

"I want to advise her of her rights," I said.

Grudgingly, he approved, and I took Francine by the arm into the kitchen. Koch joined us, and I closed the kitchen door.

"Francine," I said. "We're here to help. Are you calm enough to talk?"

She nodded, sniffing.

"Is any of that nonsense true? I mean about putting on an exhibition?"

"I was trying to stall until you got here. I had to think of something that might . . . "

"Might what?"

"Keep them from touching me."

I guess she saw Koch and me looking at each other.

"I didn't want a repeat of what Koslak did the last time. He probably told the super. They planned this."

"We need demonstrable proof of that."

"I swear I'm telling the truth."

"Unless there's proof, it's their word against yours. And there are two of them."

Francine looked utterly forlorn.

Koch asked me, "What about the knife?"

"How did that happen?" I asked her.

"I didn't know how long it would take for help to get here. I didn't even know if it would. I mean can you rely on an answering service? I didn't leave the message, they wouldn't let me phone, I had to tell him what to say in a way he wouldn't know what the message was, and I could hardly think of anything except French, hoping he wouldn't know it. I was thinking of going out the window. Do you think I wanted to do a strip for them? Koslak beat me for screaming. Nobody came. It was the only thing I could think of to buy time, only I couldn't stall them any more. I was getting desperate. I grabbed the kitchen knife, maybe I shouldn't have, but I did, and he grabbed it away from me."

"Was there anything about money?"

"I swear, nothing. They made that up."

"You shouldn't have come back here."

"It's my home. I was just picking up some clothes. For a few minutes, that's all."

Koch, looking helpless, said, "Mr. Thomassy, can I do anything?"

"I don't know if either of us can do anything."

"What do you mean?" said Francine.

"Nothing happened."

"They were going to rape me."

"But they didn't. At best, it's attempted rape, and we have no proof."

"But he did it the last time." She was crying now. Koch tried to put his arm around her again, but she shrugged it off. "Betrayed by the rules. No douching. Go straight to the hospital. Get a piece of skin or clothes for the police. I don't know what you people expect of women!"

"Don't lump us with the enemy, Francine," said Dr. Koch. "We are here to help. That's why we came."

"Then help."

The older cop poked his head in the door. "Look, mister, enough is enough. We got a call that something was going on up here. We don't know what was going on up here. These guys were fully dressed, but the girl was naked. My partner and I saw the guy with the knife, but she admitted it was her knife. We frisked them both before you got here. They were clean. I can't arrest either of them for doing nothing, right? And the one guy says he'll charge false arrest if we do, and nobody wants that kind of hassle, right? Why don't we pack everybody off and call it a night."

"Because." I pointed him into the other room, and waved Koch and Francine to follow me.

I stationed myself as close to Koslak as I could but talked to the others. I was hoping he'd make a grab for me. "I'll take this matter to the D.A. in the morning," I said, "so you'd better file an accurate and complete report, officer. The woman would have no reason to call for help unless help was needed. May I have both of your names and I.D. please?"

I could feel Koslak bristling as I took the information down. Then I went up to the bearded man without the arm.

"You're the superintendent of this building?"

"This one and the two next door."

"You came up here to turn the kitchen water off because there was a leak down below?"

"That's what I said."

"Officer," I said, "would you check with the apartment below to see if they've had a ceiling leak or any other leak this evening?"

The older cop nodded and the younger one went out.

"How long have you been superintendent of this building?"

"Two years." He turned to the cop. "Do I have to answer his questions?"

"I'm no lawyer," said the cop.

"Well, I'm an officer of the court, as you know, and there is an obligation to investigate certain facts at the scene of any alleged crime. A crime has been alleged here. And if the police don't do a thorough job of investigation, it'll only make the D.A.'s job harder, so I'm trying to help you avoid being criticized later, do you understand, officer? Okay." Then to the one-armed man, I said, "When you applied for the position of superintendent here, did you fill out an employment application for the landlord?"

"No, it was just an interview. I saw his ad. He was desperate for somebody. The previous super was a wino and a crook."

"Did your employer ascertain whether you had been in trouble with the law?"

"Hey, what is this?"

"You heard what this is. We're investigating a complaint. Do you have a police record?"

From his expression I would guess our fishing expedition was leading somewhere.

The super was sullen and silent.

"Never mind. We'll note there was no response. We can check his record easy enough. Now you." I turned to Koslak. "How did you gain entrance to this apartment?"

"He let me in."

"Did you think it was his apartment?"

"No. He lives in the basement next door."

"What made you think he had the right to invite you into this apartment?"

"There was this show."

"What show?"

Koslak looked at Francine with hatred.

"There was no show when you entered and none after you entered, isn't that right? You were trespassing. Is trespass a proper charge, officer?"

"I'll sue for false arrest."

"Do whatever you like, mister," I said.

Just then the younger cop came up from downstairs. "The lady says there was no leak in her apartment."

"Did you take her name?"

He looked dumbfounded.

"Officer, would you mind taking her full name, address, and her exact words since you'll be filing a complete report on this matter."

He looked at the older cop. The older cop nodded. He went back down.

"Okay," I said to the super. "You made that story up."

"I'm not saying anything without a lawyer."

"Call your lawyer. There's a phone in the kitchen."

"It's nighttime."

"He'll have an answering service for emergencies."

"I don't have a lawyer."

"You'd better get one." I turned to Koslak. "You have a lawyer, mister?"

"You're damn right."

"Well, you better call him and tell him that you're being charged with slander. You did say in front of witnesses that this young woman offered to perform certain sexually enticing acts for pay. Considering the nature of her employment as an official of an international organization, such defamation could be most injurious. Would you note the allegation, officer?"

"I don't have to book him for anything like that."

"I just want to make sure you note the additional charge. You're booking him for trespass."

"You'll have to come along to the station," the officer said sadly to Koslak.

"My wife'll be worried."

"I'll be happy to tell your wife where you are," I said to Koslak.

"Fuck you!" said Koslak.

"Hey, let's watch it," said the officer. To me, he said, "You coming along?"

"We're all coming along," I said, taking Francine by the arm.

SEVENTEEN

Thomassy

Widmer got me on the phone early. "George," he said, "Francine was very upset last night."

"I'm not surprised."

"What happened?"

"Did you ask her?"

"She wouldn't say anything."

"Then it's not my place to."

"Please?"

"There was a trespassing incident involving the man who raped her, Ned. Fortunately, the police were able to intervene. I've lodged a trespassing complaint."

"George, I want her out of that apartment. I don't care what it costs."

"She doesn't take instruction from me, Ned. You'd better talk to her yourself. Remember, there's that damn lease."

"I don't give a damn about the lease! Anyway, breaking leases should be child's play for you, George."

"Ned, there are leases and leases. I don't even know who owns that building. It might take good money."

"I don't care."

"One thing's sure, Ned. There won't be an escape clause on the grounds that the folks upstairs include a rapist and the super is a one-armed freak."

"What's this about the super?"

"He was with Koslak last night. He was the one who let him in the apartment."

"Jesus, George, there must be a way."

"Sure, let's run a sublease ad. Wanted: tenant for apartment under rapist. Ned, you can't even say 'Gentlemen Only' in an ad any more! Want to take the responsibility of a sublease to another young woman without telling her what she's getting into?"

"I don't care if the apartment sits empty. George, are you pursuing the original complaint?"

"You bet your life."

"When?"

"Right now. Today."

"Keep me posted, George. And one other thing."

"What?"

"Don't tell Francine I called."

Thank heaven for disbarred lawyers. Without someone like Fat Tarbell, my investigative work would be a lot more time-consuming. If a disbarred lawyer doesn't want to spend the rest of his life clerking for paralegal wages, he's got to develop a specialty. Tarbell is a sucker fish on the body of the Westchester D.A.'s office.

I can tell Tarbell likes me. He follows the cases for which he supplies information, and keeps score. He knows what my score is, and it is through him that at least part of my reputation among lawyers in this county is built.

I doubt anybody'd go after Tarbell. Not any more. He knows too much.

I phoned him, asked about his Mrs. and his kid John—John's at Yale Law School and I can tell you he's one lawyer who's never going to get caught doing anything that'd get him disbarred. Then I got down to it.

"I'd like to talk Cunham into a criminal prosecution."

"Shame on you. Who do you want to get?"

"Somebody a client wants to get. How's Cunham fixed?"

"Up to his ass. He's shuffling troublemakers like you off on a kid named Lefkowitz. Know him?"

I didn't and asked Tarbell to fill me in.

"I'll tell you. He wears a key chain."

"Thanks a lot."

"How many guys you know today wear a key chain? He's Harvard *summa*, Columbia Law, listen, he's had the same girl friend since high school. He weekends in Amagansett where he breaks the law smoking grass with some other unmarried couples they share a rental with. Twenty-seven, an assistant D.A., he thinks he's riding shotgun for God. He's going to be Attorney General by the time he's forty."

"I'll bet."

"Well, there are two ways of dealing with a kid like Lefkowitz," Tarbell went on. "You can Stepin Fetchit, kiss young massa's ass, make him feel so big and so good he'll get his rocks off doing a favor for Big Shot Thomassy. However, George Thomassy no good as Stepin Fetchit. You better zap him. He's chicken shit if you come on strong. What's the complaint?"

"Rape," I said.

"Forget it. Not this year."

"Want to bet a case of wine?"

"I never gamble," said Tarbell. "You'd have to have Cunham's family jewels in your safe."

"You got anything useful?" I asked.

"Don't I always? Except this particular bit takes a very tough character to use."

I didn't say a thing.

"It'll cost you two hundred if you use it, four hundred if it works."

"Photograph?"

"Newspaper clip."

"I'll be over."

"Look, do me a favor," said Tarbell, "don't come to my place this time."

"You keeping an underage mistress?"

"Just meet me in the Gristede's parking lot in half an hour."

"I hope whoever's tapping your phone isn't listening."

"I pay real good to have it cleaned regularly."

"You think of everything."

"If I thought of everything, I wouldn't have lost my license. I'd be making a fortune like you guys."

*   *   *

I spotted Fat Tarbell in his Ford before he saw me. I walked over to the driver's window and said, "Don't move."

Tarbell laughed. "Come on, I saw you in the mirror. Here, put this in your wallet. I don't want you to lose it unless you lose your wallet."

"This is a Xerox."

"I've got the original if you ever need it. No extra charge."

"I wish there were easier ways."

"Fuck that. I'd be out of business."

As I watched him drive off, I thought if I ever got disbarred, what would I do to make a living?

When I phoned Lefkowitz I said I wanted to see him at 3:00 P.M. that day and I hoped it wouldn't be too inconvenient. He started to say something about a previous appointment, which I told him he could blame me for in canceling and I would be there at three sharp.

When I arrived I told the secretary not to bother I knew the way and went right past her, around the L, and into the office marked "Gerald R. Lefkowitz." He looked up from his newspaper, actually blushed folding it up like he had been caught masturbating, and I said, "Three o'clock on the button."

"I'm very pleased to meet you, Mr. Thomassy," said the boy lawyer, holding out a flustered hand.

"Lefkowitz," I said, "I'm not much for sitting around offices. Why don't we take a walk. Okay?"

He glanced over at the armchair he had been planning to seat me in as if to apologize to it for it missing this opportunity to have George Thomassy's celebrated ass sitting in it for half an hour.

"I hope you walk with a brisk stride," I said.

"I hope so," said Lefkowitz. In two minutes we were outside, and I set the pace at Thomassy's not-quite-marathon walking speed.

"Exercising the body stimulates the mind," I said. "Don't you agree?"

He agreed.

I was going to get him to agree to a lot more before the walk was over. First I filled him in on the facts. Then I said, "Lefkowitz, we're not going to have trouble over the sexual aspects because you're a member of a smart new generation with no hang-ups, so we can talk frankly, right?"

When he said "right" he was already short of breath. Good.

"You didn't by any chance row at Harvard?"

He shook his head.

"Pity," I said. "Great sport. Now. What happened to Miss Widmer, you'll recall that's the name of the complainant, was a crime of violence, that's what we have to keep foremost in our minds. I'd wanted to be sure to brief you thoroughly before I see Gary."

His speech was beginning to crack up into breathy stretches. "There are . . . certain kinds of cases . . . rape is one of them . . . that Mr. Cunham is not fond of putting before mixed company."

"I've heard he uses that expression about the Grand Jury. You tired? You want to sit down on that bench?"

Lefkowitz declined the chance to rest. Foolish.

"When you've added to your experience," I said, "you'll find that the majority of so-called sex crimes have nothing to do with sex. I don't mean your peeping tom or your run-of-the-mill exhibitionist. I'm talking about forcing sex on someone."

"Rape," said Lefkowitz.

"Right. Maybe it'll be easier to judge my conclusion—and I want you to be the judge, Lefkowitz—if you consider a case of male-to-male rape, say in prison."

"Happens every day."

"Right. But is it sexually motivated? Look, if a convict deprived of normal company builds up a head of steam, he can always use his hand. It's convenient—I almost said it's handy—doesn't bother anybody, relief is quick, and nobody gets hurt. However—" I stopped walking and looked straight at Lefkowitz. "Your heart okay? You're puffing a bit."

"Don't do much walking. Should do more."

"Continue?"

"Why not?"

"Okay. We were talking about a prisoner. If he wants some variety, there's always someone else's hand around for fair exchange. No big deal. Why then, I ask you, doesn't a day go by in any sizable jail without one or more single or gang rapes? I mean it's trouble compared to jacking off. They take the trouble because it's a method of control, of putting someone down, or keeping someone in line. Got it? If the guy who leads a gang rape lets everyone else have a piece afterwards, it's he who's the permission-giver. Rape is a function of power. The sex is incidental. The violence or threat of violence isn't. Which is back where we started. Rape is a crime of violence having relatively little to do with sex urges that can be satisfied in different and lots less complicated ways."

"That's a very interesting point of view, Mr. Thomassy."

I stopped, giving Lefkowitz a chance to puff while stationary.

"I am not in the habit," I told him, "of espousing interesting points of view. That's what law school teachers do. They're exercising their students' minds. I have to deal with the practical realities of crime in this county, and I wouldn't hold the view I have about rape if it wasn't—based on my experience—true. Follow?"

I had turned around and could see the relief in his face at the prospect of heading back toward his office.

"I would like to reflect on what you have said, Mr. Thomassy."

"I wish there were more time. But it's imperative that we get the Widmer case to the Grand Jury as soon as possible, and while you—" I gave him eyeball-to-eyeball for two seconds— "undoubtedly have the authority to do so yourself, I expect you will want to consult Gary since he has pronounced views on the matter. I could see him almost any time next week. Does that allow you enough time?"

Lefkowitz did not respond.

"I know what's troubling you," I said. "You don't like to have the boss say no. I want to assure you he won't."

"I don't mean to question your confidence, Mr. Thomassy, but on what basis do you think that Mr. Cunham would agree to put a difficult case on an unpopular subject before the jurors?"

"First, you will persuade him that we are talking about a crime of violence. Gary's very into violence, he uses it in all his speeches about how permissive Democrats in New York have reaped the whirlwind and how Cunham's Republican Westchester is a safe place to live because violence is not condoned, correct? Do you know a Mr. Morrell?"

"A who?"

"Charles Morrell?"

I could see his mind going like a pinball machine registering *tilt*.

"I used to see him in Amagansett," I said, "on my way out to East Hampton. Don't worry, he doesn't let me copy his customer list. The point is that smoking grass doesn't seem to harm people the way violence does, which is why you, and I, and Gary Cunham are concentrating on stopping violence, not victimless crimes that haven't been wiped off the statute books yet."

Mr. Gerald R. Lefkowitz, Amagansett weekend potsmoker, showed visible relief.

"Third, I know Gary will agree with your recommendation that the Widmer case go before the jury because of this."

I looked left and right as if I was about to slip Lefkowitz the Pentagon Papers. From my breast wallet I took the Xerox of the clipping from the Buffalo student newspaper. It was a mild little thing, really, Charles Cunham, identified as the son of Westchester's D.A., was lauded for his leadership role in two "controversial" student organizations, LEMAR and the Gay Activists Alliance. Lefkowitz looked at the clipping, at me, back at the clipping.

"Let me explain. I think it's fine that Gary's son is working for the legalization of marijuana, especially because of his background. It's not as if he's defying his father because he's working for legalization, right, of a harmless substance, right? I just think that Gary, and I really don't know him that well, I'm sure you've gotten to know him better working with him as closely as you do, I don't think he likes to advertise the fact that his son's sexual preference is what it is, perhaps he takes it as some kind of sign of personal failure on his part in raising the boy or setting an example. Who knows? Probably a very old-fashioned view. I know for a fact that one reporter in the Gannett chain is looking for a Cunham story. I don't know the background of that vendetta, whatever it is, but I don't think he ought to be prodded onto this one, don't you agree?"

I had to give Lefkowitz credit. He looked me straight in the eye when he said, "Mr. Thomassy, I believe you are trying to influence both my attitude toward this case and Mr. Cunham's attitude as well by an implicit threat."

"Did you think it was implicit? Mr. Lefkowitz, you're in the early part of what I am certain will be a marvelous career in the justice system. I can sum up by saying that above all, I don't believe in people getting hurt."

I slipped the clipping back in my wallet.

"I suppose you'll feel an obligation to alert Mr. Cunham to the fact that I don't believe in people getting hurt?"

"Goodbye, Mr. Thomassy." He held out his hand. I shook it.

"Goodbye, Mr. Lefkowitz. Please let my secretary know when I'm to see Mr. Cunham."

I watched young Lefkowitz trundle back to his office, a bit more knowledgeable about the facts of life than he had been before 3:00 P.M.

EIGHTEEN

Francine

When it became obvious that the case was going to be taking me out of the office more than I could cover with ordinary excuses, I decided to tell X about the rape. I kept it to a minimum. I'd been attacked. Chances are that the man would be prosecuted. I was cooperating. I didn't tell him that it was me who was determined to get Koslak behind bars.

"I'm sorry it happened," X said. "I'm glad it didn't make the papers."

"The trial might," I told him.

"It could blow your security clearance."

"Is that all you're concerned about?"

"Don't get angry, Francine," he said. "No clearance, no job."

I couldn't allow myself to think about that. I immersed myself in my assignment, one I really liked. X was preparing a two-page insert on hypocrisy for a speech to be given by the American Ambassador to the U.N. It wasn't for a particular speech, but was to be kept on hand for any occasion that might prompt a speech in the Assembly. It was my boss's idea to round up ten or twelve quickly told examples of hypocritical conduct on the highest level. My job was to scour around for historical incidents in odd parts of the world so that it wouldn't look like we were picking on Western Europe or the Soviet Union. Every continent had to be included, except Australia. And the personages involved had to be immediately identifiable. The idea was that the insert would be used when the Ambassador addressed the Assembly as an adversary against a position taken by "the other side," which by this time included most of the world. It was assumed that whatever the Ambassador was speaking against could be attacked as hypocritical. I think the point of the exercise was to convey to the people who could still bear to listen to the U.N. on radio or watch snippets on TV that the Ambassador was a master of political history and irony, someone who could send up the enemy and therefore might be in line for high elective office. Of course the taxpayers' money was not supposed to be spent on promoting a domestic political candidate, so the exercise on hypocrisy was itself hypocritical, and I was having a good time ferreting out material for my boss to choose from.

I had left word with Margo, who fended my calls, to take messages except for dire emergencies. When she buzzed me in the middle of Hypocrisy Number Nine, she said, "This isn't a dire emergency, it's your lawyer. Later?"

"No," I said, "I'll take it."

Sometimes as I answer a phone call, I see myself as if I were a camera watching me.

"Hello, hello," I said, as though saying it twice made the announcement more personal.

"Hello yourself," Thomassy's voice said, "I've got good news." I pictured him sitting, then standing.

"Are you sitting or standing?" I asked.

"Running," he said. "Aren't you interested in the good news?"

"Of course."

"One D.A. down, one to go."

"You see," I said, "even members of the legal establishment can be reasonable."

"Don't be so sure. I had him by the short hairs."

"How affectionate."

"It wasn't affection. I had some information I didn't think the D.A. wanted to see circulated further. When can you come see me?"

"Today?"

"Preferably. I want to bring you up to date."

"I should be finished in an hour, but it's pretty late now."

"I'll wait for you."

Thomassy the Impregnable sounded human. He added, "Do you have a dinner date?"

"I was going to eat my parents'."

He laughed. "Why don't you call and tell them you won't be home."

"At all?"

"For dinner, I meant."

"They're at a worrying stage."

"Tell them you're with me."

"After hours? They'll worry more. Especially my father. He thinks all men think as he does about me."

By the time I arrived Thomassy's secretary had gone. The outer door wasn't locked. I went in quietly. The door to his office was open. I coughed to catch his attention. He looked up from his paperwork, came out bearing a smile I couldn't associate with the man I had first met. He plunked himself down on the couch in the reception area.

"Please don't stand," he said, gesturing at one of the armchairs. "You feeling better?"

"Got lost in work today," I said. "Helped."

"Good." Though I was ten feet away, I felt as if he were examining my face with his hands.

"This is a business meeting?" I asked.

"Yes."

"You're going to tell me what happened with the Assistant D.A."

He shifted his eyes from their examination of me.

"Yes," he said.

And so he told me about his meeting with Lefkowitz. He stood up to act out the part about sweeping past Lefkowitz's secretary, taking the young lawyer for a breathless walk. He had me laughing. Thomassy should have been an actor.

On the phone it sounded like blackmail. He's making light of it.

"I have a feeling," I said, "that you don't usually fill in your clients along the way."

"You're damn right."

"Why are you doing it now?"

He hesitated. We both knew why.

"You're pretty proud of the way you overwhelmed the poor kid," I said.

"He's about your age. He ought to be able to take care of himself. You can, can't you?"

"Yes I can. If I were up against a blackmailer like you, I'd call the cops."

Thomassy laughed, then immediately apologized. "I'm sorry," he said, "I keep forgetting how naive most people are about the police."

"And about life?"

"Right."

"Like they think the ends don't justify the means."

He had picked up a magazine from the table. Now he put it down carefully as if he was restraining himself from slamming it. "All right, Miss Philosophy Major."

"Political science," I said.

"Life is not school. A lawyer's job is to manipulate the skeletons in other people's closets. If a woman has a starving child and steals food, those means justify the ends. I'll bet you're for euthanasia."

"Where warranted."

"Okay, you're justifying killing on grounds that it's merciful. You blink the means to secure the end. Think of yourself in a packed life-boat at sea, filled to capacity, and there's that extra swimmer coming up, wanting to climb aboard. You know the boat won't hold him, do you smash his hands as he tries to hoist himself aboard? What right do you think you have to decide whether someone else is going to live?"

"Maybe one more wouldn't sink the boat."

"Maybe it would. And you'd find out by taking the guy aboard."

"Yes I would."

"Endangering fifteen people maybe. Maybe drowning them."

"I'm civilized."

"To whom, the fifteen already aboard the boat?"

"What would you do?"

"Save the people in the boat."

"By shoving off the fellow trying to get in?"

"If necessary, yes. A bad means to a good end."

"I suppose it'd be easy for you."

A flash of anger reddened his face. He let it pass, then said, "It's a matter of experience. It gets easier to make realistic decisions. Even tough ones."

"You're saying it's easy for you to use a kid like Lefkowitz to twist the D.A.'s—"

"On your account!" he interrupted.

"—after a lifetime of using courtroom tricks."

"I haven't lived a lifetime," he said.

Thomassy was what, fortyish? How few years ago I used to think of that as an age beyond the divide of us and them, over the hill, old people. We move the borderline of acceptability away from us as the years slip. *I haven't lived a lifetime,* says the vital man.

He continued in a different voice, the mentor trying to be patient with a slow pupil.

"I bet your best teachers in school taught by tricks. I can give you half a dozen examples from my own . . ."

"Yes?"

"Tricks. Bad means to good ends."

"Not blackmail."

"You want to be a bishop, says the cardinal, you do as I say. I don't know of any area of life where blackmail doesn't get used. It's just we feel more comfortable being hypocritical about it. Why are you laughing?"

I had to tell him what I'd spent the day doing.

"Well," he said, "nice girl spends day cooking up hypocrisy examples to use hypocritically. Bad boy spends day twisting the D.A.'s arm to prosecute a crime."

"What if I said it offended me to have blackmail used for me?"

"I'd say don't get caught doing anything for the rest of your life and you'll be okay. And drop this case."

The gulf I was getting to know was the one between two lawyers, this man and my father. My father lived by the protections afforded by propriety, forms, the sure knowledge that the right people will continue to pretend. Thomassy was man with the mask off, cutting through the bullshit my father thought of as those things that made people civil. Had the barbarians come? The barbarians have always been here. The Widmers were a permanent minority, dwindling as mobile classes cottoned onto the rules the world was governed by.

"You haven't said a thing in two minutes," said Thomassy.

"I've been thinking."

"That disqualifies you from a lot of occupations."

"You think," I said.

"Yes I do."

"Not enough," I said.

"Some things don't have to be rethought every week. Some people learn from experience."

"I thought you were inviting me to dinner tonight."

"I am."

"The Annapolis?"

"I had in mind a place that makes a very interesting light meal."

"Has it got ambience?"

"You'll see."

He took me to his house.

Dear Father, this is one of those open letters I never send. You recommended him as a lawyer who could shepherd my anger through the courts. Now I'm involved with the shepherd. If you knew, it'd make you angrier than the fact of my rape.

Thomassy's house was on a street with six or seven houses, not too close to each other, each set back a hundred feet from the road, enough space for a lawn with a single specimen tree. In the middle of the block, between two of the houses, there seemed to be a house missing. There was only a gravel driveway going back more than a hundred yards into a wooded area. You had to go most of the way before you saw the small house nestled among the trees. In the middle of civilization, Thomassy had gotten himself a forest home, seclusion in the suburbs, invisible to strangers.

"Like it?" he asked.

"A hermit's keep."

"Let's go inside."

Inside, the place was a surprise, a den of opulence, walnut walls, expensive furniture, lots of places to sit comfortably or lounge, bookshelves floor to ceiling on one long wall, a carpet that looked authentic Turkish, swirls of blue-grey against a background of burnt umber and a subdued maroon. Over the couch, lit by a recessed ceiling light of its own, was a single painting of a long-necked woman.

He was looking at me as I looked at the Modigliani.

"Cost a fortune?" I asked.

"Half. I bought it quite some time ago."

"It's beautiful."

"Yes," he said, then looked away from me.

"This isn't the kind of bachelor pad one expects," I said.

"What did you expect? First, let me get you a drink."

"Anything. With soda."

He busied himself.

"I guess I expected something that looked like a couple of furnished rooms."

"A man without a woman equals poor taste."

"Right."

He handed me the drink. "Well, there's a lot of chauvinism around on both sides," he said. "You are the first female visitor I've had who'd know who painted that picture."

"Maybe you've gotten into the habit of fucking down."

"What does that mean?"

One second I feel I can say anything to Thomassy the way I would to a close girl friend, the next it's like this, trapped on the giving end of something that startled him.

"You choose the women you go with."

"Sure I do."

"And they're like Jane what's-her-name?"

"More or less."

"Less. Maybe you fuck down because it minimizes the whole procedure."

I couldn't tell what he was thinking. He was avoiding looking directly at me. Uncharacteristic. I felt cruel joy. Thomassy was vulnerable. He was a human being, just like the rest of us.

The dinner he prepared was an avocado with a choice of lemon or vinaigrette, a Basque omelet that may have been the best omelet of any kind I had ever had, an endive salad made with walnut oil and an unlabeled vinegar he said he bought privately. The coffee had a touch of chocolate and was served with whipped cream.

We ate in the short leg of the L that connected the living room and the kitchen. In the corner where the walls met there was an arrangement of plants, a three-foot dracaena in a tub on the floor, and three or four hanging pots with ivies and ferns. In the center of the long wall hung a large painting, perhaps four feet wide, of a grain field in a high wind, done with thousands of small strokes. It was very close to abstraction, yet one knew it was a field ready for harvest and that the velocity of the wind was a danger to the high stalks.

"Who?" I asked.

"Hyde Solomon."

"A newcomer?"

"No. He started making it in the fifties I guess. He's got bad eyes. Very nearly blind."

"He's got good eyes," I said.

"What's left of them. I was introduced to him at an opening after I bought that. He's a tall man, stammers, painfully shy, knows his work is good that's all. In one respect I envy him."

I tried to guess, unsuccessfully.

"When he's finished, some of his work, maybe just a few, will survive. Nothing I do survives. A lawyer is a member of the performing arts, though not even movies are taken to preserve the act."

He was right, of course. Cocksure success, master of his profession, winner, finds life wanting. Wanting posterity. Denied Dr. Koch, denied doctors, lawyers, teachers, except for the innovating genius, the legend. Art, if it survives, lingers. The rest of us head for the dustbin. I'm surprised artists aren't hated more by the transients.

"I'm a salesman," he said. "I sell cases to juries. Or to punk D.A.s. Get that look off your face," he said to me, "I'm not fishing for sympathy. It's just that sometimes I wish I made something that might last. I cook up an act that vanishes as fast as this meal."

"It was very good." I touched my napkin to my lips.

"You expected a TV dinner."

"Sort of."

"You're a treasury of prejudices," he said.

"So it seems."

"Attractively packaged."

"Thank you," I said.

"With a good mind."

"That surprises me," I said.

"That you have a good mind?"

"That you think I do. I know I have."

"I know you know you have."

"Two modest folks," I said. "I thought opposites attract."

At ten o'clock George snapped on the TV for the news.

"Good news or bad?" I asked.

"Always bad," he said. "People watch to be sure others are worse off."

"Why watch?"

Out of habit, I'd run the sink water and started cleaning off the few dinner dishes.

"I'm not," he said.

I turned around. He was watching me. Suddenly he was on his feet. "I'll do those," he said.

He came up behind me. The front of his body was touching the back of mine. I felt his lips on the lobe of my right ear, just for a second.

"It's all right," I said. "A woman doesn't want to be admired just for her mind."

He put his arms around me and took the dish I was rinsing carefully out of my hands and put it aside.

"I'll do those later," he said.

"I should be going soon."

He turned me toward him.

"My hands are wet," I said.

He took my head in both his hands and touched his lips to mine, a skim for a split second.

I kept my wet hands wide apart as he kissed me again, this time mouth to mouth.

I broke away. "My hands are wet," I said, breathless.

"I don't care."

And then I put my wet hands around him as our mouths met. I could feel his body's warmth and my own heart pound. And suddenly he was kissing the side of my neck, then below and behind my ear, I could feel his tongue flicker, and then our mouths were together again until, to breathe, I pulled away, feeling the blood in my face, and I was quickly drying my hands on the dish towel when he pulled me into his arms again and I knew we both knew it was no use fighting it any more and we were holding each other tightly and desperately, and then we were moving each other to the couch, not wanting to let go, but we had to, to open the couch, and then it was kissing again, and clothes coming off, his and mine, and we were lying clasped, kissing lips, faces, shoulders, then holding on, sealed against each other, until he raised his head and realized there were tears in my eyes and his bewildered look was begging for an explanation.

I could hear the thud of my heart.

"What's the matter?" he whispered.

I couldn't find my voice.

"Tell me," he said.

It was like the anxiety attacks I would get in the middle of the night when insomnia stole my sleeping hours, a fear that my heart would burst from the thudding.

"It's like driving the first time after an accident," I said.

We lay side by side for a while. I tried not to think of Koslak. The harder I tried, the more I thought of it, detail by detail.

"I want to get drunk," I said.

"I wouldn't recommend it. Do you get drunk often?"

"No. Not in ten years."

When I was in my last year in high school, I had gone on a triple date, the jocks enjoying their own company. We girls felt dragged along, I wanted to leave, I didn't want to be a spoilsport, I drank too much of whatever we were all drinking, and I was sick all over the ladies' room and wretched all night and the day afterwards.

"I am not a drinker," I said.

George smiled. "I know that."

He got up, naked and unashamed, and went somewhere, returning with two elegant glasses filled halfway with something I didn't recognize.

"Madeira," he said. "Rainwater." He took a sip. "Magic," he said, and handed me my glass. "It's a one-drink drink. Safe."

I looked at the glass skeptically.

"It's okay," he said. "Try it."

I took a sip.

"Lovely," I said, licking it from my lips.

"Don't do that," he said.

"What?" I took another sip. He leaned over and licked my lower lip. No one had ever done that. He slid onto the bed, holding his glass upright as if it were a gyroscope. Then he tipped it slightly and let a few drops splash onto my breasts.

"Don't move," he said, and gave me his glass to hold. There I was, helplessly holding one glass in each hand, unable to move, and he licked the Madeira from each breast and from the valley between.

He borrowed his glass back, tipped it lower down, then handed it back, my handcuff. I looked at the two glasses, at the ceiling, then at the soft hair of his head as he licked the drops of Madeira from below my navel and from the inside of my thighs. I concentrated on the two glasses, trying not to think of the tongue that was now moving in a way that I felt down the stems of my legs and upwards to my chest, as my breathing gasped again and again until I felt a sudden thick shudder of release, eros flooding, I clasped his head with my thighs like a vise, hoping I wasn't hurting him, and then he was suddenly alongside me, taking the glasses away, putting them on the floor, and clasping me with the full length of his body as the waves slowly waned and I was at peace.

"Was the Madeira good?" I asked.

"Delicious," he said.

I turned my attentions to him, hoping I could make love to him with half the skill he had, and when we both seemed ready for our first joining, I turned him over onto me, and saw the surprise in his eyes as he was suddenly, terribly impotent.

"It's because I was raped," I said.

"No, no," he said. "I swear. It makes no difference."

"Then what is it?"

"I don't know."

I felt at fault and desperate. I tried to arouse him in every way I remembered. The harder I tried, the less his response. It was no use. Finally, I collapsed back in defeat.

I took his offer of a lit cigarette.

"I thought you have a lot of women," I said.

"I have had."

"This happen often?"

"Not for years."

"Why single me out?" Then quickly, "I didn't mean it to sound that way." I kissed him, but he was not there to receive it.

Finally he said, "We can come up with a lot of suppositions, but we'd never know if we were right, so let's not."

"Next time," I said.

"We don't know," he said.

We must have both slept for a bit. At least I did. When I opened my eyes, he was propped up against two pillows, staring into space.

He had seemed to me a man who could do anything.

NINETEEN

Thomassy

A professional is someone you can count on to deliver. Up in Oswego you don't get to see much in the way of real baseball. When I was growing up, we had radio not television, and baseball is something you have to see. So when I finally emigrated south to the suburbs of New York City, I made up for all those years in Oswego by going to Yankee Stadium two, three times a month. Box seats weren't expensive, and you could bloat yourself and a woman on hot dogs and beer without going broke.

One day—I think the Yanks were up against Minnesota, but I wouldn't swear to it—we sat next to a yeller. You know, one of those guys who screams encouragement and instructions to the side he's rooting for and abuse at the other players and the umpires. The yeller was popping up and down in his seat, "Show 'em, Joe," "We need a hit," "You're blind as a bat!" It was the rookie year of a young slugger who'd just come up from the minors. The Yanks had used him as a pinch hitter and on account of somebody or other's injury this particular game was the first that he was on the starting lineup, in fifth place. The first two batters struck out and then one of those things happened, the third popped one up to center field, an easy one, but the sun must have blinded the center fielder one crucial second because he reached for the ball like a blind man. It actually hit leather, but he couldn't hold on to it, and so with twenty or thirty thousand people watching him, he chased the ball, got it, bobbled it, and by the time he threw it, it had to go to short because the runner was on second. The yeller went crazy, popped a paper bag, screamed as if he'd been knifed. The Yanks had a man on with two out.

For a minute, I thought they were going to walk the fourth batter, which didn't make sense, but it was just the Minnesota pitcher being nervous. The third pitch went right down the middle, no curve, no chance at the corners, and the batter, served up this piece of insurance, put his back and shoulders into his swing and clouted a line drive past the infield that put himself on second and the runner on third. I thought I'd go deaf before the yeller lost his voice.

My heart went out to the rookie as he stepped up to the plate. Men on second and third, two away. He had yet to hit his first home run in the majors. A single would do it. I felt myself inside his head, eyeing the ball as it came in. It cut the outside corner low for a called strike. You could feel the tension in the park. The kid sort of backed out of the batter's box, calling time, and played around with the bat, glanced toward the Yankee dugout as if he expected a miracle in the form of instruction, blew on his left hand, then his right, then stepped back into the box and took his stance.

The second pitch was a change of pace, and the rookie watched it as if he were just hoping it wouldn't cross the plate, which it did for a second called strike. The yeller leaned into my ear and said to me, "That fucker better hit that ball."

The third pitch was wild and I could feel the rookie's relief as the catcher collected it quickly and the runners returned to their bases. I wanted that rookie to hit that ball more than I had wanted anything ever at a ball game.

The fourth pitch was a fast ball, perfect for a slugger, and he stepped into it, swung. Instead of the crack of bat against a ball headed for the outfield, the sound was barely audible, the ball hitting the bat near the handle, rolling just in front of the plate, a perfect bunt—who needed it?—and the catcher was on top of it at once. The rookie, like a trooper, ran like hell for first. The catcher threw the ball to first with disdain, and the side was retired. What an ignominious moment for the rookie! The yeller was joined by half the ball park crying its derision.

"Too bad," I said to no one in particular.

The yeller was trying to say something to me in the midst of the bedlam. There had to be a reason for an important failure, and the yeller had seized on mankind's oldest nightmare. *He couldn't get it up* was what he was saying.

I knew why I remembered that incident. With two cases coming to trial, I wished I had a law partner I could pass at least one of them to, or that I had a goddamn associate I could rely on for help. My head was not with either trial. It was remembering the baseball game and the yeller's conclusion. It was remembering Francine and the night of Thomassy's floppola.

I tried to get the judge to give me a week's postponement on the Connolly case. When things are bad, they usually get worse. Judge Bracton, who had never refused me before, refused me now the way my own organ had refused me.

Connolly was charged with holding up a gas station at gunpoint. He denied it. He had a record. They picked him up, put him in a lineup, and Wilson, the gas station operator, identified him. Fortunately I had been able to question two of the detectives who had been present at the lineup. I studied up on Wilson. I was ready to pulverize him on cross-examination. Maybe because he was a gas station owner like Koslak. Maybe because Koslak had gotten into Francine and I couldn't.

It was a short trial. The D.A. put Wilson on the stand and had him recite the facts of the robbery, the usual stuff. He had closed up, switched on the night light, locked the door, was getting into his own car when a guy comes out of the shadows, puts something hard in his ribs, and says "Gimme the paper bag." I don't know why gas station owners put their day's cash in paper bags, but a lot of them do.

To elicit sympathy for Wilson, the D.A. tried to get in testimony from him to the effect that he had been robbed twice before in the same year, but I objected, and the objection was sustained. Then I had my go at him.

"Mr. Wilson," I asked, "how tall are you?"

Up popped the D.A. muttering "irrelevant" and Judge Bracton told him to sit down. I said I would show it was a material line of questioning.

Wilson said he was six feet tall.

"Is that the height given on your driver's license?"

"Yes, it is."

"Mr. Wilson," I said, my eyes checking the judge to make sure he'd go along, "would you mind stepping off the stand and coming over here." I motioned him over to where I'd had a doctor's scale brought in, the kind that has an L-shaped measuring rod for height, too. Wilson was reluctant. He looked at the D.A., the D.A. looked at the judge, the judge nodded. Wilson stepped on the scale as if it was covered with broken glass and he had bare feet. I lowered the measuring rod till it brushed his skull.

"According to this," I said, "you're five feet ten inches. Does that mean your license application was false?"

Well, there was a flurry at the bench, but I had gotten my point across.

"Mr. Wilson," I said when he had returned to the stand, "you testified that the person who robbed you came out of the shadows near where your car was parked. Could you tell whether the robber had a moustache?"

"He didn't have no moustache."

"I see. Was he close enough for you to tell whether he was clean shaven, whether he had shaved that day or had a few days' growth?"

"I didn't notice that close."

"Could you tell if he had pimples or not?"

The judge had to quiet a titter among the spectators.

"I don't know. I didn't notice."

"What did you notice?"

"You know, a general impression of what he looked like."

"In the dark?" I shot a disbelieving look at the spectators. "Did you notice his height?"

"He was the same height as me."

"Is that six feet or five feet ten?"

I had gone for the laugh and gotten it.

"Mr. Wilson," I continued, "when you were taken to the lineup, how many men were in it?"

"Seven or eight."

"You sure it was seven or eight?"

Wilson was getting nervous. Actually, there were six people in the lineup, but I was saving that piece of information.

"Mr. Wilson, is it true that when you were asked if you saw the man who robbed you in the lineup, you said and I quote 'It was either him or him' and when a second later you learned that one of the hims was a police officer you settled for the other one, namely the defendant?"

Wilson looked at the D.A.

The judge told him to answer.

"That's the way it was," he said.

"No more questions."

They don't teach it to you in law school, but you'd damn well better latch on quick to the Rules of Human Tolerance. If someone exaggerates his height by a quarter or half an inch, people think what the hell. But two inches, that's more than vanity, it's perverse. And if you say you recognize somebody, you have to notice not just the general configuration of a face, but some specific details.

My summation was brief. Wilson was held up in relative darkness, he hadn't really gotten a good look at the robber. In the station house, he hadn't been sure, he had guessed. You don't guess when people are accused of serious crimes. Wilson filled out a license application not erroneously, he had been willfully false. He was an unreliable witness, and there were no other witnesses. Connolly had been picked up not because there was anything linking him to this crime but because he'd been in trouble in the past. When arrested he had no paper bag full of money, no gun. I didn't blame the arresting officer for his zeal, I just pointed out that you can't go picking up suspects willy-nilly on the street. I said there were more reasonable doubts in this case than there were hard facts, the only hard fact was the one we stipulated, that Wilson had been robbed and hadn't merely hidden it somewhere to collect on the insurance. The jury was back in fifteen minutes with a not guilty verdict, which was no surprise to me or Wilson or the D.A. Only Connolly breathed a sigh of relief, probably because he did it.

At least I could still get it up in the courtroom.

I was standing at the urinal shaking the last drops out and thinking *You bastard, you let me down, you ought to be cut off,* when a voice from the next urinal says to me, "That was an easy one."

"Yeah," I said to the D.A., "that was an easy one."

Widmer bills his clients. You think I'd collect from guys like Connolly if I billed them?

"I'm very grateful to you," he said when I came out of the john.

His wife, a mouse he probably beat up on regularly, said, "I can't tell you how grateful we all are, Mr. Thomassy. It would be awful for the children if Charles went to jail again."

Charles. The formality was for my sake.

"What do I owe you?" he asked.

Your freedom, you jerk.

"The retainer covered all but five hundred," I said. The five thousand retainer was intended to cover all of it in case he got socked away. The five hundred extra was my tip for getting him off.

"I have it right here," he said. He peeled off ten fifties. I wondered if it was gas station money.

"You shouldn't carry that much cash with you," I said. "You might get robbed."

His wife laughed, but he shut her up with one look.

"Connolly," I said, motioning him away so his wife wouldn't hear. "You better stick to your job, period. Know what I mean?"

He nodded.

"I won't take you on for another armed robbery, understand."

"You won't have to. I'm staying clean. You were terrific."

That's my consolation. The threat of not defending him again might be more effective than any jail term. He'd have to make an honest living. Like me.

I wasn't used to self-hatred. I had my pecker to blame.

Can you imagine yourself famished, looking at a table laden with ripe fruit, and you can't get your mouth to work. I mean you actually bring a peach up to your mouth and it won't open, won't move, won't cooperate. You can't eat a peach intravenously, you need your mouth. I mean there's no other part of the body that behaves like a pecker with a mind of its own, an uncooperative, stubborn, unpersuadable prick. What is it telling me?

COMMENT BY FRANCINE WIDMER

In high school and college I thought the trouble with men was that they were an army of erect penises marching around all day long looking for a home. You danced with a fellow and soon there was that stiffening coming between you and the idiot would look at you with a kind of how-can-I-help-it expression. They perform on signal like jumping dogs, touch it with a hand and it curves up like a banana head ready to take a bow. But when you need one, when you want one, not for its own sake but as the best last step in bringing you together with someone you want to be together with, and what do you get, a pathetic lump of overcooked pasta looking like it's ready to fall off its owner's body.

Now I appreciate the great advantage of a really skilled performance, the faked orgasm done so perfectly even you begin to believe it was more than an act. God was extra good to women, if it isn't working, you don't have to advertise failure, you just make believe, hypocrisy to the rescue, like in every other avenue of life a bit of fraud will see you through. I remember once I was faking it, and suddenly the real thing caught me by surprise. Poor men, an inborn lie detector hanging off each of them, ready to rat. To be betrayed by a friend is terrible, but to be betrayed by the organ you feel most protective about, treason!

The truth is: some part of him doesn't want me. Not *that* part of him, some other part. That part is just the message carrier. Jane yes. Rosemary yes. Edna yes. Francine no.

❁

I stared at the telephone. Then I dialed Jane.
"Hello, stranger," she said.
"Don't be coy, Jane. It's only been a few days."
"You left me something to think about."
"Your husband on the road tonight?"
"Wait, I'll ask him."
"Don't be stu- . . ." I heard her laughing.
Then she said, "What time?"
"Seven all right?"
"See you at seven."

It was damn near seven-thirty when I got to Jane's. Oh I had left my office on time all right, it's just that I found every nondirect street in that part of the county to keep me from getting there. I built up a head of steam that should have warned me to call her and call it off.
"Sorry, I'm late," I said.

She made drinks. Not a word.

"I'm sorry about the way that other evening worked out," I said.

"Did you see her again?"

"Yes."

"How did it work out?"

"Well, as a matter of fact not too good."

"Oh?"

"Would you believe old Thomassy just couldn't get it up?"

She put her drink down.

"You never had that kind of trouble with me."

"No I haven't."

"And you're here to try it out again to see if it's a permanent malfunction or just the other broad who puts you off."

I like directness in women only to a degree.

Affecting calm, I said in my best judicial voice, "Now Jane, your relationship, I mean yours with me, preceded my knowing the other lady by—"

"Francine, in case you've forgotten her name."

"You sound angry."

"Me? Angry?"

"Well, bitter?"

"Me? Bitter? I've just been waiting here for my favorite lawyer, knowing he would turn up sooner or later for a quick bang. I just hadn't expected it to be a litmus paper test to find if the fire'd gone out."

"You keeping talking that way," I said, "and it will stay out."

"That'd be an interesting revenge. For me. And for several others."

"I thought you liked my company."

"I did. But I felt like a Martian when that other woman was here. You had special all over your face. You falling in love, George, at your age?"

"Don't be silly."

"If falling in love is silly, I'm not silly. I haven't been in love in twenty-two years. It doesn't interfere."

"Jane, you're a smart woman."

"I thought I was a good lay."

"A good lay and a smart woman. Can I move over to where you are?"

"You never asked for permission before. That's a bad sign."

TWENTY

Koch

She is back, back, back, twice a week Francine will be coming after work, a reunion, I welcome her, how well she appears (Aphrodite, Venus, Helen!) wafting into my study, at a gesture from me lying down, smoothing her skirt over her mound as if to level it into insignificance, but I know it is there, fur over flesh over bone guarding the inviolate—violated—lips over lips. I sit behind her head where I can steal with my eyes the configuration of her unbound breasts as she lies there spilling words from which I must pluck the clues to feed back to her so that she will understand herself. How will she understand that I am in violation of everything except honesty in my feelings for her?

Talk.

I will listen.

Of course I want her to talk about me, and if not, about herself. But how many women over the years have lain on that couch and talked to the air about how their lovers talk to them about their wives, and the men, caught in the vortex of two women, who cannot keep from telling each about the other under the disguise of news or gossip. And now what does Francine tell me, who lusts to hear almost anything else except what she now says.

Thomassy, she says, is not particularly good looking, not in the way a Robert Redford or a Paul Newman seems attractive to so many women, he has a face that is his, she says, dark without the sun, intent features focusing all business one moment, laughing the next, it is his vitality, his command, he has the law in his hands because he understands how minds work!

The mind, I want to interrupt her, is my province, not Thomassy's!

Other men, she says, drift like boys drift.

Perhaps Thomassy drifts, I suggest. If he is such a great courtroom performer, such a skilled people-manipulator, should he not be on a bigger stage, fighting front-page cases, making a fortune like other lawyers?

He is not interested in publicity, she says. She is giving him a medal. An award. The award is herself.

Has she thought about the discrepancy in their backgrounds?

Yes, she says, he's not like Bill, not like her father and her father's friends, isn't it wonderful?

Has she thought about the difference in their ages? I ask.

Yes, it would be better if there were not so many years between.

Why does she think so?

Because he will die too soon.

Can you understand how I am near to going out of my mind listening to my sweet Francine in love?

I must take risks.

Why did you return to therapy? I ask.

He was impotent with me, she says.

I am ready to scream *Look at me behind you a man of sixty with a thick bulge in his pants from watching and wanting you, there is no justice in this world!*

I only speak the last words: "no justice in this world."

That, she says, is why Thomassy attracts her so, he has long ago recognized there is no justice in the justice system, and he fills the void with his manipulative skills. He is not like the hypocrites she works with, she says, or the people in Washington, Paris, London, Moscow, Peking, in the throne rooms and in the streets, there isn't a shred of false idealism left in his bones.

Why does he not fill me? she says.

I am silent.

Why is a man sometimes impotent?

I am silent.

It can't be guilt, he has no obligation to any other. It can't be shame, he has been a lover of others for decades, women who come and go.

Perhaps, I say, he thinks you won't go.

Now she is silent.

Perhaps, I say, he is afraid of permanence.

I don't want to be a quick fuck, she says angrily.

No one wants to be, I say. If you admire realism so much, why are you not a realist? Perhaps you threaten him.

With what? she says, up on an elbow, turning to face me. I motion her back to a lying position. Am I protecting the anguish on my own face?

With what am I threatening him? she repeats.

With love.

We are both silent. Then I say, love disarms. It is impervious to reason and to control. If both love, there is nothing to win.

The aim of Thomassy's existence, I say, is to win. Just as mine is to cure. You cannot always win.

You cannot always cure, she says.

Ah, I say, but in love something happens. Do you know the form of glue that is called epoxy, made of two substances which when melded become another? The process is called curing. Love always cures, changes from heart-thumping, irrational, wild cacophony to something different, also called love, a peace with each other.

That is beautiful, she says.

I have had a lifetime to think about it, I say. Then I add: epoxy, when cured, is hard. In all the years of my practice I have never heard of a case of impotence that did not change if circumstances changed enough. Sometimes merely habit is enough.

She is quiet. I watch her body breathe. I have turned her over to my rival not because I am a good man but because I am a weak man, accustomed to helping others be strong. It is time to go, I tell her. The hour is up. I will see you Thursday.

She gets up, brushes down her skirt over her hips as if I am invisible, then leaves, a flurry of hips and buttocks and legs through the door, going to find Thomassy, pushed by me.

TWENTY-ONE

Francine

Koch is a saint. I left without saying goodbye. I had to get to a phone.

The West Side streets were full of lolling people who watched me as if I were hurrying too fast. One of four stoop poker players whistled. Steeled, I headed for my car, key in hand, saw the street-corner phone booth empty, searched through my bag for a dime, called. Answering service. Of course, it was after hours! I fussed through the bag for the pack of matches on which I had scribbled his home phone, found a second dime, dialed. It took him a long time to answer.

"It's me, Francine," I said.

"What's up?"

You could kill a man who talked that way.

"Can I come on up?"

"I don't think so."

"Look," I said, "it was just the first time."

Then I heard her voice in the background saying purposely loud enough for me to hear, "Who is it, George?"

What else could I do but hang up?

Home, I went through charades of conversation with my parents, what did you do today?, I didn't pay attention to what I did today, what did *you* do today?

"You seem distraught, dear."

You bet your ass I'm distraught. I'm going to steal your gun and keep it loaded on a table facing my door, and if Koslak or the super gets through the door, I'm going to shoot them where the guy said I should kick them.

"How is Mr. Thomassy doing with your case?"

"I'm going to fire him," I said.

My father's face adjusted itself to a totally unexpected piece of news. "We should discuss this," he said.

Now father, under the same set of circumstances in your pied-à-terre—*you do have one, don't you?—would you have been flaccid with me, you wouldn't find incest an inhibition, it'd be an encouragement, after all, you've had all these years to get used to the idea, haven't you?*

"I think we should discuss this," he repeated.

"By all means."

"Do you find him unsatisfactory in the way he is handling the case?"

No, idiot, I find him unsatisfactory in the way he is handling me.

"I don't want to pursue the case."

"What caused your change of heart?"

Father, you could choose your expressions better.

"It is pointless to force the District Attorney to prosecute a case the government doesn't want to prosecute."

"That's why you have Thomassy."

I don't have Thomassy. One strike and he went fishing with what's-her-name.

"You'd be appalled at the methods he uses."

"I wouldn't be appalled. I just prefer that others use them."

Fastidious. Say, would you mind rubbing out a few people for me over the weekend? Usual rate? Father, would you please go to sleep so I can find the gun I need. Please?

"You don't seem inclined to talk this evening. Don't do anything precipitous. We'll talk about it again. I'm going up to bed."

I sat at the desk in my room, writing the letter.

Dear Mr. Thomassy, I appreciate everything you've tried to do to me, I mean everything you've tried to do for me, but I see no point in pursuing the matter. Koslak is an admitted danger, but I've got good news I forgot to tell you in the rush of things.

My boss is due for reassignment momentarily, Paris probably, and I don't see how I could resist the opportunity. Please send me your bill for services rendered, insofar as they were rendered, or were attempted to be rendered. I am letting you go. Yours sincerely, Francine Widmer.

In the morning I put that letter in a book on the top shelf where I used to hide things from the cleaning woman. The letter I sent was shorter.

Dear George, I can see that by pursuing this case I could turn myself into an injustice collector. If the government doesn't want to deal with rape on its own initiative, I don't want to be the one to force it to. It's not just the expense. It could make me one-tracked, single-minded, a crank. As to Harry Koslak, don't worry. I'll be moving out of the apartment. The landlord will have to find me. Please send me your bill, which I'll pay promptly. With best wishes, Francine.

I kept a carbon of the letter, which I reread the next morning. It seemed too quick and cold. Thomassy had gone out of his way for me. I needed to pick up the phone.

"This is Francine Widmer," I told his secretary. "Did he get my letter?"

"Not yesterday."

"I only mailed it yesterday."

"There was nothing this morning."

"Well, maybe that's good. Can I talk to him, please?"

"He had a first-thing appointment with Mr. Cunham this morning. About your case, in fact."

"Oh God."

"What's the matter?"

"There's been a development."

"If it's important, I could try to reach him at Mr. Cunham's office, though he dislikes being disturbed during outside appointments. Shall I—I see it's after ten. He's probably in with Mr. Cunham already. Shall I try just in case? I'll put you on hold."

When she came back on she said, "He's already in with him. I could leave a message with Mr. Cunham's secretary."

Tell him he's fired.

"Is Mr. Cunham's office in the county courthouse in White Plains?"

"Miss Widmer?"

"Yes."

"I wouldn't do that if I were you."

"You're not me."

TWENTY-TWO

Thomassy

Like some doctors and dentists, Cunham measures his worth by the number of people wasting life in his outer office, and so I was surprised to find the waiting room empty. His secretary buzzed him, and I was on my way in. Second surprise. He got up from behind his desk to pump my hand as if I was really welcome.

Gary Cunham was big, easily six-six, played right guard for Army, still had a handsome baby face when he became the youngest bird colonel judge advocate in Vietnam. They say he tried cases wholesale, sent kids to the stockade on punk evidence, got a taste for power, which, as anyone who has had both can testify, tastes better than money. Baby Face Cunham, nearly bald now, was the most famous D.A. Westchester ever had, all ready for lift-off into big league politics. His ruddy cheeks inflated and deflated like a fish when he talked. I wondered what Cunham looked like when he was getting laid. His wife must be blind. Maybe she only lets him in from behind so she can look at the pillow instead.

"You look well, George," Cunham said.

That's his standard opener. Everybody likes to be told they look well.

"I'll try one of your cigars." I pointed to the box on his desk.

He nodded. I took one.

"Didn't know you smoked cigars, George."

"Only defensively." I gestured at the haze of blue-grey smoke.

He sat back down into his brown leather high-backed chair. West Point is good for the spine. Gary looked as straight-backed sitting as standing.

"What brings you here?"

The Armenian massacres. I would have loved to say it out loud. He wasn't waiting for an answer.

"What's this business about a clipping, George?"

"Oh that's nothing important, Gary."

"What can I do for you?"

"I assume you were briefed?"

"Sure, sure," he said, trying to minimize the process. I'd have bet he spent some sweaty minutes over whatever Lefkowitz said to him.

"You know the girl's father? Ned Widmer?"

"Met him. Republican dinners, that sort of thing."

"I'd like to see that case get before the Grand Jury. I'd appreciate it real well if it could happen fast. That maniac is still a threat to her."

"Alleged maniac," said Cunham, making a laugh.

"This county is not exactly known for deliberate speed," I said.

"Except on the thruway."

"Gary, if this were attempted murder one, you wouldn't make jokes. It's rape one, and the attempt succeeded. And there was a second attempt by the same party."

"Alleged rape," he said. "No witnesses. No objectively verifiables. Where'd you get that expression rape one anyway?"

"It was premeditated."

"That's got to be proven. In fact, the act itself has to be proven."

"Gary, I think I can teach whoever you assign to take this before the jury how to convince somebody Koslak didn't effect his entrance to the woman's apartment to borrow a cup of sugar."

"Oh? You're going to prove he had enough sugar at home?"

I mustered zero pitch in my voice. "I think the man's wife would make a very interesting witness."

"Now George, you know the man's wife can't be called."

"Says who? If Koslak had admitted to his wife that he raped Widmer that'd be privileged, but do you think he has? If Koslak alluded to it with a third party present, even if the third party was real friendly, the privilege is gone. Mrs. Koslak wasn't an accomplice, was she? She can't take the fifth amendment, can she? What she can do is get her ass on the witness stand and tell us, under oath, whether she had sugar in the house or not when her husband wandered downstairs for a cupful. If she had, and I'll bet you she had, then his empty cup did not lead to Widmer enticing him but his going down there on a needless errand because he had something else in mind, follow?"

"You've done a lot of homework, George. Do you know what this case could cost the county?"

"About your annual salary?"

"I don't make that much, George."

"I'm not the IRS. I live in this county."

"Are you implying—"

"Nothing," I cut him off. "You wouldn't think twice about the expense if it were murder one."

"Rape isn't murder."

The Armenian women, wailing, killed themselves rather than let their living bodies be used. "Gary," I said, "I'm sure you knew this once, but let me remind you. Under Saxon law, rape was more serious than murder. A man with property needed a son. Once the blood line ran out, his property would revert to the crown. In desperation, a husband would order a manservant to rape his wife to beget an heir. Rape could become an act against the crown. It was only when the Normans took over the judicial system that rape became a kind of property crime. All right, let's think of it that way, a form of armed robbery. You give the robber or you get it. Like that better, Gary? I can't see you turning away from a juicy armed robbery because of the cost."

"George, you're going to an awful lot of trouble lecturing me. Why are you pushing this case?"

"My client . . ." I stopped when I saw the expression on his face. "If you're insinuating something, Gary, spill it."

"You're not a virgin, George. You've had a lot of ass in this county over the years. Don't ask us to pay for this one."

"Okay," I said, taking the clipping out of my wallet. "No gloves." I put it on the desk in front of him.

He looked at it for about two seconds, and said, "So what? Some college paper, who cares?"

"You do. You wouldn't have seen me unless you did."

"What'd you pay to get the clipping?"

"Two hundred dollars."

"You can buy a lot of ass for two hundred."

I stood up. "Gary, I have never paid for ass in my life. And if I did, it wouldn't be relevant. This was my client's money."

"You didn't have to show it to Lefkowitz."

"If I hadn't, I might not have gotten to see you quickly. He's not going to broadcast it unless you give him cause."

"You've put me in a very awkward posture, George. Now I've got two potential blackmailers on my hands. I'll have to coddle him as well as you. Why don't you sit down?"

I sat and said, "You've been privy to more plea bargaining than any other lawyer in this county. You're too smart to need a lecture from me. The state's got something on you and you plead guilty to something less than you might get in court. Isn't that blackmail? No, it's the essence of our system, if I remember your Lincoln's Birthday speech correctly. Our justice system would be swamped if it wasn't for plea bargaining. Well, Gary, I'm suggesting you bargain. Put the case in front of the Grand Jury. If they don't move it, you've lost nothing. And you've gained a lot."

"The Gannett papers wouldn't print rubbish like that!"

"It's local news."

"My son's in Buffalo. That clip's from a student newspaper."

"You're local news. You and anything about you or your family. You think I couldn't get one reporter on one Gannett paper to be tempted to get behind something a little bit bigger than the last accident on Route 9A?"

"You're a bastard, George."

"I'm a good lawyer. Good for my clients. You know any clients who want to lose?"

"Sometime, somewhere along the line, George, you're going to make a big mistake. I'll be waiting for it."

"I'll work on that assumption."

"You know I've got a lot of friends in a lot of places."

"Don't try getting affidavits from all of them. I'll tell you something, Gary. I've got one friend who's worth all of yours rolled in one because he's one hundred percent dependable."

"Who?"

"Me." I'd hardly taken two puffs on the cigar. I put it down on his ashtray. "You might save that for the next guy who's in here."

"Are you leaving?"

"Soon as I hear that you're assigning this case. Well?"

I could see him swallow. He didn't say a word. Just nodded.

"Thanks," I said.

I turned my back and walked from the room. I figured he'd be thinking how soon he could get his hooks into me.

Outside, his secretary said, "Oh Mr. Thomassy, there's a message from your office."

"Never mind the message," said Francine, coming through the outer door. "I want to talk to you."

She stopped ten feet away. Cunham's secretary stared at the arena between us. Then the inner door opened and six-foot-six was standing there, obviously expecting me to be gone. Then he saw Francine.

"Is that the girl, George?" he asked. "I'd like to meet her."

As they were shaking hands I said, "Girls of twenty-seven are called women today, Gary."

TWENTY-THREE

Francine

Phrases out of 1940s movies. We laugh at all those women who used to say, "I want a tall man" or "I want a guy that's handsome." What difference does it make how *tall* a man is? A man can be too short, a midget whose size would be in the forefront of your mind, you'd be making too much of it. Well, what about the man who's just a bit on the short side, say five feet two, if he were intelligent, attractive, a go-getter, and sensitive? At the same time, do you want somebody seven feet tall, you couldn't help feeling you were always looking up, that compared to other men, he was standing on something, an elongation of mankind, a freak? You see, it gets it down to something in between. You want a man to be not too short and not too tall because you don't want to be concerned about his tallness.

Yet when I saw Gary Cunham looming up there, I have to admit I was impressed by his tallness. What good is common sense if you react that way?

"I am the rapee," I said, shaking his hand.

I caught a reproving glance from Thomassy.

Cunham was one of those men who extend a finger or two along your wrist when they shake your hand. Nobody ever got their face slapped for it. *Does it feel good?*

"You'd be a temptation to anybody," he said. Then he added, "That's a compliment."

"I don't mind compliments," I said. "I don't want my apartment or my body trespassed on."

"I thought young people made light of body contact between strangers," he said.

"Well," I said, taking Thomassy and Cunham as a joint audience, "why don't we take rape off the books. For people under thirty. And over twelve."

"Rape is a serious crime, of course," said Cunham, his height shrinking with every syllable. "It is also—as I'm sure your counsel has explained—the most amorphous of all crimes, the most difficult to pin down with substantiated evidence."

Thomassy unchecked his tongue. "Well, we've solved all that for the future, Gary. Miss Widmer and I have patented a miniaturized version of the cameras in banks that start clicking when a robbery's in progress. It's smaller than a Minox, and you wear it around your neck on a chain. When rape is threatened, a touch of the hand over the heart starts its silent clicking, recording the attacker and the attack. When it's over, you rush to the hospital, get swabbed, and rush to a film lab and get it developed. Open and shut cases. Very little for us lawyers to do except indict and convict."

Cunham laughed. "A great invention, George. What do we do in the meantime?"

"We indict by the usual procedures, which I'm glad you've agreed to do. If the Grand Jury is unresponsive, I guess Miss Widmer'll just have to wear the camera next time the assailant comes around—he's been twice—and record the action."

"Sounds like entrapment."

"Where there's a will, there's a way," said Thomassy. "Come, Miss Widmer, Mr. Cunham runs a busy office."

"I'm very glad to have met you, Miss Widmer. I trust we'll be seeing you again."

And again the bastard shook my hand, his fingers extended along my wrist. A bit less sophisticated and he'd have tickled my palm.

Outside on the street, I turned on Thomassy and said, "What that friend of yours wants is easy cases."

"Right."

"What he wants is the rape of a forty-year-old Roman Catholic lady who goes to church every day and who was examined by a Roman Catholic physician the day before who would testify that she had her hymen intact. It makes me furious. Don't try to pacify me. What I would have liked to do in there is pull a gun on your friend and make him open his fly and pull his thing out."

"Using force."

"You're damn right. The only way you can identify with someone who gets raped is to feel it happening to you."

"Not true. Look, do you want to win or do you want to prove something?"

"Both," I said, "both, damn it!"

"I've watched plenty of professional civil liberties lawyers at work, and I'll tell you something. They're so intent on proving something they sometimes forget their clients want to win. I'm not a politician and I'm not a preacher. You wanted Cunham to take your case to the Grand Jury and I think he's going to. What more do you want?"

"You," I said.

I had wanted to fire him. The moment I saw him, I knew I had been racked with jealousy because I loved him.

After a moment, I said, "We've got two cars in the parking lot. Why don't we leave mine there. Drive me up to your place. Please?"

"You going to be merciful to the fellow who disappointed you?"

"You disappointed yourself. George, I'm grateful for what you did with Cunham, but this hasn't got anything to do with that."

"All I did was supply Cunham with a piece of information that will eventually show up on your bill for two hundred dollars."

"Please don't rob me of my idealistic youth all at once," I said. "Moreover, I'm not as naive as you think. I just wish our . . . relationship didn't threaten you."

"I don't feel threatened."

"Then please."

"Please what?"

"Take me home with you. Let's try again."

"No."

"I don't care if you get it up or not. You will when you sort out the marbles in your head. Please."

"I've got a better idea. Can I pick you up Saturday morning? I want to take us on a trip."

"If a change in environment will make a difference, sure. Where to?"

"LaGuardia."

"I hate to fly."

"Driving to where we're going takes too long."

"Where?"

"Trust me."

"Can you trust me in turn, George?"

He paused a second too long. "Sure," he said.

"There's a letter in the mail, from me to you. When it arrives, tear it up without reading it. Think you can do that?"

TWENTY-FOUR

Haig Thomassian

Every day except God's day I am already up at five, working the horses. Every day my hands hurt from holding leather at the other end of which is a big-eye horse what don't want to do what I want him to do. This game I win every day. I stop with horses when five is on my watch again. My neck aches. My worse tiredness is in the bottoms of my feet. When I was young man, never tired, not morning, not night. Now sometimes tired in morning, bad. Anyway, five in evening is good time. I sit with my tea, staring into the fire, dreaming good parts my life long ago. I call this my "little sleep."

So this day I am having my little sleep I hear a car stop. My shotgun is on wall. The door is safely locked. I go to window, pull curtain, see George.

I unlock door, pull open, yell at him, "Who died?"

"Hello, Pop," he says. "There's no one left to die, just you and me."

"You drive five hours without telephone first? You crazy?"

"You don't answer the telephone."

"Why should I answer?" I say to him. "Who is there I want to talk to?"

"People will think you died."

"That's why you come? To pack up my things for yourself?"

George shakes his head. I let him in. "Have some tea," I say, "five hours is long drive."

"I rented the car at the airport," he says. "I didn't drive all the way to Oswego."

"Then what you want?"

George says, "I wanted to be sure you were all right."

"Why?" I say. "You think if I die I stink too much. Nobody here to smell."

Well, we talk lots of things, I tell him I got a man comes three times a week help with the horses, if I'm dead, the man knows where to look for George's telephone number on the first page of my little book that says Police, Fire, Vet, Undertaker, George.

George kids me, why don't I take a woman into the house since Marya died, I tell him I take care of myself, cook, clean house, little sex, everything. He tells me I am married to the horses. I yell at him who he married to, criminals? Judges? Floozies? Forty-four years a bachelor, everybody must think he's a you-know-what or a eunuch.

"You never bring me a woman to inspect so I know you are serious!"

That's when he tells me there's a woman in the car. "Why you not bring her in, stupid!" I yell at him. I go outside, pull open car door, say "Come in, come in."

Inside, I look at her better. She's a baby, compared to George.

I give her my hand. I give her my name. I ask her if she is a woman lawyer.

"No," she says.

I am surprised.

Well, we talk a lot that evening. I apologize for the franks and beans, it's all I got that's enough for three, they say never mind, we drink beer, it's almost like the old days when George was a boy. This girl smart. This girl has a lot of class. I ask her if she is an Armenian, knowing what the answer will be. I tell her it's okay anyway. After two hours I ask her to write down her telephone number. She looks at George. George says it's okay. I take my little book and after Police Fire Vet Undertaker I cross out George's number and write her number in. George laughs so hard I think he'll die. He understands I approve.

They have to drive back to airport. I don't kiss her cheek or anything, I haven't shaved. I pull George aside, tell him he's a lousy son but maybe I can have a nice daughter.

"Don't jump to conclusions," he tells me. "We hardly know each other."

"Liar," I say.

They get in the car. I wave. I say something. He doesn't hear me. He rolls the window down. I say again, "Tell her about the Armenians."

The next morning, 5:00 A.M., I go to my horses a new man.

TWENTY-FIVE

Francine

I suggested that we might stay in a motel near Oswego and not head straight home.

"I don't like motels," said Thomassy.

"I don't think anyone likes motels. I thought, just on the spur of the moment, for the night, it might be fun."

He looked at me as if the word "fun" were repulsive to him.

On the flight back I asked him why we had gone to Oswego. To visit his father, he said. I meant why did we go to visit his father. Why do you think? he said. I said I didn't know. He said he didn't know either.

The flight took under fifty minutes. We got a clear view of the city as we came in to LaGuardia over the sound. In his car, I asked if he had planned to whip up a dinner for us. He hadn't. I volunteered to cook one with whatever I could find in his place.

"There isn't much."

"I'll try."

While he was slouched on the sofa, his legs sticking straight out, coddling Jack Daniels on ice, I asked, "What would you normally be doing on a Saturday evening?"

"Recovering from flying," he said.

"You don't usually fly around on Saturdays, do you?"

"I fly all week."

You couldn't call it a conversation. I did the best I could with eggs and cheese. I found a bottle of Château Giscours '66, but there wasn't time to air it.

After dinner, I sat three feet away from him on the couch. "What are you thinking?" I finally dared.

"Nothing."

"Are you in a bad mood?" I asked.

"No."

"I was thinking of Beckett. Those two people in ash cans on opposite sides of the stage."

"Nothing compared to Héloïse and Abélard," he said. He wasn't smiling. Wasn't it better getting lost with Bill on a date, anything, than this sitting around with nothing happening? Except that I felt something *was* happening.

COMMENT BY THOMASSY

Of course she took it for granted you'd spend the night together, idiot. You don't take other women to Oswego. You take her to Oswego. Where do you take her next? The head bone's connected to the neck bone. You take an option on a woman. The thigh bone's connected to the ham bone. The binder connects to the contract. Joint tenancy. Great. Either or the survivor. Terrific. Stop thinking like a lawyer, Thomassy. A lover doesn't think.

I have to acquaint this woman with who I am. Look here, Francine, I have to say, I was brought up in a certain period. I am a period piece. Any fellow brought up in my period had to know the rules of four games: baseball, basketball, football, and mating. Francine, here's how mating was played, not just by me and my crowd but by everybody. You were supposed to go around the broad as if she was some kind of Monopoly game. Player One, male, is supposed to move from lips to tits to you-know-where and get as much as he could without making the big commitment. Player Number Two, female, has to lead him on, step by step, toward the contract, the steps consisting of One: fraternity pin or reasonable facsimile; Two: engagement ring; Three: you're out, game called permanently on account of marriage.

Moreover, I ought to tell her in those days you *had* to play or pretend to play or Player Number Two, female, and all her friends would say you were not a man. *I don't want to* was not a male election. Francine, in my hung-up generation, that was the highest form of social coercion, just a hairline away from rape without a weapon: you play or you forfeit. You can fuck bad girls all you want to. But if you go steady with a good girl and fuck, you better be prepared to visit a jeweler.

You kids live in cloud-cuckoo land, no past, no worries about the future, just have a piece of now, pass it around, have a drag, use my body it doesn't wear out. Save it for a rainy day? Suppose it never rains, you say. Think of the future. What future—oxygen, plutonium, hydrogen? I never knew whether it was Armenian or Thomassian but my father used to say *What would you do six years from now?* Apply that idea to almost anything and it changes what you're thinking of doing. Six years from now I'd be bumping the half-century mark. What if you got pregnant now—oh yes, pregnancy was always around the corner—you'd end up with a kid that in six years would have a fifty-year-old father, and what kid wants that?

I have got to sit ye down, Francine, and give you a lecture on a minor, temporary affliction of mankind more prevalent than the common cold. It's called loin-tingle. It doesn't require a relationship, it requires scratching and it goes away. You need a man of thirty. I know all that garbage, mommas' boys, deep-freeze neurotics, or if not, two youngsters fumbling around for experience, it doesn't have to be permanent, first marriages are for experience-gathering.

Let me throw cold water on it. Just turn the sexes around. Young man, older woman, and what do you get? Fag hags? Young woman, older man, you're just catering to the society-for-the-admiration-of-tight-bellies. The experienced lover with the child needing guidance, care, money, a parental substitute?

Oh yes, I can hear your answer all right, you are the magnificent age of twenty-seven, you've skipped the first marriage, and so have I. You have an answer for everything. Maybe that's why I'm having this conversation with you safely inside my head. I don't like back talk from opposing counsel. My court is my court and your court is my court.

All of this noodling is probably just a cover-up for my own disinclination to hook up with another person. It's hard enough living with yourself. You learn your own likes and dislikes, you take shortcuts, you convince yourself. And there's no one to blame. How often can you fight with yourself over something trivial? Married people fight all the time over trivial things.

Look at her, she's fallen asleep with her clothes on.

❁

Oh yes it's sinful to pretend I'm still asleep while he turns me over gently and unhooks the one link at the top of the dress, then slides the zipper open. There's no way he can get this off me without cooperation. I am a stone. Catatonic.

He's managed it. I ought to wake up and applaud. Don't spoil it. He's managing. Aren't you glad there's no bra to fuss with, counselor? He is kissing my back between the shoulder blades, not exactly kissing, I can feel the rough surface of his tongue as he moves down each vertebra, to the left side, then the right, he knows I'm awake, he knows I'm feeling it.

His mouth is now at the indentation of my waist, on the right, and if I didn't have an erogenous area there before I do now, God do I feel it, and his hands are cueing me to turn over, and I turn slowly, and he is at my belly, one side, his tongue moving teasingly down, I was glad he turned me over, I thought he was going to kiss my butt, now his tongue is on the other side of my belly sort of sliding down, saying something to me like a promise, but stopping and moving up again, the anticipation is exquisite. No one ever did anything like this, I guess it's experience I'm experiencing. He moved up to kiss my lips softly, gently, and I admit I felt alarm he wasn't going down any farther any more! His hand went down there, just a touch past the mound, and I could feel, barely, a finger circling, not touching it, just on the hood and then to the side and the other side, just as a woman would do it, I mean a person who'd felt it herself. Men, boys really, sometimes just go with the finger like it was a hacksaw till you could scream idiot that hurts, but George was doing it so right I thought the top of my head was coming off, he was down there and I could feel it in my nipples, and he knew it, I don't know how he knew it, but his hands were up to my breasts, just teasing around the nipples, then flicking fingers over them, over them, over them, and suddenly his mouth was moving down again, fast this time, to where his finger'd been and I felt the first flickers of his tongue on my centerpiece, my breath was choking me, my own breath from my chest heaving, and everything just pointing beautiful arrows down there, the epicenter of everything getting ready, I could feel it, my hips were rising to meet his tongue, and then my hips were into a rhythm, and he was cupping his hands under me, helping, and I was thrusting as if everything, my whole body, was coming together in one place, meeting where his tongue was now circling it, and for a second I thought he was going to stop but he was only moving his mouth down where I felt so excruciatingly sensitive, and he moved just a bit, circling the epicenter again, and I heard myself saying, "George, come up here," and in an instant he was kissing me and entering me and then plunging again and again, and it was if every beautiful nerve ending was singing, and I said, "Don't stop, oh God, don't" and I let go in unbearable waves of joy, and he said, "Hey," because I was moaning so loud, and I never felt so good as when I pulled his head to mine so I could kiss him again, and hold him, and love him without end into eternity amen.

TWENTY-SIX

Koch

Last night when I went down for the newspaper, a boy of seventeen, eighteen, dark, bumped into me on purpose. In a Spanish accent he says to me so that everyone can hear, "Watch where you're going, mister!" I look right and left. No policeman anywhere. Not a friendly face. Just other Spanish-speaking people, young, old, waiting to see if a fight will start.

I walk back to my house without my newspaper. I go upstairs, double-lock my door, imprisoning myself in my apartment. I cannot talk about the change in the streets to Marta. Can I call a friend like Allanberg and tell him what happened? He will think me crazy to worry about a teen-ager who bumps me in the street. Do I call 911? The police will think I'm crazy too. I go to sleep thinking what is the matter with me, a small thing happens and I make some apocalypse out of it.

In the morning, my mood is still somber, but soon I have a phone call from my angel Francine and I am suddenly manic like a child. She says she has an unexpected conference at work, she will have to miss the regular hour, could she make it late in the day. I seize the opportunity like a gift. How late in the day, the last appointment? She says yes, that will be all right, is it convenient, and I say oh yes, and immediately put myself to calling the Murkoff boy's mother and say can he be brought right after school, I need his regular hour for an emergency patient (lie! lie!), and I am all set, Francine will be Iago's last patient of the day. With my heart high, I hope that once the hour is over she will be led by me from the study to the living room where we will sit and drink tea as friends while my eyes see her from a more direct angle than I enjoy on the couch. Or do I hope that from the couch of my study I can lead her to the bed of the bedroom once she sees the enormity of my need? How many fantasies I collect in the wastebasket of my head, what she does, what I do, what we do together. I begin to believe that *it may come true.* Is that the supreme fantasy?

She greets me, as usual we shake hands, a concession to my being European. In Vienna I would brush the back of her delicate hand with my lips. Here it is mine to hold for a second, feel its warmth, and the softness of its skin. I think of the skin I have never seen, at the small of her back, at the back of her knees.

On her face she has a certain expression we analysts have come to recognize: *today I am going to give you a present.* What this means is she will tell me something she thinks I have been waiting to hear. I gesture at the couch, I wait for the ceremony of her lying down, the placement of her body, sitting first, then swinging her legs up, then lying back supported by one elbow, then flat, the line of her unconstricted bosom rising with each breath. There is the prolonged silence that sometimes means *I refuse to talk* but today I am certain means that the mind's podium is being dusted in preparation for a declaration. Ah, here it comes.

"That time, right after I was raped, when I came here for help, you told me I had no vocation."

"Yes."

"That I didn't know what to do with my life."

"Yes."

"Isn't it dangerous telling someone something like that when they're in a state of distress?"

"I would be a poor analyst if I did not sometimes take a chance."

"Take chances with your own life, not mine."

"Now, Francine, listen. You were under great stress. But your anger at my lack of tact helped keep the thought about vocation in your mind so that now, perhaps when you are prepared to deal with it, it is waiting."

Suddenly, Francine is sitting up, swinging her legs off the couch, facing me.

"I could have killed myself," she said.

"Francine, there are people who can kill themselves, and people who cannot. You are among the latter."

"You were playing with my life."

"I was not playing."

"How could you be sure I wouldn't do something drastic?"

"Oh one is never sure," I said, "but experience is a good guide."

Her face reddened with anger. "The risk wasn't yours!"

"Please lie back down."

"No. You're supposed to be a doctor. If I come in with a broken arm, I want it set."

"If you come in with the flu and demand a useless shot of penicillin, I will not give it to you just to make my lot easier. This is not instant therapy. Now please lie back down."

Instead, she stood up. "This is an impossible relationship, Dr. Koch. I talk, you listen. I'm supposed to be candid, but you're not candid with me. It isn't give and take, it isn't normal."

I remained seated. "My dear Francine," I said. "If I say something at the wrong time, you condemn me. If I say nothing, you condemn me equally. I am not a magician. Psychoanalysis is a learning process. Did you hear process? I am the backboard. You are the player with the ball."

"Why can't we talk like two people?"

"Please lie back down. One does not talk to the priest in the confessional as if he is a friend who talks back."

"Oh so that's what you think you are!"

"You know very well I'm not, my dear. The priest has the church's formulas for absolution. I have only yourself to offer yourself."

"Very prettily put."

"You are entitled to your sarcasm. Now may I ask you to please leave or please lie back down."

"You're ordering me!"

"I am suggesting."

These are the risks we take. Like governments practicing brinksmanship. I watch Francine sit down on the edge of the couch. I say nothing. She looks at me. I say, "We have locked antlers. One of us cannot leave."

Finally she lay back down. I waited a few moments, then I said, "Can you define vocation for me? Think a minute."

"It's not just making a living."

"Correct."

"It's a whole scene that gets you excited. It's your thing."

"What about your father's vocation?"

"My father counsels his clients. He's a friend to a lot of them. He does contracts for them. He's sort of a general consultant in the guise of a lawyer."

"Guise?"

"His work doesn't excite him."

"What does then?" *Besides you,* I thought.

"I don't know," she said. "Perhaps nothing does. He could do lots of things."

"Such as?"

"He could have been a businessman or an ambassador, something like that."

"Listen carefully. What would he enjoy being?"

"Someone else."

She knew she had said something terrible. I gave her a moment to reflect, then said, "The other lawyer. Thomassy. Do you think he wants to be somebody else?"

"You've gotta be crazy, he loves doing what he does so much he doesn't want to have anything to do with anyone else!"

"Meaning you?"

"Anyone."

"Do you feel he is a competent lawyer?"

"He's a fucking genius. He's a fanatic about manipulating people, cases, laws."

"To what end?"

"It's an end in itself, he loves it!"

"He has a vocation."

"It's an obsession with him."

"Yes."

Then she said, "You don't like George."

"I wouldn't say that."

"I'll say it. You don't like George."

"My likes are not relevant. It happens I am not a policeman or a criminal. I live outside those things that obsess Mr. Thomassy. I do not need him in my life. Do you?"

"You're giving me the willies."

"How?"

"You make me think maybe I'm not like George."

"You want to be more like George?"

"It's his vitality."

"You have vitality. Don't you like your work?"

"I like some of the things I do at the job."

"Would Mr. Thomassy say that about his work?"

"No. He's a zealot about the whole lot."

"He has a vocation."

"All right! I don't! And I am about to fuck up my life by attaching it to his, living off the excitement of his drive. I don't want to do that. I want to be my own man."

We lingered in the silence that followed. Finally, she said, "I meant my own woman."

"There is nothing to be embarrassed about. Saying 'your own man' doesn't make you homosexual. The terms of our language are male. That is the only significance of your remark."

"You mean I'm not suddenly turning queer."

"Not suddenly."

"Now what the hell do you mean by that?"

"You spoke of yourself once or twice as having a crazy side. Tell me about that."

Experience has taught me to expect a long silence before she answers.

"Ever since I was a kid, every once in a while I just let all my crazy thoughts and words hang out, like I was letting some other nature out of me, some . . ."

"Uncontrolled?"

"My mother and father never let any crazy side of them show."

"Concealment?"

"Yes. To be decorous. Proper. Unexcitable. It's the essence of Waspdom."

"You were saying before that excitement was part of vocation."

"Yes," she said. "My vocation is not to be a Wasp. Like needling people, shocking the bourgeoisie, fucking blacks, you know."

"Or Turks?"

"What do you mean?"

"I meant Armenians."

"But they were enemies."

"Of whom?"

"Of each other."

"And?"

"My parents. They don't want to know people who are emotional, who dance wildly, who kill, who . . ."

"Say it."

"Who rape. They think the ethnics, all of them, are raping our world."

"Whose world?"

"My parents' fucking world!"

"Not yours?"

"I want out of that world. Look, Dr. Koch, there was a world of people before my mother and father and me, before any Wasps. It's a temporary stage. Their time is up."

"You fled from your parents into Cambridge, you befriended all sorts of types, talents, eccentrics, lunatics."

"Weirdos."

"You want to be like them?"

"I want to be like myself. Only . . ."

"Yes?"

"I want to be obsessed like George."

"Vocation. Yes. Well, I think that's all for today."

"Jesus, it's like coitus interruptus, right when I'm getting somewhere, you stop."

"Yes."

"It's part of the technique, right?"

She was sitting up, looking at me. I nodded.

"There aren't a lot of Wasps in your profession, are there?"

"Some," I said.

"Not many, I'll bet. Too embarrassing."

"Is your car parked nearby?"

"Just a couple of blocks away."

"I need some exercise after sitting all day. I will walk downstairs with you."

She looked at me, a slight smile subverting her countenance for the first time that day.

"Our antlers aren't locked any more?" she said.

I shook my head.

In the street she said, "It's like coming out of a movie into real life." She turned left. I went with her.

"Were there Spanish-speaking people in the area when you moved here?"

"It was a very long time ago. Maybe a few. I never noticed. Now it is the *lingua franca.*"

"*Lingua hispánica,*" she said, laughing.

"Yes."

So soon the tables turn. Before me, I think, came generations of refugees whose children wanted only to look and act and feel more like the ruling Wasps than their parents. Now the Francines are slithering out of the Wasp compound, finding their way out into the world, looking for the other inhabitants of the planet. She is becoming a European. She has been raped by a Slovak. We are two refugees in this West Side mini-ghetto of mine that shrinks every day like a grape drying. All around we hear the language of Torquemada. Look at those three young toughs eyeing us, sucking machismo from cigarettes, laughing. I feel the fibrillating panic: *the bars on the cages are being lifted, the animals are being let loose, the holocaust is coming again.*

"Are you all right, Dr. Koch?"

"Fine, fine." Dear God, I have lived in this neighborhood for twenty-six years, with Marta and after Marta, will I have to move, become a refugee once more?

As she reaches her car, she says, "It's a very colorful neighborhood you live in."

"Yes. Full of life." *And death.*

She shakes my hand. "Thank you for accompanying me."

"*De nada,*" I say in the language of the enemy, as she gets in and I close the door. She ignites the engine, backs up turning the wheel, then pulls away from the curb with a roar, my Francine, waving with one hand. I walk to the corner newsstand, and amidst the Spanish magazines, I find the evening paper, and walk warily back across no man's land to where, I suppose, I live.

TWENTY-SEVEN

Thomassy

Making love to Francine isn't a commitment! I don't want to get on an emotional roller coaster, or get trapped in those phone calls, hanging on to each other like spider spit. I need to get this over with by getting the case closed my way quick.

The excuse for a lot of her phone calls to me was what was happening at the Grand Jury. I phoned Lefkowitz to volunteer some help to whoever was presenting the case, and all I could get was his secretary saying he had left a message that if I wanted any information I had to call Mr. Cunham directly. So I called Gary and all I could get was his secretary saying her beloved Mr. Cunham could not speak to me at the present time. Of course the runaround was deliberate. I kept checking the *Daily News*, which is a more reliable place than the *Times* to get the first flash of a rape indictment, especially white on white. Could Cunham be stalling? Was he testing to see if I would do what I said I would? Was he setting a trap for me?

I searched the grand jurors list for a familiar name. Luckily, Muscreve was still sitting. God how a man can waste his life between playing Republican potsy and public service. He remembered me.

"Mr. Muscreve," I said, "I'd heard that the Widmer rape case might be coming before the jury along about now, but I haven't seen anything in the papers."

"Well, Mr. Thomassy, we sent down the true bill on that only today."

I tried to keep my voice light. "No wonder I haven't seen it in the papers."

"You won't," he said. "The D.A. ordered it sealed."

"What the hell for?"

"I don't recall anybody went into detail about that. You know how it is on the Grand Jury. The D.A. wants something, no reason not to co-operate. He's serving the people."

"Yes. Thank you very much, Mr. Muscreve."

"Any time, Mr. Thomassy. My friends and I have a lot of respect for you in this county."

I didn't lose much time wondering when I'd get a call for a return favor. I called Francine.

"News," I said.

"The indictment?"

"Yep."

"When?"

"Yesterday. Sealed. That means it won't appear in the papers."

"Is that good?"

"It'll save your father some sleep. I don't know what Cunham's up to. Anyway, I expect your friend Koslak's been picked up."

TWENTY-EIGHT

Koslak

Shit if I was going to get up this early just because some boob pushed our doorbell by mistake. I could feel Mary getting out of bed. Then she's shaking me saying it's the police, and I look past her and there is this cop standing in the doorway of the bedroom. I shook my head to wake up faster. "Don't tell me, I left my car by a fire hydrant," I said.

"I wouldn't know," said the cop. No smile. He had a piece of paper in his hand.

"What's the problem?" I said, and got my feet on the floor. "My station get hit?"

"You're under arrest," says this cop, and looks at Mary.

"What for?" she says.

"Nothing," I said. "I didn't do anything."

"Get your clothes on, Mr. Koslak," said the cop.

"What'd he do?" Mary says.

"You going to watch me getting dressed?" I says to the cop.

"I'll turn around," he says, standing in the doorway.

I'm getting into my clothes, and Mary is at the cop, badgering him. The cop says, "I've got to take him down to the station and get him booked."

"For what, for Christ's sake!" I yelled, and that did it.

"Rape," he says. "You've been indicted by the Grand Jury."

COMMENT BY MARY KOSLAK

All my life I've imagined hearing certain things that change everything. I hear a doctor telling me one of the kids has leukemia, and it's like an explosion in my brain. Everything stops. No doctor ever said that to me. None of the kids been sick serious, but I think leukemia—blam! Hearing rape was like that. Look, I'm no stupid thinks her husband never dips his wick somewhere else, they all do, don't they? But rape? What for?! I give it to him whenever he wants it, even when I don't want it, what the fuck does he have to go out and rape somebody?

It was like I answered my own question. He didn't need to do it, that's why he didn't do it, he's being framed, it's a mistake, something like that. I wouldn't put a frame past some of the people he mixes with. Next thing I hear the kids and I go in to shush them, only it's too late, and Mike, he sees the cop, I hope he didn't hear nothing. I pat his head and tell him to get back in bed, it's too early, I'll be back in soon, and I shut the door. By this time, Harry's dressed, he's brushing his teeth, and I say to him he doesn't want to go down to the station house without a shave. The cop says hurry up.

He's getting ready to go and I give him a glass of orange juice. He says he can't go nowhere without a cup of coffee, but the cop says come on, and they go. The door closes and I feel like I'm going to go out of my mind waiting to hear what happens. I open the window and when I see them I yell, "Call a lawyer!"

Harry gives me a dirty look, and I realize people in the street can hear me. They watch him getting into the cop car. Whatever I do is wrong!

❋

Mary should've kept her big mouth shut. I don't need the neighbors knowing nothing. This'll all get cleared up. When you fuck some broads, they'll squawk to hurt you. I just need to think my way out of this.

The cop has a buddy in the car. The buddy sits with me in the back.

He don't need to put cuffs on. I hold my hands in my lap and concentrate on thinking. Mary is right. I got to think lawyer. They know how to fuck the law before this kind of thing gets out of hand.

So I'm riding along thinking this here friend of mine Tony Ludo once got into real trouble over what started out like nothing. You know how you get to talking to a woman in a bar, she says something to you, you answer, you talk some more, and somewhere along the line she puts her hand not too accidentally on your leg, some sign like that, and you ask to take her home. So Tony takes this woman, Angie was her name, something like that, to her place, and they do the normal, you know, couple more drinks, a feel, and pretty soon he's throwing it to her on the bed.

The way Tony tells it this Angie was real hungry. Tony's got this thing he does, he works out on the parallel bars and all that and he's got strong arms, and he just positions his whole body forward so his head's past the woman's head. He explained it, this is so her clit gets the action, and this woman Angie, she likes what Tony's doing so much she comes like a maniac, yelling and all, and Tony, he's just about to let go when he hears the door. I tell you he's got ears like a dog to hear like that. He says what's that, and Angie slides out from under, leaving Tony hung up, and there's this guy standing there with keys in his hand. Tony knows he's gotta be Angie's husband, right, and this guy says to Angie why doesn't she finish him off as if he's used to finding her screwing somebody. Tony figures to get out of there fast, pulls his clothes on while this guy's making cracks at him, and Tony tells him to shut up, and *that* gets the guy mad. Listen how crazy this is, the guy isn't mad at Tony for screwing his wife, he's mad because Tony told him to shut up! Well, according to Tony, this guy shoves him, and anybody knows Tony'll tell you you don't shove Tony Ludo, he smashes his fist into the guy's face, the guy reaches for something on the table, and Tony don't want to get hurt so he smashes the guy again, remember he's got these arms from the parallel bars, right, and the guy crumples up out cold. The woman is crying, it's a mess, and Tony splits. It's all right to go to a little bit of trouble to get laid, but that was too much. Tony goes back to the bar, and he's not there half an hour when the cops come in and arrest him and take him down to the station house and book him for murder cause Angie's husband is dead.

Dead? Jesus, you can imagine how Tony reacted. He's been in a hundred fights like that, somebody gets hurt, but dead? And wait'll his wife finds out what the fight was about, how's he gonna explain? I mean Tony was just collecting a piece of ass that was offered him, no big thing, right?

The cops, they let Tony call a lawyer and he calls Brady. Brady's the one who keeps Tony's Shylock friends out of the cooler and he works for Teamsters and the garbage people, he's gotta be good. He gets Tony sprung on bail, gets the charge reduced to manslaughter two, it goes to trial. Brady goes to see the widow, commiserates with her, sees what kind of animal she is, hints that Tony wouldn't mind coming around once in a while to do his parallel bars trick, but he couldn't do it if he was in jail, could he? Besides, he finds out that her husband reached for a screwdriver after he got hit the first time, and a screwdriver can be one lethal weapon, right? So he goes to trial with the guy's widow as the chief defense witness, I mean he's a genius, and Tony gets off innocent. I figure Brady's my man.

Meanwhile they're taking my picture and fingerprinting me just like in the movies, so I say how about a lawyer.

"Make it fast," they tell me, just to be tough. I tell this cop, he's a sergeant, "I'm innocent till proved guilty, right? Well, I'm innocent, so don't hustle me. I got to look up the number." Brady's number is in the book all right, but that cockamamie secretary of his tells me he's busy. Busy? I'm gonna end up in the can unless I get Brady. So I says to the cop the sergeant left with me, "I got a right to talk to my lawyer privately," and he moves to the other side of the room, but watches me like I'm a crook going to steal something, and I cover the mouthpiece some and turn my back to the cop and I say to Brady's secretary, "Look, pussy, I'm gonna come up there and spread your legs unless you let me talk to him," and in a minute he's on the phone saying, "Were you threatening my secretary?" and I say, "Nah, nah, it was just my way of getting to talk to you." He starts to dish me that real busy crap and I say I was referenced by Tony Ludo. "Okay," he says, "you come up and we'll talk and I'll recommend somebody for you."

"Are you kidding?" I say. "I been arrested. I'm calling from the station. I been mugged and printed and all."

"What's the charge?" he asks.

I look to see if the cop can hear me. "Rape," I whisper.

I could hear Brady say, "Jesus!" He talks to someone in his office, I don't know what, and then he comes back on the line and says, "Koslak, I'll have to get you before a judge so we can get you bailed. What police station are you at?"

I tell him and say "Hurry," and he hangs up. "We wait here for the lawyer?" I ask the cop. The cop says, "Follow me," and would you know he puts me in the slammer to wait?

It must have been hours before someone shows, a fellow who looks so young I figure he can't be Brady. I say, "Are you Brady?" and he says "I'm an associate."

"What's an associate?"

"I work with Mr. Brady."

This associate ain't giving anything to anybody. You could hardly figure him for a human being. No sign of friendliness or anything. We're put in this tiny room alone and he asks me some stupid questions and then I put it to him, "How come you're so friendly?"

This young punk says to me, "I'm here to do a job."

"Mr. Brady know you're this friendly with the people who pay him?" I ask.

"If you have to know," he says, "I don't give a damn. I don't care if a guy bangs his wife, or his girl friend, or his mother for all I care, there's enough ass around you don't have to force it."

"Wait a minute, kid," I says. "You're working as my lawyer. You know the law. I'm innocent till somebody says I'm guilty."

"Sure."

I could break this kid's neck. I answer his goddamn questions, you know, where do I work, do I own the station, how do I know the woman, what did I do, what did she do, what was my alibi, that kind of thing, and then we get taken by cop car to the courthouse, and there's this runt behind a desk who turns out to be a judge and he looks at me like he can tell from my face whether I'm to be trusted or not. I don't give him any crap, I talk respectful, and then this kid lawyer talks to him so no one can hear, whisper whisper, but whatever he says it works, and the judge says something about my roots in the community—what the fuck is that?—and names ten gees as the bail. Ten gees? But it turns out this kid's got a bail bondsman with him and he asks me all kinds of questions, how much I make, how come I don't own a house, what's the make of my car, things like that, and finally I sign some papers, and the kid is driving me to his office. He says something to Brady's secretary, she looks at me like she could spit. After I cool my heels for a while, wondering about Mary, what she's thinking about this, the secretary says okay for me to go in. I look around for the kid, but he's disappeared somewhere in the back, I guess into his own office, and I go in to see Brady.

Well, sure, I go in there expecting Brady to be six feet tall and he's a midget, I mean shorter than Abe Beame, and he's got these eyebrows that go all the way across the bridge of his nose, one straight black line. His chair and his desk are on a raised platform. I know guys wear boosters in their shoes, but he's got his whole setup up in the air. He says, "Sit down!" and that's what I do, down, looking up at him, and I tell him my story, and he sits there chewing on his cigar. I'm trying to figure what'll make him take the case himself, and I say, "Mr. Brady, I realize you're a busy man, but it's not like I'm a charity case, I can pay a retainer in cash."

"Five thousand?"

"That's okay."

"A check isn't cash," he says.

"I can pay cash."

"When?"

"Tomorrow okay?"

I swear I can't tell from his expression what he thinks, he just chews the cigar. Maybe he's thinking of pocketing some of the cash and turning the rest over to some other lawyer to handle me. What he does is buzz his secretary.

"Get Mr. Cunham for me," he says.

We wait. I start to say something but Brady holds a finger in front of his lips. His brain is on that phone call.

The intercom buzzes. Brady listens, looks mad, says, "Try Lefkowitz."

We wait again. Is he trying to pass me off?

The intercom buzzes again. This time Brady smiles. "Lefkowitz," he says, "good day to you, too. Question. How come the boss decided to put an alleged snatch invasion to the Grand Jury? Doesn't sound like him. That's right, Koslak. He's with me now. Who? Well, thank you very much."

That black line across Brady's forehead, it lifts up in two places, over each eye. He seems happy. He buzzes his secretary again, and says, "Get me George Thomassy."

To me he says, "Just have to confirm something. Take a minute."

I watch him. He watches out the window. The phone buzzes. He picks up, smiles, pushes one of the buttons, says, "Hello, George. How you doing?"

I can't hear what Thomassy is saying, but then Brady says, "You representing a woman named, let's see here," he looks at the yellow pad he's been scribbling on, "Francine Widmer?" Brady listens, says "That's all I want to know," hangs up, stands up, pumps my hand, and says "You're on. Bring the money tomorrow." He seemed so happy about his call you'd think Thomassy was a broad he wanted to fuck instead of another lawyer!

Brady buzzed for the associate. The kid comes in. "Find out who Francine Widmer sees outside her office. Boy friends. Doctors. Everybody."

Brady winks at me, tells me I can go.

When I leave I tell Brady's secretary I was sorry about what I said on the phone and she says she accepts my apology so that's okay. I'm so high that Brady's taking the case I could go right into that Widmer broad's apartment with a cup of sugar in my hand all over again. I know she's not there, and besides, I'm not stupid. I go home and I grab Mary by the right ass and shove her into the bedroom and without taking any of her or my clothes off, just ripping down her pants and opening my zipper, fuck her fast just for old times' sake! Whee!

TWENTY-NINE

Koch

Dr. Allanberg and his wife, bless them both, took me to Lincoln Center to hear Moussorgsky, and I come home in a cab, euphoric, a bit tired, happy, the music still in my ears. The doorman tells me a patient is waiting for me in the lobby. Who? I have no appointments this late at night, no new patients to see, and the doorman brings me over to a very short man sitting in a lobby chair and he shakes my hand and says, "My name is Brady, Dr. Koch."

This man, whose eyebrows go straight across his forehead in a most unusual way, glances at the doorman who has retreated out of earshot out of politeness, then says, "I must talk to you."

"Who are you?"

"I'm a lawyer," he says. "I've come to see you about a psychiatric patient of yours who you are treating for mental illness, and who is accusing a client of mine of an imaginary rape, and I am terribly concerned about the man's wife, his children, and I need your suggestions. Please, Dr. Koch."

"I'm afraid I cannot talk about a case to anyone except the patient." *What has this tiny man to do with Francine?*

"I think it's imperative that I see you now, Dr. Koch. You'll understand the moment I explain."

"Impossible," I say. Yet I am curious. "Perhaps we could make an appointment," I say. "When a patient cancels, I could call you . . . "

I can see the doorman staring at us. Shall I order the man away?

"Dr. Koch," says Brady, "this is a private matter."

Of course it is private, between Francine and myself and no one else.

"It is essential," says Brady.

I am a European idiot. Is it politeness to this stranger that makes me invite him up? Or my curiosity?

As we go into the living room I say, "I am really very tired." *Why is he looking around the apartment that way?*

"I'll be brief," says this Mr. Brady, sitting down. He puts each hand, fingers extended, on one knee, very symmetrical. "I am a lawyer. I represent Harry Koslak, who has been indicted for an alleged offense against a patient of yours, Francine Widmer. In the event that this case is not dismissed and we go to trial, I intend calling you as a witness for the defense."

I start to object and he says, "One moment. My client will of course pay at the usual specialist rates for your time when you testify and any preparatory time involved, or we can subpoena you, as you wish. I have studied the case and I believe your patient is a high-strung woman of easy morals who has a history of sexual relations with others in extralegal circumstances. Please let me continue. I know you have a confidential relationship to your patient, but at the same time you have the reputation, I have checked, of a kindly man, and I assume you would not want to see the father of two young children go to jail for accepting the favors of a young woman who has given those favors to others on repeated occasions. It is making too much of a minor thing. It is possible that Miss Widmer's testimony on the stand over several days would be too trying for her. Perhaps this whole matter can be disposed of expeditiously, without unnecessary pain to anybody, but to do so I would need to review the record of her treatment. I could, of course, have another psychiatrist testify as to her psychological condition based on her testimony or any pretrial testimony that is admissible, and you might then be subpoenaed to support or contradict specific points in his testimony, but as you can see, that would make for a very long drawn-out procedure painful to all parties. If you cooperate now, it would speed things up immeasurably, and as a courtesy, for your cooperation, I would be pleased to arrange for a donation of a thousand dollars to your favorite charity, or if you would prefer the cash so that you could make the donation yourself, that could also be arranged, what do you say?"

This is unbelievable. I have heard of such people. "One moment," I say. I go to my study and dial Thomassy's home number—thank heaven I have it—and apologize for waking him at that late hour. He says he was not asleep. In the background I can hear a woman's voice. Is it Francine? I tell Thomassy who I am being visited by and the essence of what he has said.

"Let me talk to him," says Thomassy.

I go to the living room where Brady is now pacing and I point to the extension phone and say, "Could you pick up please?" and then I hurry back to my study like a mischievous child to listen in.

"Brady," he says, "what the fuck are you doing there?"

It is a very short conversation, an exchange of expletives and tough legal phrases I do not grasp, and they hang up. I put the telephone on the cradle and go back to the living room, but Brady, glaring at me, says not so much as a good night, and leaves.

I feel a tightness like a pre-angina condition as I prepare for bed. I try to read. Hopeless. This man Brady will get what he wants if he has to disembowel me. Can one fight back against people like that? Or does one wait in bed, foredoomed, for the sounds of *Kristallnacht?*

THIRTY

Francine

One successful fuck does not a summer make. The next time it could all collapse, and we'd be back where we started. Was I wrong to be nervous?

George didn't want to eat out, so we drove to his place and I extracted enough from his fridge to cook us a passable dinner. He pushed the food around on his plate as if it was pieces of a jigsaw puzzle.

Afterwards I put on some Mozart the Peacemaker. It almost always works for me. In his armchair, without looking up from his law book, Machiavelli says, "Could you turn that down?"

"I thought you liked Mozart?"

He didn't answer me.

Eventually I said, "This is just like being married, I suppose."

He put a place marker in the book, shut it, sighed, and said, "I'm sorry."

"What's the matter, George?" I went to turn off the phonograph.

"You don't have to turn it off. I just said turn it down."

"My generation hasn't learned to listen to music when it's barely audible. Can I read something to you?"

"I haven't been read to since ten years before you were born."

He's feeling his age tonight.

"What did you want to read?"

I took the sheets out of my briefcase. " 'In Praise of Limestone.' Auden. Know it?"

"No."

"It's my cure-all."

"It's illegal to copy books," he said.

"It's my book. If I copied it by hand, would that be illegal? Jesus, the law is cockeyed. May I read?"

"Is it long?"

"It's the right length. Don't let me force it on you."

"Look, my head's full of something else. I won't be able to concentrate."

"Tell me what's the matter."

"Not right now."

"What've you been reading?"

"Cases."

"Is that all you're going to say?"

"Rape cases. Look, Brady's going to try to battle this out before we ever get to court. His strategy's to harass you into dropping the whole thing. The prosecution's nowhere without you."

"I know I won't quit. Let me read Auden to you."

"I've dealt with Brady. He's a certifiable sadist. When he wants his jollies, he gets them. He looks for situations where he can twist someone's balls."

"Then I'm safe."

"Brady's not after you. He's after me, don't you see? I'd love to push his face into the gravel, but this time I've got a handicap I'm not used to."

"Me?"

"My relationship with you. He's got to find out about it if you keep coming here."

"Want me to stay away?"

"As a lawyer? Yes."

I lay there on the couch, trying to let the music soak into me, thinking *Josephine de Beauharnais wouldn't have just sat around listening to music, she'd have found something to distract him.*

I sat up. He didn't look up.

I stood. If I stood on my head, would he notice? I went to the john, took off blouse, shoes, slacks, pantyhose. I rubbed my hand across the elastic marks. I was tempted to rub lower. Opening the door of the john a smidge, I could see him making notes demonically. I got all the way to the couch stark naked, stretched myself out. *He didn't notice.*

The record, thank heaven, stopped. I didn't go to turn it over. He noticed the absence of the music. That's when he looked up.

"Dear God," he said.

I turned part way to the wall. *Thata girl. He thinks you're shy. You're showing him your fantastic ass.* My ears, like rabbits' ears, listened for sound. He was putting the book down. He put the yellow pad aside. He was coming across the room. I turned toward him. He had dropped to his knees beside the couch.

"You look lovely," he said.

He put a hand on the flat of my belly and said, "You feel good, too."

The flash of light came from the window straight across the room.

"Jesus!" He was on his feet in a second, bolting across the room, opening the window, trying to grab at something, cursing. He ran to the hall and out the door like a maniac. I could hear footsteps racing down the gravel driveway.

I hurried my nakedness back to the john, got his bathrobe off the knob on the back of the door, and wrapped it around me.

When he got back, George's face was livid. "The son of a bitch got away."

"Someone took a photograph."

"You can bet everything you own to a nickel that that photograph is for Brady."

"We weren't doing anything."

"Oh no, just you lying naked and me with my hand on you, how much do you think you need for a blackmail photograph?"

"That's ridiculous," I said. "Nothing I've done with you is embarrassing to me."

"I'm not thinking of you being embarrassed. I'm thinking of who he'll show that photograph to."

"In court?"

"Brady's not stupid. That's not the kind of thing you can show in a courtroom. If I know Brady, he's going to use it now."

"Who?"

"Put yourself into his head, think what he would do. Damn it, you should have pulled the curtain if you were going to take your clothes off!"

"I didn't think anyone could see here in the woods. I mean there're no windows across the way."

"That guy was no amateur."

"I was only trying to distract you. I thought you need some R and R."

"Oh I do, I do."

"How can lawyers do things like that?"

"Some do it more easily than others. Some don't."

"Do you?"

He looked at his fingers at first, not answering me, then he said, "Look, Brady doesn't take those pictures, he hires people. I got something from somebody, that's all."

"A picture?"

He nodded.

"Like that?"

"No, just a newspaper clip."

"But the effect is the same?"

"How do you mean?"

"Morally," I said. "Is that what all you guys are taught in law school, dirty tricks?"

"Not in law school."

"I think I'd better get my clothes back on." Halfway to the bathroom, I stopped and asked him, "Who's he going to show that picture to?"

"It's only a guess."

"Guess for me," I said.

His face looked very tired. "Your father," he said.

THIRTY-ONE

Widmer

My secretary said that a Mr. Brady was telephoning. He wanted to speak to me, she said, about my daughter. Which daughter? When she got back on the line, she said it was Francine. I didn't know any Brady, but I wondered what had happened to Francine now.

"I'll speak to him," I said.

It is modulation rather than accent that conveys breeding in an American voice. Brady's rasp belonged to a man who had never given any thought to how he sounded.

"I have a photograph of your daughter I think you ought to see," he said.

"I have a great many photographs of my children, Mr. Brady, and I'm quite busy right now."

"I bet you'd have to go back to baby days to find a picture of Francine without anything on."

Oh how I would have loved to tell this Brady person about my treasured photograph and then hang up. "We don't take baby pictures in our family," I said.

"Mr. Widmer, this picture of your baby was taken this week."

I must keep him at a distance. "To what end?" I asked.

"You mean why did she take her clothes off?"

"No. I meant why did she have the picture taken."

"Oh," said Mr. Brady. "I don't think she wanted this picture taken. It was through a window. At some risk to the photographer. It's an expensive picture, Mr. Widmer, and I think you should see it."

I thought it best to ignore this kind of extortion ploy.

"I'm really not interested in seeing pictures of my daughter nude," I said. "Goodbye, Mr. Brady."

Before I could hang up, he said, "One moment, Mr. Widmer. There is one element in this photograph that may make it of special interest to you."

My "yes?" was hesitant.

"It was taken in a man's apartment."

"My daughter is twenty-seven years of age, Mr. Brady, and is free to do as she chooses. Goodbye, Mr. Brady."

"Don't hang up! This is George Thomassy's house the picture was taken in."

I was silent for a moment. I could hear him breathing on the line. Then I said, "Is he in the picture, too?"

"You bet."

It was as if someone had announced that I was in the picture of Francine that I had secreted away. George Thomassy was closer to my age than to hers.

"Mr. Brady, is the object of your call to sell that photograph?"

"Oh no, no. I want to *give* it to you. After we discuss one or two things."

"Do I get the negative also?"

"There is no negative, Mr. Widmer. It's a Polaroid. Avoids questions from whoever's doing the developing. Can you come up to my office at four this afternoon?"

He gave me his address. It was out of the way.

"I'd feel safer in my office, if you don't mind, Mr. Brady."

"Oh Mr. Widmer, I'm a lawyer."

"Yes, well, could you make it here at four?"

"Of course," said Brady. "Anything to oblige a colleague."

He knew I would be offended by a word suggesting that he and I had anything in common. Time passed as slowly as an inchworm till four o'clock.

Mr. Brady turned out to be a very short man. On my couch, he had to sit far forward so that his feet could touch the floor. In person, he seemed far less menacing than on the phone.

He held up the snapshot by the top corners, close enough for me to see that Thomassy was fully dressed. I thought Francine looked as graceful as an odalisque. The photo was anything but pornographic. I guess I had expected to see them copulating.

Brady put the snapshot in his pocket. "I want you to have that," he said, "as soon as we agree on a course of action concerning the case."

"What case?" I wasn't going to help.

"The Grand Jury has handed down an indictment charging that my client, Harry Koslak, forced his attentions on your daughter. I have a good deal of information that it may well have been otherwise. Hold on, Mr. Widmer, maybe it was, maybe it wasn't. The point is that Koslak is married, has two kids, and if he goes to jail because of your daughter's complaint, you're not going to feed those kids, and I'm not going to feed those kids. I don't want to see an injustice done here to either party. You know how rough a rape trial can get. And believe me, for the sake of those kids, this one's going to be plenty rough. I don't think the judge will be able to bar the press. Through a friend I've already arranged for coverage from the *Daily News*. Broadcast media won't be hard to get for a sensational trial involving the daughter of a prominent attorney."

"What do you want, Mr. Brady?"

"I wish you'd give me a ring by the close of business tomorrow and tell me that the charges have been dropped. Cunham'd be relieved not to prosecute. We'd all feel better, wouldn't we? I'd give you the picture now. I trust you. But just in case you can't persuade your daughter, I'll need it along with the others for the trial. I'm sure you understand."

I must explain something about my temperament lest you think that my hesitation about the next step was a personal failing; it was a failing of my heritage. I made no attempt to avoid active service during the war, and though I spent a good deal of it behind a desk, I had no fear of seeing action. In boarding school I was in brawls repeatedly. When Priscilla's cat was the merest kitten it once got itself out onto the overhang of the roof from which it could not retreat, nor did it yet dare spring. I don't know whether it was my neck or my limbs I was risking, but I did crawl out there without anything solid to hang on to, to rescue the damned cat. You can see I am not a coward about ordinary hazards to life and limb. It is the *embarrassments* that I usually seek to avoid, the phone call to someone who may hang up on me, the near stranger to whom I should volunteer an apology, above all, the confrontation on the kind of subject matter I would choose to be sheltered from. In some respects life has prepared Priscilla better than it has me for such encounters; perhaps it is the leavening power of Gristede's that has accustomed her to the occasional necessity of overriding her heritage. Yet I cannot ask her to speak to Francine in my stead while I hide in the closet. And suppose it is not only Francine but Thomassy as well who has to be confronted?

It took forever tracking her down at her office. With staff available from all of the bloody United Nations, I had to connect with an American black who pronounced the name "Wimmer" and kept asking me to call back when I explained as tactfully as possible that I was Miss Widmer's father and that I had to reach her now. Finally, her familiar voice, a bit breathless, was on the phone.

I should have rehearsed what I was going to say because my head was a sudden jumble of questions which I reduced to a simple appeal to see her at once.

"Oh I can't, Dad, I really can't," she said. "I've got hours to go before I can get out of here tonight."

On my desk I have one of those baseball-sized glass balls with a country scene in it. If you shake the ball, as I did now with one hand, you have a snowstorm in the ball, hundreds of minute white flecks whirling about, falling on the house and barn and miniature farm animals. I like to watch the artificial snow settling when I think.

"Dad, I really can't hang on long now."

"That photo that was taken of you recently . . ."

A second's delay, then "Yes?"

"It was just offered to me."

"Blackmailer?"

"The lawyer who's representing Koslak. Will I see you?"

"Can I pick you up right after work?"

"Of course."

"If George can come down, shall he join us?"

"George?"

"Thomassy."

"Shouldn't we have our chat first?"

"I don't have any secrets."

"We have confidences, Francine. But do as you wish."

She would always do as she wished in any event. I was curious to see if she would bring Thomassy or not.

THIRTY-TWO

Thomassy

I'm sure everyone gets a queasy feeling when you're about to meet with someone for the first time after they and you know you've been fucking a relative of theirs. I could have done without that trip to Widmer's office, but better office than home.

I got there after Francine arrived. The secretary showed me in. Widmer was behind his desk. Francine was slouched on the couch across the room. I don't know what the hell was said before I got there, but the twenty feet between was jumping with family electricity.

"Hi, Ned," I said.

He reached across the desk to shake hands. Christ, I bet he usually comes around the side of the desk to greet a visitor. He's keeping that big piece of furniture between us.

"Hello, Francine."

She kind of opened the fingers of one hand at me, like a kid being taught to say bye-bye. I wish I knew what had transpired before I came.

I decided to sit on a chair down Francine's end of the room, to pull Ned away from the desk. Maybe he'd sit next to Francine on the couch.

I was waiting for Widmer to take the initiative. It was his meeting. He said, "You must have found traffic heavy coming down this time of day."

Jesus! If not the weather, it's traffic. "Not too bad," I said. "It was worse for the people coming up out of the city."

"Of course."

Francine, I thought, maybe you could bake a cake during the silence.

"Okay," I said. "We're here to talk about Brady."

"The photograph . . ." Widmer began.

"Is incidental," I said. "It's like a burglar's tool, one of several. The question is what to do about the burglar."

"One moment, George."

I looked at Widmer, and he looked slightly away as he continued.

"This isn't just a photograph Brady showed me. It's a picture of you and my daughter."

"Ned, we're past the point where you ask a father for his daughter's hand or any other part of her anatomy."

"I understand that." He pronounced it *I hate that.*

"We're here to talk about a legal situation," I said, "and it would be best for us to consider the subjects in that photograph as two consenting adults, and get on with the real problem, which is that it's being used to attempt to blackmail Francine into dropping the case. Ned, let's deal with Brady. If we win, we'll discuss the other matter. If we lose, I think perhaps none of us will be talking to each other."

I can't say it was a sigh that Ned emitted. I wished he would move from behind that damn desk.

"All right," he said. "Brady."

"First, Ned," I said. "I want to take the blame for Brady's interest."

"How's that?"

"I guess," I said, "I'm the only one present who's dealt with Brady before. He's in this because I'm in this. He's got money coming out of his ears in retainers. He has to be on call for all his regulars, and they keep real funny hours sometimes. The last thing he needs is a one-shot like Koslak. But he'd love to crack my head, in or out of the courtroom, and he's smart. Rape is a good subject for someone who works his way."

"What way is that, George?" Widmer asked.

"He starts by figuring out who his opponent really is. It's not always the accuser or the accuser's lawyer. Then he figures what's his opponent's most vulnerable point. What could he use to jab that point? How does he get the jabber? Then he does it, a, b, c. It won't do any good for me to drop off the case, now—don't worry, Francine, I wasn't intending to suggest that—once started he'd stick with it. Even if you put another lawyer onto it, he'd keep thinking of it as Thomassy's case. I'd be the losing pitcher even if I was taken out of the game."

At last old man Widmer came around the desk and sat down on the couch three feet away from Francine. It's a good thing we're not drinking coffee. We'd have to get up to pass the sugar and the cream.

"George, you said rape is a good subject."

"Terrific. For the defense. Murder, you've got a body. Dead is dead. Rape you've got a body that *says* it was violated against its will. You've got to prove the violation and the will. With murder, if a stranger does it, the question is was it planned or did the opportunity come up in the middle of something else? Even if it's in the middle of a robbery, it's murder one. If it's in an ongoing fight between relatives or good friends, it's obviously murder two. We've always got the possibility of murder in our hearts for beloved friends and kin. But that's the ball park. The uncertainties have to do with degree, not did it happen. With rape, you're back to the beginning of the hard questions. Was there an element of seduction? Was the rapee a temptress? Then there's a whole set of other kinds of questions: Did penetration take place? Penetration of what? How do you prove it? You see what I mean?"

"All too graphically," said Widmer without smiling.

"Look," I said, "I'm sorry, but that happens to be the subject matter. Let me go on to something else. You've seen Brady, Ned, so you know how short he is. I knew a kid like that in high school. Everybody else was still growing and he stopped. They called him 'midget,' something sweet like that. I remember things like 'Midget, while you're down there, why don't you kiss my ass?' Short kids grow up riding the one universal human emotion nobody much talks about, vengeance. Except they want to revenge themselves against nearly everybody because nearly everybody is taller. That's Napoleon. I could name four or five classy lawyers you know, Ned, who fit that category. And there's Brady. No class. His connections are garbage people, junk dealers, Shylocks, mob people. In some ways, the Shylocks are Brady's favorites. They charge something like ten percent a week. There's no way you can pay back. Soon you're paying interest on the interest. It's a room without doors. You're trapped. And they love it. You make money for them until you can't do anything any more. Then they beat you to death, or dump you somewhere. I know one case where they left the guy alone, because he was committed to an institution. They'd driven him nuts. These Shylocks are lovely people. They need a good lawyer to represent them because they are in an activity that happens to be illegal. A good lawyer for them is one who specializes in winning outside the courtroom, because they don't like courtrooms. Most of all, a good lawyer for them is one who is animated by a desire to beat up on the legitimate, taller-than-five-feet world. Brady's their man. Now let's talk about him and our problem. Francine, you haven't said a word."

Francine looked straight at me and said, "I love you."

I could see the pulse in Ned's temple. I said to her, "If you think that's helpful under these circumstances, you're crazy."

"That, too," she said, smiling.

I wouldn't have liked to be inside Widmer's skin.

Finally, he spoke. "The photograph, from what you've said, I suppose you both know what's in it?"

"Approximately. But Brady's already lost its biggest asset. You've seen it. Francine knows you've seen it. I know you've seen it. Nobody got hit with lightning. We're all sitting in one room peaceably together discussing it. We've disarmed that photograph, just as I'd like to see Brady kept from slipping in any kind of sexual innuendoes about Francine in front of the jury before the judge can shut him up. I think the D.A. in his direct examination of Francine should make it clear she is not Queen Victoria, just that she wants to choose what she does and a rapist doesn't give her a choice."

I looked at Widmer. He seemed lost in his own office, with his own daughter.

"Is there a room nearby from which I could make a private phone call?" I asked.

"Of course," said Widmer. "My secretary will show you the way."

At the door I turned and said, "Francine, you might want to chat with your father a bit. I'll pick you up in a few minutes."

When I was alone, I dialed Fat Tarbell's number. Busy. I doodled on the scratch pad, then dialed again.

"Yes," said Fats.

"George Thomassy," I said. "I've got a heavy one."

"Shoot."

It was a risk asking Fats. The other fellow was also undoubtedly a client of his. "Brady," I said. "What have you got on his sex life, if he has one?"

Fat Tarbell laughed. "Oh he's got one. You're looking to get me into trouble. He gives me more business than you do."

"On his sex life?"

"No."

"Then we're not competing."

He laughed. "You got a sense of humor, Thomassy. This'll be expensive."

"How expensive?"

"Who's your client?"

I would have liked time to reflect on that one. "I guess," I said, "that I'm the client."

"Well. Didn't know you get yourself in trouble, George. Thought you kept your nose clean. Oh well, thousand sound too much?"

"Five hundred sounds better. And it better be something quick and good."

"Well, let's see. Amsterdam or New York?"

"New York'd be a lot easier."

"Right. Affidavit from a lady he visits about once a month."

"Straight lady?"

Fat Tarbell laughed. "Prostitute. Own brownstone. No other women. Privacy. Expensive."

"How'd you get the affidavit?"

"Listen, George, you thinking of getting disbarred and going into competition with me?"

"Not on your life."

"She got into a bad hassle with someone on the Mayor's staff. I fixed it in exchange for the affidavit. Sixteen people covered, but you're the first to put it to use. Now that I'm looking at it, George, I think five hundred's too cheap, even if it's for you."

"Five hundred to see. Seven fifty if I get to use it."

"How'll I know?"

"I'll see that you know."

"I trust you, George. You got a deal."

"Thanks. The Gristede parking lot?"

"Not this late. Come up to my place."

"I'll have a girl with me."

"Leave her in the car."

"As you say."

"How long will it take you to get here?"

"I'm still in the city. About an hour."

"Bring cash will you? I could use it tomorrow."

"Make it an hour and a half then."

"Take your time. I ain't going nowhere tonight. Bye, George."

When I went back into Widmer's office, he had his arm around Francine, and she looked like she might have been crying.

"Everything all right?" I asked.

Neither of them answered me. God, you leave a father and daughter alone together for a few minutes and what happens?

"I have to get up to Westchester fairly fast. Ned, you don't keep cash in your vault by any chance, do you? The banks are closed."

"How much?"

"Could you cash a check for five hundred?"

He nodded, disappeared for a few minutes, returned with an envelope. In my circles, he'd have handed me the money, counting it as he did so.

"It's in there," he said.

I gave him the check.

"Can I give either of you a lift to Westchester?"

Widmer shook his head.

Francine nodded at the same time.

As we left I said to Widmer, "I think I may be buying us some good news."

He had a puzzled expression on his face. I felt sorry for him. What I did for a living was sometimes fun.

"I think we're going to be able to do some interesting pretrial plea bargaining with Mr. Brady."

"Oh?" was all he said. I had a feeling that somewhere inside his vest was a little boy wanting to come along for the ride.

THIRTY-THREE

Koch

I am walking home from the Thalia Theater, lost in thought, imperiled by traffic, agitated not by what I have seen in the movie house, but what is going on inside my head. I think: in this neighborhood if a man walking on a block empty of people suddenly feels the clutch of a heart attack does he cry out? To whom, there is no one in the street, and the people in their apartments have immunized themselves against cries from the world outside. He slumps to the ground and dies in silence, his throat filled with the anguish of having no one to call to. However, if the same man sees one other person on the street, he calls loudly for help, hoping that one other person will come quickly. And if the same victim feels the thump of an attack in the middle of a crowded street, does he cry out for help? He knows he will be noticed by the crowd, and despite a sudden fear of immediate death, he doesn't want his reputation besmirched by being thought a coward or a crybaby. He crumbles in stoic silence. It is his environment, the circumstance of other people, that governs whether a man speaks and, to an even greater degree, what he says.

Imagine a presidential candidate addressing the nation on television, saying, "I woke in the middle of the night from a dream in which the platform I was standing on was collapsing in slow motion and I was trying to grab on to people and they were shrinking away from my grasp, not wanting to go down with me, and suddenly I was awake in bed, my pajama top drenched in cold sweat. I need your vote." Yes, but that same man lying on the couch in my darkened office tells his analyst exactly that, the dream of the night before, and reaches out for the vote of the analyst that he is, nevertheless, a rational human being, anxious and frightened that he will not win in a career where winning is everything and losing is not second best but the beginning of severe depression. He wants to be sustained by me, and he speaks in a way he never would to his wife, or closest confidants, or the world. The speeches of our life are orchestrated not by what we want to say at any given moment but by who is listening.

I think of these things as I walk home from the Thalia, where I went to see *Potemkin*, which I cannot bear to see on the small screen of my television and which I have not seen in a movie theater for perhaps fifteen years. I looked forward to this evening. When I sat in the lighted theater, one or two dozen people scattered among the seats, I saw that everyone else was in twos and that only I was alone. I wasn't afraid that a prostitute would come sit next to me or a man cruising would mistake me for an aging homosexual. It is only when the lights dim and the movie comes on that I suddenly feel that such occasions call for an audience of at least two. The other people in the theater have brought their own companionship. I cannot at a moment of recognition on the screen turn to Marta to see if she is reacting as well, or nudge her with my elbow, a touch of shared experience. I am too conscious of myself. One person is an insufficient audience for a motion picture. I feel a wave of anxiety. I am half an audience.

The picture had hardly started, I was just getting used to squinting at the English subtitles when the impulse to see *Potemkin* again is overriden by the knowledge that movies are not to be seen alone, they exaggerate the loneliness, the inappropriateness of solitary viewing, the not being part of an audience within the audience. I must leave.

The ticket taker looks at me. After all, it is crazy to spend three dollars to be admitted and then to leave, he thinks I came on the wrong night, that I wanted to see another film, that I will demand to have my money returned, all this I see in his expression as I go by, demanding not money or anything else but the chance to leave and, walking home, to think of the man having a heart attack in the street, and that I have been a fool among fools to have abjured a lasting companionship since Marta's death. The newsstands on Broadway shout at me with their pornographic magazines, the great behinds and breasts visible from a distance, barking at lonely men by the millions.

I remember the first time I saw the inside of such a magazine, on the coffee table of my waiting room. I was certain it was not there before Shenker arrived, therefore Shenker must have left it. I turn the pages. The central attraction seems to be the orifices of women, some tight-mouthed as in life, some pink lips within lips, open and moist. One looks up and these orifices belong to faces that reduce one's incipient erection to instant disappointment, faces not guided by an interior intelligence, or even a sensible look, but a put-on petulance or a talentless simulacrum of passion. Did Shenker leave this as a sign that at the age of forty-two he is no longer cringingly afraid of a female body, or something much simpler, that this distinguished biochemist has at long last reached the stage where he can masturbate to orgasm without guilt and is now ready for the next step, to develop a relationship with another person? For Shenker it would be a triumph! I cannot leave this magazine on the table, I put it away in a drawer in my study. Is it to study my reaction to it once again? I look and I am forming analyses of each of the women in my head, a ridiculous exercise. A rose is a rose, but to me the vagina is a flower with a stem that leads straight up the spinal cord to the brain. When Shenker comes the next time I hand him the magazine and say "I believe you left this." He says "It's not mine," and I know I have lost him for another year of circumlocutions and evasions of the fact that his mother taught him to despise his sexuality as she despised hers.

And so, as I walk, my thoughts lead me inevitably to where they have led again and again, Francine, the intelligent child on the couch rehearsing her yesterdays in order to rationalize her tomorrows, talking, talking, while I see her stretched out, hips and legs and breasts and beautiful hair within touching distance of my two hands, which clasp each other for safety. Gunther, I tell myself, an old penis attached to an experienced brain is a dangerous weapon. My loins fill, my testes rise, I hurry my walk to a brisk pace, taking deeper breaths of the night air I can feel filling my lungs, determined to go home and call one after another of my widow friends, to make dates, to see them on a regular basis in the hope that the prospect of a continuing life with one of them will be acceptable so that once again, as with Marta, I can go to movies in peace. What a liar I have become! It is in bed I long for companionship much more than in the movie house. I camouflage my lust for Francine in intellectual garbage! Do you think I could make anyone understand this? Perhaps my own analyst, long dead. I must keep my silence like the man who is having a heart attack in a street empty of people.

I turn the key in the lock. Did I leave the door unlocked? Never! No one has the key except the superintendent. This is New York, home of drug addicts, burglars, thieves, psychopaths who kill without reason, had I better go back down and telephone the police? If I telephone they may or may not come these days. And if they find nothing, if it is all anxiety in my head nurtured by my apocalyptic epiphany on the way home from the movies, I will be put down as another of the aged cranks who sees substance in shadows.

I go in. Do I hear any sound that is out of place? If I did, it has stopped. I look in the living room, the bedroom, nothing. But I hear it again, and I swear I know what it is, the unmistakable sound of a drawer in a file cabinet closing slowly.

"What is it?" I say in a loud voice, opening the door to my study, and it is not my imagination, but a man I have dreaded seeing all my adult life. I don't know who he is, this man who is taller than I am, in his thirties, wearing sports clothes, holding a group of file folders in his hands as he turns toward me. He is the intruder of my fears.

Calmly, he says to me, "I thought you were at the movies." This is not an accidental intrusion, a burglar trying random doors of an evening, he has come here now because he knows I was supposed to be elsewhere. Fool, I should have obeyed my first instinct and called the police!

"What do you want?" I say, wishing my voice were as calm as his.

"You sit right down there, doctor," says the man. He points with the file folders to the chair behind my desk.

We are all of us inexperienced when finally a nightmare visits us. Who makes up our dialogue on such occasions? Though we may have imagined, as I did, a dozen times, what an intruder would say and how we would answer, it is a useless rehearsal. I say, "You cannot take anything. Those are private patient files of no value to anyone except me."

The man reaches into his jacket and pulls out a pistol. He doesn't point it at me, just puts it down on the file cabinet. "Sit down the way I told you and you won't get hurt, doctor."

He is so calm you would think he has done this a hundred times. Maybe this is his regular occupation. I sit obediently at my desk. I think I bought a four-drawer cabinet for patients' files that has a lock at the top that I never push in. What is the use of an unused lock? Would it have made a difference? Don't these people all know how to open locks? Such locks benefit only the lockmaker. How much money do I have in my wallet? At least fifty dollars that I remember.

My mouth dry, I say to the man, quietly, reasonably, "Those are private files. They are very precious to my work and to my patients. They are of no use to anyone else."

"Shut up!" he says.

"I will give you fifty dollars to leave the files alone."

He laughs out loud this Nazi. At that moment, squatting near the bottom drawer, he finds the file he is looking for. Toward the end of the alphabet. Intuition tells me it is Francine Widmer's.

I take the five tens out of my wallet and put them down on the far side of the desk.

"Thanks," he says, taking them.

"Now please go."

"Sure." He leaves the files he doesn't want on top of the cabinet, takes the pistol and puts it in his jacket pocket. He has the file he wants and he is at the door of the study. There will be no way to find him. I do not know who he is.

"You took the fifty dollars. You must leave the file."

He looks at me as if I am mad.

"We agreed."

"Fuck you, doc."

I have to tell you I have noticed the darts before this and have put them out of my mind, but his breach of what I thought was our agreement stings me, and his insult stings me, and I feel the energy of all my lifelong complaints against the injustices of the world, as I pick up the dart and throw it straight at him, instantly thinking he will pull out that pistol and shoot me dead, but the man screams the most impossible scream I have ever heard, falls back against the door jamb, and slides down to a sitting position, pulling at the dart, screaming, the blood running down his face, and I see all too clearly that it has gone into his right eye nearly up to the feathers. He tries to pluck at it, but it must cause greater pain, and I pick up the telephone and dial 911, and thank God there is an answer soon, a Spanish-accented policeman, and I tell him an intruder in my apartment, with a gun, I have wounded the intruder, he gets the address, the apartment number, and I hang up, my hands shaking, my heart beating, I cannot go past his thrashing body on the floor, what is he doing?

I realize he is trying to get the gun. The file folder, its contents spilled, with blood on the pages, scattered all over. He has the gun, can he see me to shoot?

"You fuck!" he yells like an animal. I crouch behind the desk as the gun goes off, an explosion of noise, the bullet landing somewhere behind me. Do I dare crawl to the other side of the room, farther away, or is the safety of this desk my best protection, God God, what have I done? It is impossible not to look, so around the corner of the desk I stare to see him suddenly retch, vomiting over the hand with the gun, the files, the carpet, this once human being, out of his bloody eye a dart sticking thrown by my own hand.

Every minute of waiting seems an hour, then, at last, I hear unmistakably the sound of the elevator in the hallway, the clatter of feet, the front door open, and I see the two policemen as in slow motion, their guns drawn, and they see the vomit-covered disgust of the man against the door jamb, and I stand only to see that one of the policemen is pointing his gun at me, and I shake my head and point to the slumped man. He takes the gun out of the man's hand almost without effort.

"Jesus!" says one of them, looking at the face with the dart. The man's lips now open and close like a fish, pink bubbles appearing when the lips part.

"You throw that dart?"

I nod.

The policeman wraps the man's gun in something—a handkerchief?—and the other one says some gibberish about anything I say can be held against me, I have the right to observe silence, I am under arrest.

"I am Dr. Koch. This is my apartment. This man is a burglar. I came in when he was looting my file cabinet. He threatened me with his gun." And I stop. Had he actually threatened me? It is so hard to be sure. "The dart was the only weapon I had. It was self-defense."

"I'm sorry, doctor," says the policeman, looking back at the mess, "we'll have to book you. You can call your lawyer if you want, after I call for the ambulance."

THIRTY-FOUR

Thomassy

I told Francine she'd have to wait in the car.

"I didn't bring anything to read," she said.

"I'll leave the key. Turn on the radio."

"It'll drain the battery."

"I won't be long. Lock the doors from inside. Sit behind the wheel. If anybody tries to bother you, take off. When you get somewhere, call this number." I gave her a slip with Tarbell's phone. "Don't memorize the number," I said. "It's one you don't ever want to have to use without me fronting for you."

Tarbell answered the door, a large, curved pipe hanging from the side of his mouth. He removed it to grunt a greeting, led the way through the disorderly wilderness of his apartment, down a long hallway with closed doors on both sides like sentinels. We passed the open door to the kitchen. A woman sitting at the kitchen table nursing a cup of coffee nodded at me. His wife? Cleaning woman? What was behind all those doors? I'd been in the apartment only once before. I glanced around his so-called study at the end of the hall. I'd forgotten what a mess of papers and casebooks littered the room.

"A flash fire'd put you out of business," I said.

"Nah," said Tarbell. "The best stuff's on microfilm."

"Brady's?"

"Natch. Have a seat." He flopped a fish hand at a Naugahyde arm-chair with a stack of file folders in the seat. "Just put them on the floor," he said, plopping his three hundred pounds into a swivel chair and passing me a stapled affidavit of about a dozen pages. "You'll see she signs it both ways. That Anna Costello, that's her real name. Her customers know her as Anna Smith. Her good customers know her as Anna Banana."

I was trying to be polite enough to pay attention to him, but my eyes were skimming the affidavit.

"Why Anna Banana?"

"Oh it's a thing she does. It's in there."

"What does she do for Brady that Mrs. Brady doesn't do?"

"Brady's on page seven. She refers to him as Mr. B."

"How do I prove it's Brady if I have to?"

"His social security number's in there. Anna's a smart lady."

I skim-read pages seven and eight.

"Useful?" asked Tarbell.

"The kind of people he works for wouldn't like to think their mouthpiece was into something this kinky. They'd think he freaked out."

"Other people's sex always looks crazy."

"This is straight out of Krafft-Ebing."

"Let me unstaple it. You can take pages seven and eight. Just bring them back."

"I'd like to take the whole affidavit."

"You're not paying for the whole affidavit."

"I'd like to fill myself in on Anna's kind of shtick, just in case I need to know more about her than how she services Brady."

"Well, skim it."

"I've got a lady waiting in the car."

"Skim it here."

I did. It was pretty awful stuff. I like to think I'm broad-minded, nothing human is alien to me and all that, but maybe some of this stuff isn't human. "Okay," I said when I had finished.

Tarbell took the staple out and handed me pages seven and eight. Then as an afterthought, he handed me the first and last pages also. "You might need those, the beginning, and then the signature page."

I stood up. I guess I wanted to get out of there.

Tarbell held his hand out.

"Sorry. Almost forgot." I gave him the envelope with the bills. I waited till he counted them. He wasn't part of Widmer's trusting world.

"By the way," he said. "He goes to Amsterdam at least once a year. Interesting."

"How'd you get that?"

"Other people go to Amsterdam. A little money helps finance their trip, and builds my inventory."

"Tarbell," I said, "do you have a file on me?"

I could swear his cheeks reddened. "Sure," he said. "Small one."

"Think I could guess what's in it?"

"Doubt it."

"Could I buy my own file?"

"What the hell would you want to do that for, George?" he said.

"Just testing."

"Get the hell out of here before I get angry."

"I should be the angry one."

"If I'm not covering everybody, people won't come to me first, they'll go to Broderick in New Rochelle. Listen, you don't like what I do for a living, you just get me reinstated in the bar, okay?"

I didn't want to get on the wrong side of Fat Tarbell. "Don't think I don't understand," I said. "My life is your business."

He laughed. "You're okay, George." He showed me down the long hallway to the door. "Come back soon."

Francine was sitting in the driver's seat. She unlocked the door and slid over when she saw me coming.

"Sorry it took so long," I said. "Some of the stuff I had to read on the premises."

"What's he got on Brady?"

"I'd just as soon not talk about it. It might put me off sex for a week."

I had meant to phone my service from Tarbell's. I guess reading that junk had distracted me. I pulled up at a public phone and called.

"A Dr. Koch called. Sounded very upset. Asked you to call soonest." She gave me Koch's number. I wondered what was up. I looked over at Francine in the parked car. She seemed restless. I decided I'd return Koch's call when we got home.

When we reached my place, I took my jacket off, lowered the knot of my tie, and sat down to read the Brady pages in Anna Banana's affidavit once more before putting them somewhere Francine wouldn't come upon them accidentally. I guess she'd say I had an old-fashioned point of view as to what a woman should and should not be exposed to. A double standard for kinkiness.

Francine got the ice, made the drinks as if it was her place. The whole thing had a domestic feeling about it. Was I bothered by that? I didn't want a woman to wait on me. Some guys get married for the service. A bachelor gets used to doing his own.

Jesus, I nearly forgot about old Koch. I stashed the Brady stuff away in the other room, then dialed Koch's number. "Oh," said the lady in the answering service as if she was waiting for my call. "He's very anxious to talk to you. As soon as possible." She gave me an unfamiliar number. I wrote it down, thanked her, and redialed.

"Sergeant Heller." It was a police station. A wave of thoughts skittered through my head. Koch'd been mugged. Couldn't be too bad or the old man'd be in the hospital.

I identified myself and told the sergeant I was trying to reach Dr. Gunther Koch. Francine had come into the room. She pointed at my glass. I must have gulped my drink without thinking. She was wanting to know if I needed another. I shook my head. Meanwhile, the sergeant had passed my call upstairs to the detectives. "Just a minute," somebody said, and I could hear the telephone clatter onto a desk top at the other end. It took forever till somebody else picked up, another voice, saying, "You the doctor's lawyer?"

"What happened?" I asked. "Did he get mugged?"

"No," said the rough voice. "The doctor's the perpetrator."

God, police use words like that every chance they get.

"What did he do for Christ's sake?" I couldn't believe that mild-mannered man would do anything harmful to anybody.

"He hit a guy in the eye with a dart."

I looked up at Francine.

"Could I speak to the doctor, please?" I asked.

"Hold on, I'll get him." Again, the receiver clunking on a desk top.

When Dr. Koch got on, he talked so fast in that accent of his I could barely make out what he was saying.

"Slow down," I said to him.

I could hear him take a deep breath. "It is unbelievable," he said. "They have taken my picture. They have taken my fingerprints. I am booked as if I am the criminal. Please help me."

"Tell me what happened. Slowly."

"This man, he had a gun."

"Start at the beginning," I said.

Then he told me about coming home from the movies, finding the door open, seeing the man at the file cabinet, the man forcing him to sit behind his desk. "I offered him fifty dollars to go," he said. "He took the fifty dollars and was taking Miss Widmer's file anyway. On my desk I have these three darts . . ."

"You threw one at him. He could have shot you."

"I didn't think, really. It just happened."

"You hit him."

"Yes."

I thought of a guy getting a dart in the eye. Jesus!

"Is he hurt bad?"

"Quite bad, I'm afraid. Please help."

He sounded like a child, this doctor of the child in us, suddenly at sea.

"Who do you normally use for a lawyer?" I asked.

"An old friend from Vienna, who makes out my will. He will not know what to do in this . . . police station. Can *you* help me? We are . . ." He hesitated. "In this together, are we not?"

I was very tired. Manhattan was a long way away.

"Get the address from the cop," I said. "I'll be down."

Francine wanted to know what was going on. I buttoned my collar and shoved my tie back up in place and put my jacket on. "Mind the house while I'm gone," I said. "I'll probably be half the night."

"I'll come with you."

"You don't want to see your shrink in the lockup. It won't help your analysis. I've got to get going."

"Please let me come with you."

"It would embarrass him. He's embarrassed enough."

"What happened?"

"You happened." I didn't realize how awful that was until I said it. "An intruder in his apartment was after your file. Koch hit him in the eye with a dart."

* * *

As I raced the car down to Manhattan for the second time that day, I tried not to think of Francine or what she might be thinking. I read the road signs out loud. I pushed the station buttons on the radio. Nothing, nothing, and nothing. I had to stay awake. Just keep driving, I told myself, *drive.*

THIRTY-FIVE

Brady

I don't give a fuck for Harry Koslak's freedom. I got him out on bail so that I can prepare him for trial. Jail is no environment for rehearsals. Because the incident took place in the apartment directly below Koslak's, I suggested we meet in his apartment so he could walk me around the incident, so to speak. His wife seemed scared of me. I told her to take a long walk with the kids. As for the story Koslak then told me, I'm sure I didn't get it as it happened exactly. Koslak makes it sound as if he controls his cock like a light cord. That man I have yet to meet.

So when he finished what he called his explanation, I sat him down in his living room in one of those armchairs with plastic covers, next to the fake fireplace that never fooled anybody.

"Harry," I said, "let's handle the rest of this conversation in the following way. If I ask a question, you answer truthfully. If a question makes you uncomfortable, instead of giving in to the temptation to lie a little, just say you'd rather not answer that one, okay?"

"I'll tell you the truth," he said. "Ain't I been telling you the truth?"

"How did the Widmer girl first come to your attention?"

"You mean when'd I notice her?"

"Sure."

"On the stairs. Going up and down. You know, I'm going to work, I'm coming home from work, she's going someplace, she's coming from someplace."

"Did she say hello to you?"

"Not so's I remember."

"Did she nod the way people do when you live in the same building?"

"Yeah, I think so."

"Did you nod back?"

"Probably."

"Did you ever nod first at her?"

"I don't do that kind of thing."

"You mean she made the first overture, she nodded first."

"You might say so."

"Was there anything provocative in her manner?"

"What do you mean?"

"Did she act sexy in any way?"

"Well, when I come up the stairs after her, you know, she's got one ass going up while the other's going down, back and forth. That's sexy."

"Would you say she walked that way on purpose?"

"What do you mean?"

"Harry, you know damn well what I mean. Some women just walk as if it's transportation and some roll their melons when there's someone to watch."

"Well, I'd have to guess."

"Go ahead, guess."

"From the way she dresses, I'd say she's probably walking sexy."

"What about her dress?"

"She don't wear dresses."

"I mean the way she dresses, what she wears, Harry." I was getting impatient.

"She don't wear no brassiere."

"Sometimes or always?"

"I never seen her that she didn't wear nothing under her blouse or sweater or whatever, even going to work."

"Did you find that sexy?"

"Yeah, yeah."

"Did you find that provocative?"

"How do you mean?"

"Did her lack of a brassiere make you think things or want to do things?"

"You bet."

"Do you find all women of that age make you think things or was there something special about Miss Widmer?"

"Look, she is a real special-looking dame. She's got class the way Grace Kelly has class, you know what I mean? Not cheap. Class."

"That attracts you."

"It makes me want to poke my thing in there to see if it's real."

"How do you think she thinks about you?"

"Now?"

"Before all this happened."

"I don't know she noticed me except to nod. I was embarrassed, to tell the truth."

"Embarrassed?"

"Yeah, well I was often wearing overalls, right? I mean if I was wearing a business suit and a tie I'd a felt better about what she might be thinking."

"Did you feel, Harry, that she was beyond your reach?"

"Yeah, in a way, but I tell you, any dame walks around with tits like that is looking to get them grabbed, right?"

"You said the second time, when you and the janitor paid her a visit, that she was more cooperative."

"Yeah, she took her top off. Wouldn't you call that cooperative?"

"Maybe she thought that would interest you both."

"It sure did."

"Maybe, Harry, she was stalling until help could come."

"Stalling? I'd say she was moving things along. Listen, I never met a dame that'd volunteer a strip that wasn't a whore. Anyway, I don't pay for pussy. I don't respect anybody has to."

"Let's stick to the subject, Harry." I could have caved in his skull. "Would you say the janitor instigated the second visit?"

"What?"

"Put you up to it."

"Jason? I was the one told him. Listen, I don't want to get old Jason into dutch."

"Not even if it helps your case?"

"I'm not that kind of guy."

"But you thought that by bringing him along, if he had a piece of it too, you'd be convincing everybody that Miss Widmer'd ball anyone who came along, right?"

"Right."

"So you were thinking of your defense?"

"Sure."

"Why did you think you'd need a defense?"

"Be prepared, I say. To tell you the truth, I was surprised as hell when she did something about it. Most dames don't say nothing."

"Harry, how many women did you rape before this?"

He was silent.

"That's it," I said. "If you're tempted to lie, just don't answer."

"I'm not lying. I never raped nobody. Listen, Mr. Brady, you ever meet a woman you weren't married to who just invited you in? They all need a little sales talk, a little pressure, some more than others."

"What do you mean by pressure?"

"You know, what they like, you threaten them a bit, you joke about it or maybe you don't joke about it, you twist an arm a little, just as a reminder."

"A normal part of the mating game."

"What's that?"

"Never mind. You've had women resist like Miss Widmer?"

"Sure."

"But never call the cops before?"

"That's right."

"How many women?"

"Exactly?"

"Estimate."

"A dozen?"

"You asking or telling?"

"About a dozen. Maybe two dozen."

"Harry, I don't know if I want you testifying in your own behalf. I'd have liked to have you tell the story the way we plan it together, understand? Let's go back. You said you were thinking of your defense. Does that mean you thought you had done something wrong?"

Harry laughed real nervous like. "Look, Mr. Brady," he said, "don't you think you're doing something wrong whenever you have sex? I mean with anybody?"

"We're talking about you, Harry, not me. Keep to the subject. You said Miss Widmer tried to talk you out of it. What did she say?"

"Like I said, all dames try to talk you out of it. Christ, Mary even used to. She still does once in a while, and I'm her fucking husband!"

"What did Miss Widmer say to try to talk you out of it?"

"She said I could go to a prostitute or something like that."

I'd had enough. I got up to go.

"Wait a minute," he said. "What's all this talk about? How's it going to do me any good?"

"Well, Harry, you're the customer. You're entitled to hear it the way I hear it. Let me play it back to you. You met her on the stairs many times. She said hello to you first. You never said hello to her first. When she walked ahead of you, it was your impression that she walked provocatively. You couldn't help noticing that she never wore a brassiere. You found that provocative, too. Naturally. She looked very lady-like to you, yet very enticing. You had the impression that she wanted it. You had the impression she wanted it not just from you, which is why you brought along the janitor the second time. You thought you were doing something she wanted. You get the picture?"

Harry seemed very pleased.

"We'll have a chance to go over this again, Harry."

"You sure know how to put things, Mr. Brady," he said. "I'm glad you're my lawyer on this case."

That remark would cost the stupid idiot at least an additional thousand dollars, which I better hit him for before he goes to jail.

THIRTY-SIX

Thomassy

You sometimes forget that policemen are government workers, meaning no significant economic motivation, lots of useless paperwork, a life of time spent waiting for something to happen or someone to move a process along a little. To survive, a policeman like a doctor has to immunize himself against the waves of rage and rancor splashed at him by perpetrators and victims alike. A chief of police, who as a young man probably had a surfeit of vitality, is eventually as discouraged as a beat slogger. I pity them. You can't talk to a cop man to man. You're either a supplicant or a superior.

Which leads me to the duty sergeant at the precinct that was holding Koch.

"That psychiatrist needs a psychiatrist," he said.

"What's the problem?"

"He acts like we done something wrong to bring him here."

"Sergeant," I said, "this isn't one of my usual clients or your usual clients. He's a senior professional person and being in this place is like his suddenly finding himself on Mars. I want to talk to him in a private room."

So Koch and I were led to a cubicle on the second floor, where he tried to say six thousand things at once. Trying to calm him down reminded me of the time my car's engine wouldn't shut off when I took the key out and kept shuddering for minutes till it finally collapsed into silence. For the moment I was the psychiatrist and he was the patient. When he was finally quiet, I asked him what he was thinking.

"In Vienna," he said, "my passport was stamped with a red J." His voice fluttered. "Please, Mr. Thomassy, I have never been in a place like this. Get me out of here. I beseech you."

I didn't want to be beseeched by anybody. I told him the routine.

"Listen carefully, Dr. Koch. You had to be booked because an action of yours injured another person. The circumstances are what the judge will listen to, not a policeman. I will get you down to night court and ask for bail. But I need to know the facts. Just the facts, if you can."

"I realize you are being very helpful to me," he said. "I am just a stranger to you."

"You're less of a stranger than most of my clients when I first meet up with them. Please tell me what happened in your apartment."

So he recapped the thing. I asked him to wait in the room while I went out to talk to the detective.

"That's the first psychiatrist we've had in here," said the detective.

"Congratulations," I said. "Let's get him down to night court right now while he's calm."

"Look, mister, we've got seven guys in the lockup got here before he did. I can't spare anybody to go with you now."

"How long?"

"Morning."

"Can I use your phone?"

"Local?"

"Local."

"Sure."

You couldn't dial out. You got the policeman at the switchboard.

"Please get me the officer on duty in the commissioner's office. The number is—"

He knew the number and was already dialing. The detective stopped penciling the form in front of him. He was listening.

When I was connected, I said, "This is George Thomassy. I don't want to bother the commissioner this time of night. I'm up at the twenty-fourth precinct. I've got to get some red tape untangled before a distinguished citizen loses his cool and talks to the newspapers. Yes, I'll wait."

When he got back on he said, "What's the problem?"

"No problem. An intruder was caught in this citizen's apartment, threatened him with a gun, and got injured in the process. All we need to do is get the doctor—"

"A legit doctor?"

"A psychiatrist. Just want to get him down to a judge so we can get him home before he starts talking to the papers."

I looked at the detective. "He wants to talk to you," I said.

The detective took the phone. I could have guessed the conversation. The detective hung up, and without saying a word to me went into another room and came back out with a young cop. "This is Patrolman Mincioni. He'll ride you and the doctor down."

"No cuffs," I said.

"No cuffs."

It would have been easier with one of the Westchester judges. Judge Sprague was a new face for me.

"Your Honor," I said after he read the report the cop put in front of him, "there are several possibilities. If the doctor had had nothing to use in his defense, the intruder would have walked off with a file that is essential to a rape case being tried in Westchester. The people might have lost that case if the file was not available, or was available only to the defendant's counsel. Your Honor, I believe the intruder may have been employed by defense counsel through channels. If Dr. Koch had been brave enough to use the only defense weapon at hand, an ordinary practice dart, and missed, or merely nicked the intruder, the intruder, who was used to carrying a gun, wouldn't have missed Dr. Koch when he shot him and we'd have a corpse instead of a doctor, and a killer on the loose. Because this doctor—and this is not true of all doctors as you know, Your Honor—was not a passive citizen in the face of crime, and luckily disabled the intruder with the one and only dart thrown, the people can proceed with their case in Westchester. Dr. Koch probably deserves a medal instead of the fingerprinting, mugging, and humiliation of the station house, but right now I want to get him home and to bed after his harrowing experience as a good citizen. I don't have to tell you that Dr. Koch's roots in the community suggest that he be released on his own recognizance."

Well, here is this judge in front of a night court full of inner-city ethnics and he's got to let a white middle-class physician off. His face rigid, severe, mock contemplative. Then he said, "Two hundred fifty dollars bail."

I asked Dr. Koch if he had his checkbook with him. He didn't.

"Will it please the court to have the defendant paroled in the custody of counsel?"

"That will be acceptable," said Judge Sprague.

And in no more than ten minutes we were outside. The doctor shook hands with Patrolman Mincioni. Mincioni was respectful, as to a priest.

I drove Koch home. When we got there, he didn't move to get out of the car.

"What's the matter?" I asked.

For a moment he said nothing. Then, "I was thinking of what I will find up there. I don't like hotels, or I might stay in a hotel tonight. Oh well," he said, opening the car door, "we are here." He turned to me. "I don't know—truly—how I would have managed without your help. Please come up for a cup of coffee before you drive home."

I was beat. It was after 3:00 A.M. I wasn't up to conversation. Maybe the old man was scared. Half a cup of coffee was probably a good idea anyway. I double-parked.

"That's all right," said Koch. "Everybody double-parks here."

He showed me the disarray in his study. It was a mess, particularly near the door, where the man had slumped. He pointed to where the bullet had gone into the wall.

"Perhaps my Saturday cleaning woman can come tomorrow," he said. "If I can find her. I will have to see patients in the living room. This has to be cleaned before I can see patients in here."

He started to push one of the file drawers back in and I said, "Don't." I startled him. I guess I said it too sharply. "I think I'd better send a forensic photographer up here in the morning. The police didn't take pictures, did they?"

"No."

"It'll cost, but it's worth it in case I don't get this dismissed."

"What does that mean?"

"Nothing to worry about. Leave it to me."

In his kitchen I watched him empty a small paper bag of beans into a hand grinder. He passed the shallow dish of powdered beans in front of my nose. I had to agree the aroma was pleasing. He then dripped hot water through them and offered me exactly what I had asked for, half a cup.

"I won't join you, if you don't mind," he said. "It'll be hard enough to sleep as it is. I wonder how that poor man is doing. The one I hurt."

"I can check for you tomorrow if you'd like to know."

"Oh don't bother yourself."

"No bother. Just a phone call. This coffee tastes as good as the aroma of the beans promised. What is it?"

"Ethiopian Harrar. Zabar's has it sometimes. How old did you tell me you were?"

"I'm forty-four. Why do you ask?"

"Do you think Francine Widmer is in love with you?"

"I wouldn't say that."

"Well, I am saying it. You see—" Koch hesitated just a second— "I also have an inordinate response to her."

I sipped at the coffee.

"That makes two of us," he continued, "with the combined ages—" he laughed— "of one hundred and four, in love with a twenty-seven-year-old. In China they used to venerate age because it represented the wisdom of experience. In Europe, maturity still is respected a bit. In this country, age is despised. America may become a terrible country as the population gets older and older."

I stood up. "Time to go."

"Thank you for coming up. May I give you my check for the bail while you are here?"

"Just mail it to me."

He extended his hand in a warm, sure grip.

"I am not a serious rival," he said. "Except here." And he pointed to his leonine head. "Good night."

I found Francine asleep on top of my bed, her knees drawn up, her two hands under her cheek, a naked child. I rejected the child in me when I was still a child, Koch would say. He'd say that because my father refused to venture out into America, I'd have to do it for both of us. I am my father's keeper. I am my own keeper. I don't need anybody. Not that body on my bed. I have kept myself free of family tyranny by staying single, not fathering any tadpole of my own, observing the bodies of innumerable women the way I am watching her now, from a distance, objects in a Sears catalogue, tools to play with for a week or a season. They went home, sooner or later, to the rest of their lives.

Looking at her lying there contently asleep, I thought how recently I've come to understand about the bodies of women. When you're young, you're exposed to enough locker rooms to know in a few years' time that no two men undressed look alike, and that most parts of most men are pretty damn funny if you don't look at them with loving eyes. But we stereotype the women according to what Francine's father would call the paradigm of an age. Not the rotundness of the Renoirs or of the Latin American women, but the sleek, flat-tummied, long-legged look-alikes who can be photographed almost wholly nude, with or without body make-up, and seem to women as enticing to men, and yet I've never dated a woman who filled the prescription flawlessly. There are always the too-thin eyebrows, the few long hairs growing from the areola, the butt that naked is a bit too big, the thighs that wrinkle a bit from fat that will not come off with exercise. The thing about Francine is that I note those minor imperfections as I did with the others and have feelings about them because they are part of the whole of her. Love isn't blind, and it isn't tolerant. It is encompassing. It doesn't make virtues out of warts, it makes them part of an over-whelming affection for the corpus that envelops the vital organs of someone whom you unreasonably love. When love strikes, reason be-comes inoperative. When it becomes operative again, it is probably a sign that that particular love is on the wane, or settling for the kind of lifelong affection and attachment in which warts are condoned.

And it's not just the physical appearances that work that way. I've never known a woman for long who did not, on some occasion, have a breath temporarily worth avoiding. Or one who did not, in the middle of some night, let some flatulence escape. Where is the woman whose stomach does not percolate like a chemistry beaker if you put your ear to it. It could happen with a one-night stand, or during an affair. You can count on these demonstrations that the woman is alive. But when you love the person, the effect of all these demonstrations is different. They are less to be observed and noted than your own breath, which, when foul, you tolerate less. Love is what, acceptance?

Love puts you in a dangerous magnetic field. You can be anywhere, she can be anywhere, the field of force operates. If you can't close the field with your arms, the pain can be exquisite. The operator of person-to-person radar, a force stronger than conscience. It isn't commitment, a conscious act, but a gravitational pull that works your heart, your adrenaline, your breathing, and your balls. Thomassy, don't ruminate, I tell myself, it's not your style. You're used to cases that conclude. Love—even if experience and statistics show how very often it slackens and disappears—is *at the time* seemingly unending. It's a new experience for you. Don't knock it. Enjoy it.

Francine stirred, opened her eyes, stretched, saw herself naked, and pulled the sheet and blanket up to her chin.

"You could have covered me," she said.

"Not a chance," I answered.

THIRTY-SEVEN

Widmer

When I was a young man I would have dismissed the notion of precognition as unsuitable for discussion. Buck Rogers was fiction. Laser beams were comic book devices. Men flew, but not in space. You see how the very science I accepted with faith has now turned me into Square Alice at the Mad Hatter's table. Today, young people like Francine take precognition for granted, as the Greeks did. The period in which rationalism flourished was historically short. It was a comfortable period for well-brought-up people. Then the carpet was yanked.

It was thoughts such as these that I brought with me to the meeting in Lefkowitz's office because I did in fact have a clear precognition that it would be a remarkable meeting. Francine was to be there, and her attorney, of course.

Once upon a time the bride was brought by the father, but on this occasion I arrived in the anteroom alone, minutes before Francine arrived with Thomassy. My thought was that they had come straight from their shared pillow. Then I thought the pillow had most probably been under her hips.

We greeted each other with inane pleasantries, and were spared the possibility of extended conversation by being ushered into the disappointing presence. Lefkowitz, a rotund young man, attempted to conceal his incipient corpulence with a vest; the Phi Beta Kappa key and chain across it merely called attention to the concealment. Of course I was prejudiced. This young assistant district attorney, undoubtedly with political ambitions, was probably from a recently well-to-do background, unmistakably Jewish in his physiognomy as well as name. He deferred to Thomassy a bit too much. He called me sir, but his gesture to take a seat was casual; with Thomassy, I thought he would put the chair under the man. He designated Francine as the most minor of his visitors by giving her a chair to one side, as if he expected her to be an auditor only.

Lefkowitz ordered coffee. This meeting was too serious for coffee. The others declined also. Lefkowitz, his hospitality drained, retreated behind his desk and spoke.

"I am going to be trying the Koslak case," he said, "and I thought it would be useful if we met for a general discussion. I could then see Miss Widmer separately to go over the details."

It was as if a midshipman had announced himself the new captain of an aircraft carrier.

Thomassy said he was pleased that Lefkowitz would be personally involved in this important case and asked him what tack he proposed to take in its prosecution.

Lefkowitz, addressing himself to Thomassy and me and pointedly ignoring Francine, gave the schoolbook answers, summarizing the facts, declaring the crime would be proved by the testimony of the victim and corroborated by other circumstantial but condemning evidence, and he would be calling for punishment for the perpetrator as a lesson to others. Under different circumstances, I could have allowed myself a moment's amusement, but I saw the tic in Thomassy's jaw.

"Well," said Thomassy, standing, "we might as well drop the case."

"Please sit," said Lefkowitz, alarmed and standing.

They both sat at once.

"All right," said Thomassy. "Let's put the problem on the table. If you use the textbook approach, it'll come down to her word, his word, reasonable doubt. We can't depend on passing pieces of paper in the courtroom. The strategy has got to be worked out right here, putting together all the experience we can muster."

"Of course," said Lefkowitz, fingering his key. "I will be discussing the details of the presentation with other prosecutors on the staff and with Mr. Cunham, and my presentation will have the benefit of their combined experience."

"To be realistic," said Thomassy, "the track record of this office on rape prosecutions is . . ."

He was going to give Lefkowitz a precise figure from his notes. Into the momentary silence, I said, "Deplorable."

To my surprise, Lefkowitz said, "Quite right, Mr. Widmer. But I'm sure you know the pitfalls in the way of getting convictions."

"George," said Francine.

I could see Thomassy didn't like being called George in front of me.

"George," she said, "how would you present the case?"

"Yes," said Lefkowitz, "I was about to ask."

"Do you want your stenographer in here?" Thomassy asked Lefkowitz.

"I'll take notes if they become necessary."

I had the distinct impression that his embarrassment stemmed not from Thomassy's seniority but from the presence of a woman of his own age in the room.

"All right," said Thomassy. "How this case goes depends in some measure on the opening presentation. I'm sure you can put it in your ball park before Brady tries to put it into his ball park. Mr. Lefkowitz, I'm positive you've arrived at the same conclusion I have. Your theme is force. That's the issue. But before you press that, the jury has got to get used to the idea that sex is not the issue. Otherwise, we're in Brady's ball park, the victim is not a virgin, she's experienced, sexy looking, maybe sexy feeling, all you need is a hint that she's concupiscent and it could raise a reasonable doubt in the minds of the jurors as to whether she tempted Koslak, and Brady's off and running. We have to create an atmosphere in that courtroom right from the start that defuses talk about sex, that takes the Victorian dirty-mindedness that still infests us all to one degree or another and puts it on the table as something that is not at issue. Force is the issue, not standards of moral conduct."

Thomassy took a deep breath. He looked at me, at Francine, and then at Lefkowitz. His audience was paying attention.

"Okay," Thomassy continued, "how do we do it? How do we play back to the jury a tape recording of what they themselves really think when they think sex? Mr. Lefkowitz, every lawyer handles things a bit differently, but suppose you were to get up close to the jury and ask them, each of them, to think of the worst kind of sex they ever heard about, the sexual thoughts that most repel them. Suppose you got them to play the tapes inside their heads, gave them a chance to think of whatever kinky things clutter their consciences. Then let them off the hook. Remind them everybody thinks things like that from time to time. We're not here to evaluate anyone's sex life except as force is used to push it on other people."

For a moment I thought Francine was going to put her hand on Thomassy's. I wished her not to do that, not for my sake, but for Lefkowitz's. He had enough to contend with without being exposed to the personal relationship between victim and advocate.

Lefkowitz wrote down one word on his yellow pad. I prayed the word was "force."

Then Thomassy continued. "From your presentation the jury is certain to conclude that the issue is not temptation. Of course the victim is not at age twenty-seven a virgin. She has the same moral standards as innumerable scientific surveys have shown to be predominant in her generation—which is different from the jury's generation unless you're damn lucky and can get some younger people impaneled. She is a professional woman. Educated. She lived alone out of choice. She had no reason to suspect that a neighbor she saw frequently in the building would introduce himself into the apartment by deceit, as the testimony will show, and then use force to foist his sexual demands upon an unwilling person. I'm certain you'll set it up so that when Brady goes through his shtik, the jury will hear it against the background of what they remember from your presentation."

I wished Lefkowitz took more notes. A man like Brady could eat him alive.

"I'm sure most of this has occurred to you," said Thomassy.

"Yes, but do go on," said Lefkowitz. "It's useful to hear you frame it your way."

I concealed my smile. That young pup has learned his tricks.

"Good," Thomassy continued. "It won't hurt to consider the point that ordinary men and women have very little understanding of the enormity of rape as an experience.

"Suppose you were to convey to the jury the idea that everybody hears all the time and nobody believes. The two big crimes are supposed to be murder and rape, but everybody thinks murder is terrible and rape is something to be discussed with the women's movement.

"Why the different attitudes to rape and murder? You've got to get the answer across. We're used to murder. All the literature we're exposed to from the time we're kids deals in murder. Start with the Bible, Cain kills Abel. Take the jury through Mickey Spillane, if you have to. Murder is commonplace in our imaginative lives. The ten commandments put it straight, Thou shalt not kill. When it comes to forcing sex, the commandments hedge. Thou shalt not covet thy neighbor's wife. Hell, everyone covets his neighbor's wife from time to time. The issue is force. The commandments may fudge it, but the law does not. Rape and murder have been the two big capital crimes. You've got to bring them together in people's heads. I mean the people on the jury.

"Some judges will let you get away with a hypothetical instance. Let's try this. If you eliminate all other people except the potential victim, murder is still possible in the form of self-murder, suicide, still a crime on the books. But if you eliminate all other people, rape is impossible. What you're left with is masturbation, and that's not a crime. In a rape case, we need to focus on the other person. There's no doubt about who the other person is. Koslak. He just says he didn't force it. So we concentrate on the issue of force."

The thought occurred to me that if I had heard a lecturer like Thomassy in law school, I might possibly have been tempted in a different direction. Law as the theater of ideas in a forum of power? Ah well, for me it was too late. Thomassy was going on. I couldn't afford to miss any part of it. To Lefkowitz he was saying, "You're Jewish, aren't you? Well, let me suggest something else for your consideration.

"There are a lot of things one can't suggest directly to a jury. Every lawyer has a different way of getting things across by body language, intonations, allusions, subliminally. I'm sure you'll be able to find a way to reminisce about various things. There'll be a lawyer at the accuser's side who is of Armenian extraction. Perhaps that lawyer has a strong feeling about rape because the Armenians, the first Christian community in modern times, were early in this century subjected to rape as well as murder by the Turks on a scale that, in your reflections, can only be described as genocide. In fact, you yourself can allude—you'll know how to do it without rattling the judge—to the fact that you, representing the people's case in this courtroom, cannot forget that in this century, in which six million of your coreligionists were exterminated, many of the women, the attractive ones, had the option of choosing repeated rape in the SS brothels instead of death, and that after the experience of rape, many chose death. You'll have alluded to the Christians and the Jews, and if you can keep Brady from objecting, you'll have covered everyone in this jurisdiction. What you are accomplishing with all the finesse you can muster, all the indirection at your command, is to get the jury to see rape in all its historical enormity. Once you do that, Brady won't be able to mock, disparage, or trivialize what happened. I'm certain you can do it."

Lefkowitz poured himself an inch of water from the carafe on his desk. "Mr. Thomassy," he said, "I respect your experience, but do you really think the judge would let me get away with that?"

"It all depends on how you do it," said Thomassy. "Look, one thing you can count on is that none of those jurors will have been a victim of rape or be related to a rape victim. Brady'll knock them off for cause before they're impaneled. Therefore, it is your obligation, you explain to the judge, because people know so little about the crime of rape, to give them some background, some filling in."

"I was hoping," said Lefkowitz, "to avoid emotionalism in my presentation."

"I don't expect you to be emotional at all," said Thomassy. "You're far too skilled for that. You're just alluding to facts about the historical context quietly. Be as cool as you want to be. The emotion will be in your listeners."

Thomassy's puffing up of Lefkowitz seemed to be working. The young man billowed with each stroke. He turned to me, and said, I thought a touch condescendingly, "Mr. Widmer, you've had longer experience at the bar than either of us. Do you have any points you'd care to have me consider?"

I would have had him consider his youth and his mortality. What I said was, "Mr. Lefkowitz, my practice, as you may know, is very different from Mr. Thomassy's. I've never uttered a word inside a courtroom. I would find it exceedingly difficult to present this case."

"Mr. Widmer," said Lefkowitz, "I've had a good deal of experience these last two years, in criminal matters I mean, and my percentage of convictions, on cases where I presented the cases not just prepared them, is significant and rewarding."

I could guess that Francine was not entirely happy with Mr. Lefkowitz, but Thomassy, with a glance, kept her from saying something. They had had a previous agreement on the point, I was certain.

"I think it would be useful in the opening presentation," said Thomassy, "to cover two more points. Murder is a single act. When it's finished, that's the end of it. The victims of rape, when they are allowed to live, or when they give in so that they can live, then have to spend the rest of their existences with the disgust and terror and memory of it. Rape is a continuing crime because long after it is committed it goes on in the head of the victim."

"A good point," I said.

"Excellent," said Lefkowitz. I wonder what he wrote down on that pad of his.

"My last point," said Thomassy, "has to do with the importance of this particular case. From time to time we've had the experience in this county of a rapist who focuses on youngsters, ten- and twelve- and fourteen-year-olds. When he's caught, the mother refuses to let the child testify. She takes the child to a psychiatrist, and the psychiatrist discourages public testimony because it could be traumatic for the child. He doesn't worry too much about the private testimony the child is giving him because that's therapy and he's being paid for it. Well, we're all against child rapists, right, and we're furious when the guilty escape the law because the underage victims aren't allowed to testify. But the truth is that many women who are raped feel exactly as the mothers of the children do, they don't want to go through the public experience, the drawing out of their private lives, the humiliation, the obscenity of the details. They fink out. In this case, the jury is going to hear from an extraordinary victim, the rare, brave young woman with the strength to testify, the moral strength to be unwilling to duck her responsibility to the rest of humanity. Don't make her into Joan of Arc. Just make damn sure that in your opening she comes across as someone deserving of respect. That's the word to write down: respect."

"I already have," said Lefkowitz.

"It's your meeting," said Thomassy.

"I think I've got what I need out of this larger meeting," he said. "I'd like to go over the details of the actual event from my notes with Miss Widmer, if that's all right with you gentlemen."

I said Thomassy and I would wait for her in the anteroom and take her to lunch afterwards.

Outside, we went to the men's room, the bridegroom and the father of the bride in adjoining urinals, listening to their respective tinkles. It would have been more comfortable to skip a urinal in between, but also obvious.

"Well," said Thomassy, "I think she's safe with Lefkowitz."

I had to laugh.

"I mean in the office," said Thomassy. "He could blow it in the courtroom."

I had to agree. "What do you think are our chances?"

Thomassy didn't answer. I didn't know if he was thinking or preoccupied.

"Realistically," I said.

We both took extra time to make sure the last drop went, then zipped up, washed up, and strolled down the corridor together before he replied.

"Lefkowitz is no match for Brady."

"Our case is good." Why *our* case? And how did I know it was good? I sounded like a layman.

"Ned, good cases are of no value if your advocate isn't shrewder than the other guy, or doesn't know where the power lies. We have one chance."

"What's that?"

"Work on Brady so he knows he's playing with me and not with the kid Lefkowitz."

We walked back the way we had come. "George," I said to him, "when you were in school, did you think of justice as the lady with the scales and all that?"

"In the streets of Oswego, Ned, things aren't much different from Manhattan. They don't let you get away with cock and bull. Clout counted. Not justice." He looked at me. "Were things different at Groton?"

"No. Of course not. The parents pretended, of course. And the masters. But not the boys. Did you pay the piper?"

"Piper?"

"The leader. The bully. Whatever you called him."

"I worked around him."

"A mite harder working around Lefkowitz."

"Yup."

"Well, never fear," I said. "I'm no authority on tactics, but it seems to me your suggested presentation was rather brilliant. If only we could hire an actor for the role."

"Why thank you, Ned." He seemed genuinely pleased. "Glad you steered Francine to me?"

"Not entirely."

Back in the anteroom, we sat apart. I thumbed through a *U.S. News and World Report*. When Francine emerged, Thomassy, who was not reading, went to her first. They said something to each other, I couldn't overhear, and he took both of her hands only for a split second. I thought *Are we at last mingling our genes with the barbarians', or have we found a way of protecting ourselves?*

We went to lunch. I was the supernumerary.

THIRTY-EIGHT

Thomassy

I put my briefcase against the leg of my chair so it would be sure to fall over when I got up. I didn't want to forget it. I couldn't tell you what I ordered or ate or heard as I watched the talk ping-ponging back and forth from Francine to her father, her father to Francine, meaning, really, I watched how Francine's lips moved when she talked, the way she touched them with the edge of the cloth napkin, the way her hair swayed when she tossed her head. All I'd had was a Campari and soda before lunch and I was sailing, floating, except it wasn't a casual high, easygoing or passive. I was being swept along weightlessly in space under the influence of the most potent hallucinogen in the world, the thrall of being in love.

Every once in a while Widmer would turn to me and say something. I'd nod or shake my head, possessed, not knowing what I was agreeing to! Francine, intuiting that a mad obsession had taken hold, covered for me, keeping the conversation bobbing amidst the noise of the restaurant. I felt as if she and me, me and she were the only ones mattering, stripped of all other things in life except each other. And the tremendous energy that came with it! Sitting still I felt like leaping up, whirling about, dancing like a Nijinsky even though I've never danced solo in my life. It's the omnipotence, the feeling I can do anything, I am in love.

At last father and daughter were through. We stood for the ceremony of his leaving. He pecked Francine's cheek, a cheek that I wanted
to lick with my tongue like a cat. I shook Widmer's hand, hoping mine,
its skin prickling with nerve endings, didn't feel as hot to him as it felt
to me. My face felt flushed, too. The nerve endings on my arms and
elsewhere cried out to be touched by you know who.

"Goodbye," he said.

Tra-la, I wanted to say.

"I suppose you two have things to talk about," he said.

I suppose, you suppose, he supposes. We suppose, they suppose.

He vanished into the crowd after a last little wave at his daughter
and glance at me, and the two of us were alone in that crowd. I put my
hands on the table and she covered them with her own.

"It's unbearable," I said.

"I know," she said.

Could another person feel energy bouncing around for release, the
total, total, total overwhelming joy of it all? Perhaps she felt a bit of it,
too?

"More than a bit," she said. Was she reading my thoughts or was I
talking out loud and not knowing it?

"I've got to get back to the city," she said. "The stuff on my desk is
crying out for my attention."

"I am crying out for your attentions," I said, and I knew she could
hear me, because I could hear myself now talking out loud instead of
inside my head.

"Listen," I said, "this is urgent."

"What?"

"This." I moved my hands under her hands. "I'd be dangerous in
the courtroom," I said. "To my client. To myself." I moved my face
across the table and she moved hers to meet it. From four inches away
from her lips, I said, "I've gone insane."

Francine laughed, got up. "Let's walk it off," she said.

"Terrific," I said, standing, my briefcase falling over to remind me.

I walked as if my feet were hydrofoils. Like a guardsman on parade, I
swung her hand in my hand all the way forward, then all the way back.

"We must look nuts," I said.

"Nuts we look," she said.

"There it is," I pointed. Holiday Inn.

"This is crazy," she said.

I swung my briefcase. "Crazy is as crazy does," I said.

I signed as in as Mr. and Mrs. Archibald Haig, in honor of our respective fathers. Looking over my shoulder, Francine laughed. The man at the reception desk smiled.

"I'll show you the way," he said, taking my briefcase.

Oh the absurdity of the man carrying my lone briefcase ahead of us, switching on the room lights, showing us the bath, the closet (for what?), the TV set, everything except the bed. I thanked him two dollars' worth, ridiculous, and double-locked the door. My arms went around her, clasping her close enough to meld us cheekbone to hip, deliciously hurting. She pushed us asunder, and then woosh, no two people in the history of the universe ever flung their clothes off as fast as we did, and there I stood, my heart pounding, my rod pointing, and she touched it, just barely touched it around the head, then dropped to her knees, taking it into her mouth in a way it had never been taken by anyone before, *as if it were hers.*

"No, no," I said, motioning her over to the bed, but she shook her head, fiercely in charge of my organ, which I was now moving to the rhythm of her mouth. Of course dozens of times in the past with others I had felt the mechanics of it. Jane used to hold it apprehensively just below the head as if afraid I'd suddenly lunge too far, but now Francine was alternately licking and kissing and enveloping it in a way that electrified its entire surface, and I moaned—first time in my life I ever did that—moaned with the excruciating pleasure of it, as the throb started, and she somehow cupped her hand around my balls without breaking the rhythm, and her eyes glanced up at me for a second, and then like a great pulse of energy, I started to come and come and come, and finally slipped, exhausted to the floor beside her, our arms around each other, rocking.

I remember the fantastic look of accomplishment in her eyes. She knew how good she had been for me.

"What hath the mouth that the vagina hath not?" I whispered in the curlicues of her ear.

"A tongue," she answered, laughing, and I remember we kissed in a kiss that seemed to last for all time until we broke to breathe again.

"Turning you on turns me on," she said in my ear.

"I don't believe."

"Proof," she said, holding her breasts. Her nipples were obtruding and hard. I licked one with the tip of my tongue. She turned slightly so that I could lick at the other.

I remember her taking my head in her hands and moving me down to the triangle of her once-blond hair and below, where her lips seemed to part in slow motion to reveal a pinkness where I busied my tongue, and in an instant her hips were moving to a savage rhythm on the carpeted floor. Suddenly she stopped, pulled my head up to her. I didn't know I was erect again, but somehow she knew and took it with her fingers and placed it where my mouth had been, and then we rocked in that same impatient insistent demanding rhythm of hers until she was saying *now now now* and we were both senselessly kissing and coming and kissing and coming.

We must have dozed. When we awoke, I felt drained, rag doll limp, euphoric. I kissed the end of her nose. We untangled, stretched, somehow got to our feet. I felt as if I would stumble. We held each other for support.

We dressed. I know we dressed but I don't remember it. I only remember our looking around the motel room making sure we had everything including my briefcase, and then noticing that at the center of the scene of our lust stood the fully made, unrumpled bed we had not needed.

We laughed like kids, then closed the door behind us.

THIRTY-NINE

Francine

At the office I received the funniest sort of phone call from my father. He asked me if I was still seeing George. The way he pronounced "seeing" had a private connotation. With the case still pending, I told him, of course I'd been seeing George. He sounded as if he were pleading a case that had gone askew. Weird!

I certainly wasn't going to pick up on whatever he was hinting about. In fact, I felt in an unstoppable rush to see George every possible minute. The day after the Holiday Inn episode, George and I met for lunch halfway between his office and my office and would you guess where that halfway turned out to be? The same Holiday Inn, same desk clerk, same expressions, only this time when my clothes were off I skewed my hand around to my back and showed George the Band-Aid right above my butt.

"No carpet," I said.

"Hop onto the bed," George said, but one step ahead of him, I plunked myself into the overstuffed chair near the window. Straight ahead was the mirrored bathroom door, and I have to admit I looked pretty good in it. I moved my right arm snakelike as if in a dance, watching my reflection. Then my left.

"Narcissus," said George. "Will you have a room service lunch before or after?"

"Instead," I said, as he dropped to his knees in front of the chair. It was odd, watching in the mirror, then oddly exciting, then very nearly unbearable.

We didn't muss the bed this time either. We did order a couple of sandwiches afterwards because all that appetite gave me an appetite.

That evening we went to the movies. How do I know what was playing, it was a movie, we weren't watching the movie, we were too busy with each other. That night we slept at George's, the jigsaw pieces of our limbs learning to find the perfect fit with each other. The next morning, I had my driver's license at risk as I zoomed to work, getting there late, and was greeted by X saying, "Can you make lunch?" and me answering, "You mean cook?" and he saying, "In a restaurant, idiot," and me saying, "I took a very long lunch yesterday, I should eat in," and him saying, "I'm the boss, it's okay."

Over lunch I kept thinking of yesterday's nonlunch lunch with George, and I guess I wasn't paying too much attention because X finally said, "Are you in love?"

"Yes."

"Who's the lucky man?"

"A man."

"As distinguished from a boy?"

"Yes."

X professed mock jealousy—I hope to Christ it was mock jealousy—and then invited me to sub for him on a radio panel because he had a conflicting appointment.

"I know all about your conflicting appointment," I said. "You don't want to do it."

"Right."

"Why?"

"Fair enough," said X. "Butterball is the other guest. I'd be tempted to let him have it. If I do, it's serious."

"And if I go on in your place, it's not serious because I'm just a young woman of low station and it doesn't count."

"Oh it'll count all right. Just sending an underling like you will be received by His Highness as an insult. It's beautiful."

"Thanks a lot." I wasn't really angry. Butterball, or His Highness as we sometimes called him, was the crown princeling of a new West African country with a population smaller than Harlem's, but who saw

his Harvard-educated self as the most glamorous of the spokesmen for
the new bureaucracies that had dumped all their white colonial riffraff
and were learning to master postage meters and typewriters.

"The subject," said X, "is the shrinking world."

"Lovely."

"You could have a good time at it. It'd be good experience."

"When?"

"Next Tuesday evening."

"Will you listen?"

"Wouldn't miss it."

"If I'm terrific do I get a raise?"

"You know the system."

"I do indeed."

In the meantime, there was the weekend. Friday night George took
me on the longest drive through Brooklyn to some terrific Italian restaurant in Coney Island and it was two in the morning before we got
back to his place. When I came out of the shower he was in bed asleep,
the son of a bitch, but I crawled in alongside of him, kissed the back of
his neck, and the back of his back, and he muttered sounds in his sleep.
I slept too, till sometime toward morning when I felt the scepter
stiffen. We made languorous middle-of-the-night love till daylight,
then slept till noon. Still in our nightdress, we ate a marvelous breakfast
of grits and bacon and eggs and English muffins and orange juice and
back to bed.

"Not bad for an old man," I said, flaked out from postcoital exhaustion, absolute, terminal, and slept again. I woke, refreshed, glanced at
the clock. Impossible! It was after three in the afternoon! Where had
the day gone?

"Get up," I said to George.

"After you," he answered.

"Simultaneously," I compromised, and we pulled each other up, and
then, like kids, made a game of dressing each other.

"This is a very erotic exercise," said George.

"Oh no," I said. "If you're not worn out, I'm worn out, let's go for a
walk," and we did, until the daylight faded. Having missed lunch, we
stopped for dinner early at a small Italian place. We finished half the
chianti before the spaghetti arrived. We laughed at each other mixing

the meat sauce, forks twirling the pasta in dinner spoons, shoveling it into waiting mouths. Halfway through, George made a thing of taking a single strand in his lips and sucking it in.

"People are looking," I whispered.

"Voyeurs," said George, "may they enjoy it."

"Crazy," I said.

"Crazy," he echoed.

Suddenly George said, "Let's go!" He motioned for the waiter, who came scurrying over.

"No good?" he questioned, as if to say how can spaghetti not be good.

"Marvelous," said George. "Check, please."

George overtipped, and we both skipped out of the place, and once in the street, hand in hand, ran back to the house and to bed. I didn't think I could have another orgasm, but I did, I did.

Sunday morning we were awake at dawn. It felt as if the rest of the world had disappeared. I pulled down the covers and addressed George's organ. "This," I said, "is a day of rest." All I did was tap it on the head to make my point, but I could see it stirring. "Lie still," I told it, patting it down. It wouldn't listen, thickening. "It's Sunday," I said, touching the rim of the corona, circling it as one does the rim of a martini glass. And there it was, instant yeast, the veined mast twanging up to its full height.

"A day of rest," I said to the unmoving George, as I got up to lower myself unto him, then raised myself, then lowered again, riding him first in fun and then in fury as the shudders came and I collapsed on top of him.

I was still lying half over him when we later woke.

"They shoot horses, don't they?" said George, and I had to laugh, even though I hadn't seen the movie.

I told him about the Tuesday radio show and invited him to hold my hand. "Not literally," I said, "they'll probably make you sit somewhere behind the glass, but you can watch me show off with Butterball."

"Have you ever been on the radio?" he asked.

"Nope."

"Aren't you nervous?"

"Only about us."

"What about us?"

"Continuing."

His kiss caught me by surprise.

"Sated?" he asked.

"Yes."

"I had an idea."

"No more."

"No, a different idea. How would you like to get out of being the star witness at Koslak's trial?"

"I said I would do it."

"What if you didn't need to?"

"I'm not going to let that bastard off."

"Suppose I was able to guarantee a jail sentence for him without a trial?"

"You planning a dictatorship?"

"I want to try something."

"Who's stopping you?"

To me, after all those days and nights of lovemaking, he seemed unstoppable.

FORTY

Thomassy

To avoid getting into an Alphonse-Gaston routine, I went to see Brady in his office.

"An honor," said Brady.

"Sure," I said.

I asked him if Koslak meant anything special to him.

"A fee."

"Period?"

"Period."

"What do you think Koslak will get?"

Brady laughed. "An easier piece of ass the next time. What can I do for you, Thomassy?"

"I'm not prosecuting the case. Lefkowitz is."

"Too bad in a way. Some people around the courthouse might pay to see a Brady-Thomassy play-off." Brady's face suddenly lost all expression. "I've seen that punk kid work. I'll get Koslak an acquittal or probation easy."

"Not if you have any ballsy women on that jury."

"Look, Thomassy, you know I'm not going to have *any* women on that jury. I got a little something worked up that won't even use up my peremptories. You come around. You'll enjoy it."

"I'd like to let you in on a little of my strategy."

"Lefkowitz's."

"Mine. Lefkowitz is going to be my Charlie McCarthy on this case."

"Good trick if you can do it. One step out of line and I'll have you removed from the courtroom for interference. By the judge, of course."

"I'm tutoring Lefkowitz."

"Sure."

He was wanting to hear but not to show it.

"I've got an expert witness."

"Look, Thomassy, I'm bored with all that psychiatrist shit. I'll tear him to pieces."

"I didn't have a psychiatrist in mind. I think the jury needs to understand the difference between seduction and rape, between normal sex and abnormal sex."

"And?"

"My expert is Anna Banana. The subpoena will read Anna Smith. You know this expert?"

Brady had the no-expression curtain on his face, but he couldn't immobilize the small, dancing tic near his upper lip. He picked up a paper clip and opened it into a single not very straight piece of wire. Finally, he said, "What's that to me?"

"I'm planning to have her files subpoenaed, too. There'll be a connection."

"You're bluffing. You'll never get her on the stand."

"Lefkowitz has a law school classmate in the Manhattan D.A.'s office. This friend has quite a file on Anna Banana, but Lefkowitz's friend has generously arranged for the lady to continue her eccentric livelihood. It seemed an important consideration to her, which is why we expect her to testify gladly. For a fee. I'm quite convinced her expertise in what is normal is based on more professional experience than most psychiatrists have. She's got quite a bit to say about men who, say, rape instead of paying for their special requirements."

"You finished, Thomassy?"

"There's a second and more expensive witness. However, my client is willing to foot the bill from Amsterdam."

I was certain Brady was thinking where he could get my arms and legs broken for a price.

"Oh," I said, "and of course Lefkowitz will be calling Dr. Koch."

"That son of a bitch!"

"Why'd you say that?"

"I heard he was a son of a bitch."

"Could it be you heard he managed to repel an intruder?"

Brady flinched when I touched my eye. He knew I knew.

"Thomassy, I don't know why you're rolling in all the heavy artillery. Some twat gets laid by someone she didn't pick and you're acting like there was a million-dollar construction contract at stake."

"I'd appreciate your characterizing my client differently."

"I forgot you had a piece of her."

"Anna Banana, Amsterdam, Koch. Could be an interesting array of experts."

"What's your suggestion, Thomassy?"

"Cop a plea for Koslak. No trial. You got your retainer. I might talk Lefkowitz into first degree assault."

Brady bent the wire into a circle.

"Trespass."

"You've got to be kidding, Brady. Her father's a lawyer. He sent her to me. I can't come up with a Mickey Mouse."

"I'll discuss second degree with my client."

"Thank you. Oh by the way, Brady, are you acting for the superientendent?"

"No."

"Know who is?"

"Nah. He said something about Legal Aid."

"I have a feeling, Brady, that the super didn't know what Koslak was letting him in for."

"You kidding? Koslak told me that guy bangs half the women in that block. It's better than being a milkman."

"If he gets all that ass without much hassle, what'd he want to rape the Widmer woman for? Or was he just going along for what he thought was another free ride?"

"What're you up to, Thomassy? You don't have to think of using him as a witness. I told you I'm talking to Koslak to cop a plea."

"That was the last thing on my mind, Brady. I had another idea."

Outside, I stretched my arms, pleased with myself. Francine

wouldn't have to go through with the mess. And I wouldn't have to burn on the sidelines in court, watching Lefkowitz bumble. All I had to do was get Francine out of that apartment for good. The American system of justice is a lovely way to kill two birds with one stone.

FORTY-ONE

Francine

X was right. Butterball had not been told that I was substituting for X until he arrived at the studio Tuesday night. For a minute there was some confusion because Butterball thought Thomassy was the substitute guest. The host, Colin Chapman, thought Butterball was going to walk. The instant panic proved unnecessary. Butterball could not resist any opportunity to talk to the public, especially when it couldn't talk back, and he settled down to the proffered coffee and to another dose of the American rudeness that had put him up against a mere girl. He didn't say any of those things, but it was as clear as if he had. And it stimulated me to the best twenty minutes I have ever had out of bed.

With George ensconced behind the glass next to the engineer, Colin Chapman chatted us up, then got the signal, and we were on. He introduced the subject and deferred almost immediately to Butterball, who launched into a spiel about how just two days ago he had been home for a visit and with just an eight-hour flight (first class, of course!) he had been transported from emerging Africa to New York, and since then he had talked no fewer than six times by phone to this minister and that minister back home. Colin Chapman tried to butt in a couple of times to make it a dialogue, but the only thing that worked was when I said "Mr. Ambassador" in my best stentorian contralto and put my hand over the microphone. He had to let me talk.

In fact, that was when Butterball first took notice of me.

"Mr. Ambassador," I repeated, "I have a very different idea of the shrinking world. We have seen," I said, "in recent decades, a proliferation of countries in the continent the Ambassador calls home, and in each new country, we have witnessed a growth of government agencies, a burgeoning of offices and duties and jobs where none existed, an unchecked growth of one of the most insidious forces in the modern world."

I looked up at the glass booth to make sure George was wide awake and following.

"Which is?" asked Colin Chapman brightly.

"Bureaucracy," I said, stopping and gesturing with my palm toward Butterball.

"The lady," said Butterball, "chooses to use a pejorative term for administration, the necessary functions of government if it is to keep things running."

"The lady," I said, "has a name, Mr. Ambassador."

"Francine Widmer," Colin Chapman supplied.

"Africa," said Butterball, "has found itself."

"What does that mean, Mr. Ambassador? Does it mean Africa has been found dividing itself into smaller and smaller constituencies, each with its own administrative offices, to the point where we will soon see a return in that shrinking world to the tribalism of yesteryear, except each tribe will have its own postage stamps?"

Behind the glass, George was having a good time. Butterball was trying to check his anger.

"Mr. Chapman," he said to our host, "the great leaders of emerging Africa . . ."

"Amin?" I asked.

"What did you say?"

"Amin?"

"I heard you."

"Are you including General Amin among the great leaders of emerging Africa?"

Butterball was fumbling his debits and credits. Privately he was reputed to despise Amin, but I had him boxed in.

He decided to ignore me and addressed Chapman. "Mr. Chapman," he said, "the announced subject of this broadcast was the shrinking world, and I do not see the necessity—"

"Of evasion," I said.

Chapman was loving it. In his job he had to play host to a multitude of horses' asses during the course of a year, and he obviously relished this one's discomfort.

Within five minutes I got Butterball admitting that his government actually had more government agencies than did the preceding colonialist government, that the rolls of government employees had increased by more than three hundred percent in the last two years because three semicompetents were needed to do the work of one bureaucrat who had the wrong color skin, and best of all, that he fully expected to be the subject of a forthcoming postage stamp. Behind the glass, George looked like a kid at a baseball game.

Toward the end, Butterball was panicking. "I am surprised," he said, "that the United Nations would employ a person so divisive, so intent to reverse progress, so intolerant of the change that is revolutionizing the world."

"Frankly," I answered, "I'm surprised, too. Perhaps I am like the Soviet dissenters, needles in a haystack, an almost invisible presence that cannot be ignored."

"Thank you," said Colin Chapman, "thank you both, but we've run out of time."

While Chapman was winding up, Butterball stoood, his chair making an awkward noise that went over the air. I stood and put out my hand. He had to shake it.

As soon as Butterball was out the door, Chapman said, "Lady, if I may call you lady, you were terrific. What a pleasant surprise. Whenever we get a substitution, it's usually a downhill omen. You gave us a fine program on a dull subject. I'd love to hear you give a speech at the U.N."

"Sorry," I said. "I'm not an ambassador. All I do is prepare some stuff for other people's speeches. They usually take the stingers out first."

By this time, George had come around to the studio and I introduced him to Chapman, who said, "This young lady of yours ought to be in broadcasting instead of over there with the fuddy-duddies." He stopped when he saw the man in the banker-striped suit come in the studio door.

"I agree," said the man. "My name is Straws. I'm glad I was in the building. I didn't catch all of it, but enough. You were splendid."

Straws shook hands all around.

"I'd like you to come and see me, if you would," he said, handing me a card. I glanced at it. He was general manager of programming.

"Let's go," said George.

I hadn't realized how restless he'd gotten, but the remark was rude under the circumstances.

"You couch things well," Straws said to me, "but under the camouflage a killer instinct is clearly visible. I can think of a dozen people I'd love to see you decimate."

Chapman wasn't happy either. Suddenly I had gone from being a good guest to potential competition.

"I'd be delighted to come and see you," I said to Straws. "I'll call your secretary for an appointment."

Come on, said George's eyes.

The engineer behind the glass opened his mike. "That was a very interesting program, Miss Widmer."

"Thank you," I said. I was ready to hand out autographs.

"Don't pay any attention to Art," said Chapman, gesturing at the engineer, "he's always buttering up potential hosts. He loves to work talk shows."

Straws nodded and left. "You see," said Chapman, "he didn't contradict me. I could smell his evaluation. I better look to my laurels."

"Don't be silly," I said. "I have no experience."

"You've just had a very successful audition, young lady," said Chapman. "It's a good thing Straws is set to give Lily Audrey the boot. He'll think of you as a replacement for her instead of me."

He has got to be kidding, I thought. "I've only heard her once," I said. "Isn't she the one who comes on like gangbusters?"

"You've got the right one."

George took my arm. Not gently.

"Glad you could come, Miss Widmer," said Colin Chapman.

I could feel George tugging.

We were hardly out of the building when he said, "You really fucked that poor man over, didn't you?"

"What's got into him? "I thought you were enjoying it."

"Sure thing. Love to see a picador jabbing spikes into a bull."

"That poor bull is the second most powerful man in his diminutive country and is likely to be its next head of state. He deserves every opportunity to get talked back to under circumstances where he can't decapitate his adversary."

"You do love the limelight," said George.

"Don't be silly. When I call Straws I probably won't get by his secretary. He'll have forgotten tonight by breakfast tomorrow."

"He won't forget."

"Now look, George, I've never seen you in the courtroom but I did see you give Lefkowitz the works. You like stage center as much as I do, and you've had one helluva lot more experience. I'm just catching up."

He took me by the elbow again.

"Please don't take my arm like that," I said.

"We only have the one car," he said.

"You can drop me at my place."

In the car, he said, "This is ridiculous. We've fucked ourselves silly for nearly a week and now it sounds like we're having an argument over nothing. The only reason I'm reacting to your sudden celebrity is jealousy."

"I'm glad you recognize that," I said. "It's a first step."

"To what?"

"You've probably played the lead every time you've been in a courtroom. You're used to center stage. You don't like cooling your heels in an audience. Or watching anyone else perform. Like me."

"Oh come off it, Francine. I don't think you're about to become a female David Frost. And I'm not about to become a stage door Johnny waiting for you the way I did tonight."

"This could be a break," I said. "Don't you want me to take advantage of it?"

"Sure."

"That sounded like drop dead."

"Well, I didn't mean it to sound that way. Look, Francine, you said you liked working for X."

"That's right. I'd like working for nobody even better. Like you."

"I work for my clients."

"You're fudging, George. When did you ever really think of a client as an employer? They're yours to manipulate, not vice versa. I'm not going to pass up this chance."

"I'll bet you're not."

Just as I'd let loose at Butterball, it came out of me once again in a torrent. "I'm glad this happened. It could have happened a year down the road, with our lives meshed. You just can't stand the idea of my finding something I can do well and enjoy more than my backstage work at united bedlam. You've got your vocation and that's enough for both of us. George, living alone all these years has made you into a self-centered, selfish, self-contained isolationist, and you've been that way too long for me or anyone else to rescue at your age."

I guess it was "at your age" that did it.

He didn't speak until he dropped me off at my parents' house. He didn't get out and open the door for me, the way he'd been doing all week long. He just sat glowering behind the steering wheel and said, "The good news I had for you tonight is that Brady is likely to have Koslak plead guilty to second degree assault. He'll go to jail. There won't be a trial."

"You're talking to me as if I'm a client."

"I am."

"Thank you for the good news."

"Please be sure to tell your father."

I got out and slammed the door. He roared off.

FORTY-TWO

Thomassy

I guess it was in the early years of high school that the key thought clicked: the world's got a lot of shit to hand out in the course of your lifetime, and the idea is to learn how to take as little of it as possible.

Being rich didn't always help. In those days in Oswego being rich meant owning a grocery instead of a shoe store. You could patch up last year's shoes but you couldn't eat yesterday's meal today. Joey was the grocery kid in our class. He used to dispense candy to buy favors the way John D. gave away dimes, but he got beat up more often than most because all the other kids wanted to be sure Joey and his parents got the message: being rich didn't mean being safe. My father used to say that when the Turks came, being a rich Armenian was no advantage over being a poor Armenian, it just made you complacent.

My mother, Marya, was a totally dependent person, an old-world clinging vine who would have had trouble surviving if my father had died. He instructed her, commanded her, praised her, insulted her, loved her, and she lived by his words. I didn't take her as a model. And I couldn't take my father as a model because strong-willed as he was, he couldn't defend himself against the Turks, or the prejudices of Americans toward immigrants, or the depression. The thought that clicked my life together was that I could gain and preserve my independence by fortifying myself against whatever Turks or Americans or anybody had in store. My senses told me it wasn't money or even political power that was indispensable for defense and protection, it was learning the methods. First, you had to cut through all the idealistic bullshit used to control people, you had to see how people were not how they were supposed to be. Then the techniques. A compliment would sometimes work. Other times a stare, a fist, a kick in the ass, or better yet, a way of carrying yourself and walking that made troublemakers pass you by because you didn't look like an easy mark. It got me through school. It got me to the point where I knew that I could count on one person, me. Having allies was okay, as long as privately you didn't trust them. Having friends was okay, too, provided you didn't turn your back on them when they had something to gain by knifing you in the back. I guess you could say I eventually became a lawyer because once you saw how the justice system worked, you didn't want to depend on another lawyer to get you in and around it.

I got on pretty well. People who knew me didn't tangle with me unnecessarily. I learned the rules for getting around other people's rules. I was ready for the Turks, any time. But I wasn't all strength. If I was stronger I could face up to the idea of sorting out the baggage in my head on Dr. Koch's couch, but I wasn't about to show my doctor how I had put myself together. It'd be giving some of my strength to a weaker person. I suppose that might explain why I didn't get married. When I was in my twenties, everybody else did, but the idea seemed a burden I could do without. If the Turks came, I didn't want to protect a wife also. The trouble is you meet a woman like Francine and you wonder who would be protecting whom. She's young and there's a lot she doesn't know yet, but she's learned at a rate that might put her ahead of me in know-how when she's my age. She's self-sufficient. She's willing to share her life, which makes her stronger. Once I had a crazy feeling that if I ever lived with a woman, she'd have to be a Turk to start with so I'd know I was in the enemy camp!

Well, this evening I didn't want to think about any of that, I wanted to drift, do nothing in particular, take my shoes off, read through the junk mail I should have thrown away unopened. Nothing on the television schedule made me want to turn the damn set on. I picked up a novel I'd bought at the airport and never started. In the middle of page one my mind started to wander. There was a girl in the book, not like Francine, but it started me thinking of Francine, and I didn't want to think about Francine, but there I was doing it and the phone rang.

I wanted it to be her, but it was my father, saying, "George? George?"

"It's me, Pop. What's up?"

"Nothing's up, ha-ha," he says, "too old. Want you to come visit. Important. Bring the girl."

"I'm antisocial these days, Pop. Is there anything I can do from here?"

"Say yes. Say when."

"Pop, I've got my life scrambled at the moment—"

"Soon three minutes up," he interrupted. "Hurry say yes."

"You should have called collect."

"God damn George, if I call President of United States I pay for call. If I call you, why should you pay God damn phone company racketeers? You coming, yes, no?"

"What's so urgent? Are you sick?" I asked.

"I sick making phone company rich."

"How about May," I said, "when the weather's good?"

"Now."

"Important?"

Again his silence. I could hear him swallow before he said, "Please."

I didn't remember his ever saying please to me in his life. George Thomassy, man of steel, folded like a tin cup.

"It'd have to be Saturday."

"You bring girl?"

"The girl and I aren't—Pop, I'll come alone."

"Too bad. Girl not Armenian, but very nice. You make mistake, George."

"All my life," I said. "According to you."

"What's that mean?"

"We'll talk when I get there, okay?"

"Dress warm. Cold up here."

"Yes, Pop."

"George, I have important talk with you."

"Are you all right?"

"I live to Saturday, ha-ha."

I've never been one of those work fanatics that uses the weekend to catch up on the week's undone work. For me the weekend has always been R and R time, more recreation than rest because I think it's the change that recharges the motor more than sacktime. I hadn't made my usual Friday- and Saturday-night dates for this coming weekend. I had expected to spend Saturday morning in the stand of trees around my house, cutting off deadwood and chainsawing three or four fallen trees into logs and kindling. But chainsawing can be dangerous if your mind is somewhere else, and I knew my head would be more full of images of Francine than if she were with me all the time. I felt haunted by her, hating the intrusion, and the weakness that had let me break my rules and get overinvolved with one person.

After my father's call, it was like a ping-pong match inside my head: Papa, Francine, Papa, Francine. He knew instantly she was not another one of my women. The old bastard was all instinct. Going to see him, the geographical wrench, might get Francine out of my head.

What a pain in the ass it was getting to Oswego. You got to La-Guardia by seven in the morning to catch the one and only from there to Syracuse, where the car you had reserved might or might not be there for the twenty-six-mile drive. You could get more than halfway to Los Angeles in the time it took to get to Oswego.

The flight to Syracuse was bumpy. I had broken my rule and instead of a novel, brought a case full of briefs on the plane. I couldn't concentrate on them. Her face was there. Her body, all too recent to obliterate.

It was damn cold in Syracuse, with the wind whipping around the airport like an invisible flail. I ducked inside the car rental office, and wouldn't you know: no reservation for George Thomassy.

I told the klutz behind the counter that I had made the call myself, and I had taken the name of the clerk who had confirmed the reservation. I showed Klutz the name.

"She don't work weekends," he said.

"What's that blue four-door?" I said, pointing to a car just outside the plate glass window.

"It's reserved," said Klutz.

"By whom?"

"I don't have to tell you that."

I guess I looked like I was going to hop over the counter and grab him by the throat.

Klutz looked in the box on the counter. "It's for Mr. Patterson. He called this morning."

"I called two damn days ago. What time's that reservation for?"

"Eight A.M."

"Good. It's nearly nine. I'll take that car."

"What do I do if Patterson shows up?"

"I assume you didn't walk to work this morning. You rent him your car. Let me have the form."

I signed, initialed the collision extra, took the yellow copy, and held my hand out for the key.

"It's in the ignition."

"Thanks," I said.

It's like that everywhere in this garbaged-up world. They clean the ashtrays but they lose the reservations.

Pop was waiting for me. He opened the door before I could knock, and instead of backing off when I was inside, he did what he hadn't done in thirty years. He actually put his arms around me. Just for a second.

"Cold here," he said, pouring thick, dark Turkish coffee.

"You never minded the cold."

"Mind now."

We sat in front of the fire like in the old days, side by side. Finally he said, "George, I glad you come."

I nodded.

"George, I have something to say."

I nodded again, this time looking at him.

"I die."

"What's wrong?" My heart pumped.

"Nothing wrong. Everybody die. Soon my turn. I been thinking. I got no wife, no other kids, I pop off, somebody find me, maybe, not too sure, call you, not too sure, what happen to the pictures? Worries me."

"What pictures?"

"Wait."

I followed him up the stairs. He puffed more than I remembered him to. When he reached the top, he turned around and said, "I told you wait."

Like a kid I backed off, retreated to my place at the fire. I could hear him opening doors, pulling a chair, wondered if he should be standing on a chair in his condition, whatever his condition was. I held back. I didn't want to upset him.

It took him five or six minutes to come back down with the three cardboard boxes stacked in his arms.

"Not too close to fire," he said.

The boxes were full of ancient photographs, some in a sepia tint. "You know what these are?" he asked.

"Old country?"

"Some. Some here when we first come. Some after you born. No more pictures after Marya dead." He looked at me. "Marya your mother."

That's when I first wondered if the arteries in his head were hardening, whether there wasn't something physically wrong besides age.

"You write good, George. I tell you each picture, you write on back careful, what I say."

And so we went through them, Shushan Bedrossian, a very young somewhat pudgy girl. "Write down," he said, spelling the name, "write down she a cousin of a cousin from Zeytoon."

Then he said, "Your mother sometimes cry when I take that picture out to look at it. Jealous of dead girl. Have to look, to remember. When I poof, you have to keep these pictures, look at all the dead so they are in your memory for your children."

I did not speak to him about the chances of a forty-four-year-old bachelor continuing the family.

I must have written on the back of pictures for more than two hours, spelling out the Armenian names and the Turkish names and checking them with the old man to see that I got them right.

"We ought to get these into albums," I said.

"What for?" His anger at the idea seemed very important to him.

The stew he warmed up wasn't bad. We sat at the table in silence for a while, and then he pushed himself up with his arms and went for the stairs. He had only gone up one or two when he turned to me and said, "George, by my bed, three small bottles, big white pills, small white pills, pink pills. Bring pink pills."

I went up the stairs two at a time. His room was as messy as I had remembered it. On his bedside table there was a pharmacy of bottles. But three small ones were in front and apart from the rest. I tried to read the labels for hints as to his condition. I learned nothing.

Downstairs he said, "You take too long." He swallowed the pink pill with cold coffee. "Doctor terrible," he said. "Always new medicines. Gets kickback from drugstore."

"You could try another doctor."

"All crooks. All got drugstore kickbacks."

"What's wrong with you, Pop?"

"Too old."

"You're not old, Pop, by today's standards."

"I not today. I yesterday. Tired. Stairs hard, prick soft, no good."

"Maybe it'd be a good idea to come down to the city. I'd have you checked out at one of the good hospitals. How about it?"

"What for?"

"You have to know what's wrong. Doesn't the doctor tell you?"

"Tells me mumbo-jumbo. I tell him write it down for you."

He took a piece of paper out of the drawer. It said, "Arteriosclerosis." He was watching my face.

"You can live a long time with that. If you follow the doctor's rules."

"I follow my rules. I take pills okay when I remember. Just like you, George."

"Who chops the firewood?"

"Who you think? You think I crazy buy wood with trees all over?"

"You shouldn't do strenuous things."

"Bullshit. Pretty woman walk in here, take clothes off, I do what I do, who cares strain?" He laughed through his brown teeth. "I not dead yet. You send two women, okay too." He laughed again, gestured at the coffee pot.

"Does the doctor know you drink all that black coffee?"

"George, you nuts? I think I gonna call doctor four five times a day say okay I drink coffee now?"

I made tea for us both.

Then, sitting by the fire, he sang an Armenian song. It sounded like a lullaby.

"You no remember?" he asked.

I remembered my mother singing, not him.

"I'm not sure," I said.

"You getting old up here," he said, gesturing at his head. "How's your girl?" he said. "Better make sure you don't get old down there." And he was singing again. A love song, I think. I wish I had learned Armenian, however useless it was for dealing with the world.

When it was time to leave for the last plane from Syracuse to La-Guardia, I got him to promise that next time he would come and visit me, and stay as long as he wanted to. He didn't believe I meant it.

"I mean it," I said, and I kissed his rough cheek.

At the door, he steeled himself not to let his wet eyes run. "When I dead," he shouted after me, "you can put pictures in albums, okay?"

FORTY-THREE

Francine

I have been neglecting Bill.

I have not been neglecting Bill. He doesn't interest me.

He is such a nice man.

George is not a nice man. He is an interesting man. Can't a nice man be interesting? I must ask Joan and Margaret, they're both married to such nice men.

I have been neglecting my sisters.

Joan and Margaret come in to town from their respective exurbias once each month to do Bloomingdale's, have a wicked two-cocktail lunch, take in a matinee, exchange gossip.

Dear Joan and Margaret, I thought I'd join you for lunch today. You are older, more experienced. Tell me, am I looking for trouble with George Thomassy, what do you think? I'm making him sound like a sheriff? Oh no, he's a lawyer, Gary Cooper Thomassy.

How old is he? Let's see now, Joan, your husband is two years older than you are, and Margaret, your husband is three years older than you are, and George Thomassy is seventeen years older than I am, isn't it obscene? Have I what, gone to bed with him? Now Joan, I haven't asked you about developments in your predicament, as you called it, does Bob still fall asleep in the middle of things? And Margaret, is

Harvey still too shy to you-know-what? I see, you want to know if my lawyer friend and I are compatible, considering the difference in our ages and that he's an ethnic? Well, I enjoy his company afterwards, is that a good sign?

Is he successful? Mmmmm. I assume that's a money question. I don't know about his money, he has his eye on the process, not the destination. It's called drive. I have no idea what his annual income might be. He lives modestly compared to J. Paul Getty. By the way, did I tell you I was raped? I didn't? I don't suppose either of you have ever had the experience or you would have told us, I'm sure. A gas station owner in my case, not very classy. He's going to jail, if he's not already there.

Why thank you. Without sisters, who would wish me luck?

COMMENT BY THOMASSY

I don't believe in luck. Sometimes a fortunate coincidence comes along to help, but the engine isn't driven on luck. Virtue doth not beget its own rewards. I am not a cynic. I am a realist.

What in stupid hell is a realist doing getting in deep with a kid of twenty-seven?

She is not a kid. I hate to remember what I was like at twenty-seven.

She is demanding. I have no respect for rugs and dishrags in the form of people. I am demanding, why shouldn't she be?

What evidence, Your Honor, is there that she and I are right for each other?

Is it objectively verifiable that I'm happy when I'm with her and unhappy when I'm not with her?

Your Honor, that is circumstantial evidence, at best. Besides, I got restless as hell in the studio the other night.

I was not with her? A spectator, watching her? Your Honor, if she came to this court, she would be a spectator watching me in my arena.

Should lovers watch each other performing professionally? Their acts for the world are what?

Theater.

Your Honor, life happens offstage, in private, unnoticed by strangers.

I feel convicted. I didn't do anything, Your Honor. I request a stay of sentence.

FORTY-FOUR

Francine

I couldn't wait for my interview with Mr. Straws. That show with Butterball started a chain reaction in my head. For the first time, I had not been putting stuff together for others to use, but speaking my own mind, I loved it! If my vocation wasn't in broadcast, it had to be in something like it. Dealing with Butterball not in someone's drawing room but on the air, live, with people listening to me skewer him, gave me the biggest high I've ever had in a work situation. It wasn't work, it was play, and people got paid for it! And the notoriety was not incidental. My ego was flowering.

Straws's first name turned out to be Henry. He was wearing one of those suits with overly wide lapels and slanted pockets, Cardin or something Italian. He popped up from his chair and came around to shake hands enthusiastically. His shoes had tassels.

"Do sit down," he said, hovering over me for a second or two before retreating behind his desk.

He put the fingers of both hands together as if in contemplation, which gave me a chance to observe his face. I'd guess him to be about fifty. His hair was just slightly longer than World War II. A blow-dry would have looked ridiculous with that oversized bow tie. His face had no distinguishing feature, an okay nose, everything in place, what my mother used to call "nice looking" because there wasn't a single obtrusive feature.

"It was good of you to come," he said.

This is my break, my chance, I'd have come if you worked in Alaska, I thought.

"There are a few questions I would like to ask."

"Certainly."

"I take it you have no previous broadcast experience."

"Not really," I said. *Why didn't I have the guts to just say plain no.*

"You did extremely well for a virgin the other night," he said.

"Thank you."

"Miss Audrey will be on leave for a month, five weeks actually, and I'm thinking of trying out five guest hosts, all female of course, with an eye to the future."

Nothing ventured, nothing gained. "I had thought I was being considered as a possible replacement for Miss Audrey."

"I don't know where you got that. Miss Audrey has a contract with some time to run."

"I thought there was some dissatisfaction."

"With her format. It may be correctable. You do realize that if we try you out for a week, you'd have to read commercials as well as do interviews?"

"Does Miss Audrey?"

"She did at first."

"And now?" I asked.

"She negotiated them out of her contract after her first few years. We think it was a mistake. Our advertisers believe that when the interviewer reads the commercials, it lends strength and authenticity."

Mr. Straws, I will read commercials standing on my head to get this chance. "I understand," I said.

"Some of the contenders for our fill-in spots are thinking of trying some variation in the format. I'm giving them a chance to do that. Do you have anything in mind?"

"In mind?" I sounded like an idiot to me.

"Formatwise," he said.

Look, Mr. Straws, I'm just an amateur who wandered into a lucky break. I'll have to wing it. Francine, get a hold of yourself, you're onstage.

"Mr. Straws, I'm kind of an hypocrisy specialist."

He laughed, thank God. "You practice it?"

"I study it. Mr. Straws, does a touch of vulgarity offend you?"

He liked that.

"Miss Widmer," he said, "in the media one is surrounded by it. A touch wouldn't be noticed."

"Oh I'm not thinking of a vulgar format, I just want to explain how I see myself."

He was looking at me all over. I hoped he was also listening.

"Somewhere along the line," I continued, "I developed a first-class shit detector."

He flinched at the word.

"My boss at the U.N.," I quickly continued, "has found it very helpful in his work. Hypocrisy is one of the most widely practiced and least studied phenomena. It's universally employed, not just in diplomacy and business, but even in love affairs. Therefore, a subject of interest to everyone. For instance . . ." I stopped. *Was that me talking? My wings had wings.*

"Go on," he said.

"Suppose every guest I interviewed was loosened up by being asked to tell us about who they thought was the biggest liar in public life. Two virtues. Everybody is interested in somebody publicly reciting chapter and verse about a liar they know. And if he-she is a public person, I guess we could keep it libel-proof if it weren't malicious."

"I'm amazed at the way you think," Straws said. "I mean that favorably."

"Not like a girl."

"I didn't mean that."

I looked at him and didn't say a word.

After a moment he said, "I guess I did mean that. I suppose that's what you mean by your S detector? Do you think something like that can be sustained night after night?"

"Do you think we'll run out of hypocrites?"

He made some notes on the pad in front of him.

"Miss Widmer, have you ever been given any psychological testing, TAT, Rorschach, things like that?"

"No."

"Do you think you could handle call-ins?"

"The cranks?"

"We prefer to call them our listeners."

"Mr. Straws, you saw me handle Butterball. Do you think I could handle call-ins?"

He scratched the scratch pad with his pen.

"If you were on the air, Mr. Straws, you'd have to answer or we'd be stuck with dead air."

"Unless you picked up the ball. The responsibility would always be yours."

"You've been testing me."

"Are you squeamish about sex?"

"Are we on the air or off the air?"

"On."

"Don't you get a few seconds' delay on the call-in questions?"

"Yes, of course. The producer monitors those. I meant a guest in the studio, when you're on live."

"You mean what do I do if someone tells me their preference is necrophilia? I'd say how convenient."

"I think you'll be all right on your feet."

"I thought this program was conducted sitting down."

"Very nice, Miss Widmer. Ad libbing is the whole thing. I have one reservation."

"About . . . ?"

"You. You might get bored with the trivial discussions that go on night after night."

"It'd be up to me not to bore myself. Or the listeners."

"I wouldn't worry about the listeners. They've been with Lily Audrey for years. They're used to lapses. The problem all the guest hosts will face will be their loyalty."

"To her?"

"Yes. Your advantage is that their loyalty seems to be greater to the station." He stopped doodling. "Miss Widmer, if we decide to use you as one of the substitute hosts, do you think you could get a week's leave of absence from the U.N.?"

"Oh that's no problem. It's just I'd feel inhibited on the air if I were still employed at the U.N. I'd have to resign."

"I wouldn't dream of having you resign for a one-week assignment."

"I could take that risk. Perhaps if I—" His mind seemed elsewhere.

"If in a week's trial I did as well as the other night with Butterball, you might find some other spot for me while you rode out Lily Audrey's contract. Or does that seem too speculative?"

"You're quite a daring young woman, Miss Widmer."

"I thought that might be a characteristic you were looking for." It was at that second I knew that I had given him a cue he had been looking for.

"Miss Widmer, while I wouldn't dream of you taking a risk like that for one week, I assume you don't have family responsibilities, budget obligations?"

"I'm single."

"There was a man with you the other night . . ."

"A friend."

"A good friend?"

I laughed nervously. "Not at the moment."

"I see. Well then, perhaps we can go into this further at dinner, perhaps later this week."

He stopped. I said nothing.

"In fact," he went on, "my wife's traveling in Europe, we could meet at the apartment for a drink, unless you preferred a nightcap afterward."

Clunk. It couldn't have been more explicit.

"Mr. Straws—"

"Call me Henry if you like."

"Mr. Straws, I am very excited about the prospect of this chance to show what I can do. On the air. I do want us to get to know each other better. Professionally. But I've had three very recent experiences, one rape, one attempted rape, and one seduction. I suppose the casting couch is somewhere in between, but I don't think I can hack it. If it's a job requirement, the answer is no."

He did the thing with the tips of his fingers again, then said, "You've made that clear."

"I trust it won't matter."

"Miss Widmer. I don't think you can risk giving up your existing position for a one-week trial that, frankly, has little chance now—" he paused over the *now* "—of leading somewhere more permanent here. I also think, if you will forgive me, that you are a tad ambitious for someone with negligible experience in broadcasting, and that you would soon find any routine interview show not to your liking."

"It wouldn't be routine," I protested.

"You'd get restless quickly, I can see that, you'd want to move on and up. Ambition is commendable, but without a cooperative attitude on your part . . . where are you going?"

I had stood up without realizing it.

"Mr. Straws," I said, "I am going to make it my business to find out who is the biggest competitor you have, and get a job with him paying nothing if I have to, and work my way up so fast you'll never know what happened to you when I'm on opposite your highest-rated show. I do thank you for this interview."

And I was gone. I did not slam the door. Oh George Thomassy, you would have been proud of my exit, you jealous son of a bitch.

FORTY-FIVE

Francine

You make a mistake. You *know* you've made a mistake. You don't rectify it. You compound it by making something remediable drag until it is too late.

I wasn't about to let George Thomassy escape my life without giving it one more chance. I wanted to find a way to apologize for the stupidity of our argument. I wanted him to make love to me so I could make love to him.

I didn't think I could handle it in a phone call. And I didn't want to call for an appointment. Saturday, he would be home. I drove there from my parents' house. He wasn't home. I went to a nearby coffee shop and gave it forty minutes, figuring he was out getting something or other. I could feel my courage ebbing. I went back to his place. No answer.

It was easy to decipher. He had reacted to our quarrel by spending Friday night with Jane or one of the others. He didn't spend nights with women, he said. Then why wasn't he here Saturday morning?

Perhaps spending a night with a woman—he had with me—now interested Mr. Privacy. I drove part way back home, turned around and went back to his place.

No luck. I'd leave a note. What to say?

I tore up three versions. What I left was an unsigned piece of paper wedged in the door that said *I was here. You weren't.*

That sounded like an accusation. I got out of my car and went back to the house and added to the note *Sorry.*

Maybe he won't even recognize my handwriting!

I called Bill. A date with Bill wouldn't be absolute neutrality. He would comfort me. He would compliment me and mean it. Seeing Bill wasn't a step forward in any direction for me, but would Bill understand that, or would he seize on this overture from me as a promise?

It turned out that Bill had a date for Saturday night. Succor was needed, but someone was protecting Bill from me.

Bill called back. He'd been able to get out of his Saturday-night date gracefully.

"Why?"

"You come first, Francine."

I couldn't respect his dialogue, just his decency and friendship. *Be careful, Bill,* I wanted to say, *this is a different league.* He suggested he'd pick me up at my parents' house and we'd go to an early dinner and a movie.

As expected, Father Widmer's pleasure showed when it turned out to be Bill Acton at the door.

After the amenities, I took Bill by the elbow and steered him toward the door. "We'll be late," I said for the others to hear.

When we were outside, he said, "Late for what?"

"Late for getting the hell out of the house, dummy."

"I didn't make reservations. I didn't know where you'd want to go."

"The first place I want to go is my apartment, which I wouldn't dream of going near without an escort." I put my arm through his.

"Isn't that guy still around?"

"I guess. I think he's out on bail, something like that. He's shorter than you are."

Bill looked all Adam's apple at that moment.

"I'm not worried about him, if you're not worried about him."

"Well, then," I said, "let's go."

When we got there, before we got out of the car, I looked up at the windows above mine. Dark. The whole apartment dark.

"They must have gone somewhere," I said.

"I hope to hell."

I laughed.

"You know what I meant," said Bill. "Francine, I'm not as dumb as you sometimes think I am."

"I never think that!" I lied.

"What I'm trying to say is that I sometimes actually wish you weren't as smart or as attractive as you are."

I guess I looked puzzled, because he went on, "Maybe I'd have more of a chance."

Well, what does a woman do? I liked Bill. I trusted him. I wondered if the girl he'd broken his date with went to bed with him. He preferred me, the sweet idiot.

We didn't get to dinner or the movie. I took some booze from the cupboard, made us each a light drink, put a record on, lit up a joint, caressed his head, kissed his cheek, let him kiss me on the mouth.

I took a drag—it'd been a long time, it seemed—and passed the joint to him. I could feel the desperation of his longing. He wasn't a horny guy looking to get his rocks off. It was my friend Bill, close to being my ex-friend Bill if Thomassy would have me, wanting a woman he thought himself not interesting enough for. Some people would call what happened a mercy fuck. God I hate that term, mercy for whom? For both of us! Bill made love to me instead of dinner, instead of the movies, and my urging him to stay the night after I had called home and said Bill had dropped me off at my apartment and it was okay, and then agreeing when he woke me during the night, and even letting him when what was in my mind was the note in Thomassy's door, imagining Thomassy's expression when he saw it, and why oh why wasn't he phoning?

COMMENT BY THOMASSY

The plane bumped around on the flight back from Syracuse Saturday, but my thoughts bumped around more. One moment I was thinking of the old man, we had displayed our first affection as adults, after all these years, and the next moment I was thinking of that bitch Francine, berating me for being what I was at a time when I was beginning to think I might lead a different kind of life, with another person in it. I couldn't change my age. I couldn't change into a Wasp. I wouldn't change my vocation an inch. And I wouldn't be jealous of hers if she had one. But I might learn to share what? A bed, we'd done that. A kitchen? A home? It seemed too drastic to contemplate, too important not to contemplate.

At LaGuardia I found myself loping to the cabstand only to find an impossible line. What was I doing? I'd parked my own car at the airport. I was breathless by the time I got to the lot—I couldn't remember which section I had parked in—and couldn't find my car keys in my pockets. I turned them all inside out one at a time. Had I misplaced them up in Oswego? I'd had the keys for the rented car. I'd turned that in. What had I done with my own keys? Being in love was a state of madness.

I used the key I had hidden in a magnetized metal container under the hood. I couldn't go to her now, in this state, I had to get a hold of myself, calm down, think what I would say to her.

I don't know what would have happened if I had driven straight to her parents' house from the airport. I went home, found Francine's note, took a hot bath, thought of the old man, glad I had gone, thought of Francine, knew that in the morning, my best hours, I would phone, drive over, and welcome Sunday with her. I had a crazy idea we'd drive to the city and do Central Park if the sun came out.

I had a deep sleep, not a long one. I was up at 6:00 A.M., eager to go. I put on a turtleneck and a sporty jacket I thought she'd like. Was I dressing younger? I had to put ideas like that out of my head. I breakfasted on fried eggs over and bacon and four pieces of buttered toast with my favorite dark orange marmalade. I brushed my teeth a second time that morning. I took time to stop in the self-service car wash. Crazy to wash the car when it was raining. It's only a sunshower, what the hell! I even vacuumed the inside. From a phone booth I dialed her parents' number, hoping she would answer. When it rang the fourth and fifth time I got jumpy. Then a drowsy-voiced Ned Widmer answered, "Yes?"

"I'm awfully sorry, Ned. This is George Thomassy. I'm just back from out of town and was hoping to catch Francine early this morning. Is she awake?"

"I'm not. She called late last night to say she wouldn't be staying here."

"She wouldn't have gone back to the apartment with Koslak out on bail, would she?"

"I certainly hope she didn't. She . . ." He stopped, and didn't seem to want to continue.

"Where'd she call you from yesterday evening?"

"I didn't ask. As you said, George, she's on her own now. I don't supervise her social engagements."

I thanked him, and apologized for waking him up. Was she out on a date? Was I jealous? This is stupid. I dialed her apartment. Again, several rings, and a sleepy Francine said, just as her father had, "Yes?"

I hung up. I didn't want to apologize for waking her until later. I got into the car and drove within the speed limit for a change because I sure as hell wanted to get there alive.

"Who is it?" she said through the door in a voice that grumpily indicated she had gone back to sleep.

"George."

She opened it on the chain. Didn't she believe it was me?

"Wait a minute," she said.

I was impatient, anxious, and it took at least two or three minutes for her to come back and let me in. She was wearing a housecoat. She may have run a comb through her hair, but it sure didn't look it. I didn't care. She looked as I had dreamed of her looking this morning.

"Do you realize what time it is?" she said.

I looked at my watch. It wasn't seven-thirty yet.

"Sorry to be so early," I said. "I thought we might spend the day together. There's a lot to talk about. I'm sure the rain won't last. I thought we might—"

"Where were you yesterday?"

"Oswego, with my old man."

"Did you find my note?"

"I was going to drive to Chez Widmer straight from the airport. Good thing I decided to wait till morning. I found your note. I was almost tempted to drive over then. But I waited. Woke your father. I thought you were scared to stay here alone?"

I put my hands out in the way I had done before but she did not take them. She said, "George, could you go for a walk or a drive for half an hour and come back?"

"It's raining," I said. "Besides, I want to stay right here."

"I have to dress."

"I'll watch you dress."

"Please, George."

I wasn't getting it until I noticed that the door to the bedroom was closed. Probably a mess.

"Please give me half an hour."

I guess it comes from having been a lawyer for the worst sort of clients, from handling matrimonials, from my instincts about the human race. I went to the door and before she could stop me, opened it.

The kid in bed was terrified. She'd obviously warned him.

"Who the fuck are you?" I said.

"Bill Acton."

Francine was right behind me, saying, "It's not his fault. I invited him. We can talk about it. I can explain it."

I turned to look at her. For a split second I thought of Koslak, who had forced her in this bedroom. The kid hadn't forced her. She'd invited him. *He was her age.* I was so afraid of the billowing anger inside me, I was careful not to slam the outside door.

Widmer

Saturday is my day of rest. Sunday is my day of peace. Priscilla and I had lazied around on Saturday, gone to an early evening showing at Cinema Two. When George woke me Sunday morning, I didn't go back to sleep. I was ready to commune with the out-of-doors. I planned to put on my chino pants and a T-shirt and see if I couldn't transplant the Exbury azalea that was being crowded by a fountain of weigela without mucking up the root system, the kind of thing I could do perfectly if my mind was at ease. As it was, until I pulled the drapes and saw the rain streaming down against the evergreens. Dear God, You had all week long to water the lawn and You, in Your wisdom, saved it for Sunday. The lengths You will go to to get a few reluctant parishioners into church!

In the shower, soaping myself, I thought why not take the bar of soap out-of-doors and shower in the rain? No one would see. It wouldn't be dotty. Showering in the shower was unnatural if it was raining outside. Was the peace I felt attributable to Sunday? Or to Francine going out with that nice young man again? Or to learning that Thomassy had reported that Koslak's lawyer would plead his client and the trial I didn't want to imagine would now not have to take place? I had started it with the phone call. Now it could all stop. I wish I had the talent to write a ballad, a song that could tell it all.

"You were singing in the shower," said Priscilla.

"Oh was I? I don't recall."

"Who was that who phoned so early?"

"George Thomassy. Looking for Francine," I said, toweling myself dry, wondering if I was a visual temptation to Priscilla as she was to me when she gentled a bath sheet around her.

It was early afternoon when Francine phoned. She sounded upset. "You should be in a celebratory mood," I said. "Aren't you glad you won't have to go through with the trial? By the way, did George Thomassy reach you?"

She started to cry. I couldn't make the connections, but I invited her to come over.

Priscilla poured tea for the three of us. "Damn rain wiped out my gardening for the day," I said, but I could see Francine was not up to small talk.

"What is it, Francine?"

"I seem to have mucked up my life."

"Want to talk about it?"

"Yes and no."

"You should be very pleased about Koslak going to jail. That's what you wanted, isn't it?"

"I didn't think what happens when he gets out of jail. I can't go on living in the same apartment, waiting for him to get out. Do I move to a different part of the country? Do I change my name? I'm determined to make a career for myself in broadcasting, how the hell do I do that anonymously?"

"Koslak," I tried to reassure her, "is likely to be chastened by his punishment."

"Are you kidding?" she exclaimed. "He's a nut! He'll want revenge!"

I had thought the story was over. It was apparently not to be.

"First things first," I said. "Thomassy has got to get you out of that place."

"I thought leases were unbreakable."

"No contract is unbreakable if your lawyer is good enough. I'll speak to your friend Thomassy."

"I guess you might as well know. George and I are no longer . . . friends."

I had to conceal my delight. "He's still your lawyer."

"I don't know if that's possible."

"I'll have a word with him. Now do have another cup of tea."

I had to think.

FORTY-SEVEN

Koslak

I knew a guy what did time for knocking off cars. He came to me last winter when his regular fence had the flu to see if I could lay off a Buick quick. He was the one told me the clink, when you get used to it, it's like anything else.

"But they don't let you do what you want to do," I told him.

He laughed like I'm some nut.

Well, it's worse because they make you do what you don't want to do. I wrote to Mary: Tell Brady the hacks are nothing in this place compared to the other prisoners.

When I'd asked the guy with the Buick about sex, he said, "They ain't gonna cut your hand off."

He must of knowed. He was just stringing me along, figuring I'd find out soon enough.

COMMENT BY MARY KOSLAK

The last day Harry was out on bail, that was the worst. I thought we ought to take the kids out in the park, you know, for a walk, kind of to say goodbye. I told him private before we went out that he shouldn't let on where he was going, a business trip, he would be away awhile, et cetera. The kids hear about other fathers going on business trips, so it wouldn't seem so different.

So we're in the park with Mike and little Mary. Harry sits down on a bench, the kids are standing in front of him, he brings their faces real close. I'm like turning away because it's his private discussion with them, and he says, "I got something to tell ya."

You know how kids are. They look fuzzy-faced, what's so special, you're telling us something all the time.

Harry says, "Pay attention."

Mike's a restless kid, he's ready to go running off, and Harry's got his hand on Mike's arm. Mike says, "You're hurting me," and Harry says, "I'm sorry. Look, kids, I'm going away on a business trip."

He looks at both of them, waiting for them to say something. Finally, he says, "I'm going away for a long time. Say something." And Mike says, "Goodbye," and he goes running off to play.

Harry says to little Mary, "Aren't you going to say something?" And she opens and closes her hand the way she waves bye-bye, and that's it.

So we go stash the kids with my mother, cause I figure Harry, he wants to be alone with me for a while. Last chance, and all that.

When we're going back upstairs, we pass the landing on the second floor and I'm thinking if it wasn't for the Widmer woman, we wouldn't be a family splitting up. I seen her around, her nipples showing through her dress like a whore, what did she expect?

"Listen," I say to Harry when we get up to the apartment, "you coulda won the trial."

"Who says?"

"All the women I talk to, they say rape is something you just can't prove without witnesses."

"What are you talking to them about me for?"

"They don't know I'm talking about you, Harry. Just in general. I don't know why you pleaded guilty to whatever that charge was, the other one."

"I did what I did," said Harry.

"What's that mean?"

"I pay a lawyer to listen to his advice, right? He says it's a crap shoot. If we go to trial, I could get ten years in the jug. That'd finish me. You'd be old when I got out, you wouldn't want that? This way, with good behavior, I might be out in two, three years."

"You could have won. You could stay out!"

"Now, Mary," he said, taking me by the shoulders, "Brady told me they had something, the lawyer for the other side."

"Had what?"

"Proof I guess."

"What kind of proof? I don't believe it. Maybe Brady's just too lazy to do the whole trial."

"Brady's not that kind of guy."

"How do you know?"

"I know. Anyway, I did it, it's too late."

I wasn't convinced. I watched Harry moping around the kitchen. We don't want to be arguing, this being his last day.

"What are you thinking?" I asked him.

"I was thinking," he said, "it'll seem funny not driving a car. I mean for a couple of years."

Well, I blew. "What about money?!" I let loose at him. "What am I supposed to do, go on welfare, turn tricks, what?!"

"You could get a job."

"What do I do with the kids?"

"Your mother could take care of them. It's just a couple of years."

"What about the kid in the oven," I said, tapping my belly.

"You could work for a while."

"Two months. Three months. Doing what? I have no experience."

That's when he told me about the money. "There's five hundred in each envelope." He told me where to find the first one. "Go get it," he said.

It was there. I counted the money.

"When you visit me, I'll tell you where there's another. I got enough of them stashed away."

"Why don't you tell me now?"

Harry looks at me. "How do I know I can trust you? If you had it all, you could do anything, run away with some fellow, leave the kids—"

"Are you crazy?" I shout at him. "I'm pregnant."

"So what. Lots of fellows don't care if a woman's pregnant. Listen, Mary, I want you to be faithful, you understand?"

"I'm not going to be doing anything different than what I been doing," I said, thinking of Jason. Damn Harry, anyway, he does something and I'm getting punished. Suppose he decides not to tell me where the other money is. Suppose he gets killed in prison, I'll never know where the money is.

"Oh Harry," I said to him, "what was so special about her cunt? If you stuck with mine you'da stayed outa trouble!"

That was when he whacked me across the face hard. Later, he tried to put his arms around me, to make up, but I wasn't going to fuck around with him, not after that whack in the face, not even on his last day.

❋

Once I was in the can, I thought a lot about that last day. The kids would be nearly twice as old when I got out. Slapping Mary was all wrong. Maybe in here is a good place for me to learn to control myself better.

Trouble is, there are guys in here who don't leave you alone. I figured Badger for trouble when I first seen him. Six of us sitting in the can, three facing three, and this six-foot guy with the bald head comes in, looks around, and says to me, "Hold it!"

"What do you mean hold it?" I says.

"Get up."

I'm not one of these people can let go by snapping a finger. I gotta work up to it. And here I was about ready, but I look at the other guys and get the feeling I ought to do what this guy says, so I get up, and he sits down on that pot and I gotta wait till there's another one.

I ask around about Badger. They say don't ever challenge something he says.

When I run into Badger again it's in the shower. I figure it's best to be on his good side so I say, "Hello, Badger."

I'm being friendly and what does he say?

"Hello, Cossack," he says.

There are four or five other guys in the shower, so I says slow so he can hear every syllable, "My name's Koslak."

Like he didn't hear me he says. "You know what a cossack is?"

Maybe this guy thinks I'm dumb like some of the others. "Sure," I says. "Cossacks and horses."

"What about cossacks and horses?"

"They ride 'em," I says.

"You ever ride a horse, Cossack?"

"Koslak," I say.

The other guys in the shower are like mummies. They stop soaping. They just stand under the water watching.

"Hey Cossack," Badger goes on, "you ever get ridden?"

One of the guys makes a little laugh. Badger looks at him and the guy freezes.

"I see you don't understand too much, Cossack," Badger says. "That's okay. Just lean over. Put your hands on that bench."

"Now wait a minute!" I say. I've beaten up bigger guys than Badger. Places where you can swing a bottle. I'm looking at the other guys. I don't want a couple of them grabbing me. Badger, he reaches up to the shower head. He's got something taped up there. He yanks it free of the tape and opens the blade, running his thumb on the edge.

"You copped your plea before you got here," Badger says. "Now put your hands down and spread."

I stood where I was.

"Hey, fellows," says Badger. "This virgin's shy. Why don't you all get out of here."

They jostle each other getting out, even the ones with soap still on them. The last one out is Steve, and Badger says, "Steve, hold on to this outside, okay?" and he closes the knife and flips it to him.

"We don't need that, Cossack, do we?"

"What are you going to do?" I says.

"I'm going to seduce you."

"I ain't queer," I says.

"Nobody's queer, Cossack." He puts his fingers on my shoulder and kind of runs them down my arm. It feels funny. I don't like the way it feels.

It's like as if he's reading my mind, he says, "You're gonna like everything after a while, Cossack," and suddenly he slaps me on my ass real hard.

"What'd you do that for?" I says.

"You want me to be gentle, huh?" He puts his hand on my ass and just holds it there. I move away. He puts it there again. I quick like steal a look at his dong, which is getting hard.

"You cold, Cossack?"

"Nah."

"It gets real cold sometimes," he says. "I can make you feel warm."

"I told you I'm not queer."

"Look, Cossack, if you got your eyes closed and somebody's sucking you, how do you know it's a woman or a man? I want you to be good pussy to me, right? Steve!" he calls out.

"I'm here," says Steve from outside.

"We don't want Steve with us, Cossack. Just you and me. Like a private date. Friends. Fucking good friends."

Badger has talked himself into one big hard on. Holding it he says, "Would you like to suck it?"

I shake my head.

"I didn't think so," he says quietly. "So just turn around and put your hands on that bench and spread."

"I don't want to."

"*I don't want to*," Badger imitates me in a squealing voice. He grabs my hair, twists so hard I thought my neck was going to snap. "I don't care if you want to or don't want to. *I want to*, understand!"

I'd kill this guy if he wasn't so big.

"Steve!" he yells. "You want seconds?"

"No," I say. "Just you. Just once."

"That's a nice pussy," he says, and puts his hand on my cock, all of his fingers stroking, and I don't like the idea. His thing is purple now, looks bigger than anything I ever saw, then he grabs my hips and twists me around.

"Hands on the bench," he orders, and then I feel him, it can't get in, it hurts like anything, he's shoving, shoving, and then he's in and moving in and out, and I'm thinking never again, never again, and he yells, "Hey, Steve, this virgin's got a real tight ass, come look," and I shake my head no, and Badger's saying, "Cossack, you're so good you're going to be my steady pussy, real regular," and I know when I get out of here I'm gonna find Widmer wherever she is and I'm going to kill her dead for ratting on me!

FORTY-EIGHT

Francine

I am lying on the familiar couch, listening to the familiar sound of Dr. Koch breathing, waiting for me to continue talking. I'd been telling him about the botched weekend, about Bill and Thomassy. I don't want to talk any more, to him or to anybody. Finally, I tell him I'm fed up, I don't want to be in therapy, I want to be back in life.

"You do not stop living," he says, "when you take time to stop and think."

"You just want the money."

"What money?"

"The money you get for listening to me."

"If you want to attack me," he says, "that is your prerogative. But right now you are not attacking me."

"Who am I attacking?"

"Yourself. Perhaps you do not like the way you have used that boy."

"Bill can take care of himself. He's my age."

"Here you have always talked of him as a boy."

"I didn't rape him."

"That's an interesting choice of word."

"Oh come on now, Dr. Koch. I didn't even seduce him."

"You make it sound as if rape and seduction are part of the same thing."

"Rape is force. You know that."

"Yes. Is seduction never a kind of force?"

"I didn't seduce Bill."

"You tempted him."

"I told him it was there and he took it."

"It. It. Inanimate. We are talking about people. Perhaps this Bill is like ninety percent of humanity, a weakish man you turn to as a pot to cook something in. Perhaps he does not seem very individual to you. Someone else will find him so. Perhaps someone less complex than you are. If you tempt him, he cannot resist. You are taking advantage of him. It is not the same as rape perhaps, but akin to it. Not as dangerous, but possibly, in this case, a bit inhumane also, don't you agree? Perhaps you should leave him alone."

I sat up. "I know what you'd prefer," I told him.

"Please lie down."

"You'd prefer that I give him up and Thomassy up and anybody else except you."

"I am not your lover," he says.

"You wish you were!"

He hesitated only a moment. "Yes," he said.

COMMENT BY DR. KOCH

That "yes" was perhaps the most emotionally expensive word I have ever uttered, for now, as is just, I can no longer continue as her analyst. I have admitted a personal feeling of such consequence she cannot continue her transference. I have lost her. Perhaps it is to the good. What is there possible between us? Even for my own sake it is to the good. I must redirect my libido. I cannot be so impractical. I, too, still have life to live.

✸

I couldn't bear the eye contact, so I lay back down on the couch, hoping he would speak, and, after a time, he did.

"There was a period not too long ago, Francine, when the young tried to revolutionize our conception of eros by pretending that one could live successfully in a commune in which one can turn to the left or the right at night, to a man or a woman, and it would make no differ- ence. If there were no differences, we would not need all the complex physical paraphernalia God has provided, eyes to differentiate, hands to differentiate, but most importantly a mind and sensibility that makes us feel differently about different people. Anyone who is not us is different, but it is the mind-boggling differences among all the rest that lead to our pursuit of simplicity, do you follow me?"

"I am trying to," I said. "I'm not sure."

"To say one likes all trees is less meaningful than to recognize that one likes this or that tree better than some others. We are differentiat- ing. We are expressing preferences. And so with people. We cannot commune with all people. We will never know enough of them in a lifetime. We select from among those offered to us those few whose chemistry interests us, whose looks please us, and finally whose minds and character are such that they will continue to satisfy one's emotions, even eros, when the decline begins. This is not an argument for monog- amy or exclusivity or morality, it is an assessment of experience. We prefer. If we have no preferences, we are mindless idiots. You do not prefer your Bill, or your father, or me. And so we come by theoretical circumlocution to George Thomassy, a man I have just begun to know. A Maccabee. Does that mean anything to you?"

"I hate him!"

"All right, you love him, but what I want to know—"

"I said I hate him!"

He sighed as if to a misbehaving child. "You are not listening."

I listened.

"Your Maccabee is defending me also. I trust him because he does his work so well. He is reliable. I wish my work with you was as skilled. Your friends who are revolutionaries might—"

"What revolutionaries?"

"The ones you went to college with. The ones who talk brimstone where you work. They should prize a man like Thomassy."

"He's just a damn lawyer."

"Can you see him kowtowing to brownshirts?"

"No."

"To anyone?"

"No. Not if he can help it."

"We could have used a few of him in Europe not so long ago. Have you wondered, Francine, why so many of the young public defenders are Jews here?"

Was Thomassy a reaction to the Armenian massacres? Not wanting to be in anyone's power?

"You are quiet," said Dr. Koch.

"I was thinking."

"That can be an advantage in life, surprisingly." He waited a moment. "Were you thinking about this Maccabee you hate?"

"I don't hate him."

My sentence hung in the air awaiting execution. I could feel it coming. Finally, Koch spoke again.

"Francine, you know this is not an analysis any more. We are just talking now."

"Anything wrong with that?"

"No. But I cannot charge for tutorials. We must discontinue these sessions. If you need me again, you can come again. Life is better. Go."

"What should I do?"

"What do you think you should do?"

"I should telephone him."

"Then telephone him."

It was quite possibly the most difficult telephone call I ever made in my life.

"This is Francine," I said.

"Who?"

He must have known my voice.

"Francine," I said.

"Well," he said, and was silent.

"Reasonably well," I said. "How are you?"

"I'm okay. How are you?"

"I'm alive," I said.

"I'm sure your young man will be pleased."

"Don't be stupid, George."

"Did you call me up to call me stupid?"

"I called you up to say I enjoyed the extremely brief period in which we ostensibly lived together sort of."

"I didn't move out."

"Where are we, George?"

"At opposite ends of a telephone line."

Could I not fight back just for the sake of peace?

"I owe you money," I said.

"I'll look into it."

"Maybe it would have been better to have gone through with the trial."

He didn't say one fucking word.

"If there'd been a trial, we would have had some excuse to see each other," I said, hanging up, hoping that he would call me back.

FORTY-NINE

Koch

Before the arraignment, Thomassy tells me that I should not talk except when the judge asks me a direct question, and then I am to answer in the fewest words. He makes a joke of it: I am an analyst, an experienced listener. Listen, he says, and do not talk. But it is self-defense, I insist, I must make my case. No, Thomassy cautions me, he must make my case. I am not being charged with self-defense, but with manslaughter. Marta, come back from whatever heaven you're in just this once, I trust this lawyer but I do not love him, I need someone at my side whom I love.

In the courtroom I feel alone. Here and there people buzz with each other, ignoring this ritual of justice. I am asked to stand, then to sit, I find myself nibbling at a cuticle. Finally, Thomassy is to speak and I strain to listen.

"Your Honor," he says, "this court is not the proper forum for me to express myself on a constitutional issue. I do not want to mind-read the drafters as to what precisely they had in mind when they gave the people the right to bear arms. A militiaman's rifle or a Saturday-night special? A homemade nuclear device to use against a tyrannical government? I find myself on both sides of that argument. But we are dealing with something far simpler. If an intruder has illegally entered our home to steal something and we catch him at it, and the intruder then threatens us with a loaded weapon, where are we? If we had previously been threatened and applied for a gun permit and kept a loaded gun in, say, our desk in the event of a recurrence, that would be thought of as perfectly normal. But if this was a first occurrence, we cannot reach for the gun we do not have. Our fists can't reach a gunman ten or fifteen feet away. Do we throw a rock? An ashtray? Do we throw ourselves at the intruder and become a certain victim? Dr. Koch . . ."

Thomassy looked over at me. I did not know whether I could stand. I start to rise. He motions me down.

"Dr. Koch," he continues, "has a dartboard in his office that he uses to unwind with. He keeps three darts in a holder on his desk. In the circumstances I have described, he reaches not for an ashtray, or a nonexistent rock, nor does he hopelessly lunge against the intruder. He throws a dart. Had he missed, he would have been shot dead. We know the intruder's gun was loaded. He fired it. He fired it at Dr. Koch. It was heaven-sent luck that Dr. Koch's dart hit the intruder in a vital area, the eye, and as a result Dr. Koch is alive and with us in this courtroom today. But what a miscarriage of justice it would be if the District Attorney's charge against Dr. Koch is carried any further. He has been a law-abiding citizen all his life, not even a traffic ticket to his name, and he has bravely continued his practice of helping people in a neighborhood where anarchy encroaches on lawful citizens day by day. If Dr. Koch is to be tried—and I have no doubt that he would be exonerated on grounds of self-defense—the trial would itself be a cruel and unusual punishment."

The young man who was, I suppose, my antagonist, interrupted with vehemence and anger in his voice. "This man, Your Honor," he said, pointing at me, "hit another human being in the eye with a dart."

"Your Honor," said Thomassy, "would the people rather that the doctor defended himself with a good clean pistol shot in the heart? Are we discussing the odd, perhaps even grotesque nature of the only available means of defense, or whether the doctor committed a crime in defending himself while threatened with a deadly weapon? Are the people claiming this was not self-defense?"

"The issue should be tried," said the young man. "A jury should determine whether the doctor used excessive force for the circumstances."

On what precise scale do we measure force? Should I have aimed for the chest? The dart would not have penetrated bone. The truth is I didn't think, I threw it at the center of the threat, his scornful face.

The judge, a huge-headed man with bristling eyebrows, motioned Thomassy toward him a bit. I heard him say, "Is your client all right?"

Thomassy came over to me. "Anything the matter?"

"I am drinking a glass of water," I said.

"Your face is covered with sweat."

I felt my face. I took my handkerchief and wiped my forehead, my cheeks, my neck.

"All right," said the judge. He motioned both attorneys forward for something he called a conference at the bench. He didn't want me to hear what was being said. Was I not allowed to hear at my own trial?

I watched Thomassy reply to whatever it was the judge said. I watched the young man's rebuttal. It was as if at this trial of my life I had lost my hearing. What was going on?

Then suddenly Thomassy came striding over to me and whispered, "The judge wants to be sure that you would make yourself available as a witness for the government when the man you hit recovers enough to be tried."

"Do I have to?" I asked. "Can't they just work from the police records?"

"No."

"Can I give them an affidavit?"

"They want you to testify. Please. I am trying to strike a bargain."

"The law is a bargain?"

Thomassy laughed. "Dr. Koch," he said, "you are a marvelous innocent."

Thomassy returned to the conference at the bench. After a few minutes of mumbling, he and the young man returned to their respective places looking as if they were colleagues and not enemies. Then the judge said, "The case is dismissed."

Thomassy nodded his approval, then turned to shake my hand.

"You should be happy," he said.

"I cannot be happy."

"We won," said Thomassy.

"We have not yet won. The case is not dismissed. That man is recovering, you said. He will be tried."

"He'll go to jail," Thomassy said.

"For how long?"

"I don't know. Some years."

"And be paroled sooner?"

"Probably."

"And I must lie in wait for his revenge."

I should not have betrayed my alarm. In a world where truth is a frequent danger, I should not have spoiled the gratitude he expected. I should not have told him that all he had won was a delay of my sentence. We cannot cure the world, we can only be prepared to defend ourselves again and again and again.

"Mr. Thomassy," I said, "it would give me a great deal of pleasure if you would allow me to buy you a drink. I don't usually drink, but today I will join you, if you will join me."

"Sure."

In the bar, we clinked glasses.

"Once more, thank you," I said.

He nodded.

"How much do I owe you?"

"I'll send a bill. It won't be much. Just the time."

"I am not a very good client for you, Mr. Thomassy," I said. "It took me sixty years to go before the law once. Another sixty years I do not have."

"Just keep out of trouble."

"I do, I do, I just have to keep the trouble from seeking me out. But I tell you, Francine Widmer, she will make up for me."

His face changed.

"You see," I said, "I know her probably better than anyone alive from our long hours together, and I tell you this. She is determined to confront the hypocrisy of the world not only when it intrudes on her life. She will seek it out like a ferret. That, I think, is her vocation, a female grand inquisitor. And so you see, she will be in frequent trouble, and will need a Maccabee at her side."

"Dr. Koch," he said, "you have the instincts of a matchmaker."

I had to laugh.

"Having a client like her," he said, "is too preoccupying."

"Forgive me," I said, risking all, "I am old enough to be a Dutch uncle to you, yes? It is one of the great joys of life to have a preoccupation as beautiful and intelligent as Marta."

He looked at me.

"You said Marta."

"I meant Francine," I said laughing to the point of tears, "I meant Francine."

FIFTY

Thomassy

It takes a fool to be honest with other people all the time, and something higher than a saint to be altogether honest with yourself. I wasn't about to trust myself on the phone with Francine's disembodied voice. Not now.

My secretary has a way of standing in front of my desk when she figures I'm not doing something I'm supposed to be doing.

"What's bothering you, George?" she says. She never calls me George in front of people.

I looked up at her and had to smile. "You're being a pest, Grace," I said.

"Right," she said. "How can I help?"

"All right. I want to wrap up this damn Widmer case."

"I thought you liked Miss Widmer."

"Mind your own business, Grace."

"My job is to mind your business, George."

I suppose Grace's spunk was part of her attraction for me.

"I need the landlord's name off one of her rent receipts. Will you call her?"

"Sure."

Grace is as mischievous as a Persian cat. The next thing I knew she was buzzing me on the intercom, saying, "Miss Widmer's on the line."

I didn't want to talk to her, idiot. You were supposed to . . .

"Hello."

"Hello, George," she said. Her voice exuded pheromones. It was like hearing from another time of my own life.

"I need to meet with your landlord and see if I can't get you out of that lease."

"I'd be grateful if you could."

"I don't need any more gratitude."

"You mean I haven't paid your bill yet," she said.

"I haven't sent it yet," I said. Some conversation. "I don't have his name or address. Got a rent receipt handy?"

"I'll have to look around. Don't want to keep you on the line. I'll phone it in."

"No rush. You can mail it." Thomassy the Chicken-Hearted avoiding another zombie telephone call like this one.

When the receipt arrived, Grace brought it in ahead of the rest of the mail, held it in front of me, and said, "It's here. I'll leave you alone with it." *The bitch.*

I sat staring at it between my hands as if it was a relic of the crucifixion. Francine had held it. Now I held it. Contact. Ridiculous! I've got to concentrate on getting this last bit over with period.

The landlord was the Miltmac Corporation in Manhattan, Eighth Avenue midtown, obviously two guys' names, Milton and Mac-something. No phone. Don't want calls from idiot tenants. I had my secretary try information. Can you believe an unlisted number? How do people get in touch with them? I suppose anybody they want a call from gets the number. Or gets them under another corporate name. I tell my secretary to get Fat Tarbell. His line is busy. Christ!

I sat staring through the rent receipt, paying attention to what was inside my own head.

Sometimes I doodle thoughts over and over like a broken record. On the legal pad before me I had written *A wife is a weakness.* Well, a friend is a weakness, too, male or female. Where in my life did I see a friend? My father could use a friend up in Oswego. Or a wife. *I am alone therefore I am strong.* I don't have people to compromise with, cater to, work things out with. I decide, I do. My bachelorhood hadn't bothered me up till now. Up to Francine. It's not up to Francine, it's up to me.

Grace buzzed that Fat Tarbell was on the line.

"Miltmac Corporation. Real Estate. Manhattan."

"I don't do much in Manhattan, George."

"You did Anna Banana."

"That's because Brady works up here. Let me look. Call you back."

I had written *Other people make life difficult*. I crossed out "difficult" and wrote "interesting." I crossed out "interesting." Both were true.

"Mr. Tarbell calling back."

"That was fast."

"Nothing on Miltmac, George, sorry."

"Can you at least get me their unlisted telephone number?"

"No problem."

He called back in three minutes flat and gave me the number. "No charge," he said. "Any time."

"Thanks."

No point in making a cold call. I needed the name of a person at Miltmac. I noodled a bit and remembered Arthur had a book on his desk that showed all the principals in real estate, cross-indexed by corporation and name.

I apologized for bothering him. He said it was a privilege. Miltmac's principal, as it turned out, was neither Milton nor Macsomething. His name was listed as H. Hoover. I'll bet the H stands for Herbert. He must have loved his parents for doing that.

"Mr. Hoover," I said on the phone, "my name is George Thomassy. I'm a lawyer in Westchester. I understand your firm has property in this county."

"How'd you get this phone?"

"I dialed information."

"It's unlisted. They're not supposed to give it out."

"I guess someone slipped. Anyway, do the following addresses jibe with your records?" I gave him the addresses of Francine's apartment house and the two similar houses next door.

"What's up, mister, I'm a busy man."

"Are you aware that a felony was committed on your premises by someone who is a leaseholder with you?"

"What the hell are you talking about?"

"I thought you might be aware that an employee of yours was also involved?"

"Now wait a minute."

"His name is Jason McCabe."

"That's the super."

"Right, Mr. Hoover. I was the lawyer that filed the trespass charges against him."

"What are you making trouble for? You looking for a payoff, what?"

"I'm working for my client, Mr. Hoover."

"Don't fuck me over, mister. What do you want?"

"I want to come and see you."

"I don't go in for payoffs."

"Would tomorrow at ten at your office be convenient?"

"I'll have Luigi here. He weighs three hundred pounds and can beat the shit out of a gorilla."

"I look forward to meeting you, Mr. Hoover."

There are moments in life I call high risk, high gain. You're tempted to do something that could either backfire or hit paydirt. I said to Grace that I was seeing Mr. Hoover at Miltmac the following morning at ten about Miss Widmer's lease, and it might be helpful if Miss Widmer brought the lease itself to the meeting.

Grace looked at me, not saying anything.

"Don't just stand there," I said. "Please make that call."

Grace returned with overcast on her face. Miss Widmer said she couldn't miss work, but she'd send the lease over to Miltmac by messenger addressed to me.

A jury consisting of strangers is easier to persuade.

"Please tell Miss Widmer that it's too risky sending the original to their offices, to photocopy it first and send the copy. Oh, and also tell her it might accomplish our purpose better if she was there in person, but I'll understand if she's too busy."

I stared out of the window. I'd had enough doodling.

I heard Grace's voice over my shoulder. "Miss Widmer says she'll take the day off. She'll be there."

Would you know my heart was sputtering like a chainsaw engine?

Instead of an appointment with a landlord, I felt like I had a clandestine assignation with a woman I wasn't supposed to see.

Miltmac's office was on the third floor of an Eighth Avenue building that had a porn bookshop at street level and a massage parlor on the second floor. Francine would love this.

She was already there when I arrived. The seven or eight other people in the anteroom all looked like New York messengers, pimply teenagers, middle-aged spastics, and ancient mariners. Francine was standing. There were no more chairs when she arrived and no one had bothered to offer her a seat.

I had no alternative but to go up to her and apologize for the place and the circumstance.

"I didn't know," I said.

She said, "Hello," and nothing else.

Two sticks standing.

One of the doors off the anteroom opened, and somebody beckoned one of the messengers. The kid went in. I wondered how long we'd have to wait. It was five minutes after ten.

When the second door opened, it was for us. The man waving a hand at us was a tall very thin sallow-cheeked man of at least sixty-five or seventy. He was too old to be named after Herbert Hoover. "I'm Hoover," he said, pointing to himself. "Who's the lady?"

"My client. Miss Francine Widmer."

"Pleased to meetcha," said Hoover, offering us two straight-backed wooden chairs near his desk. There was a little American flag on a stand on his desk. Behind his desk hung a faintly tinted picture of Franklin D. Roosevelt.

"Where's your gorilla?" I asked.

"I talked to Jason. He says you're supposed to be a real hotshot in Westchester. I need a lawyer up there sometimes."

I said nothing.

"That was a question," Hoover said.

"My client list is full, Mr. Hoover."

He looked at me as if I was crazy to turn down his bribe, looked at Francine, who was examining the fingernails of her left hand, shrugged his skeletal shoulders, got up, and stick-walked to the door. "Be right back," he said.

I wondered what he was up to.

I glanced over at Francine. Her face was sad and beautiful. She reminded me of the Modigliani. Of someone I once knew.

I coughed just enough to attract her attention. "Remember," I said, "the main point is to get out of the lease."

"Thank you," she said, "for telling me what the main point is."

Reach over and touch her hand? She might as well have been on another planet. Was that how I seemed to her now?

Hoover came clacking back into the room. Heel taps.

"You," he said to Francine, "are the lady who got raped in the second floor west in number twelve, right?"

Francine did not answer him. Would she look to me to answer?

Hoover glanced at me. "Is she?"

I nodded.

He glanced back at Francine.

"All right." He turned to me. "The only time I see tenants, they want the same thing. How much is it worth to you to get out of that lease?"

"How much is it worth to you, Mr. Hoover, not to have me talk to my friends in White Plains about your unsafe buildings?"

"I got no violations. I don't work that way."

"You'll have to get rid of Jason after you pay his trespassing fine."

"I ain't paying no fines for nobody."

"You know he won't pay. He'll skip."

"Mr. Thomassy, finding a super who don't steal, don't drink all day, and doesn't need to call an eighteen-dollar-an-hour plumber or electrician for every little thing that comes up is very difficult. Jason is a good boy. He tells me . . ." Hoover looked over at Francine. "He tells me this fellow Koslak invited him for what he thought was a free ride. He wasn't interested in no one who wasn't interested. Everybody knows he's got all the ass—excuse me, miss—he wants in those three buildings."

I could see the color rise in Francine's face. She looked angry and exceptionally beautiful. I wanted to say to her *Be patient, Hoover is the way the world is, we need to deal with him together.*

"Mr. Hoover," I said, hoping my voice didn't betray what I felt, "do you think your tenants approve of your superintendent's activities?"

"They love it."

"Do their husbands?"

"What're you getting at, mister?"

"If this trespassing matter gets into the papers, Mr. Hoover, you'll have to get rid of Jason. Or we can arrange for Miss Widmer to move, and leave Jason to you."

"Look, Mr. Thomassy. I ain't an unreasonable sort of person. I'll let her out of her lease for an even thousand."

"That's outrageous!" said Francine.

I touched her hand, only for a second. I was afraid she would get up and leave.

"It's less than six months' rent," said Hoover.

"Mr. Hoover," I said, "I have no intention of my client paying anything to get out of an apartment that's proved dangerous for her to live in. Moreover—" I leaned forward across the desk— "I expect you to pay for Miss Widmer's moving expenses."

"You got some nerve." The broken capillaries in his face were suddenly visible.

"Francine," I said, "would you mind stepping out into the waiting room for a minute or two? There's something I'd like to discuss with Mr. Hoover in private."

I wanted her to stay, but the fact of her leaving the room heightened the value of what I was about to try.

The door closed behind her. I hoped she would be okay in that waiting room full of drifters.

"Mr. Hoover," I said, but he cut me off.

"You just listen a minute," he said. "You think you got me by the short hairs? I've never let anyone out of a lease without a settlement and I'm not about to start now. Pay for her moving? You gotta be nuts, mister."

I remained silent.

"Say something!"

"I was waiting for you to calm down a bit. Mr. Hoover, I don't care how you make a living, what other businesses you own, like this one, or the massage parlor downstairs, or the street-floor store, you can do anything you please."

"You're damn right, mister."

I thought I heard him mumble something else.

"I didn't hear you," I said.

He thought just a second whether he should repeat what he mumbled, then he said, "I could have you taken care of, busybody."

"It'd cost you more than a thousand."

"I got people on my payroll."

"Whoever you got would have to stand in a long line of people who have threatened me. Mr. Hoover, I just want you to dial this number."

I wrote the Westchester number down on his pad.

"I'm not making no phone calls for nobody."

"That's the Westchester District Attorney's office, Mr. Hoover. His name is Gary Cunham. Just ask for him. Say George Thomassy is calling."

"You're bluffing."

"I don't bluff. That's why I asked you to place the call."

"What's he got to do with anything?"

"Mr. Cunham has a special interest in Miss Widmer's case. What he doesn't know is that the building she was raped in is part of the Miltmac smut empire. He's sworn to keep that kind of thing out of Westchester."

"We don't operate anything like that in Westchester."

"You just convince Mr. Cunham of that. Maybe he won't like the idea of the connection to your New York operations. Try him. I'll pay for the call."

I plunked two quarters down on his desk.

"You think you're smart, don'tcha?" said Hoover. "You want me to tear up that lease without any payment for the loss we'll suffer? You're crazy."

"You won't suffer any loss. She's paid through the month. There hasn't been an empty apartment in that price range up there in years. Your rental income won't skip a beat. You were just trying to steal a thousand from her and I'm stopping you, that's all."

"I'm not going to pay for her moving expenses!"

"Just to show you I'm not unreasonable," I said, "I'll settle for the cancellation if you'll sign these papers now."

I handed him the short document I had brought with me.

He skimmed it quickly. "I've got to show this to my lawyer."

"Then call Cunham."

"I don't make a move without my lawyer."

"It's in simple English, Mr. Hoover. You've seen that kind of release before."

"I ain't never released nobody, not in forty years."

"There's a time to begin anything. Want to borrow my pen?"

"What about the trespass?"

"You really want to keep Jason?"

"You're damned right."

"I'll talk to the lady. I'll use my best efforts. If you sign. I'll also need your check for the deposit on the lease."

"You're a real son of a bitch, mister."

I picked the release form up and started to put it back into my breast pocket.

"How do I know you're not bluffing?"

"Make the call," I shouted at him.

He looked at his pad where I had written the number. Then he picked up his phone and dialed the number. I guess whatever they say when you reach Cunham's office convinced him. He hung up, rubbed his chin, then motioned for the piece of paper back. I watched him sign it, put it in my pocket. I watched him make out the check for the deposit. I took it, waved goodbye at him so that I wouldn't have to shake his hand, went quickly out to the reception room. For a moment I felt panic, I couldn't see Francine. "Where is she?" I said to the receptionist. "Where did she go?"

"In the ladies' room."

George Thomassy, get a hold of yourself.

When she came back in, she returned the ladies' room key to the receptionist, then said to me, "What happened with Mr. Hoover?"

I pulled the release out of my pocket. "You're free to move," I said. *You are free to move.*

"Did you beat him up?" she asked.

"In my fashion. No violence. He's a dirty old man." *Like me.*

"George?"

"Yup." *Yup? You'd think I was a nervous kid.*

"You've been helpful to me."

I nodded.

"Really helpful. All along."

Risk rebuff. "Francine?"

She waited.

"I didn't know how long this would take, so I told Grace not to expect me back at any particular time if at all. I have a mildly crazy idea."

She waited.

Help me.

"What's your idea?"

"Since you took the day off—listen, how long since you've been to the Bronx Zoo?"

"Long time."

"Me, too. Why don't we stop there on the way to Westchester. What do you think?"

"You want to look at all of the bachelor animals who've accepted their fate?"

"What does that mean?" I asked. *Was she saying yes? Yes to what?*

She said, "There's something pathetic about the acceptance of a cage. Or the free-roaming ones who don't try to jump the moat."

I told her I'd lead our two-car caravan to the zoo.

"I've seen you drive. I won't be able to keep up with you."

"I'll watch you in my rear-view mirror."

"Thanks."

My mind wasn't on driving. Somehow our little convoy made it to the zoo without mishap. We had hot dogs and beer, got bone weary walking in a determination to see everything there was to see and smell of the animal kingdom that day. Later, we plunked ourselves down on a bench, stretching our tired legs in front of us, to watch the other people, odd as the animals, pass before us.

Finally, Francine said, "Where do we go from here?"

I have sometimes thought that the people I know are each individual parts of a jigsaw puzzle that never quite gets put together into a picture that makes sense. But at that moment, it seemed that the two pieces juxtaposed on the park bench might just possibly fit together.

We had arranged to dispose of her apartment, if not of all of its memories. It seemed natural to go to my place.

When we were inside and the door was closed, I turned the cylinder lock.

"Expecting anyone else?" she asked.

"Not today." I watched her admirable back as she ambled over to the bookshelves on the opposite side of the room. "Looking for something to read?"

"No," she said, turning toward me. "You look like a nervous school-boy. I thought you're used to stress, counselor."

"Not this kind."

"What kind?" she said.

"Us."

Francine twined her fingers into a bridge. She was fifteen feet away when she looked up from her hands and said, "Why don't you take your clothes off?"

I remembered my first experience with a girl, I can't remember her name but I see her as she looked then, pleading with me not to undress her, bargaining for the blouse and the brassiere only, not the blue jeans, not the panties, as if it was the clothes and not the body that was at issue, two awkward kids ending up half undressed doing something or other that was supposed to be sex, worried about what she would think of me, she undoubtedly worried about what I would think of her, worried that somebody would see us, catch us, punish us for ducking the parental admonition *never* to remove your clothes in the presence of someone of the opposite sex. How many grown-up couples for how many centuries fornicated with nightclothes on in the dark? It wasn't dark any more.

"You'll be more comfortable," she said, unbuttoning her blouse. Her fingers across the room affected me. I could feel the muscles of my buttocks tighten.

As she slipped from her blouse, she said, "It isn't as if we're a one-night stand."

Her breasts were beautiful because she was beautiful.

"You're very quiet for you," she said, slipping out of her skirt.

"What are we?" I asked.

She kicked her shoes off.

"I hope a little bit in love," she said.

"Yes, but what are we?"

Her expression deemed my question unnecessary. I thought she would turn her back to me as she slid her pantyhose down and pulled them off, but she faced me as if what she was doing was perfectly natural, which it might have been if I hadn't lived, like all men of my vintage, at the end of the age of embarrassment.

"I guess," she said at last, "we're somewhere between a one-night stand and a relationship that might last a bit. Who knows? Do you lawyers need a contract for everything? Take your damn clothes off!"

I felt like an idiot standing there. Quickly, I went over and put my arms around her. Her skin felt hot. I had trained myself for two decades to speak with precision and care, not to let words slip, and here I was suddenly saying, "I love you," and kissing her.

Hers didn't feel like the mouth of another person.

When, for breath, she pulled away, she said, "Your suit's scratchy."

And so George Thomassy, who like his precursors in Eden was taught that nakedness was shameful, with deliberate speed flung off his clothes and led Francine Widmer into his no longer private bedroom.